Acclaim for Christina Courtenay's enthralling time slip romances:

'Once again, Christina Courtenay takes us to the heart of the Viking world with an epic romantic tale of love and adventure'
Nicola Cornick

'*Whispers of the Runes* is the best Christina Courtenay book yet. It held me captive as I read and stayed in my mind whenever I had to put it down'
Sue Moorcroft

'A wonderful dual timeline story with captivating characters and full of vivid historical detail bringing the Viking world alive, I didn't want it to end!'
Clare Marchant

'Seals Christina Courtenay's crown as the Queen of Viking Romance. This sweeping tale . . . will leave you wanting more'
Catherine Miller

'An absorbing story, fast-paced and vividly imagined, which really brought the Viking world to life'
Pamela Hartshorne

'A love story and an adventure, all rolled up inside a huge amount of intricately-detailed, well-researched history. Thoroughly enjoyable'
Kathleen McGurl

'Prepare to be swept along in this treasure of an adventur
With a smart, courageous heroine and hunky, honourable h
at the helm, what's not to like?'
Kate Ryder

'Christina Courtenay's particular talent is to entice you into her world and capture you'
Alison Morton

'I was totally captivated by this story of love and adventure which had me racing through the pages . . . I was drawn into the Viking world so easily which felt authentic and real'
Sue Fortin

'Brought the 9th century world alive to me and made me desperate to read more about it'
Gill Stewart

Christina Courtenay is an award-winning author of historical romance and time slip (dual time) stories. She started writing so that she could be a stay-at-home mum to her two daughters, but didn't get published until daughter number one left home aged twenty-one, so that didn't quite go to plan! Since then, however, she's made up for it by having twelve novels published and winning the RNA's Romantic Novel of the Year Award for Best Historical Romantic Novel twice with *Highland Storms* (2012) and *The Gilded Fan* (2014), and once for Best Fantasy Romantic Novel with *Echoes of the Runes* (2021).

Christina is half Swedish and grew up in that country. She has also lived in Japan and Switzerland, but is now based in Herefordshire, close to the Welsh border. She's a keen amateur genealogist and loves history and archaeology (the armchair variety).

To find out more, visit **christinacourtenay.com**, find her on Facebook **/Christinacourtenayauthor** or follow her on Twitter **@PiaCCourtenay**, and Instagram **@christinacourtenayauthor**.

By Christina Courtenay

Trade Winds
Highland Storms
Monsoon Mists
The Scarlet Kimono
The Gilded Fan
The Jade Lioness
The Silent Touch of Shadows
The Secret Kiss of Darkness
The Soft Whisper of Dreams
The Velvet Cloak of Moonlight
Echoes of the Runes
The Runes of Destiny
Whispers of the Runes
Tempted by the Runes

Tempted *by the* Runes

CHRISTINA COURTENAY

First published in 2021
by HEADLINE REVIEW
An imprint of HEADLINE PUBLISHING GROUP

2

Cataloguing in Publication Data is available from the British Library

ISBN 978 1 4722 8270 5

Typeset in Minion Pro by Avon DataSet Ltd, Arden Court,
Alcester, Warwickshire

Printed and bound in Great Britain by Clays Ltd, Elcograf S.p.A.

Headline's policy is to use papers that are natural, renewable and recyclable products and made from wood grown in well-managed forests and other controlled sources. The logging and manufacturing processes are expected to conform to the environmental regulations of the country of origin.

HEADLINE PUBLISHING GROUP
An Hachette UK Company
Carmelite House
50 Victoria Embankment
London EC4Y 0DZ

www.headline.co.uk
www.hachette.co.uk

To Tina Brown
– Aussie twin soul sister and wonderful friend –
with love and thanks for everything!

Chapter One

Eskilsnes, Svíaríki, early April AD *875*

'Are you sure this is wise, brother? It could all be a pack of lies.'

'It's not.' Geir Eskilsson glared at his older brother Hrafn while continuing to place every item he possessed in his travel kist. No point leaving anything behind, because he wasn't coming back. 'The man I talked to at Kaupang had been to Ísland, and he said there is land for the taking – enough for everyone. Others said the same; I made careful enquiries. All you have to do is bring everything needed to start a new life, including cattle, and settle somewhere.'

Hrafn was pacing back and forth, but stopped to frown back at Geir. 'Cattle? On a journey across the ocean? And what if every piece of land has been claimed by the time you arrive? You'll have gone to all that trouble for nothing.'

'I doubt it. It's a huge place, by all accounts. And my mind is made up. I want my own domain, not be beholden to anyone else. Not even you.'

The brothers were close, but as the eldest, Hrafn had inherited their father's property, Eskilsnes, and everything that came with it. That made the other two, Geir and their middle brother Rurik, dependent on him unless they struck out on their own. Rurik had trained as a silversmith and was now independent, living in Birka with his wife Sara and their son, and Geir was determined to break free as well. It was past time – he'd already seen twenty-two winters.

'You're not beholden to me. I'd say it's the other way round – I need you to help me run this place. How else can I go off on trading expeditions?'

Everyone knew that Hrafn much preferred trading to running a farm, but it was a privilege to inherit holdings as vast as those their father had left him, and he'd had no choice but to take on the duties that came with it.

Geir shrugged. 'If you don't want to leave Linnea behind, just ask Rurik to come and stay here. Or Aunt Estrid – she's more than capable of taking over the running, despite her age.' When Hrafn opened his mouth as if to argue further, Geir held up a hand. 'No! Nothing you can say will sway me. I'm leaving and I'd rather do so with your good will, but if you cannot wish me well, so be it.'

His brother sighed and rubbed his stubbled chin. 'Of course I wish you well. I just don't want you living so far away. When will we see you again?'

'Come on a trading voyage to Ísland. If you can go all the way to Miklagarðr, I don't see why you can't sail west from Hordaland for a week or so across the sea.'

'Hmph.' Hrafn didn't look convinced. 'If it doesn't work out, will you give me your oath you'll come back? I know you're stubborn, but I don't want your pride to stand in the way of admitting when you've taken on too much.'

Rolling his eyes, Geir nodded. 'Fine, you have my word. But I won't fail. Just wait and see. Now come and help me load the rest of the implements I'll need, then we'll have one last feast before I leave.'

'Very well. Perhaps you'll drink so much ale you'll be incapable of steering tomorrow.'

'*Fifl!*' Geir gave his brother a good-natured shove and hefted the travelling chest. 'I can drink a barrel-load more than you and still stand up straight.'

'We'll see about that . . .'

Chapter Two

Dublin, late April 2021

'Come to Dublin, they said. It'll be fun, they said. Ha! Where's the fun if I'm not even allowed to leave the hotel? I'm nineteen, not nine. Almost twenty, in fact.'

Madison Berger poked her brother Storm in the chest, making him hold up his hands in a peace gesture. 'Don't shoot the messenger, Mads. I guess Dad is worried you'll get attacked or something.'

'I'm a black belt in karate and great at kickboxing, for Christ's sake. And why can't I go with you?'

'I'm going on a pub crawl. Who wants to bring their little sister to something like that? It's a guys-only evening, with friends I haven't seen for ages. Come on, be reasonable. It's only for one night. Tomorrow I promise we'll do something fun, just you and me, OK? Besides, you should be exhausted after a whole day of telling fortunes. Chill.'

'It's not that hard.'

The whole family – Maddie, Storm and their parents, Haakon and Mia – were in Dublin to take part in the Clontarf Viking Festival, held in St Anne's Park. Every year over five hundred living history re-enactors descended on the city from around the world. Many of them were there to recreate the Battle of Clontarf, when Irish king Brian Boru defeated a Viking army – although apparently he was killed himself afterwards – and this happened twice a day, near the site where the battle originally took place. But there were lots of other things going on the rest of the time. As well as the warriors, the festival included a Viking village with displays of weapons, crafts, food and much more, bringing this period of history to life. It was entertainment for the whole family, and tens of thousands of visitors came along every year.

For as long as Maddie could remember, her parents had been attending such events, although this was their first time in Ireland. Her dad was great at woodturning, making exquisite wooden bowls and plates on a primitive lathe, while her brother was a weapons enthusiast. If there was a battle anywhere, he wanted to be part of it. Her mum preferred to show off her skills at weaving on an upright loom. Maddie sometimes helped her, but this time she hadn't been needed, as one of Mia's friends was with them. Instead she'd been asked to do fortune-telling with runes, which was fine by her. She'd become quite proficient at it in the last couple of years, and even believed she had the second sight, as she was sometimes able to predict the future. As part of the fun, she was dressed in a Viking outfit, complete with tortoise brooches of bronze and several strings of beautiful beads. She'd bought the amber ones herself with some of her takings, and loved their honey lustre.

'Why don't you have an evening of pampering yourself or something?' Storm suggested now. 'I thought girls loved that kind of thing, and the bathrooms here at the hotel are full of those tiny bottles of smelly stuff. I'm sure Mum and Dad won't be back too late.'

Maddie shrugged. She wasn't a bubble-bath kind of person and he ought to know that.

As for their parents, there was some serious academic stuff going on in the background with a special Viking conference at the university. As Haakon was an archaeologist of some renown and Mia a respected conservator, both specialising in that era, they'd made time to attend a couple of lectures too. Because of their academic connections, they had been invited to attend some boring dinner this evening, with speeches. Maddie and Storm weren't included, but he had friends in the city and had obviously made plans. It annoyed her no end that none of the others had considered her. So was she just supposed to sit in her room and watch TV or what?

Stuff that.

'Fine. Off you go then.' She practically shoved Storm towards the door. The sooner he was gone, the better. She was going to go for a walk, and sod the others. They had no right to decide what she did with her life – she was old enough to do what she liked.

'Mads . . .' Storm tried out his serious-big-brother face, eyes narrowed as if he knew she was up to something.

'I'll be fine. But you'd better take me somewhere nice tomorrow, or else.' She pouted slightly, as if she'd given in even though she didn't like it. That seemed to do the trick.

'I will, I swear. Now be good, yeah?'

'Aren't I always?' She wasn't going to promise any such thing.

'Yes, I suppose so.' He smiled as she made a shooing motion. 'Right, I'm off then. See you in the morning.'

She waited until she was sure he'd left the hotel, then pulled a shawl around her shoulders and grabbed her key card and her mobile. She kept the iPhone in her hand in case she needed to look at a map, although she knew vaguely where she was going. It didn't matter that she was still wearing her Viking outfit; there should be plenty of other people around dressed the same way. The reception staff gave her a few funny looks as she passed them, but she ignored that. They could think what they liked.

It was late April and it had been an unseasonably warm day, with temperatures in the low twenties and plenty of sunshine. She'd caught the sun – she could feel her face burning slightly – but by now it was starting to feel a bit chilly outside as she headed south, down Capel Street. Her woollen overdress – made in an apron style usually called *hangerok* or *smokkr* – and shawl kept her warm, though, as she hurried along the pavement. Besides, she'd cheated a bit and was wearing leggings and knickers underneath so that her nether regions wouldn't get cold.

She and her family were staying in a hotel on the northern side of the River Liffey, opposite where Christ Church Cathedral and Dublin Castle were situated. As she'd been in the Viking village all day, Maddie felt like going to see the river, and she knew it wasn't far. This proved to be the case, and she quickly crossed the Grattan Bridge towards Wood Quay. To her right she could see the so-called Viking Longboat statue – like a sunken ship sticking out of water, with three benches in the middle. Two replica longships were moored nearby on the Liffey as part of the festival, and she'd been told there was a full-size one somewhere else, with re-enactors on hand to tell people all about it.

But that wasn't what she'd come to see, so instead she turned left and meandered along the river. The Liffey was enclosed with walls either side, possibly part concrete and part stone. She supposed it was to protect the streets from flooding. No chance of that at the moment, as it was low tide and there was only a small amount of water in the middle of the riverbed. This prompted a sudden urge to go down there and look at it up close, so she stopped and Googled 'Liffey' and 'tide' to make sure it wasn't going to come rushing back any time soon. Thankfully, Maddie saw that it was unusually low today, but she couldn't see any way of getting down. Surely there had to be stairs somewhere?

She carried on walking, picking up her pace a bit now. Past the Millennium Bridge and a pedestrian bridge, then another two larger double bridges. After Butt Bridge, she passed under a railway bridge that snaked overhead. Then one more bridge, and *finally* some steps leading down to the water.

'Yesss!' She gazed swiftly around her, but no one seemed to be looking her way, so she ran down the steep stairs, holding up her dress so she wouldn't trip on the hem.

'Urgh!' It wasn't a pretty sight that spread out before her. A wide band of puddle-speckled mud, that probably wasn't doing her Viking leather shoes much good. The walls towered above her, a tidal mark of mud topped with green reaching more than a third of the way up. And all around her, a whole bunch of rubbish left behind by the receding waters. But she didn't care. As she picked her way carefully along the edge, a strange excitement gripped her, and her heart began to beat faster. She'd heard of people mudlarking by the River Thames in London – perhaps she could do the same here? Who knew what might be lurking in the mire?

At first she found nothing but rubbish. 'Honestly, why are people such pigs?' she muttered. 'Haven't they ever heard of litter bins?' But every now and then something caught her eye, and she almost whooped out loud when she spotted a tiny silver coin lying right there on the surface. She picked it up and rubbed at it with the edge of her sleeve, then tried to decipher the writing. It looked like it might say 'ÆLFR' and 'AED REX' either side of a man's head.

'King Alfred? As in Alfred the Great? *No way!*'

She felt herself grinning from ear to ear. This was an amazing find and she couldn't wait to show her parents. It might be valuable too, although perhaps she wouldn't be allowed to keep it if it was treasure trove. In order to carry it safely, she wrapped it in an old tissue and stowed it in one of the two leather pouches hanging off her belt. The other one contained the fortune-telling rune staves she'd been using all day.

The mudlarking bug had well and truly bitten her now, and she carried on walking, almost bent over double so she wouldn't miss anything. She searched for ages, although she was careful not to stray too far away from the stairs in case the water came gushing back, but found nothing else of value. The light was fading and she decided it was probably time to head back to the hotel. Hopefully her parents wouldn't be too late returning, as she wanted to show them her coin before they went to bed.

She kept her eyes on the ground while walking slowly towards the steps, but just as she was about to give up, she spotted something else. It was sticking out of the edge of a puddle and she hunkered down to see what it could be. Pale in the fading light, it looked like a small piece of bone, but there were markings on it – a design of some sort. Intrigued now, she pulled it out of the mud and found herself holding a small knife.

'Oh wow, nice!'

She wiped the mud off it by rubbing it against her apron dress, unheeding of the splodges left behind on the material. The ivory was inlaid with a pattern picked out in black – coal mixed with beeswax to make it stay put. Maddie knew how this was done as she'd learned the technique on one of the many craft courses she'd attended. The end of the handle was slightly thicker, tapering towards the blade, which was fastened with what looked like two small screws. There was a deep crevice in the handle and the blade folded into it, fitting perfectly.

'A folding knife? *Awesome!*' And a fairly old one at that.

She opened and shut it a couple of times. The hinge seemed to work just fine, as if it had been oiled only yesterday, and the blade wasn't very rusty at all, which was surprising. The decoration on the handle was fairly basic, but still attractive. It consisted of a symmetrical pattern at one end, and some tiny runes etched along one side. *Wait – runes?* It was seriously old, then. Over a thousand years. She squinted at the writing in the fading light and tried to decipher the words. Given that she was dyslexic, runes weren't much easier to read than the normal alphabet, but she knew if she went slowly she'd get there.

'*Með bloð . . . skaltu . . . ferðast* . . . Huh?' Oh, hang on . . . 'No! *Shit!*'

She knew exactly what those words meant and what she was holding in her hand. A time-travel device. Yet another one. 'How the hell many of you are there?' she wondered out loud.

They existed. For real. Maddie knew that because first her sister Linnea had found one, then Linnea's best friend Sara. And now they were both living in the ninth century, courtesy of a magical artefact.

Like this one.

'Whoa, that means . . . I can time travel!'

She hugged the little knife to her chest for a moment, imagining that she could feel the power emanating from it, even though it was such a small and insignificant thing. With this, she'd be able to visit her sister in the Viking era whenever she wanted to. Or go somewhere else entirely. 'I could even have my own adventures,' she muttered, as this idea took root.

Yes, why shouldn't she have some fun by herself? Linnea loved it there, and Sara seemed equally as happy, judging by what her grandfather had said. And it wasn't as though anyone here wanted her around, was it? Not normally, anyway. Her parents were busy with their academic commitments and jobs, which always seemed so much more important than anything Maddie ever did. Even though they never said it out loud, she could feel their disappointment in her. They made allowances because her dyslexia meant she'd always had a hard time keeping up at school, but it was as though they still expected her to try harder. Make something of herself, preferably in the world of academia. As for Storm, he was living his own exciting life, training to become an officer in the Swedish army, travelling, girlfriends . . . Sure, he was always nice to her when he was around, but how often was that? And could she really expect him to want to hang out with his baby sister all the time?

No, it was up to her to strike out on her own. To show them all that she could be independent. Find her own way in life.

She bit her lip, hesitating. What if it was dangerous? Linnea had said the Viking age wasn't exactly a bed of roses. Not at first, anyway.

'Maybe I could just visit briefly? Check it out?' she murmured. It would only be for a very short time; she'd be back before anyone even realised she'd gone. What harm could it do? With the folding knife safely in her belt pouch, she could return any time. And she was already dressed for it . . .

She swallowed hard and stared out across the Liffey. With a small cut to her finger, and the recital of those words, she'd find out what this place looked like back then.

Yes, why not?

Chapter Three

Dyflin, Írland, late April AD *875*

It was the screaming and shouting that first alerted Geir to the scuffle taking place down by the river. He'd come to Írland to buy some thralls and a larger ship more suited to cargo than the one he'd brought from Svíaríki, because he'd been told this was the best place to find both those things. Now he was on his way back to the harbour after a day of haggling. He'd had to acquire cattle, sheep, goats and chickens as well, and felt bone weary. Why did it all have to take so long? He'd wanted to be on his way by now, but each day there was some new obstacle. Hopefully he'd taken care of everything now. Tomorrow they'd leave.

'*Hei*, what is happening here?'

He lengthened his stride and arrived at a group of people just as a man fell to the ground. There had been four of them, apparently attacking a young woman, but from what Geir could see, she was holding her own so far. Still, she was a female and these men didn't look like they had any right to molest her. By her clothing, she was clearly not a thrall, nor touting for business, and her furious expression showed that she wanted to be left in peace.

At first, he just stared, because there was something strange about her. She'd lifted up her gown and her legs seemed to be encased in some sort of black trousers that were so tight they were like an extra skin. He could see why she needed the skirts out of the way, when she suddenly swung round and aimed an extremely high kick at the side of one man's head, catching him with the top of her foot. *Impressive!* The attacker cried out and went down, but Geir was fairly sure he was only stunned and would return to the fray shortly. She couldn't possibly fight four men at once. It was time to intervene.

'Leave her alone! What is she to you?' He waded in and tried to step in front of her, facing another of her attackers.

'Stay out of this,' the man snarled. 'We found her first and we're having her.' He threw a punch in Geir's direction, despite the fact that the latter was nearly a head taller than him. So too was the woman, now he'd seen her up close. Unusual.

'I don't think so.' With a couple of well-aimed blows to the stomach and jaw, Geir dispatched the man, who toppled over, dead to the world. A third assailant threw himself at Geir with a roar of fury, headbutting him in the stomach. An 'Ooof!' escaped him, but he had a well-muscled body and wasn't anywhere near winded. He swiftly used the man's position to his advantage, grabbing him under the arms and heaving him aside. Small and barrel-like, but agile, the man sprang to his feet, pulling a long knife out of a sheath at his waist. So they weren't above killing for what they wanted? *Niðingar!*

'We'll see about that,' Geir muttered.

He had been in many a fight, including a skirmish with fearsome Pecheneg warriors when on a long journey with his brothers through Garðaríki, and a knife such as this was a mere trifle. While they circled each other, he had time to glance at the woman and saw her launch herself at the fourth and final man, who'd been waiting to pounce. She slashed at the attacker's throat with the side of her hand, held flat and stiff, catching him in the middle of his windpipe. The man started to gurgle and gasp, as if she'd knocked his Adam's apple down into his stomach, then staggered off, clutching his throat and moaning. Geir just stared after him for a moment, then returned his focus to his own fight.

Using a few well-practised manoeuvres, he quickly disarmed the knife-wielding man and punched him so hard he went down like an ox. He turned to the woman, who was standing stock still, panting slightly. Her eyes were wide with fright, but at the same time the light of battle still shone in them. Although afraid, on some level she had obviously relished the fight. The sight made him smile: a woman after his own heart.

'Where did you learn to do that?' he asked, copying her hand-slashing motion of a moment ago.

She shrugged. 'Not here,' she muttered.

Bending down, she picked up her shawl and a small folding knife from the dirt by her feet. She shook out the shawl, tutting at the mud that now clung to it, and brushed off the knife before putting it in one of the two leather pouches hanging off her belt. Now he had time to study her more closely, he admired the mass of long, dark, copper-coloured curls tumbling down her back. Her hair shone, despite the fading light, and he wondered how much more lustre it must have in sunlight. She wore it loose, but perhaps she'd lost her hair tie during the fight. Either way, the beautiful tresses were spread out the way they would be were she about to comb them before bedtime. He hastily blinked away the image that thought conjured up.

As she straightened up, he saw that her features were somewhat sharp – her nose especially – but they suited her, and the harsh planes of the high cheekbones were counterbalanced by a lush full mouth and big moss-green eyes. She was the embodiment of a

Valkyrie: tall, strong and courageous. He found himself wanting to know more about her.

When she ignored him and made as if to walk away, he grabbed her upper arm. 'Not so fast. A thank you wouldn't go amiss, don't you think?'

'Thank you, but I was doing fine on my own. I would have managed.'

He scowled at her ungracious words. 'To best four men? Hardly,' he scoffed. He knew their type. They would have rallied and attacked all at once, something she couldn't possibly have handled. 'What's your name? Where are you going? And what are you doing down here on your own? Shouldn't you be at home?'

'Let go of me or I will hurt you as well,' she hissed. Narrowed eyes sent sparks of fury his way, but Geir didn't loosen his grip. There was something strange about her speech. She formed the words slowly, as if she had to think about them first, and her accent was weird. Not like the locals here, and yet not quite right either.

'Not until you answer me. You owe me that much.' He took hold of her other arm as well, just to be on the safe side. 'And no, I won't let you chop at my throat. Don't even think about it – I'm a lot bigger than you.'

She snorted. 'Makes no difference. I could still beat you in a fight.'

'Not if I don't let you,' he retorted. 'Just give me a reply and I'll let you go. Much simpler.'

A mutinous expression crossed her features, but after a moment she shrugged again. 'Very well. I'm Madison. And I don't have a home here. I was just . . . out for a walk.'

'What?' None of that made any sense whatsoever. 'Mads' son?' He looked her up and down. She was definitely very tall for a woman and not massively curvy, but she had a figure – there was no mistaking her shape under the gown. Besides, her features were much too feminine for any man – the big eyes, delicate brows and beautifully shaped lips. 'You're not a man.'

'Oh, you noticed?' Obviously fed up with being held in a vice, she tried to kick his shin, but he jumped out of the way. 'Of course I'm not a man! If you don't like my name, try Maddie. Not that I want you addressing me at all, mind.'

'*Mah-dee*? That's better, I suppose. But what did you mean, you were out for a walk and you have no home? Are you from one of the ships moored here then?'

'No. I'm not from . . . anywhere here. Now leave me alone!' She performed some manoeuvre with her arms, swinging them up and around, which temporarily freed her from his grip. Her freedom lasted only an instant, as he grabbed her wrist instead and hauled her up against his chest, pinning her to his body with both arms around her. '*Hey!*' she protested, but she was well and truly stuck now.

'You can't go wandering around here on your own, woman. Are you mad? Those men . . .' he nodded in the direction two of her assailants had disappeared off in, 'were only the first of many. No lone female is safe in the *longphoirt*.'

'Then I'll go into town, if that's better. As you saw, I can look after myself. Why do you care?' Her eyes still flashed dangerously, but Geir didn't mind. She was even prettier when she was angry, and, truth be told, he was quite enjoying having her in his arms. He hadn't had a woman since long before leaving Eskilsnes and it felt good to hold her. Being so tall, she fitted perfectly against him, and he could look her in the eyes without bending down. Her riot of curls tickled the back of his right hand, and as he leaned slightly closer, he realised she smelled wonderful – like a summer meadow. Or a whole armful of flowers put together. What on earth had she been bathing in? Whatever it was, he liked it. A lot.

She had a point, though – why should he care what happened to her? He didn't. Well, not much, but he was curious. 'Hmm. So that's what you're doing now? Looking after yourself?' He tightened his arms around her, which probably wasn't such a good idea, as it made him all too aware of the curves she did have.

'Not everyone is a big brute like you! And if you'd let go of my arms, I could show you how I deal with attackers.'

'If, yes, but I'm not going to.'

Geir had been concentrating so much on the woman in his arms, he'd broken one of his own cardinal rules – always be aware of your surroundings. He heard a sudden whooshing sound and ducked out of pure instinct. One of the thugs must have recovered and was now wielding a thick tree branch. It missed Geir's skull by a hair's-breadth, but unfortunately Maddie was not so lucky. With a sickening thud, the blow connected with the side of her head above her left ear, and he felt her crumple in his arms without a sound.

'Why you . . . *aumingi*!'

After depositing Maddie on the ground in all haste, Geir surged up and caught the assailant around the waist, wrapping his arms around his midriff. He had enough momentum to send the man sprawling into the muddy riverbank, and threw himself down on top of him to pummel his face, ribs and anywhere else he could reach. Finally, a couple of well-aimed punches to the jaw had the coward's eyes rolling up into his head, then he went still. Geir hit him one last time for good measure. He wasn't usually so violent, but for some reason the sight of that branch hitting Maddie had made him go berserk.

Panting slightly, he checked to see whether the fourth man was going to give them any trouble, but he was still dead to the world. Time to leave this place before the other two came back looking for them.

Maddie was lying where he'd left her, and Geir hunkered down next to her, checking that she had a pulse. As he wanted to get away from here as quickly as possible, he lifted her up into his arms, shifting her into a more comfortable position so that her head was leaning against his shoulder. She wasn't light, but he was strong and had no trouble carrying her. With long strides he set off towards his ship.

Maddie became aware of hushed voices just as she registered the almighty pounding inside her skull. A rocking sensation soothed her somewhat, and she was warm and dry, but splashing noises and something that sounded like flapping made her frown. Where was she? Her eyes fluttered open and she groaned, putting a hand to the side of her head above her left ear, where most of the pain seemed to be concentrated. She grimaced as her fingers encountered a rough bandage. '*Ouch!*'

'Lie still and don't touch that. I think the bleeding has stopped, but you wouldn't want to set it off again.'

The big man who had come to her aid earlier swam into focus, although there wasn't enough light to see him properly. In the half-darkness his features looked handsome but unreal, wreathed in shadows, a frown of concern etched on his brow. She couldn't make out the colour of his eyes, but they were studying her intently. He pulled at her fingers and she tried to swat his hand away, just as the memory of what she'd done returned with full force, making her freeze.

Jesus, it had worked! She had time travelled back to the Viking age. She'd barely had a chance to register this before, as almost the moment she'd opened her eyes in what she'd hoped was the ninth century, those four thugs had spotted her and decided she was theirs for the taking. Their faces had lit up at the sight of her and she'd heard their cries of glee as they thought their evening's bed sport was secured. The hell it was . . .

Their exact words and the ensuing fight were a bit of a blur, but as soon as this man had started talking to her afterwards, she'd known for sure she was in the Viking era because he was speaking Old Norse. Thank goodness she'd paid attention to all the lessons she'd had recently. Linnea had insisted they all learn, just in case she visited with her husband and any kids they might have, which was fair enough.

But . . . she was still here? *No, no, no!* That wasn't how she'd planned it. She swallowed hard.

'I'm fine. Just sore. What happened?' She wasn't actually fine at all, but no way was she going to admit it to him. Parts of their conversation came back to her. He'd been interrogating her, refusing to let her be on her way. Then something had struck her head. One of his cohorts? Not that he seemed threatening in any way now, and he had tried to defend her after all, but something about him put her nerve endings on full alert. And, come to think of it, he'd been holding her much too close just before everything went black, as if he too had plans for her. Had he rescued her just so he could have her for himself?

Hell and damnation! She smothered the memory of just how wonderful it had felt to be in his arms, crushed against him. He was big and seriously fit – she'd been acutely aware of the muscles in his chest and stomach, not to mention the strong arms that had encircled her. But that was neither here nor there.

'The man you'd kicked in the head was only stunned, I think,' her saviour explained, interrupting her thoughts. 'He tried to hit me with a tree branch and I ducked, which unfortunately left you in the way. I'm sorry. I didn't react fast enough.'

'Where is he now?'

'Gone. All of them.'

She looked around her and realised she was inside some kind

of tent. His, presumably. This was not good. She was still wearing all her clothes, including her shoes, so he hadn't done anything inappropriate. Yet. Perhaps he'd been waiting for her to wake up, preferring her to be conscious? A tremor of fear shot through her. She couldn't stay here with him. It was time to disappear back to her own century, but her limbs felt weak and her head was ready to explode with pain. How was she going to get away?

Strangely enough, there was a sliver of light spilling in through the tent opening, growing brighter every minute, although she was sure it had been evening when she'd gone out for her walk. She definitely remembered the light fading. How long had she been unconscious? Her parents and Storm must be frantic wondering where she'd got to.

'Thank you for your help, but I need to go.' She tried to raise herself, but was pushed back down gently but firmly. Her heart rate increased as panic spread through her. When she tried to struggle against his hold, he just held her still, his strength so superior she doubted it took much effort.

'You are not going anywhere right now. The wisewoman was adamant. You've had a severe blow to the head and if you do not lie still, flat on your back, for at least two days, your brain could become addled. I know, because I've had the same thing happen to me in the past.'

'Wisewoman?' So he'd cared enough to call for a doctor of sorts. That was nice of him. Or maybe he was only looking out for his property? Was he going to sell her when she had recovered? A chill ran down her spine and froze her insides. This was what had happened to her sister – captured by a Viking who'd claimed her as his slave. But this man sounded solicitous and was keeping his hands to himself. Well, apart from holding her down. Perhaps she was overreacting. 'Wh-what do you want with me?' She peered at him suspiciously.

His eyebrows shot up and he looked innocent enough, although a spark of amusement briefly lit his eyes, making her unsure. 'Nothing. I'm just trying to care for you, but I'm no use when it comes to binding wounds, so I sent for help.' He shrugged. 'The old one left you some willow bark. Do you think you could swallow it now?'

'I suppose.' She knew it was an age-old remedy that had been used in the past instead of aspirin. It couldn't hurt, and she really did have the mother of all headaches. Concussion? Most probably.

'Here then, drink this.' He inserted an arm under her shoulders to lift her up and proffered a ceramic mug. When she cautiously sniffed the brew – he could be trying to drug her, after all – he smiled and added, 'It's not poison, you know.'

'It could be,' she muttered, but when he just laughed, she gave in. He supported her while she drank from the mug, which he held steady for her.

It wasn't the nicest medicine she'd ever tasted, but it wasn't so bad either. 'Thank you,' she murmured, closing her eyes for a moment as he gently laid her back down. Her fingers explored the softness she was lying on; it felt like some sort of long-haired fur. It was lovely, but she shouldn't be here.

'Where am I?'

'You're on board my ship. We left the *longphoirt* this morning.'

'Long-what?' She remembered he'd mentioned that word before, and she had no idea what it was. 'And what do you mean "left"?' Her eyes flew open as she registered what he'd said, panic flooding her once more.

'Harbour,' he explained. 'You were in Dyflin, or as the locals seem to call it, *Dubh Linn*. Apparently it means "the Dark Pool".'

'I know, but . . . were?' He had used the past tense, she was sure of it, and that one word made her gut clench. She really didn't like the way this conversation was going, and the hammering inside her skull increased.

'Yes, we're out at sea now, heading north.' He shrugged again. 'I asked around, spoke to everyone I could find, but no one knew who you were or where you belonged. I couldn't just leave you there, wounded because of my carelessness, so I decided you'd better come with us. We're going to Ísland.'

'*What?*' She shot upright, ignoring the sharp stab of pain in her head as full-blown panic erupted inside her. '*Bloody hell!*' she exclaimed in English. '*Iceland?* Noooo! But I need to go home.'

Chapter Four

Now she wanted to go home. Well, it was a bit late for that and Geir told her as much.

'You didn't appear to have a home last night,' he added. 'Or so you said.'

'Of course I have a home! Are you a thrall merchant? Is that why you've taken me? To sell me in Ísland? You can't! I won't let you!' Her eyes were wide with fright, as if he was some sort of troll.

'What are you talking about? I haven't "taken" you at all. I told you, I'm trying to care for you, not harm you. If you'd answered my questions yesterday, you wouldn't be here now.' It made him cross that she could have saved him a deal of bother. He'd had to spend silver on bribing several urchins to run around making enquiries, because he knew they always kept their eyes and ears open, but to no avail. No one had admitted to knowing a red-haired Valkyrie going by the name of Maddie.

'But . . . no! I was just going for a short walk and then . . . then going back. Home. Oh, this is a disaster!' She flung an arm across her eyes and he could see her chest rising and falling rapidly, as if she was severely agitated. It was a distracting sight, but he forced himself to concentrate on her words rather than her body.

'You are not making sense, Maddie.' He fixed her with a glare, even though she wasn't looking at him. 'For the last time, where is home?'

'Svíaríki.'

'Ah, now we're getting somewhere. So you *did* arrive by ship. Which one? I thought I'd asked all of them, but there were upwards of two hundred or so . . .' The urchins could have missed one, although he considered that unlikely.

'Not a ship. I, er . . . arrived by magic. *Trolldomr.*' Those last words were whispered, and he had to bend forward to catch them.

'You what? Magic?' He blinked as she removed her arm and stared up at him defiantly, her mouth set in an uncompromising line. Geir felt his eyebrows rise. 'You're a *vōlva*? Well, why didn't you say so?'

'Because I'm not. Not really. I just cast the runes, that's all. Wait.' She sighed and fumbled with one of the pouches at her belt, opening it and taking out the little knife he'd seen her pick up yesterday. 'I came with this. And yes, I know you won't believe me, but—'

He cut her off and snatched the knife out of her grasp. 'Odin's ravens! Don't tell me . . . you have travelled through time?'

Maddie's mouth fell open. 'Yes! But how did you know? I didn't say that.'

'I've, um, heard about this before.' He studied the handle and read the inscription. *Með blōð skaltu ferðast.* He'd been shown other items with the exact same inscription by his brothers, but neither Hrafn nor Rurik had ever explained how it worked. They'd said it was better not to know.

Before he could ask, though, Maddie put her hand on his arm and gave him a frustrated shake. 'Are you serious? You've met a time traveller? I mean, you believe me?'

'Yes, several.' He opened and closed the knife, scrutinising the runes once more. 'How does it work?'

She let go of him and frowned. 'I'm not going to tell you that! You'd steal my knife and then I'd be stuck here. In fact, I need to be getting back right now. My family will be missing me. Give me that! Please? And turn this ship around straight away. You have to take me back to Dub . . . I mean Dyflin. Now!'

Fear still flickered in the depths of her eyes, as if she was only too aware that Geir held all the power in his hands. He wasn't a mean person and would gladly have given the knife back, but he was also consumed with curiosity. Had been for ages. This was one chance he couldn't possibly pass up, and there was another thought brewing in his mind as well, something that needed mulling over before he did anything hasty.

'No, I'm sorry. We've travelled too far to turn back now. You'll have to use this when we arrive, if you still want to return to your own time. I want you to show me how it works.'

'*Nuh-uh. No way!*' she said in some foreign language, then clarified. 'I won't.'

He closed his fingers around the knife. 'We'll see about that. In any case, you're not going anywhere other than to Ísland with me.'

No! This can not *be happening!* Maddie stared at the man and tried not to groan out loud. She was only supposed to go for a quick walk in the ninth century, look around, then return to her own time straight away. Not become embroiled in a fight, get concussion and meet this . . . this stubborn bastard. Even if he hadn't kidnapped her and had no intention of molesting her, she couldn't stay with him.

There had to be some way of persuading him to give her the knife and turn back, but right now, her head hurt so much she couldn't think straight. And glancing at him, he looked dead serious. There was something else in his expression too, though. Excitement? Curiosity? Maybe she could use that to her advantage. It was astonishing that he actually believed her. She'd been prepared for total disbelief and possibly outright scorn as well. How many people knew about this time-travelling business? More than she'd thought, it would appear.

'Look, if I tell you how it works, will you take me back? I can even let you come to the future with me for a short while if you want.' She tried to keep her tone even and reasonable. Was it possible to reason with a Viking? This particular one didn't seem to be lacking in brains.

He smiled, his teeth gleaming white in the gloomy interior of the tent. 'Good try, but no. You can show me when we arrive. I assume Ísland exists in your time?'

She nodded reluctantly. 'Yes, but—'

'Excellent. Now I have a ship to steer, so unless you wish to end up at the bottom of the sea, I'd suggest you stop arguing with me. Rest and recover. You'll need your strength.'

'Hey! *Hey!* You can't just take that. It's mine. Give me back my knife!' She made to rise, but was overcome with a wave of nausea and realised she wasn't in any state to fight him for it. Not yet, anyway. She sank back down, clutching her head.

'Why should I? I'd be stupid to give up such a precious object. Now lie down. We can debate the issue later. There's plenty of time before we reach our destination.'

Maddie opened her mouth to protest, but he was gone before she could utter another word. And really, she didn't have the strength to argue right now. Nausea threatened and she desperately needed to close her eyes and keep her head still. She hadn't known it was possible for it to hurt this much.

Maybe going to Iceland wasn't so bad after all. He was right.

She could return to her own time from there and find a way to contact her parents, then they'd come and fetch her or arrange for her to travel home. Yes, no need to panic just yet. Did she still have her mobile? She opened each of her leather pouches in turn to check, then remembered she'd had it in her hand before she'd been attacked. She must have dropped it by the river while fighting off those thugs. Perhaps it got trampled into the mud? *Damn!*

But someone would surely help her. Yes, things would work out fine if only she could sleep for a while . . .

Geir had successfully steered the ship halfway through the sea channel between the northernmost part of Írland and the islands off the west coast of Skotland, the Suðureyjar. They made landfall on a beach on one of them – uninhabited, as far as he could see – as that was safer than trying to navigate past the rest after dark. He was aiming to stay close to these islands as far north as he could, then strike out for the Færeyjar, or Sheep Islands. After that, he'd been told to head north-west across the open sea and then they would hopefully arrive on the southern coast of Ísland within a week.

It all depended on winds and currents, but he had made offerings to the gods and hoped for the best. Others had made the journey and lived to tell the tale – no reason why he shouldn't.

'Men, help me to secure the ship,' he ordered. 'And pull the rowing boat further up the beach as well.' They were towing a smaller boat, as he'd been given to understand that wood was scarce in Ísland, and he'd thought they might have need of a less unwieldy vessel from time to time.

He wasn't travelling alone. Manpower would be needed in order to establish a settlement, plus there was safety in numbers, so two men from home had come with him – Steinthor, a recently qualified blacksmith, who had wanted to establish himself somewhere new; and Ingimund, one of his older brother's former tenants. The latter had been sharing a small farm with two siblings and it had become clear it wasn't large enough to support them all. Geir had hired a few others to help him sail the ship to Dyflin, but once there, the hired men had decided to stay behind. They were more interested in going off to plunder than working hard to establish a farm. To replace them, he'd bought some thralls to take with him. Cormac and Niall were young Irishmen, captured as children and raised as thralls, and Geir had chosen them for their strength and capabilities. He'd been assured they were used to working hard and could turn their hands to most tasks.

Steinthor and Ingimund each had a wife and two children, and Geir's little group was completed by two Irish thrall women and a ten-year-old boy.

Another large ship came to a halt next to his, its keel hissing into the sandy beach – other travellers also bound for Ísland, with whom he'd decided to journey in convoy. Their leader, Hjalti, was only intending to stay for a year, hunting for ivory and sealskins to sell on his return, but he'd brought a group of six men, as well as some Irish thrall women to see to their needs and help establish a temporary settlement. Geir had struck a deal with him that they would help each other if necessary, but otherwise they would create their own base and not encroach on the other's territory. Hjalti seemed trustworthy, and they'd sworn an oath to this effect. Geir had also paid him to transport extra livestock for him, since the man had the space on the outward journey.

His own men helped him to secure the ship. It was a large vessel and they had to be careful not to get it stuck completely. To make sure the tides didn't take it away, however, they tethered the mooring ropes to a nearby rocky outcrop. He wasn't taking any chances. His entire life was on board this ship; everything he owned and all he needed to fulfil his dreams. It had to be safeguarded at all costs.

'What are you going to do with the strange female?' Steinthor asked.

'I don't know yet,' Geir lied. He'd already made up his mind to try and persuade her to stay with them, at least for a while. She intrigued him. 'I'll go and see if she is awake shortly. Once the women have cooked us a meal, I'll take some food to her. It's best if she doesn't move for now. The wisewoman was adamant on that score. We don't want her to go weird in the head.'

'True. I'll go and help collect driftwood for fires.'

The women soon had food ready, and Geir took his own portion, plus a share for Maddie, and climbed on board. As he raised the tent flap, he saw her stirring with another groan. Having had concussion himself, he knew exactly how she was feeling, and it wasn't pleasant.

'Good evening. I have brought you some victuals.' He placed the two bowls on the planks next to her and hunkered down. 'There's a bucket over there in the corner if you need to avail yourself of that first?'

A fiery blush spread over her cheeks, but she nodded. 'Yes, please.'

'Here, let me help you rise.' He placed an arm around her shoulders and raised her into a sitting position. 'Just sit like that for a moment while your head adjusts. Hurts like at least ten *jötnar* are trampling you, doesn't it?'

She managed a small smile at his words. 'Something like that, yes. I can manage now, thank you.' The wary glance that accompanied her words showed that she didn't trust him yet, but that was understandable. She would soon learn that he didn't pose a threat.

'I'll wait outside. Call me when you're ready to eat.'

Soon he was back inside the tent and propping her up against his travelling kist and a bundle of furs. She stroked a hand over the top one. 'What is this? It's so soft.'

'Wolf. The darker one is bear. I killed him myself.' He indicated three bear claws hanging round his neck on leather straps. His silversmith brother Rurik had created beautiful mounts for them, and he wore them with pride. Some people said that if you killed a bear, its strength would become yours. Geir hoped it was true. He'd need all the muscle power he could get in order to succeed in this venture.

'Really? That must have been scary.' She accepted the bowl he held out to her. 'Thank you. I'm quite hungry now, and at least I don't feel sick any more.'

'Good. And no, not scary – exhilarating.'

They ate in silence. There was much he wanted to ask her, but she was in no fit state and it was better to save his questions for the morrow.

'I don't feel any movement. Have we arrived already?'

'In Ísland?' Geir started laughing. 'No, we've only been sailing for one day. It will take at least another week, if not two. We have made landfall on a deserted island. It's safer than trying to navigate in the dark, at least until we are past the Suðureyjar.'

'Oh, I see.'

He took back her now empty bowl, pleased that she had eaten it all, and handed her a leather waterskin. 'For when you're thirsty,' he said. 'Now try to go back to sleep. It's the best thing for healing.'

'I know. Thank you again.'

He noticed she didn't try to argue with him about the knife, and her gaze had lost some of the wariness he'd seen earlier. Excellent. He meant her no harm. In fact, he was beginning to think he would enjoy having her company indefinitely.

*

To her amazement, Maddie went straight back to sleep, awaking some time towards dawn. The light filtering in through the tent flaps was a pearly grey. Enough to make out shapes, but no details. She blinked, letting her eyes adjust, and then had to swallow a gasp. Her captor – she couldn't call him anything else, as he was keeping her here against her will – was lying alongside her, breathing softly, his back turned towards her.

Good grief. She'd been sleeping next to a Viking.

She'd never slept next to any man before, because she hadn't had a boyfriend.

It wasn't for lack of trying. Just like all the other girls in her class at school, she'd gone to parties and hung around the available boys, but no one she liked the look of had been interested in her. Not permanently, anyway. She was too tall, too awkward, with pale skin and flaming hair. It didn't matter how often her dad told her she was beautiful in a Pre-Raphaelite way – she didn't believe him, because no one else thought so.

A couple of times she'd drunk too much and allowed some guy to make out with her – it seemed to be what her girlfriends did, as if it was some kind of sport and something to brag about afterwards. Most of them also went all the way, but Maddie hadn't, because it felt so sordid and meaningless. She'd wanted her first time sleeping with someone to be special, or at the very least with a permanent boyfriend. But no such guy ever materialised, and although she didn't want to be left out or thought of as uncool and childish, she stuck to her guns. Even when she heard whispers about her being a 'frigid bitch'.

Bastards. At least, thanks to all her self-defence training, no one had dared say that to her face. She was very grateful to her foster brother, Ivar, for encouraging her to take up those classes. He was sixteen years older than her, but he had been bullied when he was at school and somehow he'd guessed that she was struggling.

'Being able to kick ass will give you confidence,' he'd told her, and he was right – the lessons had helped enormously, even though she'd never actually had to put her skills into practice until she met those four thugs in Dublin. *No, Dyflin, in the ninth century!* She was still having trouble getting her head round that.

She glanced at the Viking next to her and frowned. He hadn't even told her his name, but he was lying there like a protective shield. Or was he guarding his possession? She shivered, still not completely sure about his intentions towards her.

The small movement must have woken him, because he turned in an instant, gazing at her with intensity. 'Are you cold? Do you have a fever?' He put out a hand to feel her forehead, and his touch made her shiver again, although in a nicer way.

She ducked away from his fingers. 'No, I'm fine. Thank you. Sorry, I didn't mean to wake you.'

'It doesn't matter. I am due to take my turn on guard duty anyway.'

'Guard duty? Are you expecting to be attacked?' This alarmed her more than the fact that she was lying so close to a very large man in the semi-darkness of his tent. She didn't stop to analyse why.

'You never know. It pays to be vigilant.' He must have seen the fear in her eyes. 'But do not worry, we'll protect you.'

'We?' She hadn't been outside the tent yet and had no idea who else was on board this ship.

'There are five of us men, four women, a young boy and four children. Oh, and one more on the way, I believe. Also another shipload of men with whom we are travelling.'

Maddie wondered briefly if one of the women was his wife or mistress, but surely he wouldn't be sleeping here with her if that was the case? Not that it mattered, but still . . .

He sat up and dry-washed his face as if trying to wake himself fully. She heard the slight rasping as his hands came into contact with his stubble, and the noise sent a strange tremor through her. His shoulder-length hair had fallen out of the ponytail he'd tied it in the day before, and she watched as he deftly scooped it up and refastened the leather cord around it. She wished he hadn't – she'd liked it loose – then almost groaned out loud. What was she doing admiring the guy's hair? She shouldn't be noticing anything personal about him.

'Obviously I'm taking turns with the other men,' he commented, pulling her out of her thoughts.

That made her smile inwardly. How chauvinistic it sounded, but in this era it was probably obvious, although she'd heard that Viking women could be fierce too.

'Try to sleep some more.' He picked up a long-handled axe she hadn't noticed lying next to him.

She recoiled slightly. *Whoa!* That looked lethal, the edge razor-sharp.

He carried on as if he hadn't noticed her reaction to the weapon. 'It really is the best thing for what ails you. Trust me, I know.'

'You said that before. What happened to you?' She wasn't sure why she was keeping up this conversation, but for some reason she was curious about him and wanted to know more.

'I was travelling and we were caught in an ambush. Our opponents didn't fight fair, using their weapons the traditional way, and someone hit me over the head with his sword hilt. At least, I think that's what happened. My memory is a little hazy.' He smiled. 'I must go. We will speak more later.'

She nodded, looking forward to it already. No, that was wrong. She should still be angry with him, and cautious, but for the life of her she couldn't summon up the energy.

Just before ducking out of the flap, he turned back and asked, 'Do you like dogs?'

'Yes, very much. Why?'

'Good, then I'll send Blár in, if you don't mind. He usually sleeps next to me and he's been sulking because I wouldn't let him in.'

'Oh, right. Sure.'

A few seconds later, something large and furry hurtled in through the tent flap and a wet nose was shoved into her outstretched hand.

'Hello there! Blár, was it? Yes, yes, I'm pleased to see you too, but maybe you could lie down now? Down! You're a bit big, you know, and no, I don't want to be licked, thank you!'

The dog was obviously well trained, and at her command, he sank down next to her immediately but shuffled close to her legs, his tail thumping on the planks. She couldn't make out what type he was, but he seemed to be a very dark colour. 'Is that how you got your name?' she whispered, scratching him behind one ear. 'Your fur is so black it looks blue? Well, let's go to sleep now, shall we?'

And as she snuggled down once more, Blár seemed happy with that suggestion.

Chapter Five

Geir sat on a large boulder and stared out to sea. The sun hadn't risen yet, but it wouldn't be long now. He loved this time of day, when all was quiet and still, and not even the birds were awake yet. The peace was soothing and filtered right through to his very core. And it was a beautiful place this, wild and craggy, but with lush green all around. He hoped his new home would be too.

He glanced towards the ship, where all was quiet. Maddie must have gone back to sleep with Blár to guard her, and no one else was awake either. He was a light sleeper and her early-morning shiver had woken him. It had given him a jolt when he contemplated that she might be feeling worse. What if that blow to her head had really damaged something inside? He sincerely hoped that wasn't the case. She'd assured him she was fine; he had to take her word for it.

What was he to do with her? He knew what he wanted to do – make her stay. At least for a while.

The moment he'd realised that she was a time traveller, he had discerned the involvement of the gods or Norns in this. It simply couldn't be coincidence – three brothers, three time-travelling women. There was a definite pattern here. Hrafn and Rurik had both fallen in love with theirs, although it had taken time. Geir could only assume he was meant to do the same with Maddie. Why else would she be here? What other reason could there be for her ending up with him, of all people?

No, it had to be fate, destiny, or whatever one wanted to call it. Something that was meant to be.

But what would she think about that? And were they really well matched? He had no idea.

He considered what he knew of her so far. She was very tall – not a problem when he was oversized himself – beautiful in an angular sort of way, with flaming curly hair that he longed to tangle his fingers in, and she knew how to fight. Her moves had been strange, yet effective, and he liked the fact that she didn't consider herself helpless in any way. Rather the opposite – she'd been almost too sure of her abilities. Stubborn, too.

He smiled to himself. It would be a pleasure sparring with her, in every way.

Then he frowned as he recalled that there would be obstacles. The gods never did anything by halves, and even if they had intended Maddie for him, he was fairly certain she wasn't just going to fall into his arms with gratitude. *Skítr!* She didn't even want to be here; she wanted to go home. Nor was he prone to falling in love. In fact, he couldn't recall ever mooning after any woman for longer than a week, hence why he wasn't married yet. But perhaps he should leave all that to the goddess Freya; she was the expert on matters of the heart. He had to trust that if this was meant to be, it would happen somehow. Either way, Maddie had to stay at least a month or two in order for them to see if it was their destiny to be together.

'But how to persuade her?' he muttered.

He had two immediate choices: force her to remain as his captive until she too realised fate meant them to be a couple; or find a way to make her stay long enough for him to woo her and persuade her that he was the right man for her, if he felt that was the truth.

Even though he wasn't convinced of this himself, he much preferred the second option, because he had a feeling she would take badly to being forced into anything. She definitely had a strong will. And he had already told her that she wasn't his prisoner. Besides, he would much rather she was willing – he'd never forced any woman to accept his advances and he wasn't about to start now. There was no joy in that.

It was time to come up with a plan, and as the sun finally made its appearance, he knew what he had to do.

Maddie was surprised to feel the ship moving when she woke for a second time, but bright sunlight shone through the tent fabric and she guessed it must be mid morning already. She couldn't expect the crew to wait for her to rise before setting off each day. The dog had disappeared, presumably in search of breakfast, and her stomach rumbled at the thought. She supposed it was a good sign that she was feeling hungry.

'Ah, you're awake.' Her night-time protector entered through the flap, handing her a bowl containing something that looked like porridge, minus any sugar or fruit, and a horn spoon to eat it with.

'Thank you.' She managed to sit up by herself and was glad to notice that she felt a lot better. The incessant pounding in her head had calmed to a dull ache, and there was no dizziness at all. Thank goodness for that.

She took a few mouthfuls of the porridge. It wasn't particularly tasty, but she knew better than to complain. She'd had worse in some of the re-enactment camps she had stayed in, and she wasn't a fussy eater.

She looked up as he sat down cross-legged next to her. He

brought with him the tang of the sea and fresh air, and a scent that she already recognised as uniquely his – clean, male and with a hint of damp woollen garments. He'd left the tent flap partly open, and a ray of sunlight highlighted his long, messy dark blond hair with sun-bleached streaks running through it. His broad shoulders and big frame made the space seem suddenly cramped, but he wasn't intentionally crowding her.

She felt the need to make conversation and said, 'So we are sailing already?'

'Yes, no point wasting any daylight.' Grey-blue eyes framed with dark lashes searched hers. 'Are you well?'

'Better, thank you.' She did her best not to notice the faint stirring inside her caused by him looking at her like that. It was concern for her welfare, nothing else. Touching her skull with a couple of fingers, she added, 'Just hurting a little bit now. I should be able to help soon.'

'Help?' He tilted his head to one side, clearly puzzled.

'Yes, you know, with rowing and such. I'm assuming everyone has to do something on board.'

She'd been to the Viking Ship Museum in Roskilde once and gone on a trip round the harbour on a replica longship. The captain had been adamant that no freeloaders were allowed – you couldn't come along unless you were prepared to row. She'd thought the same principle would apply here.

His mouth curved into a smile and she caught a quick glint of amusement in his eyes. 'I don't think that will be necessary, but thank you for the offer. We are mostly using the sail.'

'I see.' Maddie was curious about the ship, but didn't feel up to stepping outside the tent yet. 'How long did you say it would take us to reach Ísland?' She had quickly resigned herself to having to go there once she'd realised she could still return to her own time when they arrived. Which reminded her . . . 'And are you going to give me back my knife soon? You know I can't use it out here at sea.'

'No, that would be unwise.' He shook his head, looking grave now, but there was still a distinct twinkle in his gaze. 'I'm afraid I can't return it to you yet. You see, I've been thinking, and I have a proposition for you. How would you like to stay with us and help establish our settlement before you return to your time?'

'What? Why would I want to do that? That's going to take years!' She blinked at him, surprised he'd even suggest such a thing.

'Oh, you'd only have to stay for the first year. That's going to be the most difficult time and we'll need all the help we can find.'

'A year?' Maddie's voice emerged as an outraged squeak. 'Are you insane? And what, am I supposed to be your woman or something?'

'If you're offering.' A smile tugged at the corners of his lips, drawing attention to the fact that he had a very nice mouth, framed with dark blond stubble that emphasised a strong jaw.

'I'm not! I mean, I wouldn't . . . not if you were the last man on *earth*.'

'Where's that?' He was smiling properly now, but she tried to ignore that because it was incredibly distracting.

'Miðgarðr, I think you call it.'

'I'm sure you could find a worse man than me in this realm. I have good traits. I came to your rescue, didn't I?'

'I was doing fine on my own. I didn't need you,' she insisted.

'You did, but that's beside the point – my intention was honourable. I haven't molested you—'

'That's *your* opinion. Dragging me across the sea against my will and stealing my folding knife and—'

'Oh, trust me, that's nothing. If I wanted to molest you

properly, you'd know about it.' He paused; then, as if he knew he'd teased her enough, he held up a hand. 'But no, making you my woman was not part of the proposition. We merely need your help. Another pair of hands is going to be very welcome.'

'You should have thought of that before and brought more people. What about a wife?'

He shook his head. 'Don't have one.'

'Well, perhaps there will be someone suitable there already? Or is Ísland short of women?'

'I have no idea, but I won't have time to go courting for a while. Besides, I would need to have something to offer first – a proper home and a bride price. In the meantime, I could do with having a woman in charge of my household. The others,' he nodded to the deck outside, 'are used to just following orders, but you seem to me to be someone who likes to lead.'

Was he mocking her? Maddie was known to be bossy with her family when things needed to be done, but she hadn't told him that and he didn't know her yet. Something else bothered her, and curiosity made her blurt out, 'Why didn't you marry someone back home?'

'There was no one I wanted enough. And as I said, I had nothing to offer.' He regarded her solemnly. 'You could do worse than to come with me – with us.'

She couldn't believe she was actually contemplating this, but he made it sound like an adventure. 'I know nothing about you, not even your name,' she pointed out.

'I'm Geir.'

A common enough name in Viking times, she knew, but quite nice. Not that she was going to tell him that. 'Well, Geir, I think you would regret having me with you, since I don't know much about taking care of a household. Go and find yourself a wife – there is my advice.'

That first part was a lie. She was a very practical and capable person, and knew how to do most household-related chores Viking style, including cooking and preserving, but he didn't need to know that. Yet more courses she'd attended with her parents – the Viking age was their obsession and had sort of become hers by default. She had taken part in numerous re-enactments, staying in camps for days on end, learning how to spin and weave the Viking way, and even how to milk cows and goats, turning the milk into butter and cheese. At least she'd been good at those things, because you didn't need to be able to read to excel at them. Bloody dyslexia . . .

He sighed. 'Listen, once I've been in Ísland for a year or so, I'm sure I can find a wife, but right now, I don't have time to bother about it. I have to claim a piece of land and prepare it for spring sowing and planting, else we won't survive next year. We'll need to build a house before the weather turns cold, and go hunting and fishing, as well as gather hay. All I ask is for you to stay one year. What do you say? Or at the very least to the end of the summer?'

She bit her lip and studied his face. He seemed completely in earnest, and possibly a little bit desperate. Would it really be so bad? And wasn't this what she'd wanted? Her very own Viking adventure, just like the ones Linnea and Sara had embarked upon. She must be mad to even be thinking about staying, and yet it was incredibly tempting.

'Would you give me back the knife if I said yes?'

He shook his head, his mouth quirking with amusement. 'Not at first. I'm not stupid. And I need to know I can trust you. That you won't just disappear.'

She glared at him, although it didn't look as though it was having any noticeable effect. 'And why should *I* trust *you*? If – and this is only an if at the moment – I said yes, we would need some rules. Such as, I would act like your wife in looking after the household, but you would have no right to touch me or any other . . . wifely things like that.'

Geir grinned, and his eyes twinkled again. 'Not even to sleep next to you? You might be glad of my body heat. I hear it's cold in Ísland.'

'Hmph. We could discuss that when winter comes.'

'Actually, it's cold all the time, I understand.' He became serious once more. 'But you would consider it if I agree to your rules?'

Maddie hesitated. This was insane. She'd only meant to go for a little walk around Viking-age Dublin, not sail off into the sunset with a hunky Norseman. Not that he was hunky. Much. Well, he was, but anyway . . . Now that she was here, why not grab this opportunity? She could probably find a way of taking her knife back if she got fed up. Geir couldn't have that many hiding places. Chances were he'd keep it on his person, and he had to sleep at some point, then she could retrieve it.

Yes, as long as she still had a way out, this could actually be fun. Hard work, but fun. She'd wanted to try living a green lifestyle for some time now, going on protest marches against climate change, doing her bit for the planet, and had considered joining some sort of farm collective. Here was her chance to learn how to live completely in tune with nature. And to show her family that she could do something worthwhile and be of use, even though she wasn't a book-learning nerd like the rest of them.

Her family . . . *Oh no!* Could she really do this to them? They'd be worried sick, of course, but since they'd already had other relatives and friends disappear without a trace, only to turn up safe and well a year later, hopefully they wouldn't panic too much. She'd miss them terribly as well, but she was an adult and it was past time for her to strike out on her own and try to find her place in the world. Surely they would understand? And it wasn't for ever . . .

She made up her mind. 'Very well then, I'll do it. But only for a few months, and you have to swear to give me back the knife before winter.' She didn't think she'd survive a winter in Iceland without thermal underwear and central heating.

'Excellent!' The broad smile he gave her made her stomach flutter in a most unsettling way, but Maddie told herself it was just nerves. What had she let herself in for?

It wasn't until he'd left the tent that she realised he hadn't promised anything.

Chapter Six

The following day Geir watched Maddie as she slowly ate the food she'd been given. Her movements were as dainty as a queen's, and she broke off tiny pieces of flatbread before putting them in her mouth. Her very delectable mouth.

He was beginning to think he'd done something really stupid in asking her to stay. Especially if he had to abide by her rules. Still, they'd only just met. Perhaps in a few weeks he could charm her enough that she'd agree to be his woman properly. It was what he'd intended, but she had pre-empted any such suggestion by telling him he should look for a wife in Ísland, thereby showing clearly that she wasn't open to his advances. *Skítr!* He would have to find a way to change her mind.

He wasn't as experienced with women as his older brothers had been before they married, but he'd slept with a few. They'd not seemed averse to him; quite the opposite. He had steered well clear of the kind of respectable girls of good family looking for a more permanent relationship, though. There hadn't been anyone with whom he could have contemplated marriage.

What he'd told Maddie was true – he had never come across a woman he liked enough to want to spend a lifetime with. He had known that if he was successful in Ísland – and he was determined he would be – any marriage he made might come down to alliances rather than love. Such was life for most couples, and he'd been prepared for that. But perhaps he didn't need to worry about it now, if the gods or fates had other plans for him. Time would tell.

This was the first time Maddie had ventured outside the tent that acted as shelter from the elements. It wasn't very big, as most of the space on board was taken up with livestock, supplies and farm implements, as well as a couple of tents for the other passengers. Her eyes had opened wide at the sight of cows and sheep lying down on deck, chewing desultorily on wisps of hay, while a couple of pigs snuffled their way through a pile of old turnips. Chickens cooed inside wicker cages, flapping in fright now and again as the ship rose and fell gently among the waves, and a couple of goats were tethered to the mast. It would be a wonder, Geir thought, if he managed to bring this entire menagerie safely to their destination.

She seemed to be thinking along the same lines, as she had exclaimed, 'You've brought animals? In an open boat? They must be terrified!'

'Ship, if you don't mind,' he'd corrected her. 'And do they look frightened to you?' It was true they'd been very unsettled to begin with, but now they had accepted their unusual circumstances. With the patience of most creatures, they awaited their future with equanimity.

'Actually, no. But still . . .'

He returned his gaze to her now. She had finished her meal and was absently stroking Blár's dark fur. The dog had really taken to her and was sticking to her like tree sap, as though he knew she was still fragile and needed protecting. 'How are you feeling?'

She shrugged. 'Still a dull headache, but it's much better than it was.'

To Geir's amazement, she'd done as she was told and stayed lying down except when heeding the call of nature. Most of that time had been spent asleep, and he wasn't even sure if she'd been aware of him lying next to her the few times he'd managed to snatch time to rest. It had been oddly cosy, sharing his tent with her and Blár, but he hadn't tried touching her. For one thing, she was still injured and in pain, and for another, he knew instinctively that he needed to take things slowly. She wasn't a thrall woman, to be tumbled at will. She would need proper wooing, and he had just the thing to start with.

'What are you staring at? Do I look that bad?' She frowned at him and tried to pull her fingers through her unruly mass of hair. It was like a nest of writhing snakes, and a dark red colour that shone even more in the sunlight than he'd expected. Her face was still pale from the blow to her head, but it suited her. The few times she'd smiled, he'd glimpsed a dimple on one side of her mouth. He was becoming entirely too fixated on that mouth, and forced himself to look away. Yes, it would probably feel extremely good to kiss her, but only if she was willing. He didn't hold with forcing women, not even thralls. Lovemaking was much more enjoyable if both parties were eager for it.

'No, you'll do,' he muttered. Which was an understatement if ever he'd heard one. 'But you might want to tame those tresses a bit. Have you any use for this, or would you prefer me to find you a leather thong?' He held out a long hairpin carved out of bone. He'd made it himself to while away the time at sea. One end tapered to a point, while the other was decorated with fretwork in a swirling design all his own. A snake to match her curls. Carpentry was his speciality, but carving in bone was almost the same as wood, and he'd had no trouble fashioning this simple object.

Maddie took the pin and turned it over before looking at him.

'This is beautiful! But whose is it? I don't want to take it if it's someone else's. They might need it.'

He put his hand on hers and closed her fingers around the pin. 'It's yours. I made it for you. It is but a small trinket.' He held her hand for a fraction longer than necessary, enjoying the feel of her soft skin against his callused palm.

'I . . . Thank you! That's very kind.' A blush stole over her cheeks as if she was embarrassed that someone had done something nice for her. Geir didn't know why, but rosy cheeks became her too. Lowering her gaze, she gathered up the mass of hair and tried to prevent the wind from whipping it around. She managed to twist it up on top of her head and secured the large knot with the bone pin. 'There,' she exclaimed triumphantly. 'That's better, right?' She smiled at him and something shifted inside his chest.

He cleared his throat. 'Yes, perfect,' he agreed, although in truth he'd preferred her glorious hair loose. 'But what is that on your wrist? And what have you done to your ears?'

'What? Oh, my *tattoo*.' She pulled up the sleeve of her gown to show him a design etched into her skin with black colour. It was like a thick cuff or armband, a hand's-breadth wide, and he could make out twisting animals intertwined with one another. 'Do you like it? It took ages to have this done and it hurt a lot, but it was worth it.'

'I . . . Yes. Yes, I do.' He'd seen men with marked skin before, but never a woman. There was no doubt it suited her, though, and he touched the pattern gently, following the swirl of a dragon's tail with one finger. 'I like it very much.'

He was rewarded with the biggest smile he'd seen from her so far, and it affected him like a punch in the gut. *Whoa!* This was getting a bit too intense. He cleared his throat and nodded at her ears. 'And those?'

On the right-hand side, her ear had seven gold rings piercing it at intervals, all the way up to the top, while on the other, she sported four such rings on the ear lobe. He hadn't noticed until she put her hair up with the pin. It was definitely a novel way of carrying your wealth around with you. Her family must be very rich, as the wrist without markings also had at least a dozen silver arm rings and strange chains that jingled every time she moved her hands.

She shrugged and touched the earrings self-consciously. 'Seemed like a good idea at the time.'

Geir didn't know what to say to that and was relieved when one of the thrall women came over with a platter of dried meat. 'Would you like some more to eat, mistress?' She looked at Maddie.

'Yes, please. Thank you . . . What's your name?'

'Aine, mistress.'

'What a pretty name. I'm Maddie.' She smiled at the woman, who looked both pleased and discomfited at the same time.

'Thank you kindly.' Aine quickly moved on to the group who sat at the far end of the ship near the prow: the second thrall woman, who was about the same age as herself – twenty winters, or so Geir had been told – the two young Irishmen and the ten-year-old boy. Steinthor and Ingimund's families sat at the opposite end, in the stern, their small children toddling about unsteadily while the two men took turns to steer the ship.

Maddie turned back to Geir. 'Has Aine been your servant for long?'

'What? Oh, you mean when did I buy her? Only a few days ago, but she seems capable and quick.'

Maddie choked on a piece of meat. 'You bought her?' she wheezed, in between coughing bouts.

He tried to be helpful and pat her on the back, but she ducked away, glaring at him. 'Of course,' he said. 'I needed thralls to bring with me. Dyflin has the best market for that sort of thing. Everyone knows that. I should have bought more, but I wanted to save some of my silver in case I have need of it later. Besides, it will be difficult to feed too many people the first year. I had to make sure I have enough supplies.'

She was staring at him like he was the Miðgarðr serpent. 'You're saying you own people?' She waved a hand at the rest of his crew. 'All these?'

'Not all of them, but yes, Aine and a few of the others. I need workers to help with the crops and livestock, hunting and fishing. I told you, there's a lot to do in a very short time.'

'*Thralls?*' she almost shrieked. 'That's disgusting!'

'What are you talking about?' What maggot had got into her brain now? Geir was genuinely puzzled. 'They're not dirty. I've made sure they keep themselves clean and I bought them new clothing and even some shoes. As I said, I've been told it can be cold in Ísland.'

'I don't mean how often they wash! *For Christ's sake* . . . Owning people is wrong. Just wrong. Everyone should be free. Either pay them for the work they do or let them go. I'm not staying anywhere with a thrall owner.'

'You sound just like . . . Never mind. And what has the White Christ to do with anything?' He sighed and shoved his fingers through his hair, suddenly tired beyond measure. 'Look, I've had a long day.' He'd been steering since early morning, fighting contrary winds, which had only just settled down, leaving him free to let someone else take the steering oar for a while. 'I'm not arguing with you any further. I'm going to get some rest.' He made to stand up, but she grabbed his tunic and pulled him down again.

'No, I'm serious, Geir. You can't take thralls with you to Ísland.

It isn't right for any man to own another, and that's a long way from their homeland. Offer to set them free and pay them, or I'm not going to stay or help you in any way.'

He glared at her. 'You have no choice if you wish to eat. I'll not feed anyone who doesn't do their fair share of the work. And I have your knife, remember?' He didn't want to be harangued, but then again, he'd heard these arguments before from another woman. His sister-in-law, who'd been a thrall herself for a while. The idea of everyone being entitled to their freedom had started to make sense when he'd talked to her, but he hadn't been sure he'd have enough silver to pay anyone to come and work for him. It had seemed easier to buy some thralls. He could always give them their freedom at a later date. 'Besides, I can't afford to pay anyone until my new domains become profitable. I've spent most of my hacksilver on buying supplies and livestock.'

That gave her pause, but then she nodded. 'I can understand that, but maybe if you set them free and promise to pay them when you can, they'll agree. Or offer them the possibility of their own plot of land? Trust me, people work a lot harder when they have an incentive.' She frowned. 'And I don't mean like being beaten.' Something flickered in the depths of her moss-coloured eyes. 'You wouldn't, would you? Beat them?'

'No. There's no need. Most thralls know their place, and these weren't newly captured.'

'Well, good. Then they'll want their freedom even more. Talk to them. Please, Geir? This is important.'

She stared into his eyes and he couldn't tear his gaze away. He could drown in those green depths . . . He shook his head. Maybe she really was a *vōlva* after all? But this was none of her business.

'Why should I?'

'Because it's the right thing to do. Because I'm asking you to.'

'And what will you give me in return if I grant your request?'

Her eyes widened and she jerked back. 'You want me to bargain with you? With what? My body, I suppose,' she sneered. 'I should have known. It's all you men ever think about. You're . . . *despicable*.'

That final word was flung at him in her language, and although he didn't know what it meant, he could guess as she got up and stalked off to throw herself down on to the planks at the front of the vessel, confusing poor Blár, who didn't know whether to go after her or stay with his master. Geir sighed and rubbed his tired face.

She was asking too much.

For the next few days, Maddie hardly spoke a word to Geir. He deserved the silent treatment, although on some level she could understand that the concept of not owning thralls was alien to him. She'd known this about Viking society, but it hadn't really registered until her sister had told her about her experiences. Now she wanted to reason with him, but she knew that all her arguments were twenty-first-century ones. They wouldn't affect him. In his world, thralls were commonplace and no one questioned the practice. And yet, it was wrong. So incredibly wrong. She couldn't possibly condone it.

She sighed. This wasn't an adventure; it was more like a nightmare. Stuck on a ship out on the endless ocean with a heathen and his slaves. Good grief. What had she been thinking? She'd been naïve to imagine she could just take a little trip back in time. Of course nothing was ever that easy. And to actually consider staying with him? No, that was a pipe dream.

Maddie stared out over the vast sea, rather than at Geir, who was in the stern holding on to the massive steering oar. She was sitting in the raised prow – as far away from him as she possibly could – looking out over the side. There was a little step here that formed the perfect seat, although it meant she had to have her back to the direction of travel. If she'd wanted to gaze straight ahead, she would have had to stand on her knees which wasn't very comfortable. Here, she was somewhat protected from the constant breeze, and she could see over the gunwale – not that there was much to look at other than the occasional school of dolphins, or a whale or two. And the other ship, which was shadowing them but only came close enough occasionally for a shouted conversation. If she allowed herself to contemplate how many fathoms of ocean lay beneath and around them, panic would bubble up inside her. They were so small compared to the forces of nature and it seemed to her it wouldn't take much to pitch them all into the sea. The flick of a blue whale's tail fin, a tentacle of the dreaded Kraken or even the Miðgarðr serpent . . . Or what about an iceberg, like with the *Titanic*?

'Don't even go there,' she muttered to herself. She was being fanciful now, but what if even just a really big wave could capsize them? Despite the fact that she could swim, it wouldn't do any good. The water was freezing. She'd stuck her hand in to see just how cold, and knew she wouldn't survive that for long.

It was a sturdy ship, well built and supple, she had to admit. A *knarr*, she'd heard someone call it, which was apparently some type of cargo ship – and it seemed able to withstand most of the things the sea threw at it. It hardly listed at all, even in crosswinds. So far anyway.

Curving up at either end, it was incredibly big though. Much larger than the vessel she'd helped row round Roskilde harbour. That ship had been a sleek warship, built for speed, while this one was wide and clearly made to transport large amounts of goods around. She reckoned it was at least twenty metres long, if not more, and five or six wide across the central part; she'd tried to measure it by counting her steps. An enormous woollen sail stretched above her head from a mast that was as tall as a tree. Thick ropes – Geir had said they were made of horsehair or walrus hide – tethered it to wooden cleats in several places. The creaking of the rigging and the whoosh of the waves were the only sounds to be heard, making sailing an almost surreal experience.

But Maddie was still afraid and knew she wouldn't stop being scared until they reached land safely. She was uncomfortable, too. Sitting here in the same clothes she'd worn since she left her hotel room in Dublin, she felt dirty, itchy and smelly. A couple of times she'd attempted to wash with seawater and a linen cloth, but it wasn't the same as having a bath. And when you didn't have any clean garments to change into, it seemed rather pointless. She'd considered asking if she could borrow something from one of the other women, but she knew anything they owned would be too small.

'I need to go back to my time,' she muttered. Fresh clothes, a hot shower, soap and shampoo . . . Bliss. Hopefully, she'd find all that once they reached their destination.

Iceland. She'd been there on holiday once, but who'd have thought she'd be heading back any time soon? And a thousand years earlier than last time? It was unreal.

No, actually, it was only too real. And it would seem she had no choice in the matter. But as soon as she arrived, she'd find a way to go home. She had to.

'Are you going to sulk all the way, or are you ready to listen to reason?'

Geir's voice startled her, and she turned to face him, her heart jumping into her throat. 'What?'

He was scowling, his steely eyes dark with some emotion she couldn't read – frustration, perhaps? Or anger? She stood up and realised he must be well over six foot tall, as she had to look up at him. She was used to staring most men in the face. At nearly six foot herself, she was taller than them more often than not. And he had the big frame to go with his height, too – the sleeves of his tunic outlined fairly substantial biceps and fitted snugly across broad shoulders. But strangely enough, she didn't feel threatened by his size. Rather, it comforted her, made her feel almost fragile, a thought that had her wanting to snort with laughter.

She'd never felt small or fragile in her life. She'd always been the giraffe. The girl who had to bend down to slow-dance with the boys in her class. So embarrassing for everyone concerned, although it hadn't seemed to matter as much when they were making out with her on someone's sofa . . .

'What's so amusing?' He quirked an eyebrow at her.

'Nothing. I was just thinking that I don't often meet men who make me feel tiny.'

'Well, I wouldn't say you were tiny exactly . . . A perfect size, perhaps?' His expression relaxed a fraction and he stepped closer, lifting his hand to capture some of the curls that had escaped her new hairpin and were blowing in the never-ending breeze. The small gesture seemed rather intimate and made her shiver, but she tried to concentrate on his words instead.

'Um, perfect for what?'

'For me?' His gaze was suddenly a lot warmer, and Maddie wanted to squirm, but held herself rigid. No point him getting any ideas.

'I don't think so. I'm not staying. Unless you're going to free the thralls?'

He stepped away from her, his expression hardening again. 'I can't do that. I told you. We need them to help with the work.'

'They can do that as free men and women. And children.' She glanced at the small boy, Brendan, who she'd learned was part of Geir's group of slaves, although why he'd bought such a scrawny little thing, she had no idea.

'No.' His mouth was set in an uncompromising line, and Maddie knew he wouldn't change his mind. And why should he? Her opinion was nothing to him.

She studied the two groups of people sitting at opposite ends of the ship – the free travellers and the thralls. There wasn't much difference in their clothing, she had to give Geir that; he'd obviously spent silver on proper outfits for everyone. But there the similarities ended.

Steinthor and Ingimund, the two free men, were laughing and joking with each other as they took turns steering now, surrounded by their families. Maddie had been introduced to them the day before, as well as their wives, Fridgerd and Lif. The men had been friendly in a slightly curt manner, while their wives had barely exchanged two words with her. They had two children each under the age of about four, and were kept busy looking after them. On the rare occasions the little ones weren't rampaging around, the women sat and gossiped quietly together without including Maddie. She supposed it was only natural that they should be wary of a stranger, especially one who had arrived among them so unexpectedly. And as her status here was uncertain, they probably weren't sure how to treat her. But it would have been nice if they'd shown a little more interest in her. She might have offered to help out with the kids, as she loved children.

The thralls sat in silence, their expressions stoic and resigned as they stared out over the sea. They probably weren't used to inactivity, so perhaps they were enjoying the rest, but they didn't look happy. And why would they? Taken away from the land of their birth to work for a man they didn't know in a strange country. At his beck and call every hour of the day, forced to perform the lowliest of tasks. All without any payment or even thanks for their work. It must be unbearable.

She focused on Geir again. 'So am I your thrall as well now?'

Irritation flared in his eyes. 'No, I asked you to stay as a free woman, to run the household.'

'But if I don't want to stay and you make me, I am a captive, just like them.' She nodded in the direction of the thralls.

He stepped closer again and looked down at her, his eyes narrowing. 'Ah, but you have a choice; they don't. You can make this difficult for yourself or you can agree to help me of your own free will.'

'Why would I do that? I want to go home. Back to my time. I don't belong here.'

'I think you do. And unless you remain for a while, we'll never know.'

What was that supposed to mean? She opened her mouth to ask, but he'd turned away and was striding off towards the other end of the ship, dodging the animals and tightly packed supplies that made the huge space look very cramped.

'Either way, you're staying,' he threw over his shoulder, and Maddie sighed. There was clearly no reasoning with him – it was his way or nothing.

And that meant she *was* a captive, whether he admitted it or not.

Chapter Seven

A few days later, Geir called Steinthor over to the steering oar. 'Can you take this for a moment, please? I need a quick break.'

He'd been steering for ages now, guiding the ship through rough seas. With the wind behind them, they'd been travelling at quite some speed, to the point where he'd started to feel a rumbling or vibration in the keel of the ship. The strange sensation worked its way up through the deck to his feet and into his knees, and he didn't like it. It was good that they were making progress, but he preferred a steadier pace and smaller waves, even though the prow cut through them like a hot knife through butter. He'd kept them on a straight course though, and despite the water rising up on either side of the prow like blue walls, it never came over the gunwales. They glided right through it.

He ducked into his tent to escape the relentless wind for a while. Although he was pleased that it propelled the ship towards its destination at great speed, it made the air feel much colder than it really was. And the constant breeze whipped up the waves so that everything was covered with a fine spray of brine. He was tired of feeling damp, and the tops of his ears stung. He'd have to dig out his woollen hat and mittens from his travelling kist or his extremities would likely drop off.

He stopped just inside the opening and took in the sight of Maddie, who was sitting cross-legged on the bed furs, her beautiful hair flowing across her shoulders and down her back. Even in the dim interior of the tent, the colour glowed, and he couldn't help but admire it. Not that he was going to tell her that. She'd kept to herself and hardly spoken to him, but he'd decided to give her time to get over her fit of pique before talking to her again so he had mostly ignored her. In front of her now was a small piece of white material with three concentric circles painted on it, each larger than the next. On top of these rested some rune staves, and she was staring at them with a deep frown. She looked up and met his gaze, annoyance flickering in the depths of her eyes.

'What are you doing?' he asked, although it was perfectly obvious.

She didn't reply; only raised her eyebrows to show him how stupid that question was.

He tried again. 'Whose fate are you divining?'

'My own. I wanted to know how long I'd have to endure your company.' From the accompanying glare, Geir gathered the runes hadn't given her the answer she sought.

That made him smile inwardly – he was sure the Norns were on his side, and he didn't fear what the runes would reveal. He hunkered down in front of the cloth. 'And what did you find out?'

She blew out an exasperated breath and pointed at the first rune stave. 'That one – we call it Raidho – usually means travel or moving to a new place, which is fairly obvious. I am on a journey but I'm not planning on staying.'

'Did the rune say that?'

'No,' she admitted. 'I did.' With a sigh, she picked up the next stave and shook her head in frustration. 'This one – Berkana – is the rune for new beginnings, renewal in general, or a venture that prospers. As I'm not engaged in any such thing, I have no idea why that appeared. It could also be . . . but no, I doubt it.'

'What?' Geir was curious now and sat down properly.

'Nothing.' Maddie wouldn't look at him, and he saw a tinge of pink creep up her neck and cheeks.

'Tell me. Please?'

'Well . . . Berkana is associated with love and desire sometimes, which is clearly not the case with me.'

Wisely, Geir decided not to comment on that. Instead he pointed to the third and final stave. 'And what does that mean?'

'Ehwaz is the rune for harmony and, er . . . teamwork. Sometimes progress.' She pushed a strand of hair off her face and scowled at him. 'None of this makes any sense.'

He allowed himself to smile at last. 'You mean it's not what you wanted to be told. There's a difference.'

'No! Yes. It's just . . . they can't be right.'

'Will you cast the runes for me? Please? I'd like to know what the future holds. The immediate future, at least.' Her runes had seemed to indicate success and progress, both things he wanted for himself. If she were to stay with him, then presumably they would both benefit from her good fortune.

'Very well.'

She picked up the three staves and put them into a drawstring bag made out of some lustrous black material, silk most probably. After shaking it thoroughly, she closed her eyes, dipped her hand inside and rummaged around. When she pulled it out, she was holding three staves, which she dropped on to the cloth without peeking. He noticed they were ancient-looking, but beautifully carved and smooth. She must have had them for a long time, or else she'd inherited them from someone.

'No, I don't believe it!'

Her exclamation made him peer at the cloth once more.

'What?' A frisson flashed through him. What if she saw death and failure? Did he really want to know that? It wasn't as though he could turn the ship around and sail back to Eskilsnes. That was out of the question. Hrafn would never let him hear the end of it.

She looked up at him and blinked, her eyes wide. 'They're all the same.' Her voice was somewhat hoarse and she cleared her throat.

Geir stared at the staves again. 'They don't look the same to me. There's a different rune on each one.'

'Of course there is. What I mean is . . . they're exactly as the ones I cast for me. And they have landed in very similar positions, all within the circle for the future. I . . . That's never happened before.'

Geir felt his smile widen. Oh yes, the Norns were definitely trying to tell them something, and he was fairly sure he knew what that was. The question was, would Maddie admit that they were right?

Maddie couldn't believe her eyes. The runes were normally so reliable, and she had never doubted them before. But today they were throwing her not just one, but two curveballs. How was this possible? She'd made sure to shake the pouch properly and she had heard the staves moving around inside. The three she had withdrawn earlier simply couldn't have ended up on top. It was inconceivable.

Geir tilted his head to one side. 'You're saying my future is the same as yours?'

She wanted to wipe that smug smile off his face, but was too stunned to figure out how to do that right now. 'Um, I suppose so. Although . . .' How could it be? She wasn't staying. He owned thralls and she wanted nothing to do with him. In fact, she shouldn't even be talking to him right now, never mind casting the runes for him.

He suddenly laughed, and his blue-grey eyes lit up with delight. 'I rather think you have your answer, then. You are remaining with us whether you want to or not.'

She tried to scowl at him. 'No!' she hissed. 'This changes nothing.'

'Oh, I think it does. Perhaps you should cast again?' He stood up and rummaged in his travelling chest, coming up with a pair of mittens and what looked like a crocheted beanie, which he crammed on to his head. 'Let me know what they say.'

Flashing her a grin, he left the tent and the flap settled back into place. Maddie swore out loud. She didn't want to prove him right, but on the other hand, she really didn't understand what had just happened. It had to be a fluke. With gritted teeth, she put the runes back into the bag, jiggled it almost violently for what seemed like ages, then withdrew three staves and threw them on to the cloth.

Looking down, she had to swallow very hard.

The same three runes were spread out before her. She couldn't doubt them now.

'No! I won't let you decide for me, do you hear?' She looked around, as if whoever was making this happen was here in the tent with her, then felt silly for even thinking that. But she couldn't just meekly accept her fate. That was unthinkable.

Shoving the staves back into the pouch at her belt, she stood up abruptly and ducked through the tent opening. Geir was standing not too far away, holding the steering oar, and she marched over to him and faced him, hands on hips, though the death glare she speared him with only made him look curious.

'I challenge you to single combat – *einvígi*, isn't that what you call it? Just you and me, no weapons, as soon as we reach land. If

I win, you give me back my knife immediately.'

He raised his brows, then shook his head. 'No.'

'What do you mean, no? You can't refuse such a challenge. That would be cowardly.' Maddie knew enough about Viking society to realise that no one wanted to be thought lacking in courage. It was one of the worst things you could accuse someone of.

'If you were a man, yes, but you're not. I can't fight a woman. I'd hurt you, and that would be even more cowardly.'

'You're just afraid I'll best you,' she taunted. Her fighting skills had never been questioned before, and she'd taken on and defeated men bigger than Geir in the training ring.

An infuriating smile tugged at the corner of his mouth as he scoffed, 'Only if I let you. Didn't we discuss this once before?'

Maddie clenched her fists, tempted to show him right there and then. 'And I told you I can beat you in a fair fight.'

He shook his head. 'I very much doubt it, but either way, we're not putting it to the test.' He nodded towards her belt pouch and grinned. 'Did the runes not give you the answer you wanted?'

'That's neither here nor there.' She shoved him hard in the chest, but he just laughed, not moving an inch.

'If I were you, I'd listen to the Norns. It doesn't pay to go against the wishes of the gods.'

'It does if they're wrong. And I'm not taking advice from a thrall owner.' But she knew she wasn't going to win this fight. If she wanted her freedom and her knife back, she'd have to find another way. 'Anyway, we'll just see, won't we?'

Seven days after they passed the Færeyjar, birds began to appear, and they sighted the coast of what they hoped was Ísland at last. Everyone fell silent as they contemplated their new homeland. It was stark and awe-inspiring, majestic even, as it slowly rose out of the sea on the horizon. There were snow-capped mountains inland, while along the flat coastal areas green swathes were visible among patches of dark grey, giving hope of fruitfulness and prosperity. It was a sight to behold and Geir hoped it would live up to its promise.

When they drew nearer to the coast, however, he noticed that the weather was dismal – grey, misty and rainy. He could smell vegetation on the breeze, mixed with the tang of the sea, but the air itself was freezing and strong winds carried them along. As he caught sight of the nearest beach, he frowned. It looked to be made up of sand that was so dark it was almost black, and ran along the coast for as far as the eye could see. He had never come across its like before and hoped it wasn't a bad omen. He couldn't help but feel as though they'd ended up at the very edge of Miðgarðr, the human realm. It was certainly a remote place.

Surrounding the black beaches were tall cliffs and rock formations, sea stacks, with thousands upon thousands of seabirds whirling around them, screeching, squabbling and diving for fish. They had built their nests on any available ledge, and the steep cliff faces were covered in bird droppings, making it look as though someone had thrown white splashes of paint at random intervals. Among the birds he spotted a strange black and white type with unusual-shaped flame-coloured beaks and feet of the same shade. They appeared to be numerous, and definitely stood out.

'*Puffins!*' he heard Maddie exclaim with delight.

He threw her a glance. 'Is that what they are called?'

'In my country, yes.'

'Hmm. I wonder if they are edible.'

To his surprise, her expression turned fierce and she hissed, 'Don't you dare!'

'What?' He shook his head. The woman was impossible to

understand, and as changeable as the spring weather.

As if to confirm this, in the next instant her expression was transformed into one of awe and wonder. 'Oh, a rainbow!'

The rain had stopped abruptly, and there was indeed a massive rainbow disappearing into the water in the distance. As the sun peeked out from behind a cloud, everything immediately appeared more cheerful, and he drew in a deep breath. That was better – now he felt as though this island welcomed them.

'And look over there – how magical!' Maddie enthused, as they passed a beach strewn with large blocks of ice. 'It's like giant diamonds on a bed of charcoal velvet.'

'It is indeed.' Geir stared in fascination at what looked like a frozen river flowing down the mountain behind the beach. At its bottom he glimpsed a small lagoon where bigger icebergs floated slowly towards a small opening leading into the sea. He assumed the shards on the beach had been washed up after they'd gone through. It was beautiful beyond belief.

'How will we know where to settle?' Steinthor mused out loud. He and Ingimund were standing next to Geir, who was steering.

Maddie sat behind them on the ship's planks, shielding from the breeze, and staring intently at the passing coastline. Since the incident with the runes, she'd remained largely silent and brooding, and although she hadn't protested about sharing his tent, she'd turned her back on him each night after a curt 'goodnight'. Still trying to make a point? Probably. But although she was right in that he was holding her captive in a way, it wasn't for the reasons she might imagine. He just needed her to stay long enough for him to see if she was meant to be his wife, something the runes had seemed to confirm.

Although the gods only knew why they'd sent him such a recalcitrant female.

'I'm hoping there will still be plenty of unclaimed land,' he replied now. 'Let us look for an area that has everything we'll require. I would say the ideal place would be some sort of sheltered bay with a small river running into the sea and plenty of flat land either side of it. We need grazing, arable land and somewhere to build the first dwelling house. A couple of islands would be good, then the cattle could be left to graze there without us having to worry about them disappearing before we've built fences.'

'And a hot spring,' Maddie muttered.

'What did you say?' All three men turned to stare at her in confusion.

Her cheeks turned a bit pink, as if she hadn't realised she'd spoken out loud. 'Oh, well, this island is full of mountains that, er . . . spit out fire and ash from time to time, don't you know?' She gestured to a peak that did look as though it might have an opening of some sort at the top. 'There is heat bubbling away under the ground everywhere, and numerous springs with hot water rising to the surface. Perfect for bathing and washing, although some of them are actually *too* hot.' She looked at them as if everyone ought to know this.

Geir had a suspicion that she'd learned about it in her century, and as he wasn't about to let the other two men in on that secret, he pretended to remember. 'Oh, yes, I think someone mentioned that the mountains can erupt. I had completely forgotten. Hopefully not too often.' It didn't sound good. 'Excellent idea to settle near a hot spring, though. Having our own bathing site would be extremely useful, as well as saving time and fuel.'

'You are sure they exist?' Ingimund voiced their doubts, but Geir was fairly certain she wouldn't have mentioned it unless she knew she was right.

'Yes, I believe so.' He pretended a confidence he didn't feel. 'We'll soon find out.'

He decided to question her further later on, when no one else was in earshot.

They headed west and sailed along the south coast of the island. They spotted some inhabited areas, but they were few and far between. Good. Hopefully that meant all the best land had not yet been claimed. Navigating by the sun, they rounded some sort of peninsula and turned northwards for a short while, before heading east into a large bay that formed a natural harbour. Here they encountered a couple more settlements that looked quite prosperous.

'Are we stopping to exchange greetings?' Ingimund wanted to know.

Geir hesitated, then made up his mind. 'I suppose it would be polite, but I don't want to linger here. I'll quickly go ashore on my own, then we'll continue northwards. You stay and guard the ship, please.'

Maddie had been trailing her fingers across the spray-soaked gunwale and seemed to be drawing something on the ship's planks. 'This must be Reykjavik,' she murmured.

'How do you know what this place is called?' He frowned at her and bent to study her water drawing. It looked like an island seen from above, with an extra splodge in one part. As Ingimund was steering, Geir sank down next to Maddie in the very back of the stern, a triangular area that sloped gently upwards. There wasn't a lot of room and he felt her stiffening as he squeezed in beside her, but to his relief she didn't stand up and leave.

'I've been here once before,' she whispered, clearly as unwilling to let the other two men into the secret of her origins as he was. 'Reykjavik was founded by a man called Ingólfur Arnarson, so he might be the one who owns this.' She gestured towards the settlement. 'It will become the main port and town on Ísland in the future, so I assume it's the best area to live in. If you can find somewhere not too far from here, that would be good.'

Geir couldn't fault her logic, if this was indeed the truth. He was pleased that she had thawed enough to speak whole sentences to him again. He didn't doubt that her knowledge was superior when it came to things like this, and it would behove him to listen. Perhaps that was partly why the gods had sent her to him, to help make this venture a success.

'Very well. I'll speak to the people here first to see how far their domains reach. I don't want to get into any disputes about ownership.'

There was a small jetty with a ship moored on one side. They hove to on the other and Geir jumped out. He waited for Hjalti's ship to pull up alongside his and communicated his intentions to the man. 'Do you wish to accompany me?'

Hjalti shook his head and laughed. 'No. I'm not staying here for any length of time, so I don't need to be polite. You go ahead.'

'Very well. I will try not to be long.'

They had been spotted, of course, and several people came walking towards him as he approached the main building, crossing an area of dark grey scree followed by an expanse of grass. It was a hall of sorts, but not like any he'd ever seen before, as the walls were made of turf rather than planks of wood. The impression was of a home inside a grassy hillock, the way you might imagine trolls lived, with wisps of smoke coming out of a hole in the roof. It confirmed what he had been told – that there weren't enough large trees here for any major building projects and you had to use whatever was to hand. Or perhaps the turf provided more warmth?

Other smaller buildings surrounded the hall – presumably workshops, storage huts and a smithy – and all around them were fields and meadows. He glimpsed a lake, and a forest of stunted trees stretched into the distance. Further inland hills rose up, their slopes mossy green around the bottom as though they were swathed in fabric, while the tops were dark grey. The sun cast patches of light and shadow on to the hillsides, and there were still pockets of snow dotted around, high up.

'Greetings!' he called out, holding out his hands and turning round once to show that he was unarmed and came in peace. 'I am Geir Eskilsson of Eskilsnes near Birka. Who do I have the honour of addressing?'

The man at the front of the group, who was dressed more ostentatiously than the rest, gave him a tentative smile and stepped forward. 'Ingólfur Arnarson of Vik and this is my wife, Hallveig Fróðadóttir.' He indicated the woman who came to stand beside him. 'Welcome to Ísland. I take it you have come to settle?'

'Indeed. We thought to head north of here, but I just wanted to ascertain how far your holdings stretch, so that we don't encroach upon your lands.'

Arnarson seemed to thaw further when he heard this and nodded his approval. 'Good, good, I appreciate that. As the first man here, I've claimed most of the south-west part of the island, stretching from Hvalfjördur, the first large fjord north of here, to the River Olfusá in the east. That may sound greedy, but I have friends and relatives arriving soon who will take portions of it.'

'Very well, I will go north of the next fjord then.'

'You may have to go a bit further than that, as I know of at least one other group of settlers who have taken land there, but you shouldn't have any trouble finding a good spot. Would you like to stay for a meal before you set off? All of you?' The invitation sounded slightly grudging, and Geir guessed that it wasn't because the man was inhospitable, but probably more to do with supplies being scarce at this time of year.

'I thank you, but no. It is very kind of you to offer, but we are eager to be on our way now that we are finally here. Perhaps another time? Or you are welcome to visit us once we have established ourselves.'

'Of course.' Arnarson looked relieved, thus confirming Geir's suspicion. 'I wish you luck. Thank you for having the courtesy to stop by and consult with me.'

'Not at all. It was a pleasure to meet you.'

As he set off back to his ship, Geir felt optimistic about the future. Arnarson's settlement looked prosperous enough, and everyone he'd seen appeared well fed. The man hadn't been hostile either, which was a good sign. All in all, he was pleased that he'd taken the time to stop, but now it was time to continue. They needed to find somewhere to make camp for the night.

There were smaller inlets along the larger curve of the coastline, and a couple of fjords after the large one Arnarson had mentioned. In the first, they spotted more dwellings, presumably the other settler group. The second, however, seemed empty and had a narrow offshoot. As dusk was approaching, Geir steered the ship into this. Halfway along, a tiny peninsula jutted out on the left-hand side, and behind it lay a very secluded inlet. Several islands surrounded it as well, which was even better.

'We'll stop here for the night,' he ordered, finding a sliver of that strange, dark sand where the ships could be beached. 'Tomorrow we can look around to see if this place is suitable, otherwise we'll continue.'

As he and the other men secured the ship, and the women unloaded everything they needed for cooking a proper evening meal, Geir heaved a sigh of relief.

Thank the gods – they'd made it to Ísland.

Chapter Eight

Maddie felt a bit useless, as everyone except her seemed to have their assigned tasks.

'Can I help?' she asked Aine, but the woman shook her head with a shy smile.

'We'll have everything ready in a trice.'

Guessing they would need firewood for the night – it was pretty chilly already and the sun wasn't even properly down yet – she wandered down to the water's edge and started picking up any driftwood she could find. When she dumped her load next to Aine, she received another smile, slightly wider this time. 'Thank you, mistress.'

Maddie frowned. 'I'm not your mistress. I'm a captive, like you.'

'I don't think so. That's not what the master told us. And, er, I don't know how else to address you . . . um . . .'

'Maddie will do.'

Aine nodded, her cheeks a bit rosy, as if she found this conversation embarrassing. Maddie figured the woman was probably used to being servile; it would take her a while to accept anyone being friendly to her. Presumably she'd been downtrodden for so long, it was pure habit to defer to someone.

Well, that needed to change for a start.

While she waited for their meal to be ready, she contemplated her surroundings. She found it hard to believe that she was actually in ninth-century Iceland – it was like a surreal dream, or as though she'd ended up in an alternative universe somehow. It didn't help that the vast landscape stretching into the distance was so other-worldly, almost eerie – extensive grasslands hemmed in by brooding mountains in one direction, and a never-ending sea view and coastline in the other. She felt small and insignificant. The thought that they might be the only living creatures for miles struck her, though that probably wasn't the case. Some people might call this place desolate, yet, it was too vibrant for that to be the case, and achingly beautiful in a way that affected her deeply. She couldn't explain it even to herself, but the very simplicity of it really resonated with her.

Despite being early evening, it was still fairly light, and she could see the soft green of the moss at the bottom of the mountains, interspersed with scree as if parts of the hills had slid down its slopes. It contrasted beautifully with the volcanic rock and the darker emerald of the flatlands where she was standing. In the distance, out by the coast, the screech of seabirds could still be heard, as well as a background noise of waves pounding the shore. She closed her eyes and breathed in, revelling in the fresh scents of grassland, wild flowers and a hint of brine. There was a whiff of sulphur as well, but not enough to spoil the overall impression.

No, this couldn't possibly be a dream – she really was here.

The whole group sat down in a circle around the largest fire to eat their meal. Sheepskins had been unrolled and placed on the ground to protect them from the cold, and the warmth from the fire warmed their front halves. Pulling her shawl tighter around her shoulders, Maddie nevertheless shivered in the near-constant wind that seemed to cut right through her, but the hot stew helped. They'd not eaten much in the way of cooked food for the past week, so this tasted heavenly. Although it was possible to cook on board, she'd heard Geir say he preferred it if they didn't.

'We have arrived in our new homeland at last.' Geir beamed at everyone. 'I think this calls for a small celebration. Ingimund, open that cask of ale, please. Hjalti, did you bring some? Otherwise you and your men are welcome to share.'

'We brought our own, but thank you.'

Maddie glanced at the leader of the second ship. Small and wiry, with sandy-coloured hair and a thick beard, he looked a bit rough around the edges and seemed to be an adventurer of sorts. From what she'd heard, he and his men were only here to hunt walrus, because the tusks were greatly valued back in Europe and would make them rich. The idea sickened her, but she knew that yet again her notions were twenty-first century. They called the animals *rosmhvalir* and seemed to think they were a type of whale, which secretly amused her – there was so much she could teach these people. But she also knew the poor creatures were big and clumsy, and no doubt an awful lot of them would be killed by these men. It was a depressing thought, which she didn't want to dwell on.

Beakers and mugs were produced, and soon everyone raised these in a toast to the gods, to their new home and to continued good fortune, although reluctantly on Maddie's part. 'May Tyr and Freya be with us, granting us a fruitful first year,' Geir added.

'Hear, hear!' the others concurred.

Maddie noticed that he didn't allow the ale-drinking to get out of hand, and neither did Hjalti. The latter had been talking about his eagerness to get going in the morning. The sooner they began their hunting, the more successful they'd be. Long before midnight, those who were not on guard duty drifted off to their various sleeping quarters. Some members of their party had erected makeshift tents by the shore, but Geir led Maddie back to the ship.

'We're still sleeping on board?' she asked, accepting his outstretched hand to help her clamber over the side before he boosted Blár on to the deck as well. She didn't really want his assistance, but it would have been stupid and petty to refuse.

'Yes. My tent is already raised – no point moving it until we know if we're staying put.'

'Can't I have my own, now that we're on land?' There was plenty of space here. No reason why she had to share with him.

'There are no spare ones,' he replied, his words curt. 'Why, do I snore that badly?'

'No, but . . . Oh, never mind.' What was the point of arguing? He wouldn't listen anyway.

At least on the ship's deck it was marginally warmer. Iceland appeared to be an extremely windy place, and without thermal underwear, she was feeling the cold. The ship's railing protected them from the worst of the breeze, and inside the tent it was dry and blessedly calm. She knelt on the furs and shook out two thick woollen blankets to cover herself with. There was a whole pile in one corner, so she knew she wasn't depriving Geir of his. Lying down, she caught herself thinking what an enjoyable way of camping this was. Definitely unlike any she'd tried before, although a proper sleeping bag would have been useful, of course. When the dog snuggled up to her legs, she didn't shoo him away – his body heat was very welcome.

Geir sat down next to her cross-legged, but didn't stretch out on the rest of the furs.

'Aren't you going to sleep?' she asked, glancing up at him. It was still light enough to see his expression, and she knew that soon it wouldn't get properly dark here at night at all. Being so far north, they would probably experience the midnight sun come June. Or very nearly, at any rate.

'Not yet. I'm taking the first watch. I just wanted an opportunity to speak with you alone.'

'Oh, what about?' She shuffled into a sitting position, leaning against his travelling kist, as she didn't want him towering over her.

'You seem to know a lot about this place and I just wondered if there was anything more I should know before we choose where to settle. You were right about Arnarson; that was his name, just as you said. But he called his domain Vik, not Reykjavik, although it's close enough, I suppose.' He frowned at her. 'Have you really been here, or did you learn all this by other means?'

Maddie tried to suppress a smile, but didn't quite succeed. It must be costing him dear to ask her advice when he didn't want it in other respects. 'You mean by magic? Have I had visions like a *vōlva*? No, I told you, I'm not a seeress. I can cast the runes, but I definitely can't predict the future in any other way or divine people's names. I really have been here before, and even in my time they tell the tale of how Ingólfur Arnarson was the first man to establish himself in Ísland. Actually, he came with his foster brother, because they'd both killed someone back home and were outlawed, I believe.'

'He didn't mention a brother, though he said he had relatives arriving soon.'

'That's probably because his brother died. His thralls revolted and killed him – you see why I don't think it's a good idea to have any?'

Geir snorted, but otherwise made no comment, so she continued.

'When Ingólfur heard about it, he killed all the thralls in revenge, then settled at Reykjavik. It is one of the best parts of the country, but there should be others almost as good just north of where he lives. Here, perhaps.'

'And there really are hot springs?' Geir looked dubious, as if he wasn't sure whether to believe anything she said.

'Yes, lots of them. You should look for one, as it would make everything so much easier. You'll be glad of it in winter.'

'Very well. It does seem sensible. Anything else?'

Maddie hesitated. Perhaps she shouldn't tell him anything, but that would be petty, and he wasn't the only one who would suffer if things went wrong. Not that she knew all that much anyway. She tried to remember what she'd learned during her visit. She'd done the usual tourist things and visited a few museums, but only one of them had any relevance to their current situation – the Landnámssýningin, or Settlement Exhibition. It was based on an archaeological dig at the site of what was believed to be Arnarson's original settlement.

'It's not going to be easy, but then you probably know that already. There is one piece of advice, though – don't cut down all the trees. If you do that, the rest of the area will become too exposed, and in a hundred years or so the land will not be as fertile and your descendants will starve.'

'Really? Surely trees grow back.'

'Not if you take too many all at once. They have to have a chance to regrow. There should be plenty of driftwood on the beaches. Use as much of that as you can instead. And peat for fuel, not wood.'

'Right. Thank you, I shall heed your warnings.'

She really did smile at that, because she wasn't convinced he actually wanted to listen to a woman from the future. Which reminded her . . . 'Good. Before you go, can I ask you something?'

'Of course. What is it?' He'd been about to rise, but settled down again, looking at her.

'You seem to know a lot about time travelling. Can you tell me why, please? How many others like me have you met?'

'Two.' He hesitated, then added, 'I don't suppose you know anyone by the name of Linnea, do you? Or Sara?'

Maddie couldn't help it; she gasped out loud. She felt as if someone had hit her with a battleaxe, although not in the head this time but the region of her solar plexus. 'A tall blonde woman and a shorter one with dark hair? You've met them? Both of them?' When he nodded, she muttered, '*Bloody hell*,' in English. This was weird. No, more than weird; it was downright creepy. What were the odds of him coming across those two in particular?

'So you know them? I thought that might be the case.'

'Linnea is my half-sister and Sara is her friend. Does that mean you've met Hrafn and Rurik too, their husbands?'

Geir chuckled. 'Oh yes, frequently – they're my brothers.'

'No! Truly? That is an incredible coincidence!' She stared at him and had to remind herself not to let her mouth hang open. Of all the people for her to run into in ninth-century Dublin . . . Hrafn and Rurik's brother?

'Perhaps not.' He grew serious again.

'What do you mean?'

He sighed and pushed his long hair out of the way, as if he was stalling for time. 'It is my belief that it was your destiny to find me, or for me to come across you. The gods arranged it, just as they arranged for Linnea and Sara to meet my brothers. I think . . . perhaps we are meant to be . . . together?' These last words were uttered through gritted teeth, making Maddie suspect he wasn't too happy about the situation.

Neither was she. 'You mean *together* together? As in . . . man and wife? No!'

Quite why she was so against this idea she couldn't have said, except for the fact that she resented being used as some sort of pawn of the gods. If that really was what this was about. But there were no such things as Norse gods, surely? So how could they possibly meddle in her life? She said as much out loud.

Geir raised his eyebrows at her. 'And how do you suppose you ended up here, then? Is magic not the prerogative of the gods?'

'Well, I . . .' She had no answer to that. Who knew where magic came from? Before Linnea and Sara's adventures, Maddie would have sworn it was all a scam and magic didn't exist. Now she was forced to acknowledge that it did. But as for deities . . . no, she wasn't convinced they were behind it.

'And what about your runes? You are the *vōlva*, not me, but even I would guess the gods were trying to tell you that you're destined to stay here.'

She had no response to that, because he was right about that too.

He gave her a lopsided smile that had more of an effect on her than she cared to admit. 'Trust me, I'm not sure what is happening either. All I can say is, perhaps we'd better be patient and wait to see what else the Norns have in store for us. This was why I wanted you to stay, although I wasn't lying when I said an extra pair of hands will be useful. I feel strongly that you are meant to remain, for whatever purpose. If you leave, we'll never find out.'

'I suppose.' His words had a certain logic, and yet she wasn't sure she wanted to believe him.

He frowned as if something had just occurred to him. 'You're not married already, are you? Or promised to someone in your time?'

Maddie snorted. 'Married? Me? No, of course not. I'm only nineteen! Well, almost twenty, but still . . .'

'That is way past marriageable age. Most girls are wed at fifteen.'

'Fifteen?' She was starting to sound like a parrot, but that was preposterous. At that age they were mere children, even if they might be physically mature enough.

He shrugged. 'Be that as it may, I am glad you're not spoken for. Just in case . . .'

It was her turn to grit her teeth. 'I don't *want* to be married. I told you, I'm too young. And I don't want to stay here.' She glared at him, but he sent her back what she could only interpret as a pitying look.

'You cannot fight fate, and us meeting like this . . . well, it can't be coincidence. You have been sent to me for a reason and I can only see one – we are meant to marry. Eventually.'

'No!' She couldn't believe it. It was too fantastical, and yet he knew Linnea. He'd known about time travelling. And in some weird, twisted way, his words made sense. She shook her head slowly. 'No,' she whispered again, but shivered at the possibility that he might be right about that too.

He got to his feet. 'We can discuss this more in time. No need to be hasty. Now I had best be off,' he told her as he ducked out of the tent flap. 'I bid you goodnight.'

Suddenly the tent felt very empty, but she chided herself for thinking that way. 'I mustn't get used to having him around,' she murmured to the dog, who sighed and leaned his head on her legs. 'I'm only staying here for a while, no matter what he says. We can't let the gods, or whoever, decide for us.' And yet hadn't they already done so by bringing her here? It was an annoying thought.

In fact, the whole thing was crazy. She ought to ignore Geir's theories and insist on going back to her own time immediately. But somehow that didn't feel right. Perhaps she was meant to be here, but not for the reasons he'd suggested. What if her mission, for want of a better word, was something altogether different? Like getting him to free his thralls, or preventing some disaster from befalling the group? She'd never know, if she ran away from what he'd called her destiny. Put like that, it seemed the coward's way out.

A small part of her acknowledged that staying here would be an exciting challenge, and it could also be fun – establishing a settlement, building houses, growing food, living in tune with nature. It was what she'd yearned to do in her own century, but there it was much more difficult to achieve. When she'd mentioned it to her parents, they'd scoffed and said, 'You'll soon be wanting the comforts of normal life.'

Well, here was her chance to prove them wrong. And the gods or fates as well. Or not, as the case may be. Either way, she wanted to give it a try.

But she wasn't marrying anyone. At least not unless she'd chosen him for herself. Especially not a slave owner.

Chapter Nine

The following day was spent in exploration, after the cows, ewes and nanny goats had been milked. Geir was reluctant to unload the animals until he was sure that this was the place they were staying, but Hjalti was eager to be off, so the livestock from his ship were taken to graze on the nearest island. If Geir decided not to settle here, someone would have to stay with them until he could come back and fetch them, but that was a problem for another day.

He sent everyone out in different directions, pairing them up for the sake of safety. Although he didn't think they'd be foolish enough to run away, Maddie's tale of thralls killing their master had him taking precautions. He'd warned Steinthor and Ingimund to be on their guard, and assigned each of them to accompany one of the Irishmen. Lif was told to go with the two thrall women, although he saw no need to warn her of the possibility of violence. He judged that neither Aine or Eimear would do anything untoward unless they were incited to by their male counterparts.

'Fridgerd, it's probably best if you remain here with the children. Brendan can help you,' Geir told her. 'But perhaps you can roam the immediate area and see whether there are any good spots for siting our first dwellings.'

Fridgerd nodded enthusiastically, clearly relieved at not having to traipse around an unknown landscape with all the little ones in tow. 'We will.'

Brendan said nothing, just nodded. He was a quiet child, and the only time Geir had seen him smile was when talking to Aine, who was his older sister. Even with her the smiles were few and far between, but hopefully once they'd all settled in the boy would start to relax a bit. It didn't seem right for a child that age to be so serious, but who knew what traumas he'd been through already in his short life? Geir hadn't wanted to buy a thrall that young, but he'd noticed how the boy clung to Aine at the market, and when he discovered that they were siblings, he'd found himself unable to separate them. Aine had been grateful to the point of tears when Geir bought them both.

He gave Brendan a cow horn now that made a fearful noise if you blew into it. 'If you have any trouble or concerns, just blow as hard as you can on this and hopefully one of us will hear you.'

He glanced around the small group. 'Is everyone clear on what we're looking for?' He saw a few excited expressions, which probably mirrored his own. His veins were fair bubbling with joy that this was finally happening. It was what he'd dreamt of for so long – to be master of all he surveyed, having his own domain without being beholden to anyone. He ignored the little voice in his head that reminded him that some of those present weren't here of their own free will and therefore clearly couldn't care less about what they'd find today. When – not if – he became prosperous, they'd live well too.

'Then let's be off,' he said. 'Just after midday, we turn back, agreed? I don't want anyone getting lost on our first day here.'

He headed off with Maddie at his heels, as he'd chosen to take charge of her himself. He knew she couldn't go back to her own time without the knife, which was still in his possession, so he wasn't worried about that, but he still felt the need to have her in his sight. The countryside here was very flat, with low mountains in the distance if you looked inland, their upper parts shrouded in cloud or mist. It was as though they were huddling inside an eiderdown bolster that was threatening to tumble down the slopes and smother any unwary passers-by. In one place, a high waterfall cascaded downwards, glittering in the sunlight over towards the left. In the other direction, towards the sea, there were hills and one slightly higher part. The day before, Geir had glimpsed cliffs and rock formations there, and one day soon he would go and explore further.

They walked across rough vegetation – dead, yellow grass left over from last year mixed with new green growth and scrubby bushes. Presumably this had all been covered by snow during the winter and was only now regenerating. Some spring flowers were peeking out, and it probably wouldn't be long before there were lots more. And in a small forest of birch trees nearby, the leaves were exploding out of their buds, the colour of fresh mint. It all added to the sensation of a new start, for nature as well as Geir and his group.

In some places the ground was covered in scree and large areas of the strange dark grey stone, mostly covered with moss. It wasn't the easiest terrain to traverse. 'I've never seen stone like this before,' he muttered.

Maddie must have heard him. 'That's because it's *lava*. Or used to be.' At his raised eyebrows, she elaborated. 'It forms after the mountains erupt and the melted mass coming out of them cools down.'

'I see.' He wasn't sure he liked the sound of that, and hoped it wouldn't happen in his lifetime.

Maddie drew in a deep lungful of air and closed her eyes as she slowly let it out. 'Mm, the air is so clean and crisp here, isn't it? It's almost . . .'

She couldn't seem to find the right word, so Geir guessed at '. . . heady?'

'Yes, that's it. Like a *drug*. A sort of poison, something that makes you believe you're seeing things.'

'You mean henbane? Seeresses use it to unlock their minds.'

She nodded. 'That sounds about right.'

He had to agree the air was pure and fresh, but had no idea what henbane had to do with anything.

They didn't speak for a long time after that, just scanned their surroundings, evaluating what they saw. After a while, Geir realised he was walking with his usual long strides and turned to see whether he should slow down, but his companion didn't seem to have any trouble keeping up. He smiled when he thought about the fact that her legs were almost as long as his own.

'What's so amusing?' She frowned at him.

'Nothing. Just . . . I'm not used to females who are able to walk as fast as me. You're doing well. Are you accustomed to covering long distances?' She didn't even seem out of breath.

'I run a lot. We call it *jogging*. And I train three times a week.'

'Train?'

'Fighting and such.' She made a half-hearted slashing motion with her hand.

'Ah, yes, I was meaning to ask you about that. Will you teach me sometime? It looked as though you have some useful skills.'

'Glad you think so,' she said somewhat sarcastically. She studied him, as if evaluating his potential as a fighter. 'And I might, after we've done everything else that needs doing here. If you don't mind learning from a lowly thrall?'

Geir swallowed a sigh. He didn't want to argue with her today. He'd been in such a good mood and it would spoil everything.

'I've told you, you're not my thrall.' He held up a hand when she opened her mouth to protest. 'And yes, I am well aware of your views on the subject, but I don't want to discuss them today. Can we not have a truce just for a while? Please?'

She hesitated, scowling at him, but then she shrugged. 'Very well.' She pointed a finger at him. 'But if you think I'm giving up, you're wrong.' She gave a sudden laugh. 'You have no idea how stubborn I can be.'

'I think I have an inkling,' he murmured, but he smiled at her to show that he didn't mind. He admired her for sticking to her views, even if they went against his own. He'd never liked meek women.

His comment made her smile back, just for a moment, and he tried not to notice how beautiful she looked when she was happy. Her green eyes sparkled in the sunlight, and now that she'd recovered from her injury, her skin was glowing and not as pale. The sun had changed it to a honey colour that suited her and went well with the red tresses; silky-looking strands that fell down her back for the most part, as she'd only twisted the front part up into a small knot today. He turned away, unwilling to acknowledge the sudden longing to pull her into his arms and kiss that lush mouth of hers.

She'd made it clear she didn't want him. In fact, he was still smarting from how horrified she'd seemed at the mere idea of marrying him. It wasn't the reaction he'd expected from the woman he chose as his wife. But it was early days, and he'd shocked her with his theories. She would need time to mull it over and he would give her that, even if he was convinced the outcome was never in doubt.

He forced himself to concentrate on their surroundings. 'What do you think? Will this do? It seems to me there is everything we need here in abundance.'

They had been following the course of a small stream bordered by meadowlands, but had now climbed up to stand on a low hill. The areas below them looked fertile and eminently suitable for haymaking and planting. There was the birch forest stretching into the distance, which should give them plenty of fuel and building materials, even though the trees were rather small and twisted. The stream was presumably a tributary of the larger river Steinthor and Cormac were following inland, which had cut a deep chasm through the landscape, and immediately next to it was boggier ground. This would be excellent for fuel and building material as well. He wasn't an expert on iron, but he hoped they could also find bog ore for Steinthor to smelt and turn into nails and other necessary items. With a bit of luck, there ought to be some.

'It looks perfect to me, but then I'm not really sure what is needed.' Maddie shaded her eyes with one hand and surveyed the area.

From up here, Geir could see the islands in the bay where the ship was moored. The sea looked bluey-grey in the distance. Contemplating just the one ship, he acknowledged to himself that he was relieved to have parted company with Hjalti and his crew. It wasn't that he didn't trust the man, but they had completely different aims here. Hjalti had left early that morning, heading north, where he hoped to find *rosmhvalir* – the large seal-like creatures with the valuable tusks. He'd said he would come back soon to see how things were progressing, which was fine with Geir. He'd rather not have the man around if he wasn't going to help with anything practical. Besides, Hjalti would need to build his own house somewhere if he and his group were going to overwinter.

'At least there is nothing dangerous here,' Maddie added. 'Your sheep will be safe, although I'm not so sure about the chickens.'

He turned to frown at her. 'What do you mean? I'll be putting the livestock on those islands to graze so that nothing can hurt them.'

'That's probably not necessary. If I remember correctly, the only dangerous animal living here is the *Arctic* fox. No wolves, bears or anything like that. Although I suppose *polar* bears might float over here occasionally on the ice.'

'What kind is that?' He'd never heard of those.

'White ones. Huge bears that live in the north.'

'Oh, I see.' He'd seen the pelt of a white bear once. They were very big. 'I suppose I won't be doing much hunting then. Just as well – I will have plenty of other tasks to occupy me.' He glanced at the sun. 'I think we had better turn back. Let's take a slightly different route.'

He was pleased with everything he saw, and when they stood on another hill overlooking the bay again, he noticed steam rising from the ground not too far away. He pointed it out to Maddie. 'Look. Is that one of those hot springs you were talking about?'

'Oh, I hope so! I would love a bath and to wash my clothes. Do you think one of the other women will lend me a clean serk for a while? I can't just wear my smokkr while the undergown dries.' Her cheeks turned pink and Geir couldn't resist teasing her.

'Why not? It would be a lovely sight for the rest of us.'

'Geir!' She punched him on the arm, but she was smiling so he knew she'd understood that he was joking.

'Fine. I will ask Fridgerd. Lif is a bit . . . prickly at the moment.'

He'd noticed that Steinthor's wife was a grumpy sort and hoped it wouldn't present him with problems. It was probably something to do with her being pregnant. He'd heard that it made women unpredictable, to say the least.

'Come, I want to go and have a look.' Maddie grabbed his hand and towed him down towards the wisps of steam.

He was too surprised to protest. In her excitement, she seemed to have forgotten to be angry with him, and he wasn't about to remind her. He liked her happy and carefree. As she started to run, he kept hold of her hand. It felt good – soft, but strong, with long fingers – but he told himself it was only to keep her from falling over. Not because he wanted to prolong the contact between them.

When they arrived at the spring, panting slightly from their rapid descent, they found a perfect pool surrounded by grass, stones and, in places, squishy mud. A few of the stones had white lines around them; as if some sort of mineral had washed over them repeatedly. The water was clear around the edges, and steam rose from the surface to hang in the air just above it, making the place look magical. Perhaps it was? Maddie let go of him and knelt down to stick her fingers into the water, cautiously at first. Then she sighed with bliss. 'Oh, this is wonderful!'

He copied her and felt a smile spread across his features. The water was incredibly warm, almost too hot at first. 'You're right. What an amazing thing to have on our doorstep!' Sniffing the air, he added, 'But what is that smell? It's not poisonous, is it?'

'No, that's just *sulphur*. A . . . type of ore? You find it wherever there are erupting mountains. It's not dangerous, as long as you don't eat it.'

'Good. We're definitely staying here then, and this evening we can all bathe.'

The others, when they met up back by the ship, concurred about the suitability of the place.

'The river is teeming with salmon and other fish. Some of them this big!' Steinthor told them, gesticulating to demonstrate the size of what he'd seen.

'Yes, and the meadows go on for as far as the eye can see,' Cormac added, although without the same enthusiasm. 'There won't be any shortage of fodder. Also, we won't need to clear the land of too many trees – we can just plough some of the grassland. I think there is enough for everything.'

'Excellent.' Geir turned to Ingimund and Niall. 'And what did you see?' He'd sent them in the direction of the fjord's entrance.

'Seabirds aplenty, as well as seals and *rosmhvalir*,' Ingimund said, holding out a makeshift pouch full of eggs and two enormous dead seabirds, tied together. 'We won't need to rely on the chickens for eggs this time of year. And this strange type of bird was incredibly easy to catch. There are eider ducks as well, so we'll have plenty of down for pillows.'

'Oh no! Those must be *great auks*,' he heard Maddie mutter. When he glanced at her, she looked stricken, but he had no idea why. He'd have to ask her later.

'Anything else?'

'Yes, lots of driftwood,' Niall added. 'We should probably go and collect as much as we can tomorrow. Some of the longer pieces will come in useful for building – straight and already devoid of bark.'

'Good idea. And thank you, let's hope those eggs and the birds are tasty. Lif, what about you?'

'We found some useful plants.' She pointed at Aine, who had a sack full of something. '*Hvōnn* and . . .' she nodded at Eimear, 'something she called dulse.' She made a face. 'It's seaweed, but they said it's edible.'

Geir was about to thank them when Maddie waded in. 'Seaweed is delicious,' she stated. 'And very good for your health. Great idea, Eimear!'

The Irishwoman blushed at the praise, while Lif raised an eyebrow and regarded Maddie as if she doubted anything she said. That didn't bode well for their future cooperation, so Geir quickly moved on to Fridgerd.

'Did you and Brendan find any particularly favourable spot for building on?'

'Yes, we'll show you tomorrow. The land slopes up over there with a flatter bit on top of the hill.' Fridgerd pointed. 'We thought it might be safer to be on slightly higher ground in case this river ever floods. And there is a spring of fresh water conveniently situated nearby.'

'I agree that sounds sensible.' Geir looked around with a big smile. 'I hereby claim this land from the river here to the next, and inland as far as the nearest mountain. Well done, everyone. Tomorrow we start the hard work.'

'What will you call this place?' Steinthor asked. 'Geirby? Geirsnes?'

'No, I don't think so. I'll come up with something better than that.' He had no intention of naming the settlement after himself. Arnarson hadn't done so with his, and it seemed entirely too vain. Plus it reminded him of his father, a man he'd loathed, whose property bore his name – Eskilsnes. No, he'd think of something else.

'Who wants to bathe in the hot spring Maddie and I found?' he called out. 'Women and children first, but don't stay in too long, as I'm eager to have my turn.'

Soon shrieks and high-pitched laughter rang out over the landscape. Geir smiled to himself. He was going to enjoy living here.

Chapter Ten

Maddie led the way towards the spring, the women and children following in her wake. They were all armed with what passed for towels here – large sheets of linen. Geir had found one for her in his travelling kist. She longed for a lovely fluffy one like she was used to at home, but hoped these would prove as effective, even if they were on the thin side.

'Here we are. Doesn't this look wonderful?' She gestured to the hot spring and smiled at the others. Most of them smiled back, but Lif's eyes narrowed and she wrinkled her nose.

'What if it's dangerous? I've never seen hot water in nature before, and it smells like something is rotten. It could be a trap set by a water sprite to catch out unwary travellers.'

Maddie almost spluttered with laughter, but managed to hold it in by turning it into a cough. 'Er, I don't think so, Lif. You'll have to trust me on this – it's perfectly safe. Just don't swallow it.' She wasn't sure if sulphur was poisonous, but it was probably best not to tempt fate.

'Let's get in.' Fridgerd shepherded her son over to the edge and told him to undress. She put her little daughter down on the ground while pulling her own clothes over her head, and Maddie was relieved to see that none of the women appeared to be bothered by nudity. At least not among females. She was used to Swedish pool changing rooms where women happily undressed next to each other and shared saunas naked. No men allowed, though, and hopefully Geir would keep his men away until it was their turn.

She took off her apron dress and serk, and stepped out of her shoes before tugging her leggings down with her underwear still inside them. They both desperately needed to be washed, and she intended to take them into the water with her. She never wore a bra when doing re-enactment events, and she was grateful for that now, as it would no doubt have invited lots of questions. The air was cold, not helped by the constant breeze, and she shivered, her skin turning to goose pimples in an instant. It seemed insane to undress outdoors when winter was barely over, but there was no other way if they wanted to bathe.

'Brrr! It's freezing!' She couldn't wait to get into the hot water and heard similar comments and chattering teeth from the others as well.

'What in the name of Freya were you wearing?' Lif again, frowning now.

'Er, a type of trousers common in my homeland.' It was true, after all, and the woman didn't need to know that the homeland in question was a thousand years into the future. 'They help keep me warm.'

'Hmph.'

Fortunately, Lif's children claimed her attention and Maddie was able to ball the leggings and knickers up as she gingerly stepped into the hot water. 'Oh! You'll need to be careful with the little ones,' she called out. 'Make them go in slowly to get used to the heat.'

She'd been lucky enough to visit Japan on a memorable holiday with her parents, and had tried the Japanese variety of hot bathing, the *ofuro*. She'd learned that it felt almost scalding at first, but if you inched your way in, eventually the body became acclimatised and it was the most wonderful feeling. Refreshing and relaxing, like having a sauna but in water.

It took a while, but eventually everyone was submerged. The pool wasn't massively deep, with coarse sand and some stones at the bottom, interspersed with velvety mud that clouded the water as it was churned up by their feet. Maddie leaned against a large boulder to one side and half closed her eyes, enjoying the sensation of being enveloped in heat and moisture. The two Irish thrall women stayed at one end, away from Lif and Fridgerd with their children, and looked to be whispering together. They must have caught the haughty glances Lif had thrown them, as if she didn't believe they had a right to share the water with their superiors. It made Maddie cross, but this wasn't the time to debate the issue. For now, she just wanted to wallow in the marvellous spring and forget everything else.

Staying in the ninth century definitely had some perks.

While they waited, Geir and the other men discussed the work that needed to be done with the aim of settling the area. They had to decide in which order to do things, the most important ones being cutting hay and planting their crops. Cormac and Niall were largely silent, as was the boy, Brendan, but he tried to involve them by asking their opinion. Although they were thralls, he assumed they would have a wealth of knowledge from years spent working the land, and he would be foolish not to listen to everyone. Ingimund and Steinthor gave him some funny looks, but Geir ignored them. He was the master here and he could do what he wanted.

'It's probably best if we start with haymaking,' he concluded. 'It won't take long and the hay needs time to dry. Then we can begin the ploughing, and hopefully the summer here will be long enough to give us at least a small barley harvest.'

'What about vegetables?' Cormac ventured when no one else said anything. 'They take time to grow too.' He was by far the more outspoken of the two Irishmen but still looked slightly uncomfortable to be voicing his opinion.

'Good point. Could you and Niall start preparing vegetable beds tomorrow, please? We don't all need to be cutting hay and we don't have enough tools to go round in any case.'

'Will do.' Cormac seemed on the verge of asking something else, but hesitated.

'Are you wondering what types I've brought?' Geir guessed, and the man nodded. 'Turnips, peas, beans and onions mostly, plus a few other things. Those are the most important, though.'

Tasks allotted, he and Steinthor set about sharpening the two scythes they'd brought, while they all chatted among themselves until it was their turn to bathe.

Maddie was one of the first women to return, wringing out her hair and wearing a serk that was too short for her. Geir looked away from her shapely ankles and concentrated on the sharp blade in his hand.

She came to a halt next to him and exclaimed, 'That was wonderful! Just like an *ofuro*.'

'A what?'

'A type of very hot bath to be found in a land called Japan. It's a long way from here but I was lucky enough to visit once.'

'I see. I'm looking forward to trying the spring for myself.' He contemplated her glowing cheeks, which still retained the heat from the water, and noticed her contented expression. She looked like a woman who had just been satisfactorily pleasured, languid and relaxed. He swore inwardly and tried to turn his thoughts in a different direction. Thinking about her like that was not advisable at present. 'I heard shrieking. Was it not too hot for the little ones?'

'A bit, but if you ease yourself in limb by limb, the body

becomes used to it. I showed Fridgerd and she told Lif. It's absolutely freezing when you come out, though, so make sure you have your linen sheet ready.' She gave an exaggerated shiver as if to underline this advice.

'Will do.' Geir noted that she hadn't spoken directly to Lif, which made him frown, but he didn't comment on it. Perhaps the women needed time to sort things out between them. He stood up and went to put the scythe away as the rest of the women and children came wandering back to the camp. Most of them were red in the face but smiling, while the little ones seemed drowsy and ready for bed.

If that was what the spring did to you, Geir was eager for his turn. With a nod to the other men and the boy, Brendan, he set off.

'Stormavík,' Maddie muttered the following morning, as she struggled to secure her hair in a long plait before cramming one of Geir's crocheted hats on to her head. She needed something to keep her head warm and prevent her hair from blowing in her face every five seconds. 'That's what this place should be called.'

The glorious sunshine of the previous day had disappeared, and they were being buffeted by strong winds and occasional rain showers. The clouds hung low over the nearby hills and out at sea, a mass of silvery grey with a darker edge as if tipped with steel. The air temperature had dropped as well, and she had wrapped her shawl around herself securely, tucking it into her belt to keep it in place. A pair of borrowed fingerless mittens were looped through her belt as well for when her hands became too cold. Hopefully once they started working, she'd warm up a bit, but she would need to knit herself a sweater as soon as possible. With what, she wasn't sure. It wasn't as though she could just go out and buy a pair of knitting needles, even if there was any wool available.

She'd learned knitting at an early age, as her older sister Linnea was an aficionado and claimed that it helped her relax. Maddie wouldn't go that far, but she enjoyed it and they'd spent many an evening together watching TV and knitting companionably. She'd never be as good as her sister, but she could manage simple things like plain sweaters, socks, hats and mittens. And here, she wouldn't need any fancy patterns, just a sturdy garment to keep her warm. If she could only get hold of some thick wool and something to use as needles, she'd make do.

The weather had certainly put a dampener on everyone's mood. It seemed capricious, to say the least, changing several times a day, and only Geir appeared oblivious. His handsome features were wreathed in smiles most of the time and occasionally his rich laughter rang out. The sound made her heart beat a little faster, but she told herself to stop being silly. Just because he was good-looking and occasionally charming didn't mean she should like him. He was still a slave owner and was keeping her here against her will. She had to remember that.

He and Steinthor were going to make a start on the haymaking, with Ingimund doing the raking. They were standing ready with those sinister-looking scythes in their hands, the sharp blades flashing in the light whenever they moved. Maddie knew how to use one, but preferred not to, as she found them scary. Niall and Cormac were already hard at work digging what she assumed would be a vegetable patch. That was more her kind of thing.

'You women had better begin making butter, cheese and whey,' Geir had ordered. 'And Brendan, you are in charge of the beasts. The dog will help you – it's what he's trained for. Don't let any of them out of your sight, understood? We can't afford to lose a single one.'

The cows and other animals had all been unloaded at last, although they'd had to be hobbled during the night so they didn't wander off. Geir said he was planning on letting them loose on one of the islands soon with the ones Hjalti had brought, but for today they'd keep them close. Blár was circling them, barking excitedly any time one of them strayed too far. He clearly enjoyed his guard duties and was good at them. The four cows, eight ewes and half a dozen female goats all needed milking, though, before they could be allowed to enjoy their grazing with their respective calves, lambs and kids.

'What was that you said just now?' Geir was on his way past Maddie when she'd muttered the word under her breath, but stopped to look at her.

'Stormavík,' she repeated. 'It's probably accurate. The wind hasn't stopped once since we arrived.'

There was no point mentioning that it also reminded her of her brother, whom she was missing a lot. What would he be thinking? Would he blame himself for not taking her with him on his pub crawl? Poor Storm. He couldn't have foreseen that she'd go off time travelling if he left her to her own devices. Her parents were probably also giving him hell for not looking after her, even though she was an adult. They'd be going frantic, although she still hoped they might have an inkling of where she'd gone. At least they could cling to the hope that she would return, as her sister had done.

'Hmm, I like it.' Geir gave her a quick smile, then frowned as if something had just occurred to him. 'Do you know how to milk a cow?' he whispered. 'If not, I can ask Aine to show you.'

Maddie drew herself up and glared at him. 'You should have thought of that before you decided to keep me here against my will. But as it happens, I can do most of the necessary tasks, so you needn't worry.' She was pleased to be able to inform him of this and proud that she was perfectly capable of managing the milking. 'I helped yesterday – didn't you notice?'

He seemed unruffled by her belligerent tone. 'No, can't say as

I did, but that's good. I didn't think women of your time were trained in such things. Your sister certainly had a lot to learn in that respect . . . But I'm glad.'

Goaded by his lack of reaction, she added, 'Not that I should be lifting a finger to help you, mind.'

That made his expression darken. 'Anyone who doesn't do their fair share of the work won't be given any food,' he hissed. 'That goes for you as well as everyone else.' He gestured to the land around them. 'But you're free to search for your own sustenance if you prefer?'

'No, thank you. I'd rather eat something decent.' Maddie knew when she was beaten, but it didn't mean she'd given up completely. She would do what needed to be done for now.

'Very well. I'm glad you can be reasonable about *some* things. I'll see you this evening.' To the other women he added in a louder voice, 'Maddie is in charge here. You're all to follow her orders.'

That was news to her, but she tried not to let her surprise show. Sure, he'd said he needed someone to run the household, but she hadn't thought that meant she'd always be the leader. And technically speaking they didn't even have a household yet, just a campsite.

Lif shot her a filthy look and protested, 'But I'm the oldest woman here and I'm married.'

What did that have to do with anything? Maddie wondered. She obviously had a lot to learn about hierarchy in Viking society.

Geir, who'd been on the point of leaving, turned around to fix Lif with a stern gaze. 'And I'm the owner of this land. You agreed to abide by my rules when you joined the group. Maddie is my woman, so that makes her your mistress until such time as you have your own home, understood?'

His woman? How very . . . Neanderthal. Maddie felt her cheeks turn scalding hot. She was still sharing his tent, as he'd insisted they didn't have any spare ones, and now everyone would think she was sleeping *with* him and not just next to him. She glowered at him, but he sent her a quick glance that told her clearly to play along. Fine, they could discuss it later, in private. And perhaps he was right, as his pronouncement gave her a role here, even if it wasn't true. Whether it would help or hinder in her dealings with the other women remained to be seen.

Lif opened her mouth to protest, her eyes shooting angry sparks at both Maddie and Geir. Steinthor put a hand on her elbow, murmuring a sharp, 'Lif, let it go. *Bóndi* was never going to stay unmarried for long.'

'He's not married yet,' Lif muttered.

'As good as,' her husband replied.

That too was debatable, but Maddie wasn't going to argue the point right now. 'I'm sure we can decide things together,' she interjected, not wanting to be the cause of discord so early on in the venture. 'We will divide the tasks between us, as we all know what needs to be done. We'll see you later.' She nodded at Geir to go, signalling that she could handle this, although she wasn't so sure.

Being the baby of her family, she'd never really been forced to take a leading role in any way. There had always been someone around to help her with whatever problem arose. But if she was going to stay in the Viking world for any length of time, she knew she'd have to toughen up considerably, and perhaps it was past time she grew up a bit. Stopped relying so much on others. Looking back, it was no wonder her parents had been so worried about her when she hadn't acted like a mature adult. Well, that would change as of right now. It certainly wasn't going to be easy to assume the reins, but she felt sure she could do this. It definitely beat being at Lif's beck and call, which was probably what would happen if the woman was in charge. And until she could find that damned knife, she was stuck here, whether she wanted to be or not.

She'd looked for it several times already, even going so far as checking in Geir's belt pouch while he slept, but the knife was nowhere to be found. *Wretched man!* Where had he hidden it? But now was not the time to ponder that.

The four women stood in a loose semicircle around her and she looked at each in turn. 'Right, are we all in agreement that milking is our first chore? From the noise those cows are making, I don't think they want to wait much longer.' She smiled to try and ease the tension a little. 'We'll do the ones here first, then I can row us over to the island to milk the rest.'

Fridgerd and the two Irishwomen returned her smile with tentative ones of their own, but Lif's mouth remained a thin line of disapproval. 'You know how to row?' she sneered. 'How useful.'

'Of course. Don't you?' Maddie shot back.

'I've never had cause to do anything so menial.'

'Well, then it's good that one of us can. And perhaps it's time you learned. No task is too menial here – we are all working towards the same goal.' Well, they were – Maddie might only be here temporarily, but for the moment they were a team. She turned away, refusing to be goaded further by this contrary woman. 'Let's get started. Are there enough pails and stools for all of us? Excellent.'

She found cows the easiest to milk, so she grabbed a bucket and stool and headed for the nearest one. Best not to admit that she didn't like milking goats – they could be temperamental, in her experience, and very stubborn, so she'd rather not wrestle with one if she didn't have to. Lif settled by another cow, while Aine chose a nanny goat nearby. Thankfully, the cow was docile and clearly wanted the relief of being milked, so she didn't cause any trouble. Maddie noticed Lif throwing her covert glances, but pretended she hadn't seen. Let the woman check out her technique – there was nothing wrong with it.

'Do you know what to do next with that?' Lif nodded at the milk, a challenge in her eyes.

'Yes. Why, do you have any particular suggestion?' Making butter, cheese, curds, whey and skyr, a kind of fresh sour-milk cheese with the consistency of Greek yoghurt, was what Maddie had in mind. They particularly needed whey, as that was used for preserving meat, and one could also drink it, although personally she preferred plain water. Whey tasted a bit sour, or perhaps tart was a better way to describe it.

'No. I was just curious. We don't know anything about where you've come from. You could have been raised as a thrall, like those two,' Lif nodded at Aine and Eimear, 'or you could be high-born for all we know.' Her tone indicated that she doubted the latter.

'That is true. Let's just say I am neither of those, but somewhere in between.' Obviously Maddie couldn't tell them the truth of her origins, but it was understandable that they were curious. 'I was raised a free woman and taught most household skills. If there is anything I don't know how to do, I'll ask for your help.' *Or more likely I'll ask one of the others.* Lif was the last person she'd go to for anything.

The woman just nodded and carried on with her own work. Maddie shared a look with Aine and rolled her eyes. The Irishwoman's lips twitched, but wisely she didn't say anything. It was clearly going to take a while before they all worked in harmony, but somehow they had to get there, otherwise the atmosphere in the little settlement would become unbearable. And as the appointed leader of the women, it was up to Maddie to make this happen. At least for now.

Chapter Eleven

Geir came back at dusk, hot and sweaty from a long day of scything, but pleased with what had been achieved. As he and the two men neared their encampment, he spotted a lone figure over by the raised ground where they had decided to build the first house. Maddie. She seemed to be digging straight into the hill, a large pile of soil growing rapidly next to her.

'What on earth is she doing?' he wondered out loud.

'Digging a hole?' Ingimund shot him a quick glance. 'No one has died, have they?' He hastened his steps, but Geir grabbed his shoulder and pulled him back.

'Don't be daft. If anything bad had happened, they'd have used the cow horn to call us.'

'Oh, right. Yes, of course.' Ingimund looked sheepish, but Geir didn't comment on it. The man had small children and everyone knew how vulnerable they were. A large proportion of them never made it past their tenth winter; many not even surviving one. It was always a worry and not one he was looking forward to himself when it was his turn to be a father.

Would he be the father of Maddie's children? The thought popped into his mind unbidden, but he quashed it. It was much too early to think about such things.

'I'll go and see what she's up to.' Leaving his companions with the other women, who were preparing food over two campfires, he strode over to where Maddie toiled.

'*Hei*. Have you started building my hall without me?' he joked.

She turned around and moved a strand of dark red hair off her face, leaving a smudge of dirt on one cheek, which was curiously attractive. He had to forcibly stop his hand from reaching out to wipe it off. She'd pushed up the sleeves of her serk, and the etched-in mark around her wrist was a stark contrast to her pale skin. Geir found himself wanting such a cuff himself, although he didn't know where he'd find anyone here who could produce such fine workmanship.

'Oh, you're back.' She gave him a brief smile, then turned to carry on. 'No, I'm digging a cool storage space. The weather isn't all that warm, but it's still hot enough that the dairy products might spoil. We need somewhere underground to keep them, so I thought I'd build it myself.'

Geir was impressed, although he didn't say so. She was definitely a capable woman, able to make sensible decisions, and also practical enough to carry out her plans by herself. It pleased him that he hadn't been misguided in giving her the reins over the other women. Still, she looked exhausted after a long day of working hard, and although he was very tired himself, he had the urge to help her.

'Here, let me dig for a bit. You can collect some suitable stones to line the inside with. And we'll need small timbers to shore up the corners and the roof. There might be some good ones among the driftwood pieces we've collected so far.'

'Are you sure? I can manage.'

'I know you can, but it will be faster if we work together.'

She seemed to accept this argument and began to bring stones up from the shore while he grabbed the spade. When he'd dug a hole that she said was big enough, she began to line the walls with the stones without asking for help. He gave it to her anyway. Halfway through the task, they were called to supper.

'We'll have to finish this tomorrow,' he said, and held out a grimy hand to lead her towards the hot spring. 'We'd better wash, or Lif will likely refuse to let us have any *náttverðr*.'

Maddie snorted, her dimple briefly making an appearance as she couldn't quite hold back a smile. 'Yes, I'm afraid she's still a bit cross. I think she'd been looking forward to giving orders and was hoping I'd be incompetent. The fact that I'm not completely hopeless probably annoyed her further.' She grew more serious and her cheeks turned a pale pink. 'But about what you said this morning . . .'

He knew immediately what she was referring to. 'That you're my woman? Yes, I'm sorry. I should have warned you, but it was the only thing I could think of to stop the argument. Do you mind? You said you don't belong to anyone else at the moment, so . . .'

'Well, it's just that the others will think that I . . . that we . . .' She looked away, a blush staining her cheeks.

'No. I'll make sure to let them know that is not the case. The men will believe me if I grumble about it, as if you're denying me and I'm frustrated. They'll tell their women.' It was rather close to the truth in any case, although he hadn't tried his luck in that department yet. He'd stayed on his side of the tent, with Blár acting as a shield between them. 'If it keeps the peace, one lie is a small price to pay, don't you think?'

He knew he'd been presumptuous, but in truth he thought of Maddie as his already, even though she'd refused to even consider the notion. The gods were persistent, and he was convinced they would win in the end. It was just a question of time. Besides, he could be rather persuasive himself when he put his mind to it. He just hadn't tried very hard yet. There were more important things to see to first.

'I suppose that's true.'

Nothing more was said on the subject, and as soon as they had washed their hands and faces, they joined the others for the evening meal.

As Geir looked around the circle of faces lit by the fires, he felt a deep contentment flowing through him. They had made a start, and together they would make Stormavík prosper.

Maddie was bone weary, but it was the nice kind of tiredness where you felt you'd done a good day's work. This was the sort of life she'd been wanting to live, not working in a second-hand clothes shop, just marking time until she could go home each day. Here she was doing something useful, productive, and every task was important. She was satisfied that the milking had been done in record time, and some butter, whey and curds produced. Cheese would take longer, but that was to be expected.

Brendan had proved himself useful by fishing for salmon while still keeping an eye on the cattle and sheep with Blár's help. Maddie had seen the boy using a wicked-looking fish-fork, almost a foot long and with a wooden handle. She was amazed at how good he was at spearing the fish with it, standing still in the water until an unsuspecting victim came close. He must have had a lot of practice wherever he'd lived before. Thanks to him, their evening meal was therefore a combination of succulent boiled fish, gull's eggs and some sort of strange vegetable that Aine and Eimear had picked nearby. Maddie thought it was probably what she would call angelica, although the Irishwomen had a different name for it in their own language – *ainglice* – and the Norse women called it *hvönn*.

'It's delicious,' Aine had told her, putting the leaves and

stems of the plant in a pot to simmer, together with bits of the roots.

Maddie had to agree it wasn't bad, although she'd had better-tasting vegetables in her life. No one seemed to be fussy, though, and everyone tucked in, eating heartily. She knew they needed to eat whatever fresh plant matter they could find in order to avoid getting scurvy, so she wasn't going to complain. There was one other dish available, though, that she refused to even contemplate eating – grilled great auk. In her time, these large flightless birds had become extinct because they'd been so easy to catch, and even though she realised she couldn't single-handedly save the species, she didn't want to contribute to their disappearance. She could see why the others wanted to eat them – they must weigh at least ten pounds, if not more, so there was a lot of meat on them – but not her.

She had a fleeting idea of smuggling a couple of them back to her own century, as and when Geir gave her back the knife, but realised it was a pipe dream. The magic – if that was what it was – probably didn't work on animals. If she'd understood it correctly, the time traveller had to say the special words out loud and a bird couldn't do that. Not unless it was a parrot, a thought that had her smothering a giggle. *Now you're just being ridiculous!* Either way, she was convinced that tampering with history in any way would not be allowed.

She noticed that Fridgerd and her older child ate quickly, as if they were afraid the food would be taken away from them, while the younger had a look of wonder on her face as she tried first the fish, then some egg. All three were much too thin. No wonder they'd jumped at the chance of a new life here in Iceland. The little one, a girl less than a year old, was clearly malnourished. She was still being breast-fed, but with a mother that skinny, she couldn't be getting much nutrition. It was good that she was being weaned on to proper food now, but Maddie could see that her little legs were beginning to bow in a way they shouldn't.

Rickets. The poor thing!

Having only ever seen it before on one of those harrowing films they showed on TV when there was an appeal to help starving children somewhere in the world, Maddie wasn't sure, but she couldn't think what else it could be. She racked her brain to try and remember if there was a cure. Since it was caused by vitamin D deficiency and lack of calcium, hopefully the child would recover if she was kept well fed and ate the right kind of food. She would need sunlight too, although the sun wasn't as strong here as in more southerly countries.

'What is her name?' she asked Fridgerd, nodding at the little one, who had a fist full of egg.

'Tove.'

'That's pretty. Is she crawling yet?'

A shadow passed across the woman's features. 'No, not yet. She . . . she just likes to sit and play.'

Maddie put a hand on her arm, speaking quietly so the others wouldn't hear them. 'Please don't be offended, but I can see that all is not well with little Tove's legs. I think I know what is causing it, though, and how to make it better.' She didn't say 'cure', because she wasn't sure rickets could be completely reversed, but there might be an improvement at least.

Fridgerd shot her a look of mingled suspicion and hope. 'Really?'

'Yes. Are you willing to listen?'

'Of course. Anything to help my daughter.' The woman frowned. 'I did hear someone say you're a *vōlva*. Will I have to make a sacrifice to the gods? I . . . I don't have much to give.'

Maddie swallowed a sigh, guessing that Lif was behind that piece of gossip. The woman really didn't seem to like her, which was unfortunate. 'No, no, and I'm not a *vōlva*. Not really. But I have learned a few things from, er, wisewomen.'

'Very well. What do you suggest?'

A glance at the child showed that she was now absorbed in picking out bits of yolk from the egg, seemingly entranced by the taste and feel of it in her mouth. 'Have you given her much proper food?' Maddie asked.

'No, we've not had any to spare until recently.' Fridgerd looked away, as if she was embarrassed to admit this.

'Well, from now on we'll make sure there is enough for everyone.' At least she hoped they'd be able to, although who knew what the winter would bring? If she was even here then . . . but that was a different matter altogether. 'You should stop breastfeeding her for the most part. What Tove needs is food like salmon, eggs, cheese and skyr. And we must make sure she plays in sunlight.'

'Sunlight? What has that to do with her legs?' Fridgerd looked puzzled.

'I, um . . . don't know,' Maddie lied. There was no way she could explain about the sun helping the body to absorb vitamin D. 'But the women I spoke to swore that it helped, and I have seen this for myself.'

'If you say so. I don't suppose it will do any harm. And Tove seems to be enjoying that egg. I can give her one each morning.'

'Good. Let's try that, and we'll make sure she has salmon or other fish most days too. She liked that, didn't she?'

Fridgerd nodded, then glanced towards Lif, who was on the other side of the fire with her husband. 'Please, can we keep this between ourselves for now? If . . . if it fails, Lif will tell me I shouldn't have listened to you.'

'Of course, I won't say a word, I swear.'

It was annoying that Lif held such sway over Fridgerd, but she clearly considered herself of higher status and Fridgerd must be used to being downtrodden, even though she wasn't a thrall. Maddie hoped to change that, but baby steps were called for, quite literally in this case, and she would be patient. She only hoped the new diet would help Tove.

She decided to change the subject for now and offered to cast the runes for Fridgerd. That led to her being much in demand by everyone else, and so the evening passed.

'Are you skilled at making clothes?'

Geir had been awake since first light, trying to come up with ways of wooing Maddie. Perhaps he shouldn't be so eager to comply with the gods' wishes, but he was a practical man and knew he needed a wife. They had seemingly provided him with a suitable female and he didn't want to waste time searching for another. The easiest thing would be to marry Maddie and be done with it. Besides, it was going to be agony lying next to her every night without being allowed to touch her. He could, of course, take one of the thrall women as his concubine and make it worth her while, but he didn't want to. To tell the truth, neither Aine nor Eimear appealed to him much. And what of any children that resulted from such a union? Any future wife of his would no doubt be loath to regard them with much favour. He'd seen such situations before.

No, the thralls might be persuaded to accommodate him, but he doubted it; he'd seen the way they glanced at their fellow countrymen. As their master, he shouldn't take that into account, but it would sow unnecessary discord if Cormac and Niall later had to put up with having Geir's leftovers. That would not be a good start for his settlement.

He was amazed at himself for thinking this way. Most thrall

owners cared nothing for the feelings of enslaved people, but Maddie hadn't let up in her attempts to persuade him that they were humans just like him, with the same emotions and the right to a free life. She took every opportunity to point this out, and her arguments must be wearing him down. His sister-in-law Linnea had also tried to impose her very similar views on everyone at Eskilsnes, with the result that she and Hrafn had no thralls at present. Either way, Geir had begun to look at them differently, and notice little things like those longing glances, which he was sure he never would have done in the past.

But if he couldn't have a thrall woman to warm his bed, that left only Maddie for him, and he just had to persuade her that marriage was the best course of action for them both. It was sensible as well as practical. He ignored the little voice in his head that whispered how attractive he found her and how sleeping with her wouldn't exactly be a hardship. That was irrelevant.

She looked up from the bowl of barley porridge she was consuming, her gaze slightly wary. 'Yes, I can sew, if that's what you mean. Why, do you need a new tunic?'

'No. I just thought that as you brought no extra clothing, unlike the rest of us, you might want to make some for yourself. I have cloth, both linen and woollen, and you are welcome to a length or two if you wish.'

Her expression brightened. 'Oh, well, thank you! Yes, that would be very welcome.' She glanced at the other women, who were wrangling children nearby, and lowered her voice. 'I think Lif wants her serk back, and to be honest, I don't like borrowing from her.'

She'd been forced to borrow from Lif, as Fridgerd's clothes had proved to be too threadbare. Geir would give Fridgerd some lengths of cloth as well. He had noticed Lif's reluctance to lend Maddie anything, but the woman hadn't refused an outright order from him. He tried to make light of the matter. 'She is quite a lot shorter than you, so having your own will probably be best.'

Maddie laughed. 'True.'

They both glanced towards her ankles, which were no longer exposed as she was back to wearing her own undergown at present. He found himself missing the glimpses of her slim legs, and inwardly shook his head at himself. Surely he wasn't that desperate?

'Do you want the material now or later?'

'Later, please. I'll have to sew in the evenings, as there is so much else to do during the day. Thank you.'

'You're very welcome.'

He called together his workforce to assign the day's tasks. A week had gone by and they were making good progress, but there was still a lot to do.

'I'm going to start ploughing so that we can sow the grain we brought as quickly as possible. Cormac, you're with me.' The man nodded. 'Niall, you said you had experience of shearing sheep, yes? Then that is your task for today. Brendan, you can help. Eimear, the wool will need washing – can you see to that? And Steinthor and Ingimund, can you start felling trees, please? We need to build a dwelling house for us all and a roofed structure where we can keep the hay once it's dried. In fact, the hay is probably the most important thing right now. Without it, we won't be able to keep the animals alive through the winter.'

'Will do, but I might take some time out to look for bog ore,' Steinthor said.

'Good plan. And we'll need to start cutting peat for burning, and slabs of turf soon too, as they need to dry before we can build anything with them. I thought we could use the ship's sail to cover them so that the rain doesn't increase the drying time. But that can wait a day or two.'

'Can I help with tree felling?' Maddie asked.

Geir felt his eyebrows rise. 'What? You want to—'

'Yes. And don't say it's a male task only. I know how to do it.' She gestured to the four other women. 'It doesn't take five of us to do the milking and such every day. In fact, Lif and Fridgerd are quite capable of managing it between them. If Aine comes with me, she can help carry logs.'

Geir considered Maddie's words and had to concede that she was right. If she really did know how to use an axe, she was better occupied with that than overseeing the other women, who knew what they were doing anyway. Still, it wasn't normally a task for females. 'Have you actually felled any trees or just watched how it's done?' He wasn't convinced she wouldn't do herself some damage.

'I have cut down several, and they were much bigger than the trees around here.' She looked offended at having her skills questioned, but he had to be careful. Any injuries could prove fatal, and he didn't want to lose a single member of his little group. They were all needed.

'Very well. I'll fetch an axe for you.'

He had a selection and brought her a medium-sized one, big enough to do the work but light enough for a woman to handle. He always made sure they were all sharp, but didn't protest when she asked for his hone stone. It might be needed during the day. He hesitated, his fingers meeting hers as they both held the stone. The slight touch gave him an unexpected jolt, but he ignored it and held on.

'You will be careful, won't you? I wouldn't want to lose you before you've had a chance to show me how your knife works.' He smiled to show he was joking, but only partly. The worry of anything happening to her was suddenly very real, although he didn't stop to analyse why it should matter so much to him.

She smiled back, pulled the hone stone out of his grip and gave him a small shove. 'I'll be fine. Be careful yourself – I wouldn't want to lose *you* either. At least not before you've told me where you've hidden it, in any case.'

That made him laugh. 'I'll do my best not to get in the way of the ard. It's meant to plough the soil, not harm me in any way.'

'Good. Until later.'

With a small wave, she and Aine set off towards the nearest clump of trees with the two men. Geir watched her go, a warm feeling spreading through him. Her words had indicated that perhaps she wasn't as averse to him as he'd thought, and it gave him hope. He shook himself inwardly. What was he doing, mooning about in this fashion? He had work to be getting on with.

Chapter Twelve

'Have you really done this before?' Aine glanced at the sharp axe Maddie was carrying.

'Yes.' In the re-enactment camps she'd been to, no one had had to stick to gender-specific roles unless they wanted to, and Maddie was always game to try her hand at anything. She and her brother both had a competitive streak, and she'd been something of a tomboy, copying whatever he did. Having learned a bit of woodworking from her dad and weaving from her mum, plus lots of other types of handicrafts, it had seemed like a fun challenge to attempt tree felling when Storm did, and she was glad of it now. 'Don't worry, I won't hurt either myself or anyone else. Besides, these are only small trees. You can help me make sure they fall the right way.'

'Mm-hmm.' Aine still sounded dubious, but the two of them were becoming friends, and hopefully she trusted her.

Maddie discussed with the two men which trees would be most suitable, emphasising the fact that they should leave some behind and not create any completely bare areas. Luckily, it seemed Geir had already impressed this upon them, so she didn't have to argue the point. Then they all got started. She saw Steinthor and Ingimund glancing at her to begin with, but when they were satisfied that she seemed to know what she was doing, they concentrated on their own trunks. It was tough work, but she relished the physical task and knew she was strong enough. The birch trees native to Iceland were sturdy but not massively tall. The wood was extremely hard, though – harder than oak – and felling each tree took quite a while.

She'd been taught to start with a notch somewhere around knee height. This had to be cut as deep as one third of the way through the trunk. She alternated between swinging the axe flat and downwards to create a wedge. Once that was done, she began cutting another notch on the opposite side of the tree, about a foot higher than the first one. This would help dictate the way the trunk fell. Again, a third of the way through, she stopped and went back to the original notch, deepening it. With each axe stroke, the tree became more likely to fall, and she stayed alert to any sounds of creaking that might indicate it was about to go. Sometimes this happened quickly, other times almost as if in slow motion. Either way, she didn't want to be in the way, and she told Aine to stand well back.

The Irishwoman was given a smaller axe by Steinthor and shown how to trim off all the branches. 'Just mind your fingers,' he warned.

When the trunks were clean, Maddie and Aine carried each log between them back to the site where the buildings would be erected. Brendan was taught how to strip off the bark, as this could be used as waterproofing when constructing the roof, and he set to with enthusiasm. Apparently spring was the best time for this, as the bark came off more easily, so it was good that they were cutting down trees now and not later during the summer. Maddie couldn't wait for them to start constructing actual houses – she'd seen this done in Sweden, but there the building material was all wood. She'd never tried using turf before and was looking forward to learning how that would work. It sounded as though you'd feel you were living underground, like hobbits, but perhaps that wasn't the case.

Time would tell.

'Tell me about your life, Cormac.' Geir had harnessed two of the sturdy ponies he'd brought to the ard and was concentrating on making straight furrows in the soil. The hay they'd cut had dried enough to be put into haycocks nearby, and the grass was as short as they could make it, ready to be ploughed. He could do this virtually in his sleep, though, and needed the distraction of talking to the Irishman to stave off boredom.

'My life?'

'Yes, where you came from and when you were captured. I know you weren't born a thrall.'

Cormac's expression darkened. 'No, I was not.' He was walking next to the ponies, guiding and encouraging them, but he briefly turned towards Geir at hearing his question. 'Some of your countrymen decided to raid my village, and unfortunately I received a blow to the head. When I woke up, I was far out at sea.'

'How old were you?'

'I had seen ten winters.'

'And what of your family?' Geir tried to imagine being snatched from his home at a young age, never to return. Growing up without his brothers, always toiling for others and with no reward for the hard work. It did seem wrong and he could see why Maddie and Linnea thought so. But it was the way of the world and most people needed thralls to help with the work. He had to admit that none of his thralls had been shirking their duties, and they never resisted any of his orders – in fact, they seemed to be working extremely hard. And he'd heard more complaints from Lif than from the five Irish people combined. But there was never any joy in their faces except when they spoke quietly among themselves, and they were not happy.

Well, why would they be? He certainly wouldn't, if he were in their shoes.

Perhaps Maddie had been right after all, and having the incentive of gaining a farm of their own would work better. Being free and working towards a goal. He was slowly coming round to this idea and kept mulling it over.

'My mother and father were captured too,' Cormac added, 'but they both died of illness within the first year. There was no one else.' A muscle twitched in his jaw and Geir decided not to press for more information. It was clearly a sore subject, and understandably so.

'Well, I'm glad to have you with me on this venture. You seem very capable and I appreciate your work.'

The Irishman blinked. 'I . . . Thank you.'

Geir returned his focus to the ploughing. It was all going to be hard work but he believed the rewards would be worth it. And going back to Eskilsnes with his tail between his legs was not an option.

Several weeks passed, and the group had settled into a routine. The men had finished ploughing and sowing, and had moved on to building work, while the women were occupied with milking, making dairy products, cooking, collecting foodstuffs from the wild, and dealing with the wool Niall had shorn off the sheep. Maddie also spent time sewing and now thankfully had her own spare serk and an extra smokkr. It had been a huge relief to give the borrowed one back to Lif.

But although the men worked in harmony, all was not well among the women, and this came to a head one morning. Maddie was coming back from washing their eating bowls in the nearby stream when she heard shouting. As she neared the campsite, she was in time to see Lif give Aine a hard slap that turned the thrall woman's cheek bright red and made her stumble. 'You're a clumsy fool and good for nothing! I've no idea why Geir saw fit to buy you. You're useless beyond belief . . .'

Lif raised her hand again, but Maddie hurried over and grabbed her wrist from behind. 'Stop! What is going on here?'

The woman wrenched her arm away and Maddie let her, although she kept an eye on her to make sure she didn't hit Aine again. Pointing at the ground, Lif said, 'Look, she spilled half a pail of milk, which we can ill afford to lose. She's just a clumsy oaf.'

'I didn't—' Aine began, but Lif rounded on her and cut her off mid sentence.

'It was your fault. How dare you contradict me?'

Maddie saw Brendan watching them cautiously and called over to him. 'Brendan, tell me what happened. Did you see?'

His face turned pale and his eyes widened as he gazed towards Lif, but Maddie was getting angry now and wanted the truth. 'I need you to be honest, Brendan. You won't be punished for anything you say.'

'I . . . She . . . Mistress Lif knocked over the p-pail when she tried to grab her s-son as he was hitting his little sister.' The boy's words were so quiet it was difficult to hear him, but Maddie got the gist.

She turned to Lif and glared at her. 'So how is that Aine's fault?'

'She was supposed to look after the children while I did the milking.'

'No, she wasn't. They usually play by themselves, and I thought your son had been told to keep an eye on his sister, not hurt her.'

Lif's cheeks now sported red flags of anger. 'It wasn't working and I'd told her to stop milking and see to it.'

'You said to finish with the goat first,' Aine muttered.

'Yes, and you should have been quick about it, but you were dragging your feet,' Lif shot back.

Maddie took a deep breath. 'Listen. I decide who is to perform which task, and if you need someone to look after the children, you are to ask me first. Aine had work to do – work that I had set her – and she can't possibly obey two people at once. And if you *ever* hit her again, I'm going to hit you twice as hard, is that clear? No one here – and I mean no one – is to be punished for any wrongdoing with blows or violence of any kind. That is not my way and I will not allow it. Do you understand me?'

She fixed Lif with her sternest gaze and saw the woman blanch. Maddie was bigger than her, and although she'd never hit anyone in her life except in the training ring, she would be happy to make an exception here. No way was she going to stand by and watch the thralls being mistreated like that. It was bad enough that they were slaves in the first place.

'Besides, I've never seen *bóndi* hit anyone, have you? It's not his way either.' She hoped that was true, although just because he hadn't done it yet didn't mean he wouldn't.

Lif gave a curt nod, but her eyes were stormy.

'Good, then let's all go back to our tasks, please.' Maddie turned towards Lif's four-year-old son, who'd been watching wide-eyed. 'As for you, young man, if I catch you being mean to your sister again, I'm going to lock you in my new root cellar, understand me? Little sisters are precious and need looking after. You're her protector and it's an important job, yes? As you're the oldest, you can look out for Fridgerd's little boy too.'

The child nodded solemnly and grabbed his sister's hand, then that of Fridgerd's son. 'C-come, Gerd, let's go look for seashells. You too, Ingvar.'

'Sells!' the little girl shouted happily, oblivious to the tension all around her, and somehow her joy lightened the mood.

Maddie crossed her arms over her chest and watched the others return to their work. She hadn't relished having to be harsh, but she knew it was necessary to lay down the law. She only hoped it had worked.

'Where did you learn to do carpentry?' Geir was holding a stripped birch trunk upright while Maddie expertly wielded a hammer to secure a piece of cross timber to it with a nail. At first he hadn't wanted her to help with the building work, but he was glad now that he'd given in. She knew what she was doing, that was clear, and an extra pair of hands was most welcome. He'd never seen a woman do such work before and was very curious. She was an enigma, and he found himself wanting to know everything about her.

'Um, it's hard to explain.' She cast a quick glance around to make sure no one else could overhear them. 'In my time, there are people who sometimes pretend to live the way you do. They attempt to copy your way of building to see how it was done. My parents were part of such a group, and my brother and I were always made to go with them. We both helped out and learned along with everyone else, although I wouldn't say hitting a nail on the head is particularly difficult.'

'You mean your buildings are not created this way? With timber?'

'Sometimes, but we have better tools.' She shrugged apologetically. 'Not that there is anything wrong with these, but the ones we have make the job go a lot faster. They are powered by, er . . . lightning.'

'Ah, yes, my brother Rurik let slip something about that once. I wasn't sure whether to believe him.' It had sounded too fantastical

– tools and wagons that moved of their own accord, somehow using lightning to propel them. How could that possibly work? He couldn't even begin to imagine it.

'Well, it's true. You'll have to come and see for yourself.' She grinned suddenly, green eyes sparkling in the sun.

'Me?' He was momentarily stunned by the sharp wave of attraction that rippled through him as her smile transformed her features from striking to outright beautiful. Odin's ravens, but the gods had sent him a rare gift. If only he could figure out how to persuade her that she was meant for him, but after weeks of trying, he'd made absolutely no progress at all. Their truce still held, and she seemed happy to talk to him, but that was as far as it went.

Her laughter interrupted his thoughts. 'Yes, you might like my time so much you want to stay.'

'I doubt it. I'd be a fish out of water.' Although if she was there too, perhaps it wouldn't be so bad.

'Like I am here. And yet I'm not doing too badly, am I?' She put her head to one side and regarded him quizzically.

'We-ell . . . I suppose not,' he conceded with a smile, and earned a punch on the arm for his teasing.

'Oaf.'

'Now, now. I don't want you to grow too vain by telling you how much I admire your skills.' Not that he'd seen any vain tendencies in her so far.

'Hmph. A little praise can go a long way.' She bent to pick up another nail and they carried on with the work.

'So if I tell you I find you beautiful, you'll thaw a little?'

Her brows came together and she sent him an irritated glance. 'No. I wouldn't believe you, because it's not true. I'll accept praise for my skills, but flattery for non-existent looks, never.'

It was his turn to scowl. 'How can you say that? Have you seen yourself mirrored in the spring lately?'

'Yes, and I see a *giraffe* with horrible red hair. Definitely no beauty.'

'A what?'

She sighed and hit a nail harder than was strictly necessary. 'It's a ridiculous-looking animal with incredibly long legs and neck. It's what people used to call me. Well, boys mainly, when I was taller than them. No one found me attractive, trust me.'

Her gaze was fixed on the next nail as if hammering it in was the most important thing in the world. Geir grabbed her wrist, afraid she'd hurt herself if she continued working while agitated, and when she turned to look at him, he shook his head. 'What if I do?'

'What?' She blinked, a blush staining her cheeks.

'Find you attractive. I'm taller than you, so your height does not intimidate me. Besides, I'm beginning to think that the men of your century are either blind or stupid. Maybe I *should* go there, just to teach them a lesson.'

Her frown didn't let up, though, and she snorted in disbelief. 'You're just saying that so that I'll sleep with you. Sorry, but I'm not falling for that. I know what I look like and honeyed compliments won't change anything. So spare me your lies.'

Geir opened his mouth to tell her just how serious he was, but her shoulders were now slightly hunched and he realised that this was something she truly believed. Someone – or several someones – had hurt her badly in the past and made her feel ugly. His blood boiled at the injustice of it and he wanted to throttle whoever had said such cruel things to her. A *giraffe*? Not likely. She was tall, true, but everything about her was in proportion and just perfect.

Somehow he would have to show her that she was wrong, but how? With an inner sigh, he returned to work while he mulled it over.

Steinthor had found enough bog ore to make all the nails they required, and had made charcoal which was needed as fuel for the smelting. Before starting on the main building, they'd created a small sunken hut where he'd set up his forge. The clanging of his hammer on the anvil was a constant background noise, but it was a reassuring sound. One that showed that everything was going to plan. Now that all the livestock were safely grazing on one of the islands, Geir had appointed Brendan as Steinthor's apprentice, and the boy spent as much time as he could helping out, looking like he really enjoyed learning everything the smith had to teach him. He smiled frequently and even spoke occasionally. It would seem that had been the right decision.

They were now building a frame for the main hall, around which the turf blocks creating the walls would be placed. There were two rows of upright posts, dividing the space into what looked like three aisles, and they would support the roof beams. As those had to be longer, they'd sourced them from huge trunks of driftwood. Smaller beams then radiated out from the frame at a slight angle to rest on top of the turf walls, thus forming a roof that appeared slightly hump-backed.

'Those probably came from *America* or *Canada*, across the sea,' Maddie had murmured, when studying the driftwood. 'What your people will call *Vinland* in about a hundred years.'

'I'll have to take your word for it.' Geir didn't care where they came from; they were a gift from the gods, as the birch trees were much shorter and a lot of them twisted.

The turf squares they'd cut had been left out to dry for weeks and would soon be ready for use. All the moisture in them had disappeared and there wouldn't be any further shrinkage, which was good. He'd never used them as building material before and was surprised how hard, yet light, the blocks were. Cormac and Niall, who had experience of this type of construction, were of the opinion that they'd need two layers of turf wall with sand or soil in between.

'That should ensure that the warmth stays inside during winter,' Niall had said, and Geir could see this made sense. Even though it was summertime now, the air was still much chillier than what he was used to, and winter was bound to be freezing.

'We'll put layers of stone at the bottom of each turf wall to ensure that no water can seep up from the ground either,' the Irishman added.

That, too, seemed like good advice, and they all collected suitable stones from the seashore.

'It's going to be very dark inside,' Maddie muttered now, banging in another nail. 'But I guess that's the price we have to pay for keeping warm. Are we building a *chimney*?'

'A what?' Geir hefted another upright into place and frowned at her.

'Somewhere for the smoke to escape.' She shook her head. 'Oh no, I forgot – you just have little holes in the roof on either side, right?'

'Normally, yes, although Cormac says that doesn't work as well in a turf building so we'll likely have an opening above the hearth instead. It will have to be covered with something to stop the rain and snow coming in though. He suggested the birthing sack from a calf but we won't have one of those until spring so I'll have to find something else. Why, don't you have smoke escapes like that?'

'Not exactly, but never mind. Birthing sack? That sounds, er, strange. I guess you mean the *amniotic* sac that surrounds the baby calf? Never heard of it being used for anything like that, but anyway, it will be cosy indoors.' Her cheeks became suffused with colour and she turned away.

'Is that a bad thing?' And why was it making her blush?

'No, but . . . I was just thinking we'll all be sleeping rather close to each other. Will there be enough room for everyone to have their own bench?' She wouldn't meet his eye, and Geir gathered she was asking whether she'd have to continue sharing with him.

A spurt of anger shot through him. Was he really so unattractive she'd rather sleep anywhere else than next to him? 'Perhaps. Don't you want to be my bed partner any longer?' he bit out through clenched teeth.

She shot him a startled glance. 'I don't think that's quite how I would put it, but no, I'd like my own space.' She held up a hand. 'And don't tell me – I'll regret it when I'm cold, right?'

He wanted to say that was exactly what he'd been thinking – or rather, that he'd like to have her next to him to keep him warm in other ways – but she clearly wasn't ready for this yet. He swallowed another sigh. 'I suppose we will see, won't we?'

It was galling, as he'd hoped she would have started to come round by now. He was allowing her to do more or less whatever she wanted – be it women's work or helping him and the men – but it was as if she saw this as her right, not a privilege he accorded her. And his charms, such as they were, appeared to have no effect on her whatsoever. How was he supposed to persuade her to marry him if she was completely indifferent to him? The only hold he had over her was the fact that he still had her folding knife in his possession, but she'd not mentioned it for ages. What was he to do?

He looked to the sky, seeking inspiration from the gods, and wondered if perhaps he ought to make some sort of sacrifice. He had neglected his duties in that respect since they'd arrived, but he'd been too busy. Well, he would just have to make the time. Yes, he'd pray to the goddess Freya for help, and one chicken would have to give its life in pursuit of better results.

Chapter Thirteen

Maddie bent her head over her work. Why did he have to ruin a perfectly good morning? She'd been happy helping him with the building work, and the mood had been light-hearted. At times like that she could forget that he was a cruel thrall owner who'd more or less forced her to stay here for the summer. And she had to admit she was enjoying herself.

Until he'd started flirting with her.

Stupid man! Did he really think she was going to fall for flattery? She snorted quietly. No, she was perfectly well aware of how she looked, and the fact that she was the only woman available to him. Clearly he was a practical man without a romantic bone in his body. He'd taken one look at her and decided she'd do, and now he was trying to persuade her that a relationship between them would work. Well, it wouldn't.

She had caught him staring at her quite a few times, and it was true that not once had she seen the look of disdain she'd so often been subjected to before. Maybe he wasn't as fixated by beauty as her former peers, and he was right about the fact that her height was not a problem for him. Quite the opposite. The few times they'd been standing close together, she couldn't help but notice that he was the perfect size for her, and vice versa.

But that didn't make it any better.

He wasn't in love with her. And he was still the owner of five thralls. Both were insurmountable obstacles, as far as she was concerned.

If only he wasn't so damned good-looking. Being near him, seeing those grey-blue eyes twinkle when he teased her, and watching the muscles of his arms flex as he went about every task with capability . . . it was very difficult not to be attracted to him.

Several times she'd caught herself staring at his mouth as he talked, wondering how it would feel on hers in a soft kiss. How harsh was the stubble around it? How soft his sun-bleached hair if you ran your fingers through it? It was madness even thinking about it, but she couldn't stop herself.

Still, there was no point, because she wasn't marrying him. When summer was over, she was going home.

That thought sent a pang of homesickness arrowing through her. What were her parents doing now? And Storm and Ivar, had they searched for her? She really hoped they weren't too sad and that they were keeping the faith that she'd return to them. It must be clear to them, as it was to her, that their family had been chosen by fate, the gods or whatever to have strange time-travelling adventures. It couldn't be a coincidence. While most parents would believe her dead by now, hopefully hers hadn't given up quite yet. She couldn't wait to see them.

She ignored the tiny voice in her head that told her she'd be sad to leave this place too.

'A ship! There's someone coming up the fjord!'

Ingimund shouted a warning, interrupting work just after midday. Everyone downed tools and headed for the shore, the women and children falling silent and gathering behind the men as they watched a ship being rowed towards them. It was smaller than their own, and sleeker, more suited to warriors than cargo, but thankfully it looked as though there were only a half-dozen people on board. Geir had grabbed his battleaxe from the tent and saw that the others were armed as well, just in case. They'd be five against six, not insurmountable odds by any means.

'Greetings!' An older man jumped ashore first and headed towards Geir, who was standing slightly in front of the others. The stranger was smiling, but the smile didn't quite reach his eyes, which put Geir on his guard. 'I'm Eyvínd Einarsson, and this is my son Eyjolf and some of my men. We have come from the fjord south of here – I believe we saw you pass by a few weeks ago.'

'Good day to you. I'm Geir Eskilsson,' Geir replied politely. Something about the way the man's eyes were darting around, taking in their cattle and building work as if judging their merits, seemed suspicious, but he would go along with the pretended friendliness for now. 'Yes, we could see that you had claimed that land, so we continued northwards and ended up here.'

'Ah, about that . . .' Eyvínd stepped a bit closer, his hand resting on the hilt of a sword that glimmered dully in the sunshine. 'We should have come sooner, but there is always so much to do in springtime. The thing is, I'm afraid you can't have this land. It is earmarked for my brother-in-law, who will be arriving any day now. If you'd stopped on your way past, we would have told you. I'm sorry you've done so much work for nothing, but perhaps we can come to some sort of agreement?'

Jaw clenching, Geir took a step forward himself and was pleased to find he was at least half a head taller than the man, as well as much younger. He shook his head.

'That is not how it works. We did stop to see Ingólfur Arnarson and we understood that whoever settled on a piece of land owned it. You hadn't put any markers on this domain and we were here first; we are not leaving now. Your brother-in-law will have to go elsewhere.' He gestured with one hand. 'It's not as if there isn't plenty of land to go round. In fact, he may find a better spot than this one.'

Eyvínd quickly lost his friendly expression. 'Now see here—' he began, but Geir interrupted him.

'This is not up for discussion. As you said yourself, we have done a huge amount of work here already and there is no time to start over elsewhere if we are to survive the winter. In fact, if your brother-in-law is only just arriving, he may find it a struggle to get everything done in time, and he'll have to spend the first winter with you. This is my domain now . . . unless you want to fight me for it, man to man?'

Out of the corner of his eye, he saw the son and the others move ever so slightly, readying themselves for battle, but Eyvínd hesitated and finally shook his head, plastering on another fake smile. 'Well said! I was only testing your mettle. Any man not willing to defend his property will not survive here. Welcome to Ísland.' He gestured behind him. 'The keg, Eyjolf, bring it.'

Geir raised his eyebrows as the younger man reluctantly went back to their ship and hefted a keg on to his shoulder. 'What is this?' he asked Eyvínd.

'We brought ale. A small celebration of your arrival, yes? If you wouldn't mind sharing your food, we'll contribute the drink.'

It was a strange and abrupt about-turn, and it went against the grain to spend any time in the company of this insufferable man, but for the sake of neighbourly peace, Geir accepted. He turned to Maddie. 'Is the food ready, *víf*?'

He gave her a look that he hoped conveyed his wish for her to play along, and she seemed to get the message. 'I believe so. There is always stew in the pot and there should be enough for everyone. I'll fetch out the bowls.'

Geir saw Eyjolf's eyes fix on her pert behind as she bent to retrieve the wooden bowls from their tent and her gown tightened around her momentarily, clearly outlining her shape. The look in the man's eyes was one he'd have liked to beat out of him then and there, but if they were to live in harmony, he couldn't act on the impulse. Besides, what could Eyjolf do? It was one of the unwritten rules that you never stole another man's wife, and Geir had claimed her as such.

He gritted his teeth and prepared to act the gracious host, hoping their guests would have the sense to leave sooner rather than later.

Maddie wanted to stay close to Geir, but unfortunately ended up sitting with Lif and Eyvínd's son, who had somehow manoeuvred the two women over to one side. Before she knew how it had happened, he'd pulled her down on to a sheepskin next to him, with Lif on his other side.

'What luck to be seated in between two beauties,' he murmured, throwing them each a glance. Lif giggled, but to Maddie it seemed as though his gaze was devouring her in a most unseemly manner. Should he really be talking to them like that? It was probably a good thing Geir – and Lif's husband Steinthor for that matter – couldn't hear him.

Eyjolf appeared to be about her own age, and wasn't bad-looking – dirty blond hair, even features and a lean but muscular frame – but there was something about him that made her uneasy. The few times their eyes locked, she thought she glimpsed naked lust, although to be fair, she didn't have much experience of such things. The only time a boy had looked at her with desire, he'd been more than half drunk.

He clearly had a high opinion of himself and was dressed ostentatiously. His tunic was bright blue, his belt and weapons gleaming and over-embellished, and he had a wolf pelt thrown across his shoulders despite the fact that it wasn't cold enough to be necessary, at least not during the day. A flamboyant dandy was how she would have described him in modern terms, but of course here he was just showing off his wealth. She wondered how any man settling in Iceland could be so rich already, but perhaps his father had brought raiding booty with him. She guessed they had plenty of thralls to do all the hard work, as Eyjolf didn't look the sort who'd want to get his hands dirty.

'Maddie is an unusual name,' he mused. 'But it suits you. You have the look of a Valkyrie and it fits with that image.'

'A Valkyrie? Hardly.' Was he trying to flirt with her? She squirmed at the thought. And who had told him her name? Lif? For some reason that made Maddie cross, but then it wasn't exactly a state secret.

He grinned and winked at her. 'Oh, I think so. Tall, striking and with that hair . . . magnificent!'

She felt her cheeks turn hot, but fortunately he briefly turned to Lif to heap praise on her as well. Perhaps it was just his way – some men were born flirts and couldn't help themselves.

'Where are you from?' he asked a short while later.

'Svíaríki,' she replied, somewhat reluctantly. 'And you?'

'Vestfold. But we had a small, er . . . misunderstanding with the king, and Father decided it would be best to move to Ísland for a while.' He shrugged. 'I doubt we'll stay long. There is much happening back home, and allegiances change in the blink of an eye.'

She wondered why they'd bothered coming here if they weren't interested in establishing a proper settlement, but reading between the lines, it seemed as though they hadn't had a choice. Perhaps Eyvínd or his son had been outlawed and forced to flee? From what she'd learned of them so far, it was more than likely.

'Where are your thralls?' he asked. 'Working further inland?'

'What?' The question threw her, then she rallied. 'They're all here, eating.' She gestured to the five Irish thralls, who were sitting together near one of the two campfires.

Eyjolf's eyebrows almost hit his hairline. 'They eat with you? How . . . unusual.' His expression conveyed that what he'd really meant was 'disgusting'. As if thralls were animals who ought to be fed elsewhere, and presumably on slops or leftovers.

Maddie gripped her bowl tightly to stem the tide of fury that washed through her. What the hell was wrong with these people? Lif, on his other side, was throwing her a triumphant look as if to say 'I told you so!' She was no better. But it wouldn't do to show her anger, so Maddie swallowed the furious words that hovered on her tongue. 'It's easier this way,' she bit out.

'Maddie doesn't believe in owning thralls,' Lif muttered, a malicious smile hovering on her lips. 'She wants *bóndi* to free them.' Rolling her eyes, she added, 'Even says they should be given land of their own. Can you imagine?' She pretended to shudder.

'How extraordinary!' Eyjolf turned to Lif and they began a quiet discussion on the merits of having thralls to do all the menial work. Maddie didn't want to listen, so she got up and went to fetch the cooking pot in order to offer everyone more food. She made a point of serving the thralls as well as the guests, and hoped Eyjolf was watching.

When she sat down again, he turned to her with an excited expression. 'Lif here tells me you are proficient at casting the runes. Will you do it for me? I want to know what's in my future.'

'I don't know . . .' It was the last thing she wanted to do, as it would prolong the visit.

'Please? It won't take but a moment, surely?' Eyjolf had grabbed her arm and she saw Geir scowling at them from his seat next to Eyvínd, as though he was about to come over and give the younger man a piece of his mind. It would be best to avoid a scene, and she could make it quick.

'Very well. It will cost you a piece of silver.' She'd be damned if she'd do it for free.

'Of course.' He extracted a coin of some sort from his belt and handed it over.

She opened her rune pouch and took out the staves and the little cloth with the concentric circles, placing it on the ground in front of them. Going through the usual ritual, she closed her eyes and took some deep breaths to calm her heartbeat and allow her mind to open. Not that she wanted any visions about Eyjolf and his future, but the motions were so ingrained in her, she did it almost on autopilot.

When she dropped the three rune staves on to the cloth and opened her eyes, the first thing she saw was that they had all landed upside down. She didn't tell him this was a bad sign as it meant they were reversed – the opposite of all the good qualities of the rune etched on the other side. Eyjolf's eager gaze showed that he had no idea and she decided not to enlighten him. It wasn't as though she cared about his life in any case, and most people only expected to hear good prophecies.

She picked up the first stave. 'This is Tiwaz, the symbol of honour and victory.' The former was a trait she very much doubted he possessed. 'It usually means that you will be successful over your competition and find out where your true strengths lie.' That *was* what it normally meant, and she didn't inform him of the fact that because it had landed upside down, in his case she was looking at the rune for failure and injustice. It wasn't hard to guess that he was a man who was not satisfied with his present situation but was too weak to do anything about it.

He beamed. 'Good, good, go on.'

She already had the next stave in her hand and was staring at it. 'This is Thurisaz, which tells me you will get into conflict.' She didn't add that as it was reversed, it meant potential peril and betrayal as well.

A sudden image of him covered in blood, but with a gloating look on his face, entered her mind and she had to stifle a gasp. She gripped the stave so hard it was biting into her palm, but the vision wouldn't leave. For some reason it scared her, although she didn't have the feeling she was the person he'd wounded. She saw him holding a long knife aloft, as though in celebration, and giving a great shout of satisfaction. Closing her eyes for a moment, she willed the image to disappear.

'Conflict?' he prompted. 'Ah, you mean I will be going raiding and conquering. Excellent. That is exactly what I was planning to do.'

Maddie nodded. That could be it, although she had a deep-seated feeling it wasn't. The rune in her hand was giving off vibes of danger, malice and hatred. So much so that her lungs constricted and she had to make a huge effort to breathe. These emotions could be commensurate with raiding, but in the vision she'd seen, he had seemed to be alone, perhaps battling just one person. She very much hoped it was a fight he would lose, as the first rune had indicated.

'And the third rune?' Eyjolf was clearly impatient to hear more, so she picked up the final stave.

'Fehu, meaning gains, success, happiness.' She spoke the words even though they were the complete opposite of what she should have said. The one word really echoing through her mind was 'cowardice'. She suppressed a shudder. Eyjolf might achieve success, but if he did, it would be by underhand methods and stealth.

'But this is wonderful! Thank you.' He grinned at her and winked. 'It seems the Norns will grant me everything I wish for.'

His gaze travelled along her body and back up to her face, as though to demonstrate that she was part of what he desired.

She sent him a quelling look to show him clearly that she wasn't available. 'It would appear that way, yes.'

Lif, who never liked to be left out of the spotlight, grabbed his arm to make him focus on her. 'That all sounds great. You must return to tell us about your successes.'

Maddie almost gagged. What was wrong with the woman? She had a perfectly good husband; surely she shouldn't be flirting like that? It was nauseating. Perhaps Steinthor wasn't giving her enough attention – they had all been rather busy recently, not to mention tired. Hopefully it was just Lif's way, though, and she meant nothing serious by it.

To her huge relief, the visiting party prepared to leave soon afterwards. 'We must return to our settlement before it grows dark,' Eyvínd declared. 'Wouldn't want to hinder you in your endeavours.'

'Thank you, we appreciate that,' was Geir's reply, but Maddie could tell he was holding his temper in check. If Eyvínd and his men hadn't come in the first place, they wouldn't have had to stop work on the hall for several hours. They normally didn't eat until later.

As the guests headed for the shore, Lif walked beside Eyjolf, and Maddie saw her lean closer to whisper something, then giggle. By the look the young man threw Maddie's way, it was clear they were talking about her, and another spurt of anger shot through her. What was the stupid woman up to now? Perhaps she was still going on about how Maddie always defended the thralls, as it was a subject they obviously agreed on. Yes, that had to be it. Well, too bad – Aine and the others ought to be free, and Maddie's views on that would not change, no matter what Lif thought. If she didn't like it, she could damn well go back to Sweden.

Chapter Fourteen

'Well, that was . . . interesting,' Geir mused, as they went back to their building work.

'That's not how I would put it,' Maddie muttered, throwing an angry glance in the direction of the departing vessel, whose sail could still be seen in the distance. 'I think they came here hoping to find a group they could intimidate. I'm glad you stood your ground.'

'Yes, I hope they understood me. Why in the name of all the gods would we leave when we've already sowed next year's crops? Madness.' He shook his head.

Maddie was scowling while shaping a piece of wood with a small adze. He'd watched her at first to make sure she knew what she was doing, but couldn't fault her technique. He gathered now that she was shaken by the visit, and so was he, but it had only made him realise they had to be more vigilant and prepared to defend what was theirs. 'I saw Eyvínd's son talking to you. Did he have anything of interest to impart?'

She snorted. 'Not unless you call it interesting that he thinks I'm a Valkyrie. He tried to make me believe he admired my looks. Sweet Freya – flattery twice in one day! I'm going to have my head turned at this rate.'

Geir felt his mouth twitch in amusement, but thought it best not to say the obvious – that there was a reason she was being admired. She clearly wouldn't thank him for it.

'So a smooth talker then, was he?'

'Oh yes, and how! He was complimenting Lif too. You should probably alert Steinthor to the fact that he's not praising his wife enough, as she was lapping it up. You'd think Eyjolf was starving for female attention, but from what he said, they have loads of thralls and presumably he can just take whichever one he wants, when he wants.' The adze came down with a thump and Geir put a hand on her wrist to stop her movements for the second time that day. She might have the technique right, but he could tell she hadn't had much practice at using that particular tool, and it was easy to make a mistake.

'Wait, slow down. You're going to hurt yourself.' He regarded her intently. 'Did he upset you? Touch you? I saw you cast the runes for him.'

'No, but if you could devour someone with your eyes, he would have done. As for the runes – I lied to him.'

A burst of fury coursed through Geir, and his fists clenched. 'The *aumingi*! He knew you were another man's wife. I'm glad you didn't tell him what the runes predicted, whatever it was. He didn't deserve your reading.'

She threw him a strange look, then shuddered and took a deep breath. 'Well, I'm not your wife, am I, although hopefully he'll never find that out. It was probably just his way. Don't mind me. I simply didn't like him, and I'm not used to attention from men.' She gave a sharp laugh. 'I told you, no one even looks at me twice normally.'

'Well, they should,' Geir practically growled. He was genuinely puzzled. How could they not? With that flaming hair and those stunning green eyes, let alone her graceful figure, she certainly drew his gaze. And Eyjolf's, apparently.

'Don't. We've talked about this already.' She stared at the ground and absently kicked a piece of wood out of the way.

'Maddie, look at me,' he commanded, putting his fingers under her chin to turn her face towards him. 'I don't care what you have been told in the past. You are extremely attractive, and any man would be lucky to have you for his wife.' When she opened her mouth to protest, he cut her off. 'No, I mean it. I am not trying to flatter you for my own ends. You must never denigrate your own worth, understand me? The men where you come from are utter fools.'

With that, he turned away from her before he said too much. She'd made it clear she wasn't ready to marry him, and he wouldn't pressure her, but by all the gods, he had a very strong urge to just seize her and kiss her senseless.

'Now, are you ready for the next cross beam?' he said, in the calmest voice he could manage.

'Y-yes, of course.'

He didn't look at her again for a while, because he couldn't trust himself not to haul her into his arms.

What the hell had just happened? Maddie was reeling from Geir's outburst and didn't know what to think. He'd seemed so sincere, as if he really did find her attractive, but why would he? Compared to her, he was practically a god – tall, blond and handsome beyond belief. He must have had his pick of all the beautiful ladies back home.

Perhaps he was merely being kind. He'd seen her distress over Eyjolf's comments, and had thought to calm her. Yes, that had to be it.

But dear God, what if he really did like her? What if he wanted her as his wife for his own reasons, not because he thought the gods had decreed it?

That would be . . . a different matter.

It couldn't be true, though. Their situation was unusual, and he'd said it would be expedient for them to marry. Not very romantic, and just because he'd insisted she wasn't ugly, that didn't mean he was in love with her. No, best to stick to her guns. At the end of the summer she'd demand her knife back and go home to the future.

Where no one found her attractive.

It was a lowering thought.

There was a man's chest beneath her hand – firm, unyielding and warm. A heart beat a steady rhythm on one side, and she let her palm rest on top of it, feeling the jump as it increased its pace. Her fingers trailed upwards, then raked lightly down through a sprinkling of hair. It was intriguing, enticing. She dared to dip lower, across hard abdominal muscles that were smooth ridges under her fingertips. They tightened as her touch travelled across them, as if their owner enjoyed it, and she marvelled that she could have that effect on anyone. She wondered if she dared to explore further down, but hesitated. It seemed a step too far.

Another hand began to reciprocate, travelling slowly up her leg. She knew it was a man's because it felt large, the skin work-roughened. It wasn't an unpleasant sensation, the leisurely caress leaving a tingling trail in its wake. She ought to stop it, but curiosity made her hold her breath, waiting to see how far it would go.

It stopped halfway up her thigh, and disappointment flooded her. She'd been enjoying the feeling of anticipation building inside her and felt almost bereft when there was no more. The hand hadn't gone, though; it stayed still, as if waiting for something, and in the next instant she found out what that was. Soft lips, surrounded by rough stubble, covered her own in a tentative kiss, as though the other person was asking permission with his mouth. Did she want to allow this new liberty?

Hell, yes!

She moved her own lips to signal agreement and the other person got the message. She found herself being kissed with much more intensity, a tongue teasing at her to open up. Well, why not? It was a wonderful kiss. Quite the best one she'd ever had – not that she had kissed that many men, but still, she knew instinctively that they didn't come better than this. Her tongue danced against his, joining in the game with abandon. The few times she had been kissed before, she'd been self-conscious and worried whether she was doing it right. Not so now. Her mouth knew exactly what to do, and it was glorious.

The hand that had stayed on her thigh was suddenly on the move again, skimming her bottom and up along her waist. It stopped momentarily just under her left breast, before moving up to enclose it completely. When a thumb brushed across her nipple, she jumped and her eyes flew open . . .

. . . and stared straight into Geir's blue-grey gaze, clear in the hazy light of early dawn.

'What the . . . ? Get off me!'

Maddie went from asleep to wide awake in two seconds flat as her brain connected the dots. She hadn't been dreaming at all – he'd been taking liberties. Acting purely on instinct, she rolled across to straddle him, putting an elbow against his Adam's apple. 'If you so much as lay another finger on me, I'll make sure you can't talk for the rest of the day,' she hissed, furious now. 'What do you think you're doing?'

His eyes danced with amusement, but he lay very still and raised one hand in a gesture of surrender. He slowly brought the other one out from under her gown and held that up too. 'You looked so beautiful, *unnasta*, I couldn't resist stealing a kiss. And you started it, so I thought that was what you wanted.' He managed a small shrug despite the pressure of her elbow.

'Why, you . . . I was asleep! I thought it was a dream.' As he wasn't moving, she removed her arm and instead thumped him in the chest.

He grinned. 'Must have been a good dream. Ouch!' Grabbing both her wrists so she couldn't do any more damage, he huffed out a laugh. 'I'm sorry. You can't blame a man for accepting your enthusiastic advances.'

'There. Were. No. *Advances!*' Although her cheeks grew hot as she remembered the sensation of his warm chest under her fingers, which meant she must have had her hand inside his shirt. How had that happened? She twisted her arms up and around to get out of his grip, and he let her.

'Well, then you probably shouldn't sit like that, or I might get the wrong idea and think you're trying to seduce me.' His grin widened and he wiggled his hips underneath her.

Belatedly she became aware of exactly what she was sitting on and scooted off faster than a scalded cat. Her cheeks were practically in flames now, and she swore under her breath. He was right, damn him; she probably had started the whole thing. But she'd been dreaming, unaware of what she was doing. It must have been all that talk about him finding her attractive. Her subconscious had accepted it as truth and acted on it. *God, how embarrassing!* She lay down and was about to turn away from him when he pinned her down with his chest, one hand either side of her, his mouth temptingly close to hers.

'What was that? You know, if you want me to continue, you have only to say so. And if you'd prefer to be married first, I'm ready any time.'

'I do *not* want you to continue! Oaf!' She pushed at him and he eventually moved away, but only after showing her how easy it would have been for him to just take what he wanted, by giving her a quick kiss. She supposed she should be grateful he wasn't a brute of that ilk, but she still felt disgruntled. Because the truth was she *did* want him to continue. His kisses had been wonderful and her body was still fizzing with pent-up passion. No one had ever made her want sex before – it was just something she'd considered she would have to endure at some point – but Geir did.

Damn him.

'Well, in that case I'd better go and dunk my head in some cold water. And other parts of me too . . .' He laughed and sat up to pull on his shoes. 'But if you ever change your mind, I'm here. Just so you know.'

'I won't. And I've told you, I'm not marrying you. The whole idea of the gods choosing me as your wife is ridiculous. They're laughing at us. It's a joke at our expense. If they even exist, they must be fully aware that I'd never want a husband who owns thralls.'

He rolled his eyes, but she could see a slight tightening of his mouth. The mouth that had just kissed her so expertly and which she didn't want to look at because then she'd likely throw herself at him again, and that would be a mistake.

'I still think you're wrong,' he told her softly.

The only answer he received was stony silence. She didn't trust herself to speak.

Geir wasn't sure if he was the biggest fool on earth or just too nice for his own good. Maddie had clearly wanted him just now and he could probably have persuaded her to continue. A few more kisses and caresses, and she'd have been melting into his arms, ready to surrender. But although her body said one thing, her brain was not in agreement. And until such time as she told him she would be his woman, he wouldn't force the issue. He knew instinctively that pushing her before she was ready would end in disaster.

But by Thor and all the *jötnar*, it was going to be torture now that he knew exactly how good it felt to kiss her, touch her, and caress the softness of her skin . . . He shuddered. A quick dip in the sea was what he needed right now.

Perhaps he ought to let her have her own bench once their hall was ready. It would certainly be better for his sanity. But at the same time, he was used to sleeping next to her now, and he'd miss her. What was more, he'd miss out on any other such dreams she might have.

No, he'd make sure she remained right where she was. She belonged with him.

Her parting shot stayed with him throughout the day, though. Would she reconsider if he really did free the thralls? Was that truly all it would take? And would it be such a bad thing to do?

He'd never had cause to speak to thralls before other than to give them orders, but now that they were working so closely together, he was beginning to see them as individuals. As comrades. They were unfortunate people with a tragic past and bad luck, but people nonetheless. Like Maddie kept telling him, they had feelings, wishes, ambitions, even though at the moment they had no way of fulfilling them. Linnea and Maddie's arguments had influenced his thinking, and now that he'd bothered to actually get to know the five thralls, he had to admit he was starting to like them. A lot.

They were his companions in this venture and they deserved to reap the benefits of all the hard work just like the rest of them, did they not?

What it boiled down to, though, was two things: could he trust them not to just run away if he freed them, and would other settlers laugh at him for being too soft? The first would be a major problem, as he knew he would never make a success of it here without their help. The second he couldn't care less about. He had never sought or valued anyone else's opinion, other than that of his two brothers, and he wasn't about to start now. Honour was important to a man, but was it honourable to keep others captive and use them for your own ends?

In the end, it was Lif who made up his mind for him. She'd come to view the building work and was walking around the now almost finished hall with Steinthor, who had taken a break from his smithy. Geir heard them talking as he was working nearby, but they hadn't noticed his presence, since he was hunkered down behind a pile of turf, burying some animal bones under one wall of the house. This was tradition when building a new dwelling, intended to bring good fortune to the inhabitants.

'Why are there so many benches?' Lif was saying. 'There aren't that many of us. It just makes it more crowded.'

'Geir is building enough for everyone,' Steinthor replied.

'Everyone? You mean the thralls too? They should be on the floor, surely?' Lif's voice had a slight sneer to it that made Geir want to shake her. How did Steinthor put up with such a sharp-tongued wife? The woman was unbearable. He'd never noticed it at home since he didn't spend any time with the ladies of the household, but here it was impossible not to.

He'd heard several exchanges between Lif and Maddie, and knew there was no love lost there. He judged that the latter was able to handle it, though, so he hadn't intervened, but it had been close on more than one occasion. Very close.

'It's going to be extremely cold here in winter. The floor would be too chilly for anyone to sleep on,' Steinthor answered, his tone patient. 'Thralls are no use to anyone dead.'

'I suppose, but still . . . it's not right. They should have their own hut. Perhaps a sunken one, like your smithy.'

'That's not much warmer,' Steinthor pointed out.

'It's what they're used to.'

Geir felt his fists bunching of their own accord and made up his mind then and there.

The thralls would be freed.

'I have decided we'll do it your way.'

Maddie was busy trying to build an upright loom by copying the one Lif had brought with her. She figured the woman would never let her borrow hers – she'd been reluctant enough just to allow her to look at it – and two were better than one in any case. Cloth was always needed, and the bolts Geir had brought wouldn't last for ever. As he didn't need her for building work today, she'd started making the necessary pieces, carving them out of aspen and rowan wood. These were softer to work with than birch. The loom was of a fairly simple design and she'd reckoned it shouldn't be too difficult to construct, but it was proving a lot harder than she'd thought. She'd been lost in the work, swearing under her breath, and Geir's voice startled her. She spun round, heart jumping into her throat.

'What?'

'I've spoken to Steinthor and Ingimund, and they've reluctantly agreed we should try your suggestion to free the thralls and offer them an incentive to work instead. Not that they had much choice, as I'm in charge of this venture, but still . . . I thought it only fair to consult them. There will be no payment involved, but the goal of a farm of their own to work towards. And the freedom itself, of course.'

Maddie blinked, hardly able to take in this momentous news. A thrill ran through her as it hit home, and she gave him a wide, if slightly stunned, smile. 'You're saying they will be free men and women from now on?'

Geir nodded. 'I will speak to them and ask for their oath that they will not run away. I don't know where they'd run off to, but you never know. I've heard of Irishmen travelling to Ísland in coracles. No reason they can't go back the same way if they know how to build one.'

Maddie raised her brows. 'You mean those tiny round boats made of hides stretched over a frame?' She'd seen some at a museum somewhere. 'You can't be serious. Surely no one could travel across the sea in one of those?' She gestured to the ship down by the shore. 'That was bad enough!'

'Apparently they do. Followers of the White Christ; men who seek a remote place to be alone with their thoughts.'

'That's insane.'

'I agree, but it's not impossible. And what was wrong with my ship?'

'Nothing. It was just . . . Oh, never mind.' This probably wasn't a good time to tell him how exposed she'd felt in it and how it was really nothing more than an oversized rowing boat.

'Either way, I will have their oaths and I'll make it clear that if any of them disappear, the remaining ones will suffer for it.'

That seemed rather barbaric, but a lesser evil in Maddie's eyes, and she was sure none of the thralls would be stupid enough to go anywhere. At least now she wouldn't have to work alongside any enslaved people. 'Thank you,' she said softly, and put a hand on his arm. 'I am grateful, and I think you're doing the right thing.'

'That remains to be seen.' He opened his mouth as if he was going to say something else, but changed his mind.

Something occurred to her and she frowned. 'You're not, er . . . expecting anything from me in return, are you?'

His expression darkened. 'No, the gods forbid! But if you could find it in you to stop regarding me as some sort of ogre, that would be good. Now I'd best go and speak to them. I'll see you later.'

'I don't—'

'Yes, you do. And if you want help with that,' he pointed to the bits of loom she'd been trying to carve, 'let me know. You're making a right mess of it.' Eyes briefly flashing with anger, he stomped off, but Maddie ignored the stab of guilt that shot through her. Had she judged him unfairly? Possibly, but right now she didn't want to think about that.

She felt a huge grin spread across her features. *I won!* He was going to set the thralls free and give them back their dignity. She wondered whether she'd worn him down with her nagging, or if he had just come to see sense. Either way, it didn't matter – the end result was the only important thing.

She swallowed hard as she realised he'd removed one of her objections to marrying him. Was that on purpose? Or was he merely a good man who had understood the injustice of keeping thralls? Time would tell. And the fact remained that she couldn't stay here for ever, so becoming his wife was not an option.

Chapter Fifteen

While Steinthor and Ingimund carried on with their work, Geir gathered the small group of thralls down by the shore, away from everyone else. Aine and Eimear looked wary and suspicious at this summons, while Cormac and Niall tried to appear unruffled even though he guessed they weren't. As for the boy, Brendan, he still never usually spoke unless addressed directly, except when he was working with Steinthor, when he seemed to come alive, and when he was with his sister, Aine. Geir hoped that the fact that he hadn't separated them would make her, and the others, feel somewhat indebted to him, as he needed their loyalty now.

'Sit down, please, and listen,' he ordered, indicating for them to form a semicircle around him. 'My fellow settlers and I have decided that this is a new beginning for all of us, and we'd like to try something a little bit different.' His audience was hanging on his every word, and he realised the incredible power he had over them. A power no man should have over another, according to Maddie and his sister-in-law. They were right. He could see that now.

'As you know, I have claimed a large portion of land on this newly discovered island, and I want to turn it into a prosperous holding. Not just one farm, but several eventually up along the river inland, although we will have to build it up over time and start with the one to begin with. It will not be easy, and we'll need to work together if we are to survive.'

Cormac and Niall nodded; they were with him so far. The others said nothing.

'Steinthor will be kept busy with his work. We'll be forever needing nails and implements, and if there is enough bog ore, he might be able to make objects to sell for profit as well. His wife and family will live in my hall until such time as we can build a separate dwelling for them. Ingimund was a tenant farmer to my brother, but only had a share of a smallholding, and his will be the second farm we build, perhaps next summer. I gave him my word on that before we set off.'

They were all still staring at him as though they weren't sure why he was telling them this. Owners didn't usually inform their thralls of decisions or plans; they just gave orders. Geir knew he was breaking with tradition here, but the more he'd thought about it, the more it made sense. And from listening to other travellers bound for Ísland, he'd come to realise that he hadn't brought nearly enough tenant farmers. He needed people he could trust, and trying to ally himself with strangers at this point was not an option.

'Now I bought you all because you are young and strong, and I was assured you have experience of building work and farming.' He nodded at the men, then the women. 'And you two can turn your hands to anything that is needed in a household. However, I have been led to believe that you might work even harder if you have an incentive, something to strive towards. I am therefore proposing to make you free men and women . . .' At their gasps of surprise, he held up a hand. 'On condition you swear a sacred and binding oath not to try and run away, leaving me short of the manpower I need. Should you choose to give me your word, I in turn will swear to let you have your own part of my domain as free tenants once we have established ourselves sufficiently. One farm for each couple. What do you say to that?'

They weren't couples yet, as far as he was aware, but he had no doubt that, thrown together constantly, Cormac and Niall would do their best to woo one woman each. What hale and normal man wouldn't? In fact, he'd seen signs of it already. He was faced with five open mouths and wide-eyed stares at first, but the thralls soon rallied and this turned into huge grins.

Cormac found his voice first. 'We'll be free men working towards having our own farms?'

'Yes. As I said, I am hoping we can establish a string of settlements that can work together when necessary with haymaking, harvests, slaughter and such.' Geir didn't need to spell out the fact that as the landowner, his would be the largest farm – they would understand that implicitly. These people had probably expected to die in the service of one master or other, and the promise of freedom and a home of their own was more riches than they'd ever dreamt of. Cormac said as much.

'Thank you.' He beamed from ear to ear. 'I for one am very happy to swear a sacred oath not to run anywhere. I don't believe I have anything to go back to, in any case.'

The others hurried to agree. 'We had not expected such generosity, master.'

'Not master now; just Geir, or *bóndi*.' He smiled at their delight. 'Oh, and Brendan, are you happy to continue as Steinthor's apprentice? If not, you can of course make your home with Aine and whoever she chooses as her husband.'

The boy nodded, his eyes shining. 'I want to be a smith. Please.' Being a blacksmith was a highly regarded profession, and he knew it.

'Good. When you're older, you'll be free to go and work

elsewhere if you so choose.' Geir looked at them all in turn. 'I am placing my trust in you. None of this will be easy, but together we can do it. Do we have an agreement?'

A resounding 'Aye!' came from all five.

'Then that is settled. Swear your oaths to me now and then we will all go about our business.'

They eagerly swore as he directed, and to be on the safe side, he made them swear on the White Christ as well as his own gods. Then he swore in his turn to keep his word.

Odin's ravens, but he hoped this was going to work. If not, he would be a laughing stock.

'He did what? Is he insane? Who is going to do all the hard work?'

'We all are, just as before. Nothing has changed except the fact that we can't just order the former thralls to do something; we have to ask nicely.'

Maddie took great pleasure in informing Lif and Fridgerd of Geir's decision. He had told her he was happy for her to do so, and he'd winked as he said it, which made her suspect he knew very well how much she would enjoy this moment. *Schadenfreude* was not an admirable thing, but in this case she felt justified. Lif would just have to learn to live with the new status quo.

'This is all your doing,' the woman hissed. 'You've been filling his head with stupid ideas, and because he's so in lust with you, he'll do anything you say. But it won't last, trust me on that. And when he tires of you, I'll make him see reason, see if I don't.'

With one last look of pure rage, Lif stalked off and Maddie was left looking at Fridgerd, who squirmed under her gaze and muttered, 'Sorry. She's just . . . I think it's the babe. It's been a difficult pregnancy this time and she's not herself. I—'

Maddie held up a hand. 'Don't make excuses for her. I sincerely doubt she'd be any different even if she wasn't with child. I'm sorry she can't see that this is the right decision, but perhaps in time she'll get used to it. Eventually the former thralls will move to their own farms and she will only need to see them occasionally.'

Fridgerd nodded. 'I hope so.' She put a hand on Maddie's arm and gave it a squeeze. 'You're a good woman, kind and compassionate. I like Aine and Eimear too, and we are all in this together, so it makes sense for us to be equals. As for the rest of what Lif said, don't take any notice. I doubt *bóndi* will ever tire of you. I've seen the way he looks at you. He'd be a fool to let you go.'

'Er, thank you.' Maddie felt her cheeks heat up. There seemed no point mentioning that she and Geir weren't in a relationship and never would be. Whatever Fridgerd thought she'd seen, she must have been mistaken. Or perhaps Geir was playing his part much better than Maddie was. He'd told everyone she was his woman and they had to maintain that charade in order for her to be in charge. It was better that way. Wasn't it?

She had to admit that it was becoming more and more difficult every day not to fall for his charm. He seemed to be going out of his way to please her, and often gave her little gifts – an eating knife of her own with a beautifully carved handle, another hairpin, and a bone needle case with her own set of needles so she didn't have to ask Lif or Fridgerd to lend her one. All practical items, but it was thoughtful of him nonetheless.

He was wearing down her resistance, little by little, and she wasn't sure how long she could hold out. Or even if she wanted to.

They stayed alert in case of further unwelcome visitors, but although a couple of other boatloads of people stopped by, those were new settlers on their way north looking for their own land. They didn't seem to have any wish to lay claim to Stormavík, and only came ashore out of politeness. None of them acted in a threatening manner, although some cast envious glances at what had been achieved here already. Geir began to calm down. Eyvínd and his lot must have been the exception to the rule – everyone else clearly understood that once a domain had been settled here, it couldn't be taken away from you.

And thankfully, the man didn't come back.

After weeks of hard work, they finally moved into the grandly named hall – the *skáli* – although it wasn't anywhere near the size of the building of that name back home at Eskilsnes. It looked more like a green hillock with a hump in the middle, and the turf walls and roof were sprouting long tufts of grass. Inside, there were benches for everyone, long enough for them to stretch out on rather than sleep sitting up as some people did, with shoulder-high wooden dividers in between. A substantial hearth made of stone had been placed in the centre of the room, with cooking pots hanging from hooks above it. Although the interior of the hall was dark, the flames from the fire helped and, when needed, oil lamps would be lit as well.

The entrance, a sturdy wooden door with a carved lintel, was over on the right-hand side at the front, with a small porch paved with flat stones. Geir had to duck when entering as it wasn't quite tall enough for him to get through while upright. There was a little loft area at this end of the building over an ante-room, both of which were to be used for storage. It could be reached via a ladder, and the three older children – Brendan and the other two boys – delighted in climbing up and down so it was decided that they could sleep up there. At the other end of the main room was another room, the pantry, with a bench for food preparation, shelves, barrels for storage, and hooks with all sorts of implements. From here, a rear entrance led outside to the midden, where all the household waste ended up.

To Geir's chagrin, Maddie claimed a bench for herself, as she'd wished. He chose to continue to sleep in his tent, unless the weather was really bad. It was one thing sharing a small space with people if you had to, but lying awake in the dark listening to the furtive lovemaking between Steinthor and his wife, or Ingimund and his, was more than he could cope with at the moment. Even the former thralls were pairing off, just as he'd predicted, and he could have sworn he'd heard sounds from one of those couples one night as well.

It was unbearable.

The more he watched Maddie, the fiercer his longing to possess her fully became. Their little interlude in his tent, before she'd moved into the hall, hadn't helped. His body remembered all too well the sensations her exploration of his chest had evoked. The tentative touch of her fingers as they'd raked through his stubble and tangled with his hair. The feel of her velvety skin as he'd explored in return. And those kisses . . . That had been quite something. He couldn't recall ever being so affected by merely kissing a woman. He told himself it was because she was the only one available, but deep down he knew that wasn't true. It was her he wanted, only her. And his attempts to court her had so far fallen flat.

The truth was, he was at his wits' end. What more could he do?

There were other problems too. Lif had taken the news about the former thralls badly, and was going out of her way to be unpleasant.

'Can't you speak to her?' Geir entreated Steinthor, but the man just sighed.

'I've tried, but she won't listen to me. She's got it into her head that your woman gave you this idea on purpose, just to rile her, and nothing I say to the contrary helps. I'm hoping she'll calm down eventually. The new babe should be arriving soon – that will give her other things to worry about.'

That was true, and Geir bit his tongue, hoping the smith was right. If not, he'd have to take matters into his own hands.

He arrived back at the hall one evening after a day out in the rowing boat with Niall, fishing for cod and haddock. They'd brought back a sizeable catch and he was feeling pleased, until he heard the screeching from inside the building.

'She's a thief, I tell you! She needs to be punished.' Lif's strident tones rose up to the rafters and no one could fail to hear her.

Geir rushed inside and stopped abruptly, staring from Lif to Maddie, whose eyes were flashing just as much as her opponent's. 'What is going on?'

'The thrall stole one of my amulets. It was found in her kist.' Lif pointed at Aine, who was shaking her head, silent tears streaming down her pale cheeks.

Cormac had made Aine a chest to keep her few belongings in – presumably as a courting gift – and it normally resided under the bench where she slept. Now it had been dragged out, the lid flipped open and its contents strewn around it. Lif was holding out a small silver amulet in the shape of the goddess Freya, and staring accusingly at the Irishwoman. 'It was in there,' she added, nodding at the kist.

'I never . . . I have no idea how it got in there!' Aine protested weakly. 'I wouldn't take what doesn't belong to me.'

'One of the children must have been playing and hidden it there. And Aine is *not* a thrall, as you well know,' Maddie said. Her gaze fell on Steinar, Lif's four-year-old son. She hunkered down. 'Come here a moment.' She pointed at the silver amulet. 'Have you seen that before? Did you or Ingvar hide it during one of your games? Or little Gerd, maybe? It's fine if you did. We understand it was just for fun.'

Geir watched the boy. It was a reasonable supposition, as shiny things seemed to appeal to children. Steinar frowned in confusion, however, and shook his head. 'No, Mother put it there.' Lif gasped out loud, and her son sent her a worried glance and took a step closer to Maddie, as if for protection.

Steinthor had by now arrived as well, piling into the hall behind Geir and Niall, and he pushed past them to kneel in front of his son with a massive scowl on his face. He gripped the boy's shoulders and looked him in the eyes. 'What are you saying, son? Your mother put the amulet where?'

'In . . . in the kist.' Steinar blinked, his lower lip wobbling. 'I saw her. I . . . I was under a bench, hiding from Ingvar, just for a little while. Mother came in and took it out of her pouch, then put it in Aine's kist. I thought it was a g-gift.'

Steinthor stood up and just stared at his wife for a moment. 'Is the boy telling the truth, *víf*?'

Lif had gone even paler than Aine, but her fists clenched and her gaze was still defiant. 'And what if he is? She shouldn't be living in here with us. It's not right.'

The smith, who was normally the most placid of men, literally growled as he stepped forward to grip his wife's upper arms. He gave her a little shake.

'That's *enough*, Lif! I'm tired of this constant carping. You either accept the situation or I'll divorce you and send you back to Svíaríki on your own, as soon as the new babe is old enough to do without you. Do you hear me? We came here to make a new life for ourselves. Geir has been my friend for many years and I trust him to make the right decisions. What's more, I think he has done the right thing. So does everyone else. You're the only one who can't see it.'

Lif's mouth was set in a mulish line. 'You wouldn't take my children away from me.'

'Oh yes I would. Never doubt it. Now apologise to Aine or I will have nothing more to do with you.'

Geir found that he was holding his breath, waiting to see what would happen. He was furious himself, but he knew that in this instance, Steinthor's words would have more impact. He was Lif's husband and he could divorce her if she behaved ill.

He saw the woman swallow hard, glaring at everyone present, but in the end she bowed her head and muttered, 'I apologise, Aine.'

'Good. Now let's go for a walk.' Steinthor marched his woman outside, but behind her back he nodded at Geir and then at his little son, who was standing with his mouth hanging open.

Geir got the message. He went over to the boy and swung him up into his arms. 'Thank you for telling the truth, Steinar. That is always the best way, and your father is proud of you. I'm sure he'll tell you that later.'

'R-really?' The boy's eyes were huge with fear and doubt. 'He looked angry.'

'Not with you. With your mother. She was, er . . . playing a game that's not very nice and he didn't like it. Now, what's for supper? I don't know about you, but I'm starving! And when we've eaten, you must come with me down to the boat to see how much fish we caught today. It's a magnificent sight.'

The boy's expression brightened and this diversionary tactic appeared to work. 'You brought back lots? Can I help cut them open? Father gave me my own knife.'

Geir laughed. He doubted the small and rather blunt eating knife Steinar had been given would work well on a huge cod, but there was no harm in letting him try. 'Of course. All help is welcome. Isn't that right, Maddie?'

She'd been galvanised into action by his request for food, but she looked up from stirring the pot and sent them a smile. 'Yes, indeed. I'm not overly fond of gutting fish, so if you can help, Steinar, that would be wonderful.'

Everyone slowly went back to their normal evening routine, and when Steinthor finally brought his wife back from their walk, no one mentioned the incident. Geir sincerely hoped that the message had finally sunk in and they'd have no more trouble. In such a small community, they couldn't afford to be at loggerheads, and come winter, they'd be crammed into this hall like herrings in a barrel. Any discord would be amplified a hundredfold.

May the gods give them peace for a while now.

Chapter Sixteen

Lif's third child arrived a few days after the amulet affair, as Maddie had dubbed it in her mind. Perhaps the agitation brought on the labour pains, or maybe it was just time anyway. Either way, it would hopefully serve as a good distraction.

'We'll need boiling water and clean cloths,' she told the other women. They had all congregated inside the hall, apart from Aine, who diplomatically offered to look after all the other children and keep them out of the way. The men were also banned and would have to eat outside for now.

At first, Lif muttered that she didn't need them fussing over her, but Maddie stayed firm. 'Surely you want help when the child arrives? And we can bring you food and drink, as well as wipe your brow from time to time.' Whatever the animosity between them, as women they should stick together and help each other. Not that she was sure she'd be of much use, but still.

Uncharacteristically, Lif didn't argue, and grunted in pain as the contractions continued to sweep through her. 'Something isn't right, I'm sure of it,' she moaned after several hours of struggling. 'It didn't take this long last time.'

Fear gripped Maddie. Women often died in childbirth in times gone by. What if that happened to Lif? Although Maddie knew all about these things in principle, she wasn't a doctor or a midwife. All she could do was to make sure anyone who touched Lif or the new baby was clean, hands and any implements used thoroughly washed. The rest was up to fate or the gods, whichever you believed in.

To her relief, Fridgerd took charge, for once losing her timidity. 'You'll be fine, Lif. Every time is different. Perhaps the baby is in the breech position, but you've given birth before so it's not dangerous. Now hold on to my hand, but don't push quite yet. Your pains are not coming fast enough for that.'

Her calm words seemed to have the right effect, and Lif nodded, holding her friend's hand in a death grip.

'I have heard that it helps to breathe in a certain way.' Maddie remembered watching a programme on TV about Lamaze breathing. She had no idea if it really worked, but she relayed the basic method to Lif now. It probably couldn't hurt in any case.

'Deep breath, that's it, in through your nose, out through your mouth. Hold it. Now breathe quickly as the contraction grips you – good! Another deep breath, and . . . relax.'

She positioned herself behind Lif, supporting her against a cushion, and massaged the woman's lower back and shoulders in between contractions. It seemed to be giving her some relief, and after what seemed like hours, Fridgerd finally allowed Lif to strain as hard as she was able.

'Not long now! I can see the head, so all is well – it's not a breech. Push, Lif, push! I'm ready to catch the child, never fear.'

'Did you scrub your hands?' Maddie looked up from her ministrations. 'Hot water and lye, yes?'

'I did.' The others had seemed slightly bemused by her insistence on these measures, but they were used to her being in charge now and no one questioned her orders. Eimear was standing by with hot water, a shallow bowl, and clean linen towels to dry the baby with. She'd also been plying Lif with cool spring water and mopping her brow.

Lif gave an almighty final push and screamed as the baby's head appeared, but it wasn't long before the rest of the little body slithered out.

'You have another son,' Fridgerd told her with a smile. As she rubbed the baby's back, the little one took his first breaths and cried the mewling cry of a newborn. 'And hear that? He has good strong lungs.'

Maddie wasn't convinced, as it was the reediest little noise she'd ever heard, but the infant was a normal size and hopefully he was healthy. To tell the truth, the whole birthing process was a bit out of her comfort zone, and she was just glad it was over. Even though she'd merely been a spectator, she felt as though she'd been through the wringer. The gods only knew how Lif must be feeling.

'I'll take him.' Eimear seemed to know what she was doing. A knot was tied and the umbilical cord cut, then she gently cleaned the baby with warm water while crooning something in Gaelic.

Wrapped in linen and a woollen blanket for extra warmth, the baby was given to its mother to hold after she'd struggled to produce the afterbirth. Maddie didn't think she'd ever seen such a soft expression on Lif's face, and she hoped the safe arrival of this child would help mellow her mood.

'Congratulations and well done! Steinthor will be so pleased.'

'Thank you.' Lif blinked back tears. 'And thank you for the breathing advice and all. It seemed to help.'

'I'm glad. Do you have a name for him yet?'

'That's for my husband to decide.'

The ecstatic father chose Svein rather than another name beginning with Stein, as was apparently the custom in his family, just as in Ingimund's all male names began with Ing. Maddie was glad, since she privately thought it confusing with so many similar ones, but no one else ever mentioned it so she didn't say that out loud.

The main thing was that mother and baby were both safe and well, and with a bit of luck Lif would be so wrapped up in her new child, she'd stop making trouble. When Aine brought in the older children to see the new baby for the first time, Lif even thanked her for looking after them, which was a turn-up for the books.

Maddie happened to look over at Geir, who had come into the hall with everyone else, and they exchanged a smile, both obviously thinking the same thing. It gave her a little frisson to know they were so attuned to each other, but then she told herself it was just a question of shared relief.

From now on, Stormavík might be a happier place.

Gutting fish was a vile job and no mistake, but very necessary. Geir sighed as he pulled what seemed like the hundredth fish towards himself and slit open its belly. He and Niall had been fishing again, and their catch was plentiful, for which he'd give thanks to the gods. They'd built open-ended shelters of wattle, with racks inside to hang the fish on, and these were situated near the shore, where the wind was always strongest. It was the most efficient way of turning a fresh catch into stockfish, and they had mostly cod, interspersed with haddock and ling. Smaller types, like herring, were put in barrels of brine instead.

'Would you like some help? I'm tired of sitting indoors on such a beautiful day.' Maddie put a hand on his shoulder briefly before sinking down next to him on her knees in the black sand.

Geir glanced at her. The casual touch told him she was becoming used to having him near, but she still gave no indication that his advances would be welcome in any other way. Sharing his tent with Blár felt lonely, and he missed her presence there more than he could say.

'Any assistance is very welcome indeed. I know this is necessary, but it's mighty tedious.'

She sent him a quick smile and pulled out the knife he'd given her. It flashed in the sunlight and he could see that she'd sharpened the blade.

'Why are you doing this all alone?' she asked, watching him for a moment to see how he went about the job.

'The others all have other tasks today and someone has to do it.' He shrugged and gave her a lopsided grin. 'Being a landowner isn't quite what I expected. It'll be a while before I can sit on a dais and order people around the way my half-brother Thure used to do.'

She laughed at that. 'No, I don't suppose you did this at home.' Growing more serious, she added, 'It's my fault really, isn't it? If I hadn't persuaded you to free the thralls, they'd be doing it. I'm sorry, I—'

He cut her off. 'Don't apologise. We were always going to be short of manpower, and whether I'm gutting fish or making hay, I'm still working towards establishing a prosperous settlement. I don't mind, honestly.'

'Well, if you're sure . . . ?'

He nodded. 'I will do whatever it takes.'

They worked in silence for a while, each lost in thought. It really was a lovely day, the sun warm on their faces and arms where they'd rolled up their sleeves, even though the weather in general was still a lot colder than he was used to in summer. They were surrounded by the vibrant green of the flatlands, with a hazy view of the mountains in the distance. The smell of fish ceased to register after a while as the breeze bore it away. He found this place beautiful in an austere way and didn't regret coming here. Not for a moment.

'How are you finding sleeping in the hall? Better than a tent?' He hurled a fish head as far out into the bay as he could and briefly watched as gulls swept down and squabbled over it.

'Um, honestly? It's a bit noisy, what with baby Svein wanting a feed at least twice a night, and other people . . . well, enjoying each other.' Maddie cleared her throat and added, 'Who knew a baby could have such big lungs?'

He glanced at her and saw that she was concentrating fiercely on the task at hand, while her cheeks were flaming. So she'd heard lovemaking as well. Did it make her long for it, the way it did him? Or was she repulsed by the thought? He didn't want to ask.

'Well, you can always come back and share the tent with me and Blár. We might snore, but we're not as loud as Svein,' he joked, and pretended to shudder. 'Nothing is as noisy as a hungry baby.'

Maddie smiled and the colour in her cheeks faded slightly. 'Perhaps I will. It's not too cold yet, is it? And no point sleeping inside a stuffy house until we absolutely have to.'

He blinked at her. 'You'd willingly come back to my tent?'

'Why not? Unless you would like to put one up just for me?' He opened his mouth to protest, but she laughed and gave him a shove. 'No, *fifl*, I'm joking. It will be warmer with you and the dog.'

A warm glow spread inside him at the thought that she might be lying next to him again tonight, but he couldn't resist teasing her a little bit. 'And what if you have more dreams of the kind I enjoyed immensely?'

He regretted his words immediately, as her expression darkened. Had he pushed her too far? But then a small smile tugged at the corner of her mouth. 'Then we'll just have to hope that the first thing my hands encounter is the dog and not you. That should wake me up a bit faster, as I doubt any man would be that hairy.'

Geir laughed and sent another fish head sailing through the air. 'Fair enough.'

But hopefully Blár wouldn't always stay in one place, and with a bit of luck, maybe Geir would be in the way of her questing fingers again. Right now, he couldn't think of anything he wanted more.

The fish all done, Maddie and Geir took turns bathing in the hot spring. They'd rigged up a screen of wattle so that anyone using it would be concealed from the settlement, even from a distance. She still felt rather vulnerable there, though, as if anyone could look down on her from the surrounding hills, but she was becoming used to it. And it was worth it for the sheer pleasure of wallowing in hot water, as well as the wonderful feeling of being truly clean.

She and the other women had made very basic lye soap, adding flowers and herbs for fragrance, but it wasn't as efficient as its modern equivalent. It took quite a lot of scrubbing to get rid of the stench of fish, and when she finally finished, she stepped round the wattle screen to find Geir sitting there waiting his turn. She stopped short at the sight of him and clutched her linen towel to her chest.

'How long have you been there?' Glancing back, she tried to peer through the barrier to see if anyone inside would be visible, but it seemed fairly impenetrable.

'For a while.'

'You should have said something. I thought you'd be waiting down by the shore.'

'Why?' He turned a puzzled gaze on her. 'I didn't want you to rush on my account. And it doesn't smell as bad here.' He gestured to the spring. 'It's wonderful, isn't it? I don't think I've ever enjoyed bathing more, except perhaps in the Grikklandshaf.'

'The what?' Greek sea? 'Oh, you mean the *Mediterranean*?'

He shrugged. 'If that is what you call it. The sea down by Miklagarðr. It was very warm, but then so was the air all around it, so it didn't have the same effect.'

'I know.' She remembered her last holiday on Mallorca, floating in the turquoise waters with the sun beating down on her. It wasn't an ideal place for her, with her pale skin that didn't tan easily. This far north, she fared better, and she much preferred the non-briny water of the hot spring even if it smelled like rotten eggs from the sulphur.

'You've been there too?' His eyebrows rose a fraction, then he sighed. 'There is so much I don't know about you . . . but I'd like to learn.'

As he turned those blue-grey eyes on her, Maddie felt her insides melt. He was incredibly attractive, any fool could see that, and yet he had set his sights on her. Was courting her. She had noticed, even though she'd not mentioned it – the small gifts, the surreptitious touches, backing her up on every decision and giving her more or less free rein around the settlement. He had been incredibly patient with her, it had to be said. Not like the rough, violent Vikings of legend, even though he could easily have forced her to do all manner of things. Would it really be so bad to spend more time alone with him and get to know him? Maybe even be his woman, as he'd put it? She was from the twenty-first century, where dating someone didn't mean you had to marry them.

And yet that way lay danger. If things got physical, she could become pregnant, and then how would she ever be able to leave?

Still, it was incredibly tempting. *He* was incredibly tempting. And she was only human. She held out a hand to pull him up. 'Then talk to me while I scrub your back and I'll tell you whatever you want to know. You can keep your under-trousers on; they probably need washing anyway.'

His eyes widened so much she had to laugh. 'You're offering to . . . wash my back? I . . .' He looked down at her and gave her a smile that had her melting even more. 'Thank you.'

'Don't thank me yet. I've never done it before and I might be incompetent at it. Come.'

She tugged on his hand and led him behind the screen, where she tried not to watch as he undressed. He had two pairs of trousers on, as she'd known – woollen ones on top of linen – and he left the linen pair in place as requested. She had a feeling he was tiptoeing around her, afraid of scaring her away. And he was right to, she acknowledged. She had no idea what had prompted her to offer her services as bather, but looking at his beautiful muscular body, she knew she was going to enjoy touching him. Immensely.

Geir thought he'd died and gone to Valhalla. His very own Valkyrie was kneading the knots out of his back muscles, her fingers covered in sweet-smelling lye. He closed his eyes and leaned against the edge of the pool, savouring the moment.

'I'm dreaming, am I not? Ah, that feels so good. I've been sitting hunched over for far too long.'

She chuckled. 'You and me both.'

He turned to smile at her. 'You should have asked me to do this for you. I'd be happy to, any time.'

'I'm sure you would. But unlike you, I can't just wear under-trousers and be decent. I have, um, female parts further up.'

He laughed out loud at that. 'Female parts, huh? Yes, I am well aware of that.' Too well, judging by how his body reacted to the mere thought of them. But the water and his trousers hid that part of him from her sight, and he wasn't about to scare her off now that she was finally touching him of her own accord. He felt they were getting somewhere at last.

Her fingers were firm and strong enough to massage the tension out of his shoulders and neck. She seemed to be taking her time and he was grateful for that, but he wished she would say something. Anything. Did she like what she saw? He needed to know.

'So does this mean you don't think I'm a troll then?' he blurted out eventually.

'What?' She stopped for a moment and peered at him over one shoulder.

'Well, if you are able to touch me, I can't be all that bad to look at.'

'*Fifl!*' She gave him a little push, then ran her hands down his biceps, kneading the considerable muscles there. 'I'm sure you are perfectly well aware that you are very far from a troll. I would bet you had women queuing up to jump into your bed at home, right? I'm just wondering why you didn't bring some of them with you.'

He shook his head. 'You're wrong. I'll admit I've bedded a few, but I was never the favourite. That was always my brothers. You've met them – you must have seen for yourself. Hrafn is considered incredibly handsome, and Rurik could charm anyone he set his sights on. It was ever thus.'

She halted again and stared at him with her mouth open. 'You're not serious?'

'Of course I am. The women much preferred them to me. I'm the runt of the litter. Not that I didn't have offers, but still . . .'

'Really?' Maddie blinked as if she just couldn't take this in, and it made him chuckle.

'I take it you don't agree? I'm flattered.'

'Well, I . . . No. I mean, yes. I mean . . .' She drew in a deep breath and started again. 'I have met both your brothers and I could see that they were good-looking, but you're even more so. How could the women at Eskilsnes not realise that?' She frowned. 'I don't want it to go to your head, obviously, but honestly, were they blind?'

'Clearly.' He said it with a smile, although her words made him feel all warm inside. She smacked him lightly over the head. 'No, seriously, perhaps it was just that I wasn't paying attention. I was always afraid of having to marry someone.'

She tilted her head to one side as she regarded him. 'Why? Then you'd have had a wife and wouldn't need me here. Now you're having to court the only available woman instead of having a choice of many.'

'But that's just it – I didn't want any of them. There was no one I could imagine spending my entire life with, sharing this dream with.' He gestured to the verdant landscape around them, then looked into her eyes. 'But with you, I can.'

'Oh.' She went still, then looked away.

Geir didn't know if she believed him, but he realised it was the truth. She was the only woman he could contemplate sharing Stormavík with. He'd watched her for weeks and admired everything about her – her looks, her skills, her kindness to others, the pleasure she found in life and all she did. If this was what the gods had wanted him to see, they had succeeded. He was well and truly caught. But she wasn't. Not yet.

He put up a hand to cover one of hers as it gripped his upper arm, and glanced at her. 'I know you still need more time to think about this, but rest assured I won't be changing my mind. Not even if a dozen other women arrived here.' He pulled her hand into the water to rinse off the soap, then brought it to his mouth to place a light kiss on her fingers. 'Now you'd better go, or I'll be tempted to pull you in with me. Thank you for this.' He indicated his back. 'It was wonderful.'

'You're welcome. My pleasure.' She gathered up her things and walked away quickly, as if she didn't quite trust herself not to jump into the pool with him.

Geir smiled. It was progress, and he could be patient a little while longer.

Chapter Seventeen

After she had finished a sweater for herself, Maddie had been spending her evenings knitting little garments for all the children, although she hadn't given them to their mothers yet. She wanted to wait until she had one for each child, and they wouldn't need the extra layer until autumn in any case. She'd received a few strange looks when she had first started, but when she explained that it was a craft learned from her ancestors, they didn't question it. The women here had their own way of fashioning things out of wool – *nálbinding* – and seemed content with that. She'd had to ask Steinthor to make her some knitting needles, but he was an easy-going man and happy to oblige.

The day after she'd washed Geir in the hot spring, Maddie felt restless when supper was over, and didn't want to sit down with her knitting. She ought to be tired from all the physical work she did every day, but she wasn't. She finished washing a cooking pot down by the shore and then went in search of Geir. He was sitting outside the hall carving something out of a walrus tusk and she didn't ask where he'd obtained it. There was no way she'd condone hunting such magnificent animals, but she couldn't stop it happening here, so she tried not to enquire too closely into the men's hunting expeditions.

She hovered next to him. 'Are you busy, or would you like a change?'

He looked up with the smile that always made her heart beat extra hard. 'What sort of change? More bathing?' His blue-grey gaze grew warmer and his eyes crinkled at the corners.

She shook her head and ignored the teasing. 'No. Well, not immediately anyway. I was thinking . . . you asked if I could teach you some of my fighting skills. How about now?'

He jumped up with alacrity. 'Absolutely! Let me just put this away in my kist.'

When he came back out of the hall, she led him away from the settlement. It would be embarrassing to have everyone watch them. She'd never told any of the women about her self-defence training, as the subject hadn't come up.

Geir glanced over his shoulder and chuckled. 'The others probably think you're taking me on a secret tryst.'

'What? Oh.' That hadn't occurred to her. 'Well, I—'

He put a hand on her arm. 'Don't worry about it. They already believe you to be my woman, and now you're back to sleeping in my tent, what does it matter? The men can stop teasing me about our falling-out.'

'Falling-out?'

'Yes, when you chose to sleep in the hall without me, they assumed we'd had a disagreement. I didn't disabuse them of the notion.'

'Oh, I see.'

She hadn't thought about the fact that her actions would have repercussions for him, and she felt guilty that he'd had to deal with that. It had been kind of him not to mention it or complain. It was true that everyone still thought her to be his woman, and she hadn't corrected their assumptions because it seemed easier not to. Perhaps that was wrong of her, but she didn't care.

They found a small clearing in the nearby birch forest, where the leaves had now turned from the minty green of spring to a darker hue. Maddie pulled off her sweater and apron dress, leaving only her serk. Geir's eyes widened.

'Take off your tunic,' she instructed. 'You will need to be able to move freely and you'll become very hot.'

'Right.' He did as he was told, leaving only his shirt and linen trousers, and they hung their garments off a nearby branch.

When Maddie pulled up her underdress and tucked the skirts of it into her belt, he stared at her in growing fascination. 'I need to be able to move my legs,' she explained, gesturing to the black leggings she was wearing. After Lif's comments about them, she'd started to keep them hidden at the bottom of the chest Geir had made for her, but today they were necessary, unless she wanted him to see her naked legs. That probably wouldn't help him to concentrate on the lesson, especially as the only underwear she owned was from the twenty-first century.

She began by explaining the basic principles of judo, telling him they'd do karate and kickboxing another day. 'It's for self-defence and learning to control your body mainly. The rules and exercises were established by a man in a faraway country, and the aim is to use both your physical and mental strength as effectively as possible. With the help of these techniques, even a person who is smaller and weaker than his or her opponent can be victorious, because it's all about balance and leverage.'

Geir was listening intently and she was pleased that he didn't interrupt.

She continued, 'So if you can force the other person to lose their balance, they will be vulnerable and easily defeated. You can use their own body weight against them. I'll show you.'

Learning judo took years and she didn't expect him to be able to do it instantly, but he caught on quickly and seemed to enjoy her demonstrations, even when he landed on his back in the soft, springy grass.

'Oof! That was . . . unexpected,' he huffed, and sat up shaking his head.

Maddie smiled. 'That's the point, to catch you off guard.'

'You're very good at this,' he commented. 'If I can best you, do I get a reward?'

'I don't know about that . . .' She could guess from the twinkle in his eyes what kind of reward he was envisaging, and it made butterflies dance in her stomach. 'You'd have to do exceptionally well.'

He gave her a confident grin. 'Oh, I will.'

Maddie doubted it, but by the end of the lesson, he did manage to overbalance her. He looked both alarmed and triumphant at the same time when she was the one ending up on the grass. 'Odin's ravens! Did I hurt you? I didn't mean to—'

She cut him off with a laugh. 'I'm fine. I've had worse tumbles, trust me. And that was good, very good.'

He stretched out a hand to help her up and she took it, but instead of letting go, he pulled her towards his chest and put both arms around her waist. 'Does that mean I've earned that reward then?' There was a distinct twinkle in his eyes and he gave her a slightly lopsided smile that was beyond sexy.

Her stomach did a somersault and she drew in a sharp breath, but that only had the effect of pushing her chest closer to his, which made her even more aware of his proximity. 'Well, I . . . suppose so.'

As she looked up to gauge his reaction, she barely had time to register the look of satisfaction that crossed his features before he bent to kiss her. She placed her hands flat on his chest, intent on pushing him away, but the touch of his mouth on hers was sending shock waves all the way down to her toes, and instead she just stood still.

He ended the kiss and gazed at her with a quizzical glint. 'Thank you. I shall make sure I work hard every time, if that is what awaits me.' Then he let her go and stepped back. 'Are we finished for today? I feel in need of a dip in the hot spring.'

Maddie swallowed hard and nodded. She had the urge to pull him back and ask him to continue with the kissing, but knew that would be a bad idea. 'We'll, um . . . continue tomorrow,' she managed to croak. 'You bathe first, if you wish. I, er . . . need to cool down for a while.'

He didn't comment on this strange utterance – after all, she'd get just as warm in the water – but simply nodded and left. Maddie went over to lean her forehead against a solid tree trunk. She was playing with fire and she knew it. Perhaps she shouldn't have suggested these sessions, but she missed her training and had enjoyed it hugely.

Especially that last bit.

Giving up would be the coward's way out, though, and all in all, she was pleased with Geir's progress. It wasn't just useful for him to learn – it helped her to keep her skills honed, something she had a feeling she might need here.

As for his rewards, she'd have to make sure to keep them to a minimum. Perhaps just one per evening? Surely she could cope with that.

She ignored the little voice inside her head that said she'd be looking forward to it immensely.

They continued their sessions each evening from then on, and Geir was pleased when Maddie told him he was a fast learner. Not just because it meant he might receive a reward – although she'd made a new rule that stipulated he could only have one a day – but because fighting was something he'd done almost from birth. With two older brothers it was inevitable, and he'd been doing weapons training for as long as he could remember as well. These new techniques were exciting, and he soon mastered the basics of what she called *judo*. When she judged that he knew enough of that, she started to add something she referred to as *kickboxing* and *karate* to the lessons. He was particularly fascinated by the kickboxing, where she used both her hands and feet. She was incredibly agile and quick, and able to kick as high as his head, although she deliberately held off from doing him any actual harm. Her legs in their strange trousers flashed past him in a blur, and he was sure he'd never be as fast as that.

Maddie just laughed when he grumbled about it. 'Yes, you will. It's just a question of practice. Now kick at my hand. That's it, higher. Again!'

She had fashioned some sort of mini shields for her hands out of bits of flat wood with a strap on the back, and she held these up high for him to aim at. Afterwards, he did the same for her. It was exhilarating, and he did get the hang of it eventually. It was just a shame there weren't any Pechenegs here for him to try it on.

As for the kisses, they were an added bonus and he looked forward to each evening all through the day. She deliberately kept them short, as though afraid she'd forget herself if they lasted too long, but he went along with that, although he persuaded her to let him deepen them a little further each day. Hopefully that would whet her appetite for more. It wasn't easy to keep things playful, but he managed to rein himself in somehow.

Their new-found accord was sorely tested several weeks later, when Geir came back from a hunting trip along the coast with several skins from newborn seals. To his complete and utter astonishment, Maddie went berserk.

'*Nooo!* How could you? They are only tiny and haven't even lived a few weeks yet! How could you possibly look into those little faces and kill them? That is despicable! Don't ever, *ever* do that again, do you hear?'

Geir and the other men just stared at her, stunned by this outburst. He knew she had some strange ideas, as her antipathy to eating great auk meat had shown, but this was something else.

'I didn't kill them,' he protested. 'We met up with Hjalti and he sent them as a gift for the children. These skins will be perfect for making winter garments for them. The little ones will be especially vulnerable when the cold comes, and they'll need something soft and warm.'

'I don't care! You are none of you to hunt baby seals or I'm leaving right now. Go and kill foxes or something if you must, or the older seals, but not the little ones. It makes me sick just thinking about it!'

She stormed off and Geir exchanged glances with the other men, who shrugged and went off to unload the walruses and mature seals they'd killed. The blubber would be needed for lighting soon, now that the evenings were growing darker, and the meat was a welcome addition to their diet. They had to have these things – he wasn't hunting for the enjoyment of it. And he'd left the young ones alone. He only ever hunted adult animals without dependants, in order to make sure there would be enough left for another season. That was common sense. As for Hjalti, Geir had no influence over him.

With a sigh, he followed Maddie, hoping to make her understand.

He found her sitting on a large boulder down by the shore, tears running down her cheeks. He'd never seen her cry before and didn't quite know how to deal with it. It seemed strange that she would cry for baby animals when she'd never shed a tear about her own situation. Her eyes, when she deigned to look his way, were luminous and tragic, their mossy green colour reminding him of a special gemstone his brother had shown him once. The sight cut straight to his heart, and he longed to gather her into his arms and comfort her. At the same time, though, he wanted to shake her, as he felt she was overreacting.

'Maddie?' Tentatively he sat down next to her and tried to put a hand on her shoulder, but she shook it off. 'Please, explain to me why this upsets you so much. Hunting is necessary for our survival, you know that. You've not said anything before. Is this something from your time? Is it forbidden?'

At first she didn't reply, but after a while she wiped her cheeks on her sleeve and muttered, 'Yes. The seals and lots of other animals have been hunted to the point where some of them die out completely. The great auk, for example, doesn't exist in my time at all. Some types of whale, too. They are all gone and it ruins the . . . the balance of nature. I can't bear to be here and not try to do something about it, even if what I do is a mere drop in the ocean. It's killing *me* to stay silent.' She shook her head and sniffed. 'I do understand that some hunting is necessary here, but not the babies. Never those. They are so small and defenceless, so trusting. They're probably not even afraid of you, am I right?'

Geir had to admit this was the truth. None of the wildlife here showed any fear of humans, as they had never had cause to be wary before now. He sighed.

'Look, I have no say in what Hjalti and his men do, but I can promise you that no one from our settlement will ever kill any of the young ones. From now on I won't accept such gifts from him either. And we'll eat as few of the great auk as possible. It's a shame, as they're so easy to catch, but . . .' He couldn't stand to see her so upset. And he never wanted her to look at him with disgust in her eyes again. That cut him to the quick, especially as he hadn't deserved it. 'Now, please, will you return with me? It's nearly time for the *nattverðr*.'

'You go. I need some time to think, and I'm not hungry.'

He considered arguing with her, but thought better of it. She obviously needed to reconcile her thinking with that of his time, and from what she had told him, it couldn't be an easy thing to do. He had hunted all his life, and was good at it, but he'd never given it a second thought because it was a necessity. Now he would try, for her sake, because her views mattered to him. *She* mattered to him. And he wanted to please her.

When she came back to the hall some time later, though, she refused to look at him, and she didn't come to his tent that night either. He lay awake for a long time, wondering if the gods had been wrong to send her to him, or if this was just another obstacle they'd put in his way. It was especially galling when they had so recently started to get along much better. Their lessons were a great source of enjoyment for both of them, and he'd been looking forward to their nightly meetings. Not just because of the rewards, or the fact that he was learning new skills, but because it gave him the opportunity to spend time alone with her, and to touch her.

Was it all ruined? Or would she relent and accept that he hadn't done anything wrong?

He wanted to rail at her and at fate. It wasn't as though he'd acted callously on purpose. He'd accepted a gift that was well meant, that was all. Hunting was the natural order of things. In fact, he'd been thinking of the well-being of the human pups, which surely ought to come before those of the animals. But Maddie seemed not to make any distinction between the two. It was as if she considered that animals had feelings. Did they? Geir had no idea, and quite frankly didn't want to know, because that would make him feel even worse than he did right now.

He could only hope she would forgive him in time and accept that he had done what he thought best for the people in his care.

*

Maddie knew she wasn't being fair. Yet again she had applied twenty-first-century thinking to a man who was a thousand years behind that. But she'd had to speak up or she couldn't have lived with herself. The hunting of seal pups was something she'd protested vehemently against in her own time, so how could she not do the same here?

It was one thing to accept that living in tune with nature meant hunting creatures for food and other commodities, but she drew the line at the babies. It felt like the least she could do. And she still refused to eat great auk, no matter how tasty it might be. It was the principle of the thing, even if it was silly to think that her actions could have any bearing on the future. The big lummox of a seabird was doomed, whether she personally ate any or not, but if she didn't partake of its meat, at least her conscience was clear.

But she was punishing Geir for being a man of his time – yet again – and it wasn't his fault. It had been Hjalti who'd done the actual killing; a man who seemed to hunt anything that moved.

Argh! Get over yourself!

After a few days, they continued the self-defence lessons, but some of the sparkle had gone out of the sessions and she spent most of the time setting him tasks, rather than engaging wholeheartedly. There was no joking around, and no more kissing. Finally he grabbed her by the shoulders and stared into her eyes.

'Maddie, I know you're still upset with me, but you're being unreasonable and this cannot go on. Either you come to terms with the way we live here or you will have to leave. I've promised never to kill any baby creatures, but if that isn't enough, then I don't know what else to do. I'm tired of having you look at me as though I'm the Miðgarðr serpent, and I'm done with chasing you and apologising. You know what I want from you, but I'm not going to force you and I'm certainly not about to beg. But I want an end to the uncertainty and the waiting.' He went over to root around in his belt pouch, which he'd left with the rest of his clothing, and pulled something out. 'Here. I'm giving you back your knife; now the decision is yours.'

He took hold of her hand and placed the magical folding knife on her palm, then turned to grab his clothing before storming off. Maddie just stood there, staring alternately after him and down at the item in her hand. The knife she'd wanted for so long.

But did she want it now?

Her legs gave way and she sank down on to the grass, suddenly shaking from head to toe. What was she to do? She had to make up her mind, he was right about that. He had compromised to the best of his ability, but he was responsible for the survival of the whole group of settlers here at Stormavík. For keeping the children safe and warm. There was only so much attention he could give to her qualms about their way of living. And he had been extremely patient with regard to marriage or a relationship between them as well, she had to admit.

She was so tired of the conflicting emotions warring within her; she had to make a choice once and for all. Clasping the knife tightly, she thought about going home – being reunited with her family and friends, having all the comforts of the twenty-first century and not struggling on a daily basis. Hot showers, warm clothes, hospitals, electricity, central heating, washing machines, proper soap and shampoo, and the food . . . Her mother's cooking, alongside fast food and takeaways. Everything so easy to obtain, so effortless. And yet meaningless and shallow.

Food tasted so much better when you knew you'd worked hard for it, and deserved it. Sleep came more easily after a long day's toil. What was more, she had friends here now; they felt almost like family too, so how could she leave them? And then there was Geir, always Geir . . .

With a sigh, she got to her feet. She had a lot of thinking to do.

Chapter Eighteen

Geir didn't know if he'd done something incredibly stupid or whether giving Maddie an ultimatum would make her see sense. He was hoping for the latter, but his gut told him she would take the chance to leave. It annoyed him that he'd failed to persuade her to stay, but perhaps he had been wrong and the gods were just toying with him. Either way, it was out of his hands now.

He stomped back towards the hall, but instead of going inside, he went to a small workshop he'd created nearby. It was another dug-out hut like Steinthor's, but in this one he'd built a lathe for woodworking, his favourite occupation. At the back of the hut were pieces of wood; some he'd brought with him, while others would need to be left to season. For now, he grabbed one that was already dry enough and began to create a bowl. He needed something to occupy himself with or he'd go mad with all the thoughts swirling around in his head. Woodturning was soothing and he had to concentrate – the perfect distraction.

Some time later, Steinthor came sidling in. 'Is all well?' he asked, setting down an oil lamp on a shelf.

Geir hadn't realised it was getting dark, but when he glanced out the door, he could see that dusk had fallen. 'No,' he muttered.

'She's the most obdurate female it's ever been my misfortune to come across.'

He saw Steinthor's mouth twitch, but the man had the sense not to laugh outright. 'Aye, I've noticed. She's an odd one and no mistake. Do you still want her?'

They'd been friends since childhood and Geir didn't mind the direct question. He only had one secret from the smith – the fact that Maddie was not of their time. Steinthor already knew that she wasn't really his woman, but he'd agreed to play along with that ruse.

Geir sighed. 'Yes. Yes, I do. She's . . . different to any woman I've ever met and she fires my blood like no other. But I can't force her to like me. It is for her to decide and I've told her to make up her mind. I'm done playing games.'

Steinthor nodded. 'That's probably wise. Let her stew for a while. Women are best left alone when they're being contrary.' He gave a small laugh. 'I should know – I married the most ornery one of them all.'

Geir looked up. 'Do you regret it? Lif can be even more difficult than Maddie.'

'No. She's still the one for me. And she has mellowed recently, so I have hopes that all will be well from now on. She's even talking to Aine and Eimear as if they are human. Remarkable!'

That made Geir laugh. 'Then we are definitely making progress.'

If only Maddie would stay and accept that their fate was to be together, everything would be perfect.

Maddie spent another night in the hall, tossing and turning on the hard bench, uncomfortable despite the fact that it was covered with straw and furs. She missed having Geir near. She even missed his snoring dog. But she'd needed to keep some distance between them while she made up her mind what to do.

Before going to bed, she'd hidden the folding knife in the root cellar behind a loose stone. It seemed safer not to keep it on her person or among her belongings, just in case Geir changed his mind. Now that she had it back, perversely she didn't want to use it quite yet, but it felt good to have the option.

She must have dozed off eventually, because by the time she woke, only the women and children were in the hall. Outside, soft rain was falling, so they had all found chores to do indoors.

'Where are the men?' she asked Aine when the woman brought her a bowl of barley porridge. 'Thank you.' She tried to stifle a big yawn. The night had been anything but restful.

'*Bóndi* and two of the others have gone off on yet another fishing expedition. Steinthor is in the smithy as usual with Brendan, and Cormac went to fell more trees further inland.'

Maddie nodded. Their catches had been plentiful recently and Geir was obviously making the most of it, laying in stock for the coming winter. It was the sensible thing to do. She finished her porridge and resigned herself to another day of soul-searching. At least this way she had more time to make up her mind.

Towards late afternoon, however, Steinthor and Brendan came rushing into the hall shouting something about a ship. The smith ran to retrieve his battleaxe and a shield from among his possessions, while Brendan armed himself with a vicious-looking knife and grabbed the cow horn.

'What in the name of . . . ? A ship?' Maddie's insides knotted with fear as she followed Steinthor to the door. She spotted it immediately, being dragged on to the shore, and soon after that, she saw Eyjolf running towards them with four other men, all seemingly armed to the teeth. 'They knew our men had gone,' she hissed. 'The utter *bastards*!' She exchanged looks with Steinthor, who nodded, even though he didn't know what the English word meant.

'Yes, they must have been watching us. Why else would they arrive when I'm the only man here? Go inside and barricade the door. I'll do my best, but I doubt I can hold off five men. Let's hope that door is as sturdy as Geir said it was. Brendan, you too.'

But the boy shook his head and ran towards the nearest hill, brandishing the horn. 'I'm calling for help. Cormac might hear me.'

'Good thinking.' Maddie watched him go, but even if by some miracle Geir heard the summons too, he'd never make it back here in time. 'Let him go,' she murmured to Steinthor. At least that way the boy was out of the way.

She ran back inside, but only to grab the small axe she'd used for cutting trees. It wasn't much, but it was better than nothing. 'Bar the door,' she shouted at the terrified women, but she didn't stay to see if they obeyed.

'What are you doing? Leave this to me,' Steinthor growled when she rejoined him.

Maddie shook her head. 'No, I'm going to help you.' She clenched her fists and started to bunch up her skirts, looping the hem into her belt in order to free her legs. He gasped in surprise, but there was no time to explain other than to say, 'I don't usually fight with weapons, only my body.'

They heard the horn blaring out repeatedly from the top of the hill, but Eyjolf and his men were upon them now, and Maddie threw herself into the fray. She enjoyed the feeling of triumph as she managed to kick one of the attackers in the head, but her joy was short-lived. They had dangerous weapons and she found it hard to reach them without risking getting hurt herself. Her axe wasn't as long as theirs, and although it was useful for blocking their thrusts, she couldn't do much damage to them. Time and time again she had to dance out of the way of an axe or a knife, and the few kicks and punches she did manage to deliver had no lasting effect.

While she and Steinthor fought for all they were worth, Eyjolf must have sneaked behind them and made short work of the door to the hall. She heard the sound of splintering wood, then shouts and sudden screams of terror erupted from inside.

'Steinthor, help! Noooo, my child!' Lif's voice reached them, high-pitched and almost inhuman.

'*Niðingr!*' Steinthor tried to reach the door, but he was kept at bay by two of Eyjolf's henchmen, while Maddie's progress was equally hampered by the others.

Not long afterwards, Eyjolf came outside, hauling a shrieking Steinar with him. To Maddie's utter horror, he pulled the boy close and held a knife to his small throat. The child stilled, clearly petrified, and his eyes widened in shock. 'Everyone, stop!' Eyjolf yelled, and Maddie and his men froze as though in a horror tableau.

Not so Steinthor, who tried to throw himself towards his son's attacker. With his attention solely focused on the child, however, two of the assailants took the opportunity to grab him, and despite him fighting furiously, they soon had his arms twisted up behind his back and a sword pointed at his chest. Lif came haring out of the doorway, sobbing and screaming like a banshee, her gaze wild when she caught sight of the knife being held to her son's throat. Another man caught her round the middle, slamming her against the doorpost.

'*Þegi þú*, woman!' he snarled, and she blinked as if stunned.

Behind them, in the dim interior of the hall, Fridgerd, Aine and Eimear were standing like statues, shielding the rest of the children behind their skirts, identical expressions of horror on their faces.

Maddie tried to move closer, but realised there was nothing

she could do to save the boy. She looked towards Eyjolf and saw him smirking. He pointed at her. 'This is very simple. You, come with us, and we'll spare the boy and everyone else.'

She glared at him. 'Me? Why?' But she knew why. She could read the naked lust in his eyes, just as she had on his previous visit. He obviously couldn't take no for an answer.

'Because I want you and I mean to have you. I *will* have you. Didn't your runes tell you that?' He chuckled.

'No, they didn't. I'm another man's wife. You can't do this. You'll be punished.' Fury pounded through her. She wanted to tear this smug bastard limb from limb for threatening a small defenceless boy. For terrorising a mother. And for not accepting that she'd never be his.

'Ah, but you're not, are you?' He grinned and nodded at Lif. 'She told me last time we were here that you're not wed to the *bóndi*, you're just his concubine. That means you're fair game.'

Maddie sent a death glare in Lif's direction and the woman had the grace to cringe while her eyes pleaded for forgiveness.

'For the love of Odin, woman, will you never cease your meddling?' Steinthor snarled at his wife, as tears started pouring down her cheeks.

'I . . . I didn't mean . . .'

But this was not the time for recriminations. Eyjolf had them beaten and he knew it. Maddie drew herself up to her full height, which was the same as his, and threw down her axe. 'Fine, but you're going to regret this, I swear. Geir will not let you get away with it. From now on, your life is worthless, *argr*.'

His eyes spat fury at her use of the derogatory term, but he shoved the boy towards his sobbing mother and grabbed Maddie's arms. Pulling a leather cord out of his pouch, he tied her wrists tightly in front of her, then nodded at the men who held Steinthor. One of them hit the smith on the side of the head with the handle of his axe, and he fell to the ground unconscious. Lif screamed again.

'Come, we must hurry. That little *fifl* is making enough noise to wake the dead.' Eyjolf threw a look of disgust towards the hill, where Brendan was still using the cow horn, then urged Maddie and his men in the other direction. She was grateful that at least he hadn't killed anyone. Her freedom was a small price to pay for that.

Not that she had any intention of submitting to him.

Damn, if only I'd kept the folding knife with me! What a fool. She could have used it to disappear right in front of his eyes. On the other hand, he might have searched her and found it, so there was no guarantee it would have worked. She had to rely on other methods.

She soon found herself lifted into the ship and pushed down on to the planks near the back. Eyjolf grabbed her hair and bashed her head against the gunwale. 'That's so you don't get any ideas. Just sit there quietly or I'll hurt you again,' he snarled.

Maddie blinked to clear her vision, which swam alarmingly as her head began to pound. It wasn't as bad as when she'd had concussion, but it wasn't pleasant either. She leaned against the side of the ship while the men pushed it into the water and began to row furiously. At the mouth of the fjord, they stopped to hoist the sail, and she glanced around the headland to the right, hoping against hope to see Geir coming to her rescue. Her heart leapt with joy when she spotted his small boat, but Eyjolf had seen him too.

He swore. 'Faster! We need to leave, *now*!'

Maddie knew that Geir was too far away to reach them in time. As soon as Eyjolf had the sail up, his ship would take off quicker than the others could row. But they were so close, and she couldn't go with this smug bastard. She'd rather die than be his mistress.

Without giving it further thought, she pulled herself to her feet.

'Get down, woman!' Eyjolf came rushing over, his arms snaking around her from behind, but she bent forward and surged up again with all her might, headbutting him with the back of her skull. He howled as she connected with his nose, and let go of her for a few seconds. She took her chance, and jumped.

The icy water closing over her head had her gasping, and she swallowed a mouthful of briny water. For a moment she hung suspended in the sea, paralysed from the shock of the cold, but as her lungs began to protest and the urge to cough grew, she started to move. She broke the surface and flailed wildly, pushing strands of hair out of her eyes to see where she'd ended up. Eyjolf's ship was thankfully heading away from her, pulled by the currents and the now half-raised sail, although she could hear frantic shouting.

The words were muffled, but she thought it was something like 'Turn around! Take down the sail! To the oars! *Get her!*'

Turning her head in the other direction, she saw Geir's rowing boat bearing down on her. He was still too far away, though, and she ought to swim towards the shore to save herself. She tried to move her limbs – not easy, as she was hampered by heavy skirts and shoes. Because her hands were still tied, she had to do a strange sort of doggy paddle, while kicking with her legs. But that wasn't the worst of it – it was the all-encompassing, deathly numbing cold seeping into her every pore. It was like being encased in a prison of ice. For some reason her brain came up with the word *cryonics*: freezing a body in order to revive it later – except she wasn't dead. Yet. She could feel her muscles cramping and knew she had to keep moving in order to retain any warmth at all, but she was fighting a losing battle. In water as cold as this, she probably only had minutes before hypothermia set in.

She *was* going to die, and soon.

'*No!*' Gathering all her strength, she attempted to battle the waves again, but it was impossible to move frozen legs tangled up with sodden skirts, and she could no longer feel her fingers. There was only one thing for it – to wait and let the gods decide her fate.

She'd never truly believed Geir's assertions that they were destined to be together, but she wanted to cling to that hope now, because it was all she had. 'Very well, you w-win!' she shouted at the heavens, then rolled over on to her back to float face up in the waves. 'Odin, Freya, Thor – y-you decide.' She closed her eyes, suddenly calm, awaiting her fate.

There was nothing else she could do.

Chapter Nineteen

Geir heard the cow horn and his heart stopped. He stared at Ingimund and Niall, frozen with fear for an instant, but then leapt into action. 'Row!' he shouted, flinging the fishing net to the bottom of the boat and throwing himself down on to one of the two rowing benches. 'Share those oars, I'm stronger than you both.'

They'd heard the horn and he didn't need to explain. Everyone knew it could only mean one thing – danger. On some level, he had been expecting it, but as the days passed and nothing happened, he'd let his guard down. He cursed himself for a fool. He should never have left the settlement with only one man to guard the women and children. Why had he sent Cormac off inland? What had possessed him? But he hadn't been thinking clearly this morning. All he'd known was that he needed to get away from everyone before Maddie woke up. Get away from *her*. He'd been afraid of hearing her decision.

And now he might never hear it at all, because he knew her well enough to be sure she'd be in the thick of any fighting.

They rowed like men possessed by the gods, goaded by the continuing blasts from the cow horn. Thankfully the water was relatively calm and the little craft skipped across the waves. But it wasn't quick enough. As they rounded the headland, he glanced over his shoulder and saw a larger ship turning out of the fjord, heading south. Its crew were busy hoisting a sail, and soon it would take off much faster than he could ever row. He swore out loud.

'Look, they have Maddie!' Ingimund cried.

Geir had just seen her too, standing up and apparently fighting with someone. If he wasn't mistaken, it was that *argr* Eyjolf – the ship seemed familiar, and so did that bright blue tunic. It didn't matter. Whoever it was, he had to reach them.

A loud splash followed by shouting had him glancing over his shoulder again. 'No! What is she thinking? The water is too cold. Row! We must reach her before it's too late.'

His insides had turned as icy as the water all around them, but he didn't stop rowing for even a moment. Putting all his strength into it, he matched the strokes of the other two men combined, and he was very grateful for his size.

'They're leaving,' Niall commented. He had been looking back and threw a worried glance at Geir. 'That means they've given up on her.'

'*Þegi þú!* I don't want to hear it.' He knew he was taking his anger and frustration out on a man who didn't deserve it, but until he reached Maddie, he wouldn't give up hope. He couldn't.

It seemed an eternity, but at last they drew up alongside her. Geir almost howled at the sight of her lying so still in the water, staring at the sky, with her skirts billowing around her like the tentacles of a jellyfish. His own heart stopped at the thought that she'd never argue with him again, never kiss him or tell him about life in her century. Then he saw her blink and turn to look in their direction, and he knew she was still alive. Relief flooded him and a surge of energy mobilised him.

'Help me haul her on board,' he commanded. 'Niall, hang

on the other side of the boat as a counterweight so we don't capsize.'

With Ingimund's help, he managed to lift Maddie into the boat, placing her in a sitting position leaning against the side. 'Row!' he shouted at the other two. 'We must get her home and warm.'

He knelt beside her, gazing into her eyes. 'Maddie? Can you speak? Are you able to move?'

'N-no.' Her voice was a husky whisper, but it was better than nothing.

'You're safe now. We'll take care of you. Don't move.'

She managed a tiny smile at that, and he realised it was a daft thing to say. She wasn't capable of moving and her body had started to shake violently. Ingimund and Niall had their backs to him and Maddie, but he ordered them not to look anyway. 'I have to remove some of her clothing.'

He vaguely saw them nodding, but his attention was all on Maddie. The first thing he did was to cut the cord that bound her wrists together. Next, his fingers fumbled with the two brooches that held her smokkr fastenings, and although it took a while, he managed to undo them. Getting her out of the wet garment proved a lot harder, but eventually he managed it. Her linen serk was soaked, showing her body's contours clearly, but he barely even looked. Time was of the essence and he decided not to remove it, as that would be even more of a struggle. Instead he pulled his own tunic off and threaded her into it. That too became wet, but it was warm from his body and he hoped that would suffice for now.

Turning his attention to her shoes, he managed to undo the toggles, an almost impossible task as the leather was wet and swollen. He pulled them and her socks off and saw that her feet were nearly grey with cold, the toes so pale he could almost see through them. 'Sweet Freya, help us,' he muttered, trying to rub some life into them.

'H-hold me. P-please.' The breathy request was almost snatched away by the wind, but Geir heard her. He threw himself down next to her and gathered her close, not caring that it made him as wet as she was.

'*Unnasta. Ást mín*,' he murmured. 'Don't give up. We're nearly home. You'll be warm soon, I promise.'

He hardly knew what he was saying, but he had to keep talking or he'd go mad. Maddie didn't respond, but he could feel her pulse beating feebly when he put his mouth on her throat, so he was sure she was still alive. Just.

When next he looked up, they were coming in towards the shore. As soon as the boat hit the shingle, he rose and jumped over the side. 'Hand her to me, please, Ingimund,' he ordered, holding out his arms. The man did as he was told, and Geir adjusted her weight. 'Go and see how the others have fared. I'm going to the hot spring.'

Without looking back, he took off at a sprint with his precious burden. The spring was the only thing that could help her now and he prayed to all the gods he wasn't too late.

Maddie was completely numb, and felt as if her brain was frozen too. She couldn't think, couldn't move, and speech was beyond her. Her body was shaking so much her teeth were rattling against each other, but she didn't feel part of it. She wondered if she was dying and her organs were shutting down one by one. Not really wanting to know, she kept her eyes closed.

'Almost there, *unnasta*.'

She registered that Geir kept calling her his 'dear' and his 'love', but it probably didn't mean anything. Either way, she might not be his anything for much longer so what did it matter? She wanted to tell him she was sorry about their quarrel the day before. Didn't want to die with the words unsaid. But when she tried to speak, her mouth refused to cooperate.

'We're here,' Geir murmured.

Maddie had no idea where 'here' was, but she soon found out. She heard an almighty splash, and then her entire body was immersed in water yet again. Although this time it was blessedly hot, rather than freezing.

'Take a deep breath,' Geir instructed. 'I'm going to hold you under for a moment.'

She did as she was told, although any kind of breathing was a struggle. She felt the water close over her head, her scalp tingling as the heat met her icy skin. Pins and needles assailed her and she squirmed and almost swallowed water. Geir brought her to the surface, but held her so that she was completely submerged apart from her face. She coughed and spluttered a little, but she was beginning to feel vaguely alive again, and any kind of sensations were welcome even if they were painful. Her throat was raw from the seawater earlier, and she tried to clear it without much effect.

'Just keep still. I have you.' Geir backed up and sat down in the water by the edge of the pool, where it was more shallow. He pulled her in so that she was half lying against him with her legs floating out before her. His strong arms held her close to his chest, helping to quell the tremors that still shook her. He rested his chin on top of her head for a moment.

'You're safe. You're safe, Maddie *mín*,' he murmured, kissing her hair.

Maddie didn't know how long they stayed that way, but eventually she stopped shivering apart from the occasional shudder, and all her limbs came back to life. It hurt, but it was worth it. Moving her fingers and toes cautiously, she was able to determine that they were still intact and she didn't think she had frostbite. They'd returned to their normal colour and were now rosy from the heat instead. Geir had managed to get her to the spring so fast, she hoped there wouldn't be any lasting damage at all.

'Are you feeling better?' he whispered, bending down to kiss her cheek.

'Mm-hmm. I think so. Thank you.'

'Don't thank me. This was all my fault. I shouldn't have left you without a proper guard and—'

She twisted in his arms and put a finger over his mouth. 'Shh, don't. You couldn't have known. If anything, it was Lif's fault.'

'How so?' He frowned at her, but took hold of her fingers and kissed them, trapping them against his warm mouth. The bristles that surrounded it grazed her fingertips and made her shiver in an entirely new way. She would have liked to explore this further, but instead she concentrated on trying to answer him.

'She told Eyjolf that you and I aren't married, so he thought I was anyone's for the taking.'

'Why, the utter *bikkja*! She's going to pay for this.' His voice was so savage, it made her shiver all over again.

'No, please. I have a feeling Steinthor will see to it. If he survived the blow to the head they gave him, that is.' Worry for the smith made her frown, but she pushed the thought aside for now. 'Anyway, she was punished earlier – she had the fright of her life when Eyjolf threatened to kill little Steinar.'

Geir swore quietly under his breath, then shifted her so that he could look into her eyes. 'Are you truly feeling better? Any part of you that is still numb?'

'No, I'm fine. And Geir, I'm sorry about . . . yesterday. I made my decision during the night, and when Eyjolf carried me off, I was so afraid I'd never get to tell you.'

'Go on.' His gaze was still fixed on hers and his eyes widened when she rolled over in the water so that they were chest to chest, her serk and hair billowing around them.

She put her hands on his shoulders and took a deep breath. 'I wish to stay and I want you.'

'Want me?' His steel-blue gaze became more intense.

'Yes, like this.' She leaned forward to kiss him, letting her body sink down to lie on top of his. At first he stiffened as if he was in shock, but then he tugged her closer and his mouth began to move under hers. He kissed her with reverence, as though she was made of glass and he was afraid of breaking her, but having his mouth on hers was sending shards of warmth through her entire body, and Maddie grew impatient.

'Kiss me properly,' she demanded, tangling her fingers in his hair. 'I'm not fragile.'

He huffed out a laugh, but did as she asked. Nibbling, teasing, tasting at first, his tongue delved into her mouth and she revelled in the feel of it. The taste of salt was all-pervasive, but sharing it with him made it delicious, enticing, and had her lips tingling. When his hands began to roam, she didn't stop them. Instead she moved to accommodate his questing fingers, and started exploring him in return. The palm of her hand connected with his chest, but the material of his shirt was in the way. Impatiently she pulled at the hem of it and slid her fingers inside, pushing it out of the way. She wanted to feel his skin. She wanted to feel all of him.

'*Ást mín*, do you know what you're doing?' he groaned. 'We shouldn't . . . You almost died just now! Did you swallow too much seawater and it went to your brain?'

Maddie laughed. 'No, *fifl*, and I know exactly what I'm doing. What I want you to do.'

'And what is that?' His hand had somehow found its way inside her serk and was cupping her breast, rubbing the hard nub of her nipple gently. 'This?'

'Yes. And more. Much more.' She returned to kissing him. It was impossible to get enough of his mouth, and she never wanted to break the contact between them. It was creating waves of heat that seared every part of her, and the feeling was addictive. She felt more alive than ever before in her life and she didn't want to stop.

'Are you sure?'

'Mm-hmm.'

'Let's remove your wet clothes. They're in the way,' he muttered, managing to pull his tunic, which she was still wearing, and her serk over her head and letting them float away. 'That's better. Ah, but you are so beautiful. You take my breath away.'

Maddie had never felt beautiful in her life, but as he turned her in the water and lavished kisses on both her breasts, she almost believed him. It was as though he was worshipping her with his mouth and hands and it gave her a feeling of power, especially when her stomach came into contact with the proof of how much he desired her. While his hands worked to free her from the clinging leggings, she dared to run her fingertips over the bulge in his trousers, and he sucked in a harsh breath.

'*Unnasta*,' he warned. 'You're playing with fire.'

'I know,' she murmured, 'and I'm loving it.' Loving *him*, but she didn't say that. It probably wasn't what he wanted to hear.

He hesitated. 'We really shouldn't. I can wait. You're not in any state to—'

'I am,' she insisted, boldly stroking him again. He groaned but didn't protest further. She had never felt more alive in her entire life.

Once she was naked, she realised he wasn't. 'Get undressed,' she urged, but he was already working on it. She giggled as he struggled with one of his boots. 'You jumped in here wearing those?'

'I was in a hurry, trying to save your life,' he growled. 'Ungrateful woman.' But the corners of his mouth twitched, showing that he was joking.

'Oh, I'm very grateful, trust me. I owe you.'

He stilled, on the point of pushing his trousers off, and narrowed his eyes at her. 'Is that why you're doing this? Because you feel you owe me something?' He grabbed her shoulders and stared at her intently. 'That's not how I want things to be.'

Maddie just smiled at him and tugged at the waistband of his trousers. 'That is *not* the reason at all. I'm doing this because I want you. You and no one else. Today was a wake-up call and I'm going to *carpe diem* from now on. Starting right now.'

'Karpie what?' He looked adorably confused, but quickly helped her remove the trousers.

It was her turn to draw in a sharp breath at the sight of him in all his glory, but somehow she managed to reply. 'Seize the day. Live for the moment. And I don't want to wait another instant.'

Twining her arms around his neck, she pulled him so close her breasts were squashed against him, and then she kissed him as if her life depended on it.

He got the message.

Making love in a hot spring was not what Geir had expected of this day, but he wasn't complaining. Maddie seemed to have made a miraculous recovery and an even more momentous decision. She wanted to stay. She wanted him. *Thank Freya for that!*

He didn't know if she had lain with a man before and didn't want to ruin the moment by asking. Her questing hands were hesitant, though, as if she was exploring a male body for the first time, and he decided it would be better to go slowly just in case. He took hold of her hand and firmly placed it out of reach of his nether regions. 'Not yet, *ást mín*,' he murmured. 'Patience.'

Making love in water was a novel experience for him, but he daren't leave the hot spring in case she became cold again. He slowly began to kiss and lick his way over her delectable body, caressing every inch and making her tremble in his arms. The little noises of appreciation she made almost drove him mad with lust, but he managed to rein himself in. He wanted her to enjoy this; so much so that she'd never want another man for as long as she lived. He had to get it right.

He lavished attention on her breasts, firm and beautifully shaped, and just the right size for him to cup one in the palm of his hand. 'Geir!' she whispered, her voice husky as he teased the nipple with his tongue. 'Please . . .'

'Soon, my sweet. Very soon.'

Despite being underwater, he found her slick and ready for him when his fingers skimmed her taut stomach and ventured lower. She drew in a rasping breath as he began to stroke her, then increased the tempo. He used two fingers to delve further, and she writhed underneath him. 'You!' she moaned. 'I want all of you!'

It was what he wanted too and he couldn't hold back any longer. Entering her slowly at first, then deeper in one swift thrust, he discovered that Maddie was untouched, despite having been of marriageable age for so many years. He stopped to allow her to grow accustomed to the feeling of having him inside her, but she almost growled with impatience. 'Odin's ravens, Geir, don't stop now!' she protested.

He chuckled at her very Norse way of ordering him about, but complied with her request immediately and was soon swept up in a wave of desire so strong it rocked his whole world. From then on, there was no more talking; only pure, blissful sensation, taking them both by storm.

Afterwards they leaned against the edge of the pool, resting their heads on a flat stone. He plaited his fingers with hers and just floated mindlessly, enjoying the moment.

'Was I too rough? I'm told the first time is always painful for a woman.' He leaned over to kiss her cheek and gathered her against his side. Her skin was like thistledown, and he was sure he'd never tire of touching her. In fact, he could hardly believe that this was happening at last. He'd been dreaming of her for so long now, he'd almost given up hope.

'No, not at all. I . . . loved every moment. I could never have dreamt it would be so . . . well, amazing.' She sent him a shy smile that made him hug her tight.

'I'm glad.' He had wanted her first time to be good, and knew that from now on it would get even better.

Eventually they heard Aine's voice from behind the wattle screen. '*Bóndi?* Is Maddie well? We are all becoming worried.'

'I'm fine, Aine, just keeping warm for a while longer to make sure I don't become ill,' Maddie replied. She sent Geir a conspiratorial smile and he grinned back, nibbling her ear lobe.

'We'll come to the hall soon, but it would be helpful if you could bring dry clothes and some linen drying sheets, please. All our garments are soaked,' Geir added.

'Yes, of course. I'll return shortly and will leave them here.' They heard Aine scurry off, and not long afterwards, her hand appeared around the screen with piles of clothes and a couple of lengths of linen for drying.

'Thank you!' they called out in unison, then exchanged a smile.

'I'm not sure I ever want to leave this pool.' Maddie sighed, and he hoped it was with contentment. When in the next instant she rolled on top of him, he gathered it was.

He pulled her even closer, fitting her length against his. It was astounding how well they were matched. As if the gods had created her just for him. The thought made him smile, because it would seem they had.

'Me neither,' he admitted, 'but we'll have my tent to ourselves later, and if we're going to carry on like this, I for one will need sustenance.'

Maddie laughed. 'Hmm, yes, I wouldn't want you to be too tired.'

He grinned back and stared at her, filled with awe that this incredible woman was his now and that she so obviously wanted him again. Her mouth was swollen by his kisses and her hair was plastered to her head, but even in this bedraggled state he was sure that the goddess Freya herself could not have been a more beautiful sight. He was incredibly fortunate. For now, though, she needed to rest.

'You must be sore, *unnasta*, and you've been through a lot. I'll not touch you again today unless you feel up to it.'

'I'm fine. But we should go and see how the others have fared. I'm worried about Steinthor. And Lif was bashed into the doorpost by one of those *niðingar* as well.'

'You're right. Stay there, I'll fetch the linen sheets.'

The cold air made him shiver as he climbed out of the spring to retrieve their clothing, but he barely felt it. Happiness was keeping him warm from the inside out and nothing could spoil it right now. It was time to take stock, though, and plan for the future. Because the events of this day could not go unpunished, and as long as Eyjolf remained at large, Geir would never rest easy. Maddie was his now, in every sense of the word, and he meant to keep it that way.

He'd never let her go again.

Chapter Twenty

Steinthor was lying on a bench with a bandage round his head, but he was lucid and his eyes lit up at the sight of Maddie and Geir. Lif hovered nearby, baby Svein in her arms and her other two children hanging on to her skirts as if they didn't dare let her go. Steinthor ignored her and held out a hand to Maddie, beckoning her over. She went to take it and sank down next to him on the edge of the bench.

'Are you well? Your turn to have a sore head, eh?' she tried to joke.

'I'll live. I have a thick skull, which is just as well. But Maddie . . .' he gazed at her earnestly, 'I want to thank you from the bottom of my heart, and on behalf of Lif too.' They both glanced at his wife, who was nodding, her eyes shimmering with tears. 'You saved our son. Were prepared to sacrifice yourself for him . . . for us. We can't thank you enough.'

'No need,' Maddie said. 'All has ended well. Let's put it behind us.'

He gripped her fingers harder. 'But it could so easily have turned into disaster. We will never forget this. Right, Lif?'

'No, never,' the woman whispered hoarsely. 'Thank you, and . . . forgive me. I never meant . . . that is, I did at the time, but now I don't.'

From this jumbled speech, Maddie gathered that Lif had changed her opinion about a great many things, and that was a relief. She wasn't one to hold grudges, so she stood up and went to give the woman a hug, baby and all. 'It's fine. We have to stick together and there is no point dwelling on the past. Let's just move forward.'

'Thank you,' Lif murmured again.

Maddie hunkered down and took one of Steinar's hands. 'And you were a very brave boy today. I'm sure your mother and father are very proud of you. You didn't even cry!'

He managed a small smile and a nod. 'I was, wasn't I? As brave as you?'

'Oh, much more so.' She laughed and ruffled his hair. 'Maybe it's time I started teaching you some fighting tricks too, like I've been doing with Geir. What do you say, would you like to learn?'

'Yes, please!'

'Then let's start tomorrow.'

After that, she was too tired to do more than sit down and eat the food someone put in front of her. She was aware of Geir sticking close to her side all through the evening, and eventually he led her out to their tent. She crawled inside and collapsed on the soft fur bedding with a contented sigh.

'I think I could sleep for a week.'

He sank down next to her and pulled her close, telling Blár to lie down by their feet for once. 'I hope not,' he whispered. 'I don't think I can wait a whole week to make love to you again.'

'Mm, there is that.' She snuggled into his strong arms and buried her head in his shoulder. 'Just let me have a few hours, and I'll be ready.'

'I was only joking. Your well-being comes first.' He stroked her cheek and gave her a tender kiss. 'I'll let you sleep for as long as you wish. Just answer me one thing first, please – will you marry me now?'

Maddie's eyes flew up to his. It wasn't completely dark outside, but she couldn't quite make out his expression. Did he still want to marry her for convenience? Because he needed a wife and he thought the gods had decreed this? Or did he have another reason?

She was too tired to puzzle it out, and in any case it didn't matter, because she knew what her answer would be. Had known since that terrifying moment when she'd thought all was lost. 'Yes,' she said. Her voice was husky, so she repeated herself. 'Yes, I'll marry you, Geir.'

'Thank Freya for that!' He crushed her to his chest and almost cracked a few of her ribs.

'Easy,' she muttered. 'Some of us have had quite an eventful day.'

'Sorry, I'm just so happy. Can we be married tomorrow, *ást mín*?'

'Er, yes, I don't see why not.' What was the point in waiting? She had already given herself to him, and there was no going back now. She might already be pregnant even.

That thought made panic spear through her, and she couldn't help but reflect on how different things were here compared to in her time. In the twenty-first century, they would have taken things slowly. She could have slept with Geir for months, years even, before having to decide whether they should be life partners. They would have had plenty of time to find out if they were truly compatible, but here she didn't have that choice. Here, making love had possible consequences that she couldn't influence in any way. It was difficult to accept.

She still had some doubts: that she was too young to marry, or that she'd prove to be the wrong wife for him. He was calling her his 'love' now, but he hadn't actually said he loved her. Desire was clearly not a problem, but that could diminish with time. Still, it felt right and she was sure it would all work out somehow. He trusted the gods and so should she. They had definitely been on her side today.

Now she just needed some rest.

They were to be married the following afternoon, and the other women spent hours preparing tempting dishes for a small wedding feast.

'We don't need anything special,' Maddie protested, but everyone else insisted.

Then Lif and Fridgerd dragged her off to the hot spring, helping to scrub every inch of her with flower-scented lye, as well as washing and combing her hair. It wasn't an easy task, as her curls kept getting stuck in the delicate ivory combs, but together they managed it, working one either side of her.

'You have to look your best for your husband.' Fridgerd smiled and added with a wink, 'And smell nice. We have some flowers to put on your head as well when your hair has dried properly.'

Maddie could feel her cheeks heating up. She didn't tell them that she and Geir had already anticipated their wedding night, although she'd been sure it was written all over her the day before when they returned from the spring.

She was dressed now in a clean, dry serk, and a borrowed woollen apron dress, since hers was beyond saving after its immersion in salt water, and her second one was very rudimentary and not suitable for a wedding. It was Lif's, so a tad on the short side, but it was a beautiful deep green with contrasting woven borders, and Maddie was grateful.

'That looks wonderful on you.' Lif nodded, as if satisfied with their handiwork. 'It matches your eyes. And thank goodness your brooches survived their encounter with the sea. Steinthor has polished them for you.'

'Thank you, that's very kind. I really do appreciate everything you're doing for me.' Maddie felt emotion clogging her throat, but managed to hold back the tears. She was sure now that she had made the right choice – staying here with these people who had become very dear to her. It would seem they felt the same way, which was lovely.

As she looked down at her borrowed finery, however, complemented by her own strings of beads, she couldn't help but think how different this was to any wedding day she'd ever imagined for herself. No white dress and veil, no father to give her away, no family to watch her walk down thc aisle. She would have loved to share this moment with them, but she knew it didn't matter, not really. They would just want her to be happy, and she was. A small part of her wondered if this wasn't the sort of wedding she would have chosen for herself anyway. She'd never been a girlie girl and couldn't see herself in a meringue dress; that just wasn't her style.

Anyway, today was not a day for sad thoughts; it was for celebration.

As he swore an oath to be her husband for ever more, Geir felt a surge of pride at the sight of the woman he was marrying. The gods really had known exactly what he needed, and he'd be eternally grateful to them. She was so lovely, so perfect for him in every way, his heart felt ready to burst with joy. Lif had made a wreath of wild flowers to put on her head – tiny purple-pink ones and some larger white ones combined with greenery – and her beautiful hair was flowing loose around her shoulders, the curls neatly combed and gleaming. After a night's sleep, her cheeks had their normal healthy glow, and her green eyes shone with happiness. He'd made love to her that morning, as soon as she woke up, but he wanted her again.

He would always want her.

'Are you happy?' he whispered, as they wandered back to their tent that evening, hand in hand.

'Yes, very. It's been a lovely day.' She sent him a warm smile, but her eyes took on a faraway look for an instant. 'I just wish my family could have been here. I . . . I miss them.'

He pulled her close. 'That is understandable. Perhaps we can visit them soon? You did say you could take me to the future with you, did you not?'

Her smile widened and she rested her head on his shoulder. 'Yes, of course. I can't wait to introduce you to them. But let's do that when we're more settled here. There's still so much to do, isn't there?'

'There is. As long as you're happy to wait?'

'Mm-hmm. There's no rush.'

'Good, then come here, my lovely wife.'

He pulled her down on top of the soft wolfskins, taking her in his arms and kissing her with all the passion he'd been storing up since that morning. As he slowly peeled off her clothes and worshipped her body, inch by delicious inch, she did seem very happy, and they both forgot everything else for the moment. For now, they had each other.

There was one other matter to see to, and the following day they had to return to reality. Geir was very aware that he'd have to deal with Maddie's abductor immediately, in order to show the world that such acts would not be tolerated.

'I'm going to challenge that *argr* to *hólmganga*,' he told the others over breakfast. 'First I'll go and ask Hjalti to come with me, so that the rest of you can watch over the settlement while I'm gone, then I will head south to confront Eyjolf. I cannot let this pass – it would make everyone think I'm weak and that Stormavík is easy prey.'

The other men nodded, and although Maddie didn't look too happy about his announcement, she didn't protest. He was sure she knew by now that a man's honour was the most important thing he possessed, and that by trying to abduct Geir's woman – and hurt the rest of the people in his settlement – Eyjolf had gravely insulted him. To not take revenge would be the same as declaring himself a coward, which was unthinkable.

'Can I come with you?' she asked quietly, as he prepared to leave. There was apprehension in her eyes and it pleased Geir no end that she was concerned about him.

'Not this time, *unnasta*. I'm merely going to issue the challenge today. The actual fight will be between three and seven days hence. You can come to watch then if you wish.'

'But you'll be walking into a viper's nest all alone.'

'No, I'm taking Hjalti with me, if he can spare the time. He'll be my witness.'

It wasn't ideal, but Steinthor still had a sore head and Ingimund was a farmer, not a fighter. He could have taken Cormac and Niall with him, but Eyjolf would no doubt still view them as thralls, as he couldn't know about their changed status. No, Hjalti would be best. Geir knew that the man had gone raiding in the past, before he turned to a more honourable way of earning his living, hence he was bound to be tough.

'Very well, but please have a care. I'd like you back in one piece.'

The lingering kiss that accompanied Maddie's entreaty would have made him promise anything.

He found Hjalti not too far up the coast, engaged in skinning the creatures he'd hunted recently. 'Geir! I hadn't looked to see you at this time. Has something happened?' The man came towards him with a smile, but there was caution in his gaze.

'Yes, but nothing that need worry you. I could use your help, though, if you're willing to give it.'

He told Hjalti all about Eyvínd's first visit with his son, and the subsequent abduction and rescue of Maddie. The fact that they had only been married the day before, he kept to himself. Eyjolf had been told by Lif that Maddie wasn't his wife, but that was months ago. They could have been wed any time after that, and it would be better to let him – and Hjalti – believe that was what had happened. No one in his settlement would dispute it, he'd made sure of that.

'I'll be happy to come with you,' Hjalti said when Geir had finished his tale. 'Let me just wash and tell my men where I'm off to.'

'Thank you. We need only issue the challenge today, then perhaps you and your men could watch over my settlement on the day of the *hólmganga*? I believe my wife and some of the others will want to be present for that.'

'Of course.'

It took them a while to reach Eyvínd's place, and the man himself came rushing towards the shore as they pulled the rowing boat on to the beach. His son was nowhere to be seen, but some of the other men lurked nearby and came sauntering after their master. Although no one drew a weapon, several of them put a hand on the hilt of their sword or the haft of an axe. Geir ignored this posturing – it was to be expected.

'Eskilsson.' Eyvínd nodded curtly, his gaze wary.

'Einarsson.'

'I believe I know why you are here, and can I just say that I knew nothing of my son's plans or I would have put a stop to them, I assure you.'

Geir nodded – he actually believed the man, but it made no difference now. 'Be that as it may, I am here to issue a challenge of *hólmganga* to Eyjolf Eyvíndarsson.' He indicated his companion. 'This is Hjalti Eiriksson and he is my witness. I will meet with your son on the smallest island outside my settlement in four days' time. See to it that he is there, or he will have forfeited all honour.'

In Geir's opinion the man had already done so, but it was tradition for someone to be allowed to defend himself, whether he was guilty or not.

Eyvínd's mouth tightened into a grim line. 'Very well, if you really think this is necessary. We will be there at midday.'

'Good.'

There was nothing more to be said, and although Geir glimpsed Eyjolf peering out from the doorway of the main dwelling house, he restrained the urge to rush over there and throttle him. It would keep.

Maddie didn't like this *hólmganga* business one bit, but when Steinthor patiently explained that no one needed to die, she calmed down a little.

'You are sure?' she asked, still not quite convinced. As soon as she'd heard about it, the horrible image of Eyjolf, all bloodstained and gloating, had come into her mind. She was certain now that what she'd seen when she'd cast the runes for him was this duel between the hateful man and Geir. And if her vision was right, Geir would be hurt. She couldn't bear the thought of that.

Surely it couldn't be true? She clung to the memory of the first rune she'd drawn for Eyjolf, the one that had promised failure, and very much hoped it would prove to be right. As long as Geir didn't die, that was the main thing, and she'd keep her fears to herself. She was also determined to stay on her guard – whatever happened, Eyjolf would not get his hands on her a second time.

'They will fight until someone draws blood, that is the rule,' Steinthor was saying now.

'What if Eyjolf doesn't stick to the rules, though? He's not exactly proved himself honourable so far.' Anxiety churned in her gut and she wished that this was all over and done with. She'd only been married for one day, but already she was worried about losing her husband.

Husband – how strange that sounded. She'd never in a million years imagined herself married before the age of twenty. And how could she have forgotten that she'd have a birthday soon? They'd all been so busy, she hadn't marked the days. But come September, she wouldn't be a teenager any longer, and now she was someone's wife. What on earth would her parents say when they found out? She was torn between wanting to tell them immediately and putting it off. Perhaps it was a good thing she and Geir couldn't travel to the future straight away. It would give her time to get used to the idea herself before informing anyone else.

Steinthor patted her arm. 'Stop worrying. It is my guess the *fifl* acted without his father's knowledge, and if Geir doesn't thrash him, the father surely will. Eyjolf has risked his family's honour for nothing. He failed. That will not sit well with anyone.'

'I do hope you're right.'

Geir had told her to rest for a day or two and not do anything strenuous. 'I know you said you feel well, but let's not take any chances,' he'd added.

Maddie had to admit to being a bit wobbly the day after the attempted abduction, although that might have been in part because of what she and Geir had done afterwards. It was so worth it, though, and she had no regrets. Either way, she was happy to obey in this instance, and sat on a bench doing her knitting. By now she'd completed an entire outfit for baby Svein – a tiny cardigan tied at the side, matching bonnet and trousers, and a miniature pair of socks – and a sweater each for Tove and her brother Ingvar. Next in line were Lif's two older children. She stuck to the simplest of designs, boxy with mostly straight lines so that she didn't need to worry about patterns, but that worked quite well. She was really enjoying creating such small garments, especially as it was much faster than adult-sized ones, and hoped they would keep the children warm. Lif was delighted with Svein's ensemble, which Maddie had decided to give her immediately.

'He looks adorable,' she cooed at her little son. 'And it's going to keep him from catching cold during winter. For now, he can just wear the woollen tunic and the hat in the evenings. Thank you!'

'You're very welcome.'

Geir returned towards dusk, and Maddie ran down to the shore to greet him, all thoughts of resting forgotten. Without thinking, she threw her arms around his neck and jumped up, twining her legs round his waist. 'You're back!'

'Whoa, steady, woman.' He laughed. 'Perhaps I should go away more often if that is the type of greeting I receive on my return.' He held on to her legs and proceeded to kiss her thoroughly until Maddie wasn't sure she'd be able to stand up when he finally let her go.

She grabbed his arms for support. 'Did it go well?'

'As well as could be expected. Eyvínd tried to weasel his way out of it with excuses, but I just issued the challenge and left. The duel will take place in four days' time.' He grinned and pulled her towards their tent. 'Plenty of time for us to get to know each other even better.'

'Geir! It's almost supper time. The others will—'

'The trolls take the others! We are newly married and have every right to enjoy a bit of conjugal bliss whenever we feel like it.' He tugged her inside the canvas and lowered the flap, then stopped abruptly. 'Unless you don't want to, of course? I'm sorry, I forgot you are meant to be taking things slowly. I'm an oaf. Forgive me.'

But Maddie was not in the mood to go slowly, and she'd had enough of resting. When he looked at her with that wicked glint in his eyes, she couldn't have denied him even if she'd wanted to. Which she most definitely didn't.

'Oh, I think you know the answer to that. And I feel fine. More than fine.' She pushed him down on to the furs and straddled him. 'But it's my turn to be in charge.'

His grin widened. 'Whatever you say. I've always wanted to be ravished by a Valkyrie. Can I touch?'

'Not until I say so. Now lie still.'

He obeyed her order and waited, his eyes dark with desire. It was a sight that would be imprinted on her mind for ever.

Chapter Twenty-One

The island Geir had chosen as the place for the duel was small and flat. When Eyvínd arrived with his son in tow, a large square within which the combat would take place was marked out with ropes, with posts made of hazel in each corner. This was the so-called *hólmgöngustaðr*; the two combatants had to stay within these boundaries or they forfeited victory. Stepping outside the border was considered the same as running away, which would be extreme cowardice.

In the middle of the larger area it was customary to make a smaller one with calfskins or a piece of cloth about three foot square. Geir had brought a cloth, as he didn't have any calfskins to spare. This was pegged into the ground to keep it from moving, and constituted the *hólmhringr*. The duellists were meant to stay within its bounds as much as possible. Outside this, a row of three lines were cut into the ground about a foot apart from each other, but Geir had no intention of yielding even that far. He was going to stand his ground.

Stepping into the *hólmgöngustaðr*, he gestured for silence. 'I will now recite the rules,' he said, making his voice as loud as he could so that it would carry above the constant sea breeze. 'We will be fighting with sword and shield. Each man is allowed only one sword, but three shields and someone to hold them for him, supplying a fresh one each time a shield is destroyed. Once all three are gone, the combatant has to stay upon the cloth and defend himself by parrying with only his sword. No dishonourable tactics are allowed, and neither of us is to step outside the bounds of the *hólmgöngustaðr* at any time – to do so is to acknowledge defeat. The winner is whoever draws first blood, and you will all bear witness to this fact. The loser will pay *hólmlausn* – a ransom of three pieces of silver. And no one but myself and Eyjolf is allowed to take part in this fight – the rest of you, stay out of it.'

He considered the silver a very small price to pay. He had heard of a *hólmganga* that was fought to the death, where the winner inherited all the defeated man's possessions, but he did not need to be that greedy. Taking away Eyjolf's honour was more important, and he didn't have to kill him to do that, even if he would have liked to. Besides, he had no wish to become embroiled in a blood feud with the man's relatives, which was sometimes the result if someone was slain.

'Are you ready, Eyjolf Eyvíndarsson? Then let us begin.' He indicated for the man to step inside the *hólmgöngustaðr*, and Eyjolf did so. One of his comrades stood by the ropes holding two extra shields, just like Steinthor was doing for Geir.

Geir glanced at the tense faces of his wife and friends, who surrounded the marked area. Maddie was deathly pale and her hands were held in tight fists by her sides. She hadn't said much about the duel, except to caution him to be on the lookout for cheating. He'd already been determined to do that, so her words only strengthened his resolve. When he thought about what Eyjolf had intended to do to her, righteous anger and determination surged through him. Even if she hadn't been his wife, she was still a part of his group, and the man had had no right to take her or anyone else captive. Geir was the wronged party here and surely the gods would grant him victory. A sacrifice had been made to them beforehand, but whether that would make a difference or not, he didn't know. It was up to him to determine the outcome.

The two men gripped their swords and shields and began to circle warily on the pegged cloth. Eyjolf's expression was sullen, his eyes glittering with malice.

'I only did what any red-blooded man would have done,' he muttered, so quietly only Geir could hear. 'You weren't man enough to defend what was yours and the woman wasn't your property in any case. Lif told me she didn't want you.'

Geir didn't reply. Eyjolf was trying to rile him into breaking his concentration, but he wouldn't let him. Words meant nothing, only actions. It was for Geir, as the challenger, to strike first, and he did, lashing out with the speed of an attacking snake. Eyjolf was only just in time, raising his shield to protect himself, but the blow galvanised him into action and a fierce fight began. Geir was the larger man by some margin, and knew he was stronger and probably had more experience of fighting, but Eyjolf was quick and clearly good at jumping out of the way. But if he thought to tire Geir out by this tactic, he would soon find out it wouldn't work. All the sparring and training he'd done with Maddie had kept him in shape, and he knew he wouldn't rest until his honour – and hers – had been avenged.

The fight went on and Eyjolf's shield broke in half after an almighty blow. He threw it to one side over the boundary ropes and quickly grabbed another from his friend. Geir continued his relentless onslaught – if one shield could break, so could the next, and he was determined to destroy them all, leaving the man vulnerable. His opponent was starting to show signs of panic and suddenly aimed a kick at Geir's shins.

Steinthor called out, 'Kicking is not allowed!'

Eyjolf lost concentration for a moment as he snarled an insult at Geir's shield-bearer, and that almost cost him his second shield, which creaked ominously. Soon after that, Geir's first one broke and he was forced to take a new one, but he was standing his ground and utterly determined to defeat this *argr* who had dared to try and take Maddie from him. The thought gave him added impetus, and with an unexpected feint to the right, he managed to dislodge the shield from his opponent's grip and strike it as it sailed through the air. It splintered in half as it landed on the ground and Eyjolf yelled in frustration, his face turning puce as he dashed to the side to retrieve his third, and final, shield.

'*Aumingi!* I will not let you win,' he panted. 'That woman was mine and I intend to have her. She needs to be punished for her disobedience.' He lashed out, but Geir parried, ignoring the taunts. 'What, nothing to say? You should have shown yourself to be a man and tamed her from the start. I heard she led you a merry dance. Women like that need a firm hand and . . .'

The insults were fairly gushing out of the man, but Geir continued to stay silent. He had no intention of letting them get to him, because he knew none of them were true. They were the outpourings of a man trying to justify his actions. Actions that had been dishonourable, as Eyjolf was well aware. As was everyone else present. All Geir had to do was prove it.

His opponent's third shield was showing signs of strain, a crack appearing at the top. Geir saw the man glancing at it and pretended to concentrate his efforts on the weak spot for a moment. After a couple of half-hearted blows, however, he suddenly lunged and struck Eyjolf's thigh. His blade, although dulled now by the constant battering against wood, sank into the man's flesh, and Eyjolf howled with pain and frustration. Blood seeped through his trousers and dripped on to the cloth almost instantly. There was no doubt who the victor was, and Geir felt joy and relief flood through him. *Thank Odin for that!*

'First blood to Geir!' Steinthor shouted, and everyone on Geir's side of the *hólmgöngustaðr* cheered.

Their joy was short-lived, however. Instead of yielding, as was customary, Eyjolf threw his sword and shield to the ground and, wobbling slightly, bent to pull a knife out of his boot. With a snarl and a feral glint in his eyes, he surged up and tried to sink the blade into Geir's chest. With trained reflexes, Geir brought his shield up. The knife skidded off its surface, but Eyjolf somehow managed to hold on to it, slicing into Geir's forearm before the latter could shove him away. The knife didn't become embedded, yet blood welled freely. Geir swore under his breath. He had thought the combat over with, and his opponent had caught him off guard. He should have known he wasn't dealing with an honourable man.

Eyjolf laughed and gave a great shout of satisfaction, raising his knife as if to show off the blood dripping from the blade. Geir didn't trust him not to take another swipe at him – the man was clearly unhinged. He threw away his own sword and shield and decided to put Maddie's training to good use. Before Eyjolf knew what had hit him, Geir had kicked him on the side of his head, just as she'd taught him, and followed this with a chop to his windpipe. As he went down, Eyjolf's head snapped back and he fell to the ground, clutching at his throat as he struggled to suck in air. His eyes bulged and it took a good while before he managed a much-needed breath, using it to shriek more insults at Geir, who stayed in a fighting position, ready for action if necessary. He ignored the blood dripping from his arm and felt no pain, only white-hot rage.

'*Enough!* Fool of a boy – are you completely out of your mind?' Eyvínd climbed over the ropes and grabbed his son by the back of his tunic, hauling him towards the edge. 'As Eskilsson has rightly proved, you are a *niðingr* and no son of mine. Henceforth you are banished from my lands and from this island. Get you gone! I don't wish to set eyes on you again. Thank Odin I have other, more worthy sons.'

Eyjolf was hauled away by two of Eyvínd's men. His father turned to Geir and groped in his pouch, extracting three large pieces of silver. 'I trust this will settle things, but if you wish to ask for more compensation, I will understand.'

Geir shook his head. 'No, I consider the matter closed now, as long as you make sure he leaves for good.'

'Thank you. I appreciate your forbearance. Children can be a sore trial, and I wish you better luck with yours when they arrive.'

A now subdued Eyjolf was loaded into Eyvínd's ship, while Geir and his friends stood and watched.

It was over, thank the gods. Now, hopefully, they could get on with their lives in peace.

'We have to clean that straight away, and you might need stitches.'

Maddie took Geir's good arm and gave it a little shake. He was standing as if in a trance, staring at the ship sailing down the fjord. The light of battle had gone out of his eyes, but he was still frowning. She was sure her own expression was just as grim. When Eyjolf had attacked so unexpectedly with that knife, she'd nearly had a seizure, especially as he had afterwards assumed the pose she'd seen in her vision. In that moment, she'd been sure he would strike again and kill Geir, and the mere thought of that made her unable to breathe. It wasn't until Geir had executed a particularly good kick to the head and put the vile man out of action that she'd managed to draw breath again. Her inner teacher was very proud of him, and the karate chop that had followed made her even more so.

And now it was over, thank the gods.

'What?' He turned to look at her and blinked, trying to focus his gaze. Then he glanced at his arm and back up at her, a smile beginning to tug at the corner of his mouth. 'I'll be fine. It's but a small scratch.'

'No, it isn't. It looks deep. Come, we should go back to the mainland so I can see to it.' When he showed signs of arguing, she held up a hand. 'Please, humour me. I've just been terrified nearly out of my wits. I need to do something, to make sure you stay alive, or I will go mad.'

He chuckled and pulled her into his arms, giving her a bear hug. 'You really are shaking, *unnasta*. It wasn't as bad as all that, was it? I had the upper hand throughout, and the gods were on my side because I was in the right.'

'Hmph. It was *exactly* as bad as all that. I've never been so scared in my life. Well, except for when I thought I was dying the other day.'

While she talked, she pulled him in the direction of the rowing boat, where the others waited. Steinthor ferried Maddie and Geir to the mainland first, together with the other women. He'd go back for the men afterwards.

'We'll help you with that.' Lif nodded towards Geir's arm as the group walked up towards the hall, and Maddie saw him throw the woman a surprised glance.

'What's this? You're all conspiring against me?'

Maddie shook her head. 'No, you fool, we're just concerned about you and want to keep you alive. Now please, sit down on the bench outside the hall while we boil some water. Anyone here have experience of sewing up wounds?' Although she wasn't normally squeamish, she didn't much fancy having to do this herself.

'I do.' Eimear stepped forward. 'If *bóndi* will permit.'

Geir sank on to the bench with a sigh. 'Very well, do your worst. I don't suppose I'll have any peace until you've all clucked around me like hens for a while.' He absently patted Blár, who'd come over to investigate and was trying to help by licking his hand. 'No, no, you'd better not do that or Maddie will scold you, my friend.'

She laughed. 'Ingrate,' she muttered. 'And you're right – we don't need dog slime in your wound.'

As she went inside to boil some water and fetch the necessary supplies, she was still trembling, but hoped that doing these normal tasks would calm her down. It really *had* been terrifying to watch that duel. She hadn't trusted Eyjolf to play by the rules, and he'd proved her right. It was fortunate that Geir had such quick reflexes or she could be a widow right now, only a few days after being married.

That didn't bear thinking about.

'He's fine. Let me do that so you don't scald yourself.' Lif took the pot from Maddie's shaking hands and hung it on the hook over the fire. 'You should sit down for a moment.'

'Th-thank you.' Maddie was touched at the woman's concern. Their relationship had undergone quite a transformation since she'd saved little Steinar's life, and she was glad. The atmosphere in the settlement would be so much better from now on, and she no longer dreaded the coming winter, when they'd all be cooped up together for months on end.

When she eventually went back outside, Geir was surrounded by Hjalti and his men, who wanted to hear all about the duel. He told them the tale, embroidering slightly, which made Maddie smile, while Eimear sewed up the gash in his arm. Maddie had insisted on cleaning it first, as well as boiling the needle and thread, and thankfully no one questioned her about this. When Eimear was finished, Maddie washed the cut once more, but with salt water this time, making Geir hiss at the unexpected stinging. Then she put a wad of newly collected spider web on top of the wound and bound it up with clean linen strips. She'd been taught at one of the re-enactment camps that cobwebs were excellent for knitting skin together and stopping the flow of blood, and she hoped it would help even if it seemed a bit disgusting.

'There, you'll do.'

'Thank you.' He pulled her down to sit beside him and gave her a quick kiss. She could feel her cheeks flame as Hjalti and his men smiled at this demonstration of affection, but thankfully they didn't comment, and soon afterwards, they left.

'Many thanks again for your help. Come and see us if you have any problems during the winter,' Geir called after them. 'We can all work together.'

Maddie sat with his uninjured arm around her and watched the men sail away. Peace descended on the settlement as everyone began to go about their normal business. She leaned on Geir's shoulder and sighed in contentment. Looking at the magnificent view of fields, meadows, sea and distant mountains, she felt at ease and as if she really belonged here. This enchanting island was her home now, although that could also have a lot to do with the large man holding her so tight. She drew in a deep breath of the clear, crisp air and let it out slowly, feeling the peace descend on her as she let go of all the fears of this afternoon.

'I'm so glad it's all over. I hope no one else decides to try and attack us.'

He tugged her closer and dropped a kiss on the top of her head. 'We'll be on our guard, but soon it will be winter and no one but a fool would venture out then.' He chuckled and bent to nuzzle her neck. 'And the nights are long and dark – perfect for staying in bed.'

She laughed and turned towards him, giving him a lingering kiss. 'Mm, can't wait.'

And she realised it was the truth. This was where she wanted to be, and the gods had been right – she'd fallen in love with Geir.

*

Geir's arm healed quickly and he suspected that was thanks to Maddie's ministrations. She forced him to bathe the wound in both salt water and the hot spring twice a day, and it seemed to speed up the healing process. That was just as well, since the last weeks of summer were extremely busy ones in the settlement. There was more haymaking to be done, a small barley crop as well as vegetables to harvest, constant fishing, hunting and gathering, as well as buildings to finish – a byre for the cattle in case they hadn't grown a thick enough coat to withstand the wintry weather, another storage room off the hall for food, and a latrine. No one fancied going outdoors during the worst of the snows to see to calls of nature, so they added a walkway with doors either end in between this rather stinky room and the rear entrance of the hall.

In the evenings, Geir spent his time making barrels and kists to store their supplies in. They hadn't had any problems with mice or rats so far, but that wasn't to say they didn't exist here, and it was best to keep precious produce safe.

It was all hard work, but he went about it in a state of happiness because of Maddie, and all tiredness seemed to evaporate at night when it was just the two of them in their tent. He couldn't keep his hands off her, and fortunately she seemed to feel the same.

'I'm a very lucky man.' He sighed with contentment and held her close after a languid bout of lovemaking. 'I should probably give more thanks to the gods for sending you to me. I'm not sure I've shown my gratitude enough.'

She chuckled softly and snuggled into him. 'If they are as powerful as you think, they can surely read your mind and will know exactly how you feel.'

'That's true. I hadn't thought of it like that.' He tangled his fingers in her riot of copper tresses, the curls so silky and springy he couldn't resist trying to tease them out. 'Are you still happy?'

'Mm, very.' She looked up at him. 'Can't you tell?'

'Well, I heard you earlier, but—'

She smacked him on the arm. 'You're not supposed to mention things like that. It's embarrassing. And the gods only know what will happen when we have to move into the hall. Everyone will hear us!'

Geir laughed. 'Don't worry about that, they're used to it. It will be completely dark and no one will know who is making what noises. Trust me.' He grew serious again. 'I was thinking more in general, though. You haven't mentioned anything recently about going back to your time. Are you happy to stay here with me for now? We did talk about a visit, but there's just so much to do here at the moment.'

'It's fine. We definitely have to go back at some point to let them know I'm alive and well. It's not fair to allow them to fear the worst, is it? I feel guilty about that.'

'Of course we must.' He hesitated, then added, 'You could go on your own if you wish? As long as you promise to return to me as quickly as possible.' He could understand that she must feel torn. 'Do you want to go now? We could probably manage for a few weeks if—'

She put a finger on his lips to stop him. 'No, not now. I . . . This thing between us is still so new. I'm scared that if I go home, I'll be persuaded to stay. Or what if I can't find my way back here, or end up in a completely different time or . . . No, I'll wait until spring. I want you to come with me.'

'I will, I swear.'

What she didn't say out loud was that by then she might be pregnant, and it would be more difficult for her family to make her remain in the future. At least, he hoped so, as he would want any child of his to grow up with its father around.

But that was all in the future, and he was pleased that he wasn't going to lose her any time soon.

Chapter Twenty-Two

'As soon as we finish the morning chores today, we're going berry picking,' Maddie announced one day at the end of September. At least, she thought it was September by now, but she wasn't entirely sure. Geir had called it *Haustmánuðr*, which as far as she could make out encompassed both the end of this month and all of October. After the reasonably good weather of July and August, it was getting much colder. Not that it was ever anything but chilly here – summer was far from the hot days she'd been used to at home, and she'd sometimes felt like she was permanently shivering – but it was not yet freezing, which meant it had to still be early autumn.

'All of us?' Aine asked.

'Us women and the children,' Maddie clarified. 'And Brendan, if Steinthor can spare him. The more berries we can pick, the better.'

She'd been on a quick reconnaissance walk and noticed that there were rich pickings all around the settlement. Two types of bilberry mostly – small, blue and sweet, one kind grew on boggy land and another on drier ground – but also golden cloudberries, the odd wild strawberry and something that was apparently called a crowberry, or *krækiber* in Old Norse. Shiny and black, they were everywhere. She'd brought some back and shown them to the others, and Eimear had assured her they were edible. In fact, the Irishwoman had eaten some just to prove it, which put Maddie's mind at rest, although when she tried one herself, she found it slightly bitter. They had been ripe for quite a while now and she'd already picked some in previous weeks, but the bilberries were only just ready.

'If anyone spots any edible mushrooms, we'll take those as well,' she told everyone as they set off on their foraging expedition armed with pails, baskets and wooden bowls. Blár came too, dancing around with excited barks, and occasionally herding the younger children if they strayed too far from their mothers. He clearly considered them his charges, which was sweet. She smiled at the sight of them all – picking berries and mushrooms was one of her favourite things in the autumn, something she had always done with her family back in Sweden. That thought made her smile dim, but she tried to push it aside. No point dwelling on that now; today they were going to have fun.

They worked methodically, fanning out over each area where they found either berries or mushrooms so that they wouldn't miss any. At first the children ate more than they put in their bowls, but Maddie just laughed, especially when they ended up with purple tongues. An outing such as this wouldn't be the same if you didn't allow yourself plenty of tasting, although she tried to resist it herself, as that wouldn't help with laying in stocks for winter.

'What will we do with them all?' Steinar asked, after he'd come to show her how diligent he'd been.

'Dry them, mostly, so we can enjoy them through the winter and add them to our skyr. But some we'll have tonight, with lots of cream. I saved some especially from this morning's milking. It will be like eating the food of the gods, I promise.' She was sure she wasn't exaggerating.

The chore of preserving the berries was worth the effort in order to have something sweet during the cold months ahead. It was one of the things she really missed: sugar in any shape or form – biscuits, cakes, chocolate and other treats – as there was nothing like that here. They didn't even have honey to sweeten dishes with. The mushrooms would be sliced thinly and threaded on to string, then hung up to dry. They too would make a welcome addition to their diet. It was all hard work, but Maddie didn't mind. She was enjoying herself hugely, and the satisfaction of providing for their group was enough to keep her going through the most mundane of tasks.

There was no denying everything seemed like fun now that she was married to Geir. Never having been in a relationship before, she hadn't known how satisfying it could be to share everyday tasks and burdens. Whenever they worked together, they laughed and joked with each other, and it made the time pass quickly. That and the many fleeting caresses they managed to sneak in during the day, building the anticipation for their night-time trysts.

She returned her thoughts to the task at hand. They had brought some barley bread, baked especially for the occasion, and stopped to eat this snack halfway through the day. As they all sat down on a small hill overlooking the sea in the distance, with the new settlement spread out below them, Maddie felt a huge sense of belonging and pride in what they had achieved. She admired Geir enormously for even attempting this venture, and all the other members of their group for their perseverance and hard work. It was paying off, and if they could just survive the first year, the next one would be even better, with a larger crop and more livestock.

It really was the adventure of a lifetime.

Having Geir to share it with was, of course, the icing on the cake, and she felt very fortunate. On a whim, she sent up a quick prayer of thanks to whichever gods had arranged for her to be here. She owed them.

Disaster struck on the way back to the settlement. Brendan, who had really started to come out of his shell, decided to have a race with Steinar and Ingvar. The three boys had been very well behaved and had done their fair share of the work, and Maddie figured it was good for them to let off steam a little.

'You two run first while I count to ten,' Brendan shouted, 'because I have longer legs. Then I'm coming after you. Now *go*!'

The two younger boys took off, and after counting, Brendan followed. Maddie smiled as she watched them go. The little ones had grown during the summer and lost a lot of their childish roundness – they were proper boys now, not toddlers. Whooping with glee, they moved swiftly across the grassy landscape, with Brendan in hot pursuit.

The older boy was just gaining on them when suddenly one leg seemed to partly disappear before he fell over with a cry of pain. Steinar and Ingvar glanced over their shoulders, then came to a halt before running back to see what was the matter, while Maddie and the other women and children rushed towards him from behind.

'Brendan! Are you well? What happened?' Maddie's heart was in her throat, beating hard, as she reached the boy and knelt by his side. He was lying on the ground with one leg at a strange angle, and his face was so pale it was almost grey. 'Don't move. Let me look at your leg.'

She wasn't a doctor, but even she could see the lower half of his left leg was broken. There was no way it could lie at such a weird angle if it wasn't. His foot seemed to have snagged on a hole in the ground – perhaps an animal's burrow – which had twisted the leg as a result. The boy looked dazed and she was sure he was in shock. The pain might not have hit him yet, but it would soon.

She glanced at the other women, who formed a semicircle around them. 'We have to get him back to the hall. I'll carry him if someone can take my berries, please.'

'Are you sure? I can help,' Aine offered. 'We can carry him between us.'

Maddie shook her head. 'No, we'll jolt him less if there's only one of us doing it. I'll be fine. Let's go.'

She reckoned it was better to pick him up quickly, before the first shock wore off and the pain really hit him hard. Bending down, she carefully extracted his foot from the hole it still rested in and then lifted him into her arms. He cried out and gasped for breath, and she adjusted his weight so that she could hold him as gently as possible.

'Shh, it will be fine. Just grit your teeth together for me, there's a brave boy. We're going to get you home and then you can rest.'

Of course, it wasn't as simple as that. The bone would need to be set, and that was going to hurt even worse. She swallowed hard. Poor Brendan, he'd been so happy and carefree, finally acting his age. She had loved watching him blossom, no longer the silent, serious boy he'd been when they first arrived. She very much hoped this wouldn't set him back again, and that they could heal him, although how it was to be done without antibiotics and other modern medicine, she had no idea.

As she walked, she began to pray to the Norse gods.

'Bóndi! *Bóndi!* You must come quickly. There's been an accident.'

Geir had been busy with threshing and looked up as Steinar came rushing over to tug on his arm. His insides went cold at the boy's words and he sprang into action when he saw the group of berry pickers come walking towards him. 'What happened?'

His eyes searched first for Maddie, and he was relieved to see her walking without any apparent injuries. Then he noticed her burden – a limp Brendan hanging in her arms, no sign of life on his face. 'By all the gods! Is he . . . ?' He didn't want to say the word out loud, in case that made it real.

'He's broken his leg,' Steinar said, still clinging to Geir's tunic as if he needed to hold on to something to keep him safe. 'He fell.'

Relief rushed through him. A broken leg didn't have to be fatal, and hopefully the boy had just fainted from the shock. He hurried towards the women and reached out to take Brendan from Maddie's shaking arms.

'Thank you. He's heavier than he looks,' she murmured.

'Has he spoken?' Geir studied the pale face draped over his arm. He'd come to really like the boy and had been so pleased to see him beginning to enjoy life. He had blossomed under Steinthor's tutelage and although he was much older than the other boys, it had been wonderful to see him playing with them whenever he had free time.

'Yes, a little. We need to set the bone as quickly as possible, then give him willow bark.' She went to confer with the other women and came back to Geir's side just as he passed through the doors into the hall. 'Eimear knows what to do, but she'll want your help, as it requires strength. She also says she needs two pieces of wood. Can you fashion something?'

'Of course. Here, make Brendan comfortable while I talk to Eimear.' He deposited the boy on a sleeping bench after Lif had made sure there were plenty of bed furs and cushions. He'd have to stay downstairs for the time being – there was no way they'd get him up to the loft.

It didn't take Geir long to cut two straight pieces of birch wood to Eimear's specifications, and he smoothed them a little so the boy wouldn't get splinters in his leg.

'I'm going to need you to pull sharply on the leg while I try to line the bones up,' Eimear told him while he worked. 'It's going to hurt terribly, but with a bit of luck he'll faint from the pain, allowing us time to tie the splints in place.'

'It's not going to kill him, is it?' Geir knew that Brendan was still very young and fragile.

'I hope not. As long as he doesn't develop a fever.' Eimear looked as worried as he felt himself, so he decided not to question her any further.

Brendan was awake when they returned to the hall, and was biting his lip, presumably to try and stem any tears. His trouser leg had been slashed to the knee, and someone – Maddie, presumably – had washed the dirt off his shin. The skin wasn't broken, but there was a bump where you could clearly see the bone that had become dislodged protruding. Geir had witnessed worse injuries, but never on someone so small. It made his heart clench. He ruffled the boy's hair gently and smiled at him. 'This is some scrape you've got yourself into, eh? I guess you didn't win that race.'

'No, but I hadn't planned to anyway. We were just having fun.'

'I see.' It warmed Geir to realise that Brendan had intended to be nice to the younger boys and let them win. It showed what a good nature he had. He took a deep breath and looked him in the eyes. 'Now you know you've broken your leg, don't you? And that we'll need to put it right before it can start to knit back together again.'

Brendan nodded, his lower lip trembling just a tad. 'I know.'

'You're going to have to be very courageous, but you can grip Maddie's hand as hard as you like, and Aine's holding on to you.' The Irishwoman had been instructed to grip her brother firmly under the arms so that Geir had something to pull against. 'I'm going to help Eimear and we'll make it quick, I promise. Are you ready? I'm going to count to three.'

He had already agreed with Eimear, however, that they would set the bone when he reached the number two. It was better to take the boy by surprise so he didn't stiffen in anticipation. 'One, two . . .' He tugged sharply on the foot, and as Brendan screamed in agony, Eimear swiftly aligned the bones and straightened the leg, winding a bandage tightly around it.

As they'd hoped, Brendan had fainted, which made it easier to put the splints in place and secure them with more bandages. It was imperative that they held still.

By the time the boy surfaced again, their work was done and the leg was propped up on a low pillow. Aine sat beside him with his head on her lap, looking relieved that this part was over with. She seemed almost as shaken as her little brother.

'How are you doing?' Maddie caressed the boy's cheek and brushed the hair off his forehead.

'F-fine.' Brendan was still pale, but he seemed to be trying his best to keep it together. 'Is it done?' He glanced down at his leg.

'Yes, all finished. Now you just have to rest for a couple of days and try not to move. Can you do that?'

'Mm-hmm. Will . . . will I be able to walk again?'

'Of course!' Maddie threw Geir a glance as if asking him to chime in.

'It's going to take a while,' he said, patting Brendan's shoulder. 'Maybe even months, but I'll make you a pair of crutches so that you'll be able to hobble around until the leg is healed. I'll even carve something on them for you if you like. Any favourite motifs?'

Brendan managed a small smile. 'A dragon?'

'A dragon it is. I'll do my best. Now you'd better drink this vile concoction Lif is bringing you and then sleep for a while. It will help you to heal more quickly, so take it like a man.'

'Yes, *bóndi*.'

'Good lad. Here's Blár to keep you company.' The dog had jumped up to settle next to the boy, and Geir thought it might be a good idea, as he'd keep him warm if necessary. 'I'll go and start on those crutches.'

Maddie caught up with him in his workshop and he opened his arms to her, hugging her tight. 'That was scary,' she murmured. 'I hope he's going to be all right.'

'Me too. I've come to like him a lot and I'd hate to lose anyone, let alone a boy.' He sighed. 'I feel responsible for everyone here, as if they're family.'

'I know. You're a good man, Geir.' She reached up to pull his face down for a kiss. 'That's probably why I married you.'

'Oh yes? And I thought it was just my amazing body you were after.' He nuzzled her ear and felt her tremble.

'Well, that doesn't hurt.' She put her hands on his chest and pushed him gently away. 'I'd better leave you to get on with those crutches. See you in a while. There's a feast of blueberries and cream for supper.'

'Can't wait. I think we all need a treat after today! Especially Brendan.'

And he hoped the gods would help the boy heal without giving him a limp.

Winter arrived all too soon, as Geir felt they still had much left to do. It began with an abundance of rain, which made working outdoors an unpleasant experience. As long as it wasn't too cold, however, they all persevered, and by the time the first snows came, late in the *Haustmánuðr*, they were as ready as they would ever be.

They'd built enclosures of roundpole fencing for the sheep and goats so that they'd be close enough to feed when the snow covered the ground. The animals were well used to being outdoors in all weathers and would be fine there. The cattle and ponies had to be brought into the byre and fed on their precious stores of hay, which also had to be shared with the other animals. They could potentially have been left outside as well, but Geir wasn't sure their coats had grown shaggy enough to withstand the Icelandic winter and didn't want to take any unnecessary chances.

The women and children spent most of their time in the hall – including Brendan, who was now an expert at walking with crutches – while Geir and the other men performed any necessary outdoor tasks. With all of them inside, it became very crowded, but once the thick snow came, there was no help for it.

They settled down into a daily rhythm, and for the first half of the cold season Geir was more content than he'd ever been. With happiness running through his veins, everything was easy. And as long as disaster didn't strike again in any way, he was confident they had enough supplies to last until the spring – food for everyone, ample peat stores for fuel, furs and straw for bedding, and seal blubber to burn in their soapstone lamps, as well as plenty of cotton grass to use as wicks.

Maddie seemed happy too, almost glowing, and whenever he was indoors, he found it hard to keep his eyes off her. Her gaze found his frequently as well, making arrows of heat shoot through him whenever they exchanged a glance. With his assistance, she'd built a loom out of the pieces of wood he had fashioned for her, and he'd helped her make loom weights out of stones. For part of the day, she was busy weaving *vaðmál*, ordinary homespun woollen cloth, with Aine, as it took two of them to work the loom efficiently. They stood opposite Fridgerd and Lif, who were sharing the other loom and weaving a shaggier type of *vaðmál* in which coarse locks of wool were woven into the fabric. Cloaks and blankets made of this were thick and warm. Eimear, meanwhile, saw to the cooking and made sure the children didn't come to any harm.

Maddie had adjusted to sleeping in the hall, although it took her a while to relax into making love surrounded by other people. 'I never took you for a shy woman,' he teased her at first, although he tried to make as little noise as possible just to appease her.

'I'm not normally. It's just the thought of . . . you know.' He could feel her cheek burning when he caressed it, and smiled against her mouth as he kissed her.

'Don't think about it,' he advised. 'Or listen to everyone else. It can be . . . exciting.'

She stiffened at this suggestion, but he noticed that the next time they heard anyone else moaning softly in the darkness, she became even more receptive to his advances, which amused him.

As the dark months progressed, however, he began to notice a gradual change in his wife. Both Lif and Fridgerd had announced that they were with child again, but Maddie's womb hadn't quickened. The other men had ribbed him about the possibility of having an heir for Stormavík within the year, but they stopped after a while when no such news was forthcoming. He noticed that the other women clammed up on the subject as well whenever Maddie was around. It was becoming awkward, and Geir didn't like it.

He tried to broach the subject with Maddie, cornering her in the storeroom one afternoon.

'Are you well, *unnasta*?'

'Yes, just . . . a bit tired.'

He pulled her into his arms. 'We don't have to make love every night. If I'm keeping you from your slumber, you must let me know,' he whispered, tugging playfully on her loose plait.

'No, it's fine. You know I enjoy it.' The fiery blush that spread across her cheeks told him just how much. But in the next instant she sighed and added, 'Besides, how will I ever give you that heir the others keep talking about if we don't . . .'

He tilted her face up to his by putting his fingers under her chin, then looked into her clear green eyes. 'You mustn't mind the men, *unnasta*. Not every woman conceives immediately. For some, it can take years, and we have plenty of time. I'm quite content to wait.' He chuckled. 'That doesn't mean I don't want you constantly – I do. Every time I look at you, in fact. But that has nothing to do with wanting babies, and I can be patient, so you must be sure to tell me, yes?'

'*OK*.' He knew by now what that word meant, as she'd taught him a little of her language, but she didn't sound convinced. He hoped for her sake that it didn't take too long before she was with child, as he didn't want her to be fretting, but he wasn't worried. Not yet.

'It's in the hands of the gods,' he added. And it was. If it wasn't their fate to become parents, then there was nothing they could do about it.

'Mm-hmm.' She turned her face away and buried it in his tunic, and he let the subject go for now. Instead, he made good use of the fact that they were alone inside the storeroom and there was a very convenient barrel nearby.

He knew she needed a distraction, though, so a couple of days later he sought her out again and asked if she'd ever tried skiing.

She blinked at him in surprise. 'You ski? I thought that was a modern invention. But yes, I have, as a matter of fact.'

'Then come with me on an outing today. It's a beautiful sunny day, and we could both do with a break. Put on as many layers of clothing as you can muster. I'll meet you outside shortly.'

Chapter Twenty-Three

Maddie was intrigued. Who knew Vikings could ski? It was something she'd learned at an early age – her parents put her on skis at the age of three and she'd taken to it immediately. Growing up in Sweden, near Stockholm, she'd mostly done cross-country skiing, but the whole family had gone on one trip a year up to the north, where there were perfect mountains for downhill as well, and she loved it.

As she came outside, bundled up in just about all the clothes she owned, with a felted wool cloak on top, as well as a hat and thick mittens, Geir was waiting for her. He had two pairs of skis lined up on the ground, fairly long and wide, made of birch wood and pointed at one end. They had somewhat crude toe bindings made of willow twigs, and there were leather bindings for the heel. Maddie slid her feet into these. She was wearing a pair of boots made out of fur and lined with hay for extra warmth, which seemed large and clumsy, but she knew they were necessary. The bindings didn't feel as secure as the ones on her modern skis, but then she hadn't expected them to.

'Is Blár coming with us?' The dog was always happy to follow either of them whenever they ventured outside, and loved playing fetch with snowballs, as the children had discovered to their delight.

'No, not today. I don't know how long we'll be and I don't want him getting ice stuck in his paws if he's out in the snow for too long.'

'That's sensible.'

'Here, you'll need this.' Geir handed her a long pole, sharp at one end.

'Only one?' She looked at it, wondering how she was supposed to propel herself with that. She was used to having two ski poles.

'Yes, I'll show you. Follow me.'

They set off, and she noticed that Geir was more or less just walking through the snow on his skis, without using the pole much at all. It seemed weird to her, but she followed suit and they were soon traversing the glittering landscape. She drew in deep breaths of the freezing air, feeling alive and exhilarated. It was so cold it almost hurt her lungs, but the exercise was keeping her warm and the only parts of her that stung slightly were her cheeks and nose. She'd knitted herself a scarf, as well as another thick jumper, and burrowed deep inside it.

'You were right. It is a beautiful day,' she called out, her breath emerging as a cloud in front of her.

Geir stopped to let her catch up, and grinned at her. 'Yes, it's as though we are in the land of the frost giants. Look, I think even the waterfall is frozen!' He gestured inland, where it appeared as though the waterfall they could see in the distance had turned into a giant icicle. It was a stunning sight.

They skied in that direction and reached it after an hour or so – Maddie still had trouble telling time in this era, and usually it didn't matter. But she knew they couldn't stay out for too long, as the winter days were incredibly short. She reckoned they weren't getting more than four or five hours of light each day, so they'd need to be home before darkness descended on the landscape.

'It's even more impressive close up.' Geir shaded his eyes

against the glare of the sun on sparkling snow and looked up.

'Yes, I've never seen anything like it.' How she wished she had a camera to capture this moment, but she'd have to just keep the snapshot in her memory instead.

He moved so that he was standing behind her, one ski either side of hers, and put his arms round her waist. 'It's so peaceful out here and I'm enjoying spending time with just you,' he murmured, resting his chin on her shoulder. She leaned back into him, letting out a sigh of contentment.

'Mm, me too.'

Escaping for a day was utter bliss. Although she was used to being crammed into the noisy hall with the others, it did become slightly overwhelming at times. There wasn't much space and they were literally tripping over each other, which could be incredibly frustrating at times. Sometimes it felt as though there were small children everywhere running around, laughing and chattering. The little ones didn't have much in the way of toys, but instead played with old bits of bone – Steinar even had half a sheep's jaw, complete with teeth, which Maddie found revolting. But apart from when they were outdoors in the snow or ice skating on the frozen stream on skates made of cow bones, they were continually underfoot. And the air inside was usually a fug of peat smoke, cooking smells and humanity, so being outside like this was a relief for her lungs and nose. Standing there being held by Geir, everything felt perfect, and she could almost forget the dark thoughts that had been dogging her for weeks now. Almost, but not quite.

For his sake, though, she'd push them aside for now and just enjoy their time together.

That day remained in Geir's mind as one of the highlights of the winter months, along with an evening a few weeks later on. He'd had to make a trip outside to fetch more peat for the fire, and had stopped halfway to the storehouse with his mouth practically hanging open.

The sky was an explosion of colour, undulating in front of his astonished gaze.

Forgetting the peat for the moment, he rushed inside and shouted out to everyone, 'Come! You must come outside and have a look. Find something warm to wrap up in, but hurry!'

As they all trooped out behind him, they came to a standstill and just stared at the heavens. The display of bright colours was like nothing Geir had seen before. Swirls of brilliant green and blue danced across the sky, making the most astonishing patterns. In some places this was interspersed with pink and lilac, and the whole was reflected in the snow, making the entire world feel like it was magical.

'The Northern Lights,' he heard Maddie murmur next to him. '*Aurora borealis.*'

He had no idea what that meant, or what language it was, but as she put her hand into his, he gripped it tightly and smiled. The others were oohing and aahing, and there was a look of awe on all the faces around him.

'The gods are favouring us tonight,' Steinthor said. 'That is truly a beautiful sight.'

'Yes, it was worth it to travel to Ísland just for this,' someone else chimed in.

Geir had to agree, but best of all was being able to share it with all the people here, especially Maddie. He pulled her close and let the wonder of it fill him to the brim.

One day turned into the next, and months passed by in a blur. Their days were not as physically active, but there was still plenty to do – spinning, weaving, sewing and cooking for the women, as well as keeping the children entertained and out of mischief, and other handicrafts for the men. Steinthor was the only one able to carry on working outside, as his smithy was always warmed by the forge.

Although content to do her share of the household chores, by the time spring arrived at last, Maddie was growing increasingly despondent. She'd had her period regularly every month and her body showed no signs of wanting to create a new life. At first she'd been dreading it being late, as she wasn't sure she was ready for motherhood. She wanted children, but it had been something that seemed far away in the future before she ended up here in the ninth century. As she hadn't even had a boyfriend before, the possibility of a baby had barely crossed her mind.

And yet now it was all she could think about.

She wanted one so badly, the yearning consumed her. Watching first Fridgerd, then Lif become rounder by the day was incredibly painful. What was wrong with her? Why wasn't she getting pregnant? Geir had been making love to her almost constantly ever since they got married, and yet nothing had happened. The only conclusion she could reach was that she was barren.

And that meant she would never be able to give Geir the heir he needed.

Children were important to Vikings, she knew that much. They were valued and cherished, and although a large proportion of them died – or so she'd been told by the other women – each one was loved and cared for. They were the future, the heirs to everything their parents toiled for. Geir was rightly proud of the settlement he had founded here, and he would want sons to take over one day, as well as daughters to marry off to their neighbours.

What if she couldn't provide them?

She felt sure that the joy he found in their marriage would fade quickly if she couldn't fulfil the most important function of a wife.

And with each day that passed, it became increasingly obvious that she couldn't.

'You're very quiet today.' Aine nudged her and sent her a sympathetic glance. 'Are you well?'

Aine had become her best friend among the women, and the two of them often worked together on weaving projects and other tasks. Right now, they were busy finishing off a piece of cloth on the loom Maddie had made with Geir's help. She was very pleased with the result, but the joy was fleeting. It didn't matter how skilled she was becoming in all housewifely matters if she couldn't have children.

'Sorry, I was just thinking.' She pulled the weft through the warp and Aine whacked it with the weaving sword.

'Are you missing your loved ones?'

She'd told the others her family were in Sweden and she'd been on a journey to Dublin when she'd had the accident that had led to Geir taking her on board his ship.

'No. Yes. I mean, of course I am, but that's not why . . .' She glanced at the other woman's abdomen. Aine and Cormac had been married at the midwinter feast, as had Eimear and Niall. It was only a question of time before the Irishwomen too became pregnant, she was sure. 'I still haven't conceived,' she almost whispered, taking a deep breath and staring at her feet with eyes that wanted to fill up with tears. She blinked them away.

'You mustn't fret.' Aine put a hand on her shoulder and gave it a squeeze. 'The more you worry about it, the less likely you are to become with child. Trust me. Our bodies know when we are anxious, and if you go around feeling that way, your womb will remain closed. You have to place your trust in the gods. In fate. And perhaps make an offering or two?'

Maddie never joined in when the others made sacrifices to the gods – it didn't sit right with her – but perhaps she ought to. Some ancient magic had brought her to the ninth century, and who was to say it wasn't caused by gods? She nodded. 'Maybe you're right. I . . . was taught to pray to the White Christ, but here it might be that the Norse gods hold sway. I will do as you say.'

It couldn't hurt, could it? Although she drew the line at killing animals. That was just barbaric. The gods accepted other gifts too, apparently.

'Good.' Aine smiled at her and leaned closer to whisper, 'And just enjoy what you and your man share. That is a gift from the gods in itself. I know that now.'

Maddie felt her cheeks heat up, but she couldn't help a smile from tugging at her mouth. 'That's very true. Thank you, you're a wonderful friend and I'm glad you're happy.'

It was Aine's turn to blush. 'Oh, don't mention it. You have been so kind to me, to all of us, and I appreciate it more than I can ever say.'

Trying to take her friend's advice, Maddie went for a walk into the birch forest that afternoon, bringing with her a precious piece of flatbread. They were running very low on barley now, and only consumed it on special occasions. 'But what's the point of making an offering to the gods if it isn't something you value?' she muttered to herself. She had also found some smoked meat and a handful of dried berries, and she pulled off one of her silver bangles. That would have to do.

Feeling rather self-conscious, she knelt by a large rock in the middle of a clearing. It was the place Geir had chosen for other sacrifices, but luckily it had been a while since he was here, and there were no grisly remains or discernible bloodstains. She placed her offerings on the stone and looked towards the sky.

'Goddess Freya, if you can hear me, please help me to conceive a child. For Geir's sake as much as my own. You – and maybe the other gods? – brought us together for a reason. If we are meant to stay together, then please grant my wish.' Rather self-consciously, she added 'Amen', and then almost laughed.

That was ridiculous, a word that belonged to Christianity. Perhaps she was going a little bit insane.

After that, she tried not to think about the matter any further, and threw herself into enjoying Geir's caresses. At the end of the month, however, her period still came.

Geir was growing increasingly concerned about Maddie, who was very quiet and withdrawn yet again. For a while she had gone back almost to her normal self, and he had hoped things were good between them, but after her last two monthly bleeds, it was as though all the energy had gone out of her. However, he couldn't help but wonder whether it was more than the fact that she hadn't conceived. Spring was upon them, and she'd been in his time for nearly a year now. Did she regret it? Was she sorry she had married him after all? Longing to go back to her own era? It was a lowering thought. And she hadn't talked about taking him to the future for a visit for quite a while now. Had she changed her mind about that?

He had no idea what to do about it, so he threw himself into the spring ploughing and other tasks in order not to brood.

On one of the last days of May, he heard the cow horn sound. His heart skipped a beat and he exchanged glances with Niall, who was helping to keep the ponies walking in straight lines up and down the field. 'Unhitch the ponies and follow me as quickly as you can,' he instructed. 'I'll run to see what's amiss.'

He took off and sprinted across the field, running full tilt until he came within sight of the buildings. Down by the shore, he could see a ship being pulled up on to the beach – they hadn't yet had time to build a jetty – and there were people swarming over the side and on to dry land.

'*Skítr!*' Were they to be forever targeted by unscrupulous people who couldn't be bothered to start their own settlements?

But when he came closer, one man detached himself from the rest of the newcomers and turned around to watch his progress. Geir almost stumbled, then felt a huge grin spread across his features. He ran the final stretch shouting at the top of his lungs, '*Hrafn!* By all the gods. I don't believe it!' He came to a halt in front of his brother and pulled him in for a bear hug. 'Odin's ravens, what are you doing here?'

Hrafn laughed and hugged him back. 'Nice to see you too, little brother. Although perhaps not so little any more.' He looked around. 'You have done well here. I'm impressed. Is all well? Everyone thriving?'

The other inhabitants of Stormavík were making their way down towards the shore, clearly relieved by the greeting Geir had given the newcomers. Blár was at the forefront and threw himself at Hrafn with a joyous bark, clearly recognising someone he knew.

'Hello, boy, nice to see you too.' Hrafn bent to fuss with the dog for a moment.

Geir was just about to reply to his questions when he heard a shriek and saw Maddie flying past. Blinking in surprise, he watched as she threw herself into the arms of a tall, blond man he'd never seen before. Jealousy twisted his insides and he frowned.

'Who . . . ?'

'*Ivar!* What on earth are you doing here?' Maddie was grinning from ear to ear, and the blond man crushed her to him and lifted her up to swing her around, laughing. He replied in the language Geir knew to be the *Engilskr tungu*, and the two of them chattered away, oblivious to everyone around them. Geir looked at Hrafn and raised his brows.

'Er, who's he? That's my wife he's manhandling.'

'Wife?' After staring at him incredulously, Hrafn burst out laughing and punched him on the shoulder. 'Calm yourself. He's her brother, Ivar. Although I don't think he had any idea he'd find her here. Neither did I, for that matter. How does this come about? And . . . did you really say wife?' He chuckled. 'You should see your expression. I never thought the day would come when you'd fall in love. Priceless!'

'Who says I'm in love?' Geir muttered, but that just made Hrafn laugh even more.

'You looked like you were going to tear Ivar limb from limb. I recognise that expression, trust me.'

'*Fifl*,' Geir muttered sheepishly. Hrafn knew him too well. 'So what has made you journey all this way? Didn't trust me to stay alive without your help?'

'Of course I did, but you said there might be trading opportunities here, and you know me – always up for a business venture. I brought a few extra supplies, too, in case you were running short.'

'Ha, I knew it! You thought we'd be starving by now. Well, you're wrong.' Although stocks were low, they were surviving just fine.

'Not at all, and I'm very glad to hear it. Now come, show me your new domain.'

The two men turned towards the hall, although Geir threw one last glance over his shoulder at Maddie and the man Ivar. He hadn't seen her this animated for weeks now, and it made him feel grumpy and frustrated. An arrow of concern shot through him. If she was regretting their marriage already, seeing this stranger who must be from her own time wouldn't help. No doubt he'd remind her of all she had left behind and tempt her to go back. It was a thoroughly depressing thought.

Someone cleared their throat behind them. 'Hrafn? May we accompany you?'

'Oh, yes, um . . . So sorry. Geir, you remember Vigdis, don't you?' Hrafn's expression turned slightly wary. 'Er, I brought her along because she lost her husband last year and she, um . . . wanted to go on an adventure. Well, her and her little daughter, Hilda.'

Shock shimmered through Geir. He remembered Vigdis very well indeed. Small and curvaceous, she was pretty and blond in a rather insipid way, although he noticed that her beauty had already faded somewhat since he'd seen her last. She was a couple of years older than him and had been one of the women who had pursued him for a while when he was younger. He knew her to be more tenacious than most, but luckily he'd managed to avoid her clutches that time.

Behind her, he glimpsed a small girl of about three winters, her hand held in her mother's firm grip. He raised his eyebrows at his brother, who appeared to be having trouble looking him in the eye. It was fairly obvious that he'd brought Vigdis because she was looking for a new husband, and Hrafn had thought to meddle. Well, too bad. He clenched his teeth together. As long as that Ivar didn't persuade Maddie to go back to her own time, Geir was married already.

'Welcome to Stormavík,' he said rather curtly. 'Please, do come with us if you wish.'

'Stormavík? I like it,' Hrafn murmured. He shot Geir a look as if to say he'd explain – and possibly apologise – later. This was not the time. Geir agreed, but he would give his brother a piece of his mind in the not-too-distant future.

'This way. Let me show you around.'

With one last glance at Maddie and Ivar, he led the way up the hill.

Chapter Twenty-Four

'I just can't believe it! What are you doing here? And in this time? Did you go and visit Linnea?' The questions were pouring out of Maddie in a torrent of English mixed with Swedish. It was the way they'd always talked in their family, since her mother was from the UK, but it felt unfamiliar now after speaking only Old Norse for so long. Ivar was her foster brother, having been in the care of her parents since he lost his own at the age of fourteen, and she was so happy to see him, she was close to tears.

'No, I travelled back in time by other means, but that's a story for another day. Anyway, I could ask you the same. And how on earth did you get to Iceland of all places? I thought you got lost in Ireland. Do your parents know where you are? Before I left, they were extremely worried about you, although they hadn't lost hope of you turning up eventually.'

He was still holding on to her hands, as if he couldn't believe she was real, and she was clutching his just as tightly. She shook her head. 'No, they don't, but I'm hoping they've guessed by now. It seems to be becoming a habit in our family.' She laughed. 'Gosh, it's so good to see you. I hadn't realised quite how much I missed everyone. But why is Hrafn here? Has something happened? Is Linnea OK?'

'Yes, everything is fine. I think he was just worried about his little brother, and as soon as the weather turned better, he wanted to come and check on him. Linnea would have come too, except she's pregnant again and feeling very sick. A sea voyage wasn't something she could handle right now.' He glanced at Geir's broad back heading up towards the hall. 'Not that the little brother looks like he needs looking after.'

Maddie snorted. Geir was more than capable of taking care of himself. 'No, he's done well here. We all have, although it's been hard work at times. But Geir is a great leader, a wonderful man. If anyone could succeed here, it's him.'

Ivar narrowed his eyes at her. 'Do I detect a certain partiality?' he teased.

Maddie was sure she went very pink. 'Um, well, actually he's my husband,' she blurted out.

'Husband?' Ivar's eyebrows rose almost to his hairline. 'You're kidding me! But you're just a—'

She thumped him in the chest. 'Don't even *dare* say I'm just a baby. I'm twenty. A full-grown woman.'

'But you've never even—'

'*Ivar!* Just because no one back in our time appreciated my charms, such as they are, doesn't mean Geir can't. He . . . I . . . Well, it seemed like it was meant to be when I ended up here with him.'

'Meant to be?' Ivar gave her a sceptical look. 'You're going to have to do better than that, little sis.'

'OK, fine. So maybe I fell in love with him. Or lust. Or whatever . . . The point is, we've been married since last autumn and he's not tired of me yet. Although he probably will be soon because . . . Oh, never mind. It's complicated.'

'What? You're not making sense.' He shook his head. 'But we've got plenty of time to talk. I think Hrafn plans to stay for at least a week, just to make sure Geir hasn't changed his mind about going home.'

She laughed. 'I doubt that very much. Wait till I show you what we've accomplished so far.'

'Looking forward to it.'

'Oh, isn't this . . . sturdy. Could do with a few more feminine touches, obviously, but that's easily remedied.'

Geir watched the widow as she peered around the dim interior of the hall. *His* hall. She was obviously trying to be polite, but he could tell she wasn't impressed. No doubt she was used to a large hall made out of wood, the way Hrafn's was, but that wasn't an option here. Admittedly it was a bit cramped, and the turf walls were not exactly luxurious, but they fulfilled a function and he was proud of the building. They had plans to extend it during the summer as well, adding a *stofa* – a living room where the women could have more space for their looms and benches to sit and talk or do handicrafts – and building a separate dwelling for Steinthor and Lif. If Vigdis was so fussy, it was a good thing she wasn't staying.

'Tall trees are scarce here, so we have to use whatever building materials are to hand,' he explained. He knew he sounded defensive, but really, what business did she have being critical of his home? Maddie was perfectly content to live here, as were the others in his group. 'And the women have been busy all winter adding to our comfort.'

He didn't mention that he and the other men had taken the time to cover the inside walls with planks, so that the turf wouldn't be on show. Geir had also patiently carved wooden edges, complete with various motifs of serpents and dragons, for the sleeping benches to keep the straw in place, and he was pleased with how they looked. If Vigdis couldn't see the craftsmanship that had gone into creating this dwelling, that was her problem.

'I think it's admirable, the way you've utilised what you have,' Hrafn put in. 'I'm sure these thick walls kept you snug during the winter.'

'Yes, as a matter of fact, they did. And we all survived, even the little one.' He was proud of that, as he had feared that at least one of the children would succumb to some illness or other when the cold weather arrived.

'Little one? You mean . . . ?'

'Oh no, no, not mine. Maddie and I have no children. Yet. I meant Steinthor's youngest, Svein. He was born last summer.'

'Ah, I see.'

'You have a concubine?' Vigdis's eyes had swivelled in Geir's direction at the mention of Maddie, and she frowned slightly.

'No, I have a wife,' he stated firmly, and sent Hrafn a quick glare. *The trolls take him!* What had he been promising the woman? True, as the oldest member of the family, technically he should probably have had a hand in choosing a bride for Geir, but by all the gods, he'd had no right to make promises without at least consulting him.

'But I thought Hrafn said . . .' Vigdis's mouth had the look of someone who had swallowed something sour. Her daughter chose that moment to whine and tug at her hand, and received a hissed reprimand for her trouble. Geir narrowed his eyes at the woman – there was no need to take her bad temper out on the child.

'I'm sorry, Vigdis, I had no idea my brother had decided to find himself a wife along the way,' Hrafn interjected, his voice soothing. 'It's no great matter, is it? You are enjoying this journey, wasn't that what you said?'

'Well, I . . . Yes. Yes, of course.'

Geir could tell she didn't mean it, but it was not his problem. His brother could sort out his own mess.

At that moment, Maddie came into the hall with Ivar, the pair of them laughing about something. She stopped when she caught sight of Geir, and her smile dimmed a little. He swore inwardly. That wasn't the reaction he wanted from her – not now, not ever. He wanted the happy, carefree Maddie of the previous autumn, not this downcast one. The one who'd practically flown into his arms any time he'd been away for even a short while. But nothing he said or did seemed to help these days. If she was regretting their marriage, he had no idea how to change that. And now her brother was here, presumably reminding her of everything she had left behind. How could he compete with that?

Determined not to think about it now, or to seem churlish to his new brother-in-law, he strode over and smiled at the man, while Maddie greeted Hrafn. 'Welcome to Stormavík. I'm Geir, Maddie's husband.'

'Thank you. I'm Ivar, her foster brother. Glad to meet you.' Ivar smiled back, then gave his sister a small push. 'I'm sorry, but I'm finding it hard to believe this little one is married. She's never even—'

'Shut *up*, Ivar!' Maddie gave as good as she got and shoved her brother into the nearest wall.

Geir laughed. 'I can see you two are siblings, but are you sure we're talking about the same person? "Little one"? She's one of the tallest women I've come across.'

'Ah, well, she's the baby of our family. I'm sixteen years older than her, so to me she'll always be young. Forgive me, I didn't mean to offend you or your wife.'

'Don't worry about it. I know Maddie can look out for herself. Come, sit down and we'll all have some ale. Hrafn tells me he brought several barrels, which will be most welcome.'

They sat and chatted to their guests for a while, and then showed them around the rest of the settlement. Geir noticed that

Vigdis managed to stay fairly close to him and Hrafn the whole time, but he paid her no heed. He shuddered when he recalled how single-minded she'd been when they were younger. She had tried to ensnare him, but he'd been on his guard, because he hadn't been anywhere near ready to settle down and marry. And even if he had, she'd been much too obvious in her pursuit, which had put him off. As he recalled, he'd been saved by his sister-in-law, and soon afterwards Vigdis had announced her betrothal to some other man. He hadn't given her a moment's thought until now.

Well, Hrafn could just take her back home with him when he left.

Later that evening, Maddie was coming back from a visit to the privy when she heard an argument in progress behind the byre. She pricked up her ears when she heard her name mentioned, and without thinking about it, she inched closer and strained to hear more.

'What were you thinking? That I'd be so desperate for a woman after a year here that I'd marry anyone you brought me?' Geir, sounding angry and frustrated.

'No, but Vigdis is comely and she has a good dowry now, so I just thought I would reintroduce her to you.' Hrafn's voice, clearly trying his best to be placating. 'I wasn't going to force you, just give you the option to—'

'Good, because you can't. I'm my own man.' Geir cut his brother off rudely.

'I know that, and I'm sorry. I only thought to help because I heard rumours that women are scarce here, and of course the decision would have been entirely yours. She has a small daughter, but no son, so I knew she was able to produce children—'

'What does that matter?' Again Geir cut Hrafn off. 'Either way, you can take her back with you, because she's not staying here. I have a wife already, one chosen for me by the gods, just like yours was.'

'Yes, so it would seem. Come, let us not quarrel about this. I can see that I was wrong to bring Vigdis, and I apologise. Forgive me?'

There was a slight hesitation, then Geir gave in. 'Of course.'

Maddie thought it best to remove herself, as the conversation was mostly over, and she headed back to the hall. As she neared the door, the woman they'd been talking about came out, stepping carefully over the threshold and dusting her hands together as if she didn't relish touching the dusty turf walls next to the door. She was small and dainty, but with an hourglass figure and a pretty face. Her pale blond hair hung in a long plait over one shoulder. She looked up and caught sight of Maddie, her limpid gaze hardening a tad.

'Oh, er, Maidie, was it? Would you happen to know where Hrafn went? I need a word with him.'

'It's Maddie, and no, I haven't seen him.' It wasn't a complete lie, because she hadn't actually clapped eyes on him, even though she knew where he was. 'You'd better be careful that you don't get lost out here in the darkness.'

'Thank you. I'll just sit on the bench here and wait for him to come back.'

'As you wish.' Maddie was sure Hrafn didn't want to have a discussion with the widow, especially if he had promised her a husband.

She swallowed hard. The woman had a daughter, and Hrafn's words rang in her ears – Vigdis was able to produce children. Had Geir told his brother that Maddie couldn't? That she might be barren? Perhaps he would prefer to divorce her and marry Vigdis instead. At least then he could have an heir. A whole brood of children, probably. Sure, he was angry at the moment because he didn't like his older brother trying to meddle in his life, but once he had time to reflect, perhaps he'd realise that Vigdis would be a much better proposition.

The thought made her want to howl with anguish.

As if to rub it in, Steinar, Ingvar and their little sisters rushed past the open door, shrieking with laughter in some game of catch. Vigdis's daughter toddled after them, bringing up the rear as if she couldn't quite bring herself to join in properly, or was afraid of being rebuffed. The woman glanced after her child, then turned her gaze on Maddie.

'Which one of them is yours?' she asked sweetly, but there was something ugly lurking in the depths of her eyes, making Maddie realise she already knew very well that none of them belonged to her and Geir.

'I don't have any children yet.' She tried to sound as nonchalant as she could, but probably didn't succeed, as the widow gave her a condescending smile.

'We can't all be blessed by the gods, I suppose, but perhaps your time will come. Although you've been married a while now, or so I hear.'

Wanting to retaliate a little, Maddie asked, 'How come you only have the one? I understand you were married for years.'

A flash of annoyance crossed Vigdis's features. 'The others died soon after birth. Not all babies survive, as I'm sure you know. But I'm convinced my next one will. I just need to choose a strong father for it.'

At that moment, Geir and Hrafn came strolling back towards the hall, and a small smile played about the woman's mouth as she caught sight of them. It was fairly clear who she wanted that father to be, even though she knew he was already taken. *The utter bitch!* But if it was what he wanted too . . . Maddie couldn't bear to stay for the ensuing conversation, and decided to leave them to it.

'Hey, are you OK, sis?'

She looked up and realised she'd stumbled into the hall and sat down next to Ivar without noticing. 'I . . . er, yes. I'm fine.'

'Come on, don't give me that. I can see something's the matter. What's up? Spill.' He slung an arm round her shoulders and gave her a little shake. 'Tell big brother what's bothering you.'

Maddie sighed. Why not? It would be so nice to share her worries with someone. 'I don't think I can have children,' she blurted out. Luckily they were speaking English, so no one else would understand. They were all noisily debating something anyway, Steinthor and Ingimund obviously happy to be reunited with some of their friends from home.

'What do you mean?' Ivar peered at her with concern.

'I've been with Geir since August or September – I'm not sure what month it was – and we've . . . I mean, we have slept together all that time and not once have I so much as missed a period. It's just hopeless. I must be infertile.' She swallowed convulsively, trying to keep the tears at bay, but Ivar knew her well and took her hand to pull her off the bench.

'Come, let's go for a walk,' he said loudly in Old Norse. 'It's so warm in here, I need fresh air.'

She allowed him to lead her out and past Vigdis, who stared after them but thankfully made no comment. They wandered towards the hot spring and sank down on a boulder. Ivar let her cry for a while, just holding her tight. 'I'm sure you're worrying for nothing,' he murmured. 'Surely not everyone gets pregnant at the drop of a hat?'

'It's been, like, eight months. And we've . . .' No, she couldn't tell her brother how often or how passionately she and Geir had made love. That would be too embarrassing for words.

'Have you talked to him about it?' he asked gently.

'Yes, sort of. He said the same as you, that it doesn't always happen quickly. That he can be patient. But Ivar, what if it never happens? He's a Viking, the owner of all this.' She gestured at their surroundings. 'He needs children. Sons. And if I can't give them to him, surely he'll tire of me?'

Ivar gave a low chuckle. 'I doubt that very much. The man looks at you like he's besotted.'

'No, he doesn't. Don't be silly.'

'I'm serious!'

'Well, even if he does now, it won't be long before he becomes disillusioned.' She ground her teeth together. 'Maybe I should go home.'

'What? No! Maddie, it's not that bad. Some people take years to get pregnant. You mustn't give up so soon.'

She jerked out of his hold and stood up, starting to pace back and forth. 'But don't you see? Hrafn has brought Geir a better bride, one who can definitely give him children. If I go, he'll be free to marry again. It will spare us both years of misery, waiting for something that probably won't happen. Back in our time, I'd have a chance to become a mother one day with the help of IVF. And even if I can't, being childless isn't such a big thing. Lots of women choose not to have a family, and that's normal. I probably wouldn't care so much there. Here, though, there's no hope.'

And she wanted Geir's baby so much . . .

Ivar stood up and stopped her perambulations by stepping in front of her. 'Come on, this isn't my fierce little sister talking. Where's the girl who survived the bullies at school? The one who got herself a black belt in karate? At least give it some more thought. Don't be hasty.'

'OK, fine, I'll think about it some more, though it's been on my mind for weeks now. Months, actually. It's not a spur-of-the-moment thing. But if I decide I want to leave, will you come with me? Please? I'm not sure I could cope with arriving in modern-day Iceland without money or a passport or anything . . .'

'Sure. I'll help you in any way, you know that. It's what big brothers are for. Even foster brothers.' He smiled at her. 'But for what it's worth, I think you're wrong, and you should talk it over with your husband.'

'Maybe.'

But she knew this wasn't something she could discuss with Geir. He'd persuade her to stay by making love to her, and she could never resist that. If she was going to go, she'd have to be strong and just leave. It was the only way.

Chapter Twenty-Five

Hrafn was eager to make the most of any trading opportunities while he was here, and to that end, it was decided that half the group would take a trip down the coast to visit Ingólfur Arnarson of Vik. There was no point going to see Hjalti, as he'd want to keep whatever ivory and pelts he'd collected for himself, and as for Eyvínd's settlement, nothing would induce Geir to set foot in it again.

Ivar wanted to come as he was keen to see as much of the island as he could while he was here, and naturally he asked Maddie to accompany them. Geir had been going to do so himself, but Ivar beat him to it, which annoyed him no end. Still, the result was the same so no point thinking about it. To his further annoyance, Vigdis also announced that she would come.

'No one asked you,' he muttered, so quietly that only Hrafn heard him, but despite the snort that escaped his brother, he was the one who replied with equanimity.

'Of course you must. We are here to see this place after all.'

'I shall leave my daughter at Stormavík, though. Your thralls can look after her,' Vigdis declared.

'We have no thralls,' Geir told her through partially clenched teeth. 'As I'm sure you must have gathered by now.'

'How extraordinary! I thought it was just something your, er . . . wife said to tease me.' She put a hand on his arm and smiled coquettishly at him. He shrugged her off, irritated by the slight hesitation she'd taken to adopting every time she mentioned Maddie. It was as if she couldn't bring herself to believe they were truly married. Did she honestly think he'd go around saying it if it wasn't true?

'No, but I'm sure if you ask Lif and Fridgerd nicely, they won't mind looking after Hilda for a few days,' he bit out curtly. The way she ignored her daughter most of the time, the poor child would probably be happier left behind. She'd been having the time of her life playing with the other children, from what he could gather.

'Oh, you know her name!' Vigdis beamed at him. 'I knew you'd take to her. She's such a sweet little thing, isn't she?'

'She is indeed.' He couldn't dispute that. *Unlike her mother.*

The party set off in Hrafn's ship and made good time, arriving at Arnarson's settlement that afternoon. They were courteously received, and the man seemed happy to discuss business with Hrafn, while his wife Hallveig invited them into their home for a meal. As they'd brought gifts of produce, Geir wasn't worried that they would deplete Arnarson's stocks too much, despite being a large group. He took Maddie's hand and led her to a bench near the hearth. Her brother followed, as though he was watching over her, and another spurt of exasperation shot through Geir. He was perfectly capable of looking after his own wife.

Unless Ivar was protecting her from him?

The thought was most unwelcome, and he pushed it aside. That was ridiculous.

Vigdis, who had entered the hall behind them, seemed to have every intention of seating herself on Geir's other side, but was distracted by the keen attentions of a group of men, who pounced on her as if they hadn't seen a female in years. Perhaps they hadn't, although by listening carefully, he soon gathered that it was a woman available for marriage they were after.

'There's such a dearth of girls to marry here,' Arnarson's wife confided, after she'd plied her guests with food and drink. 'You mustn't mind them.' She gestured to the hopeful swains. 'If she is already spoken for in your settlement, I'll make sure they don't importune her unduly.'

Geir smiled – possibly the first genuine smile of the day. 'Not at all. As far as I know, she is entirely free, and they'd be welcome to her.'

He turned to find Maddie frowning slightly at him, but when he raised his eyebrows at her, she looked away. 'What? You want Vigdis to stay at Stormavík?' he asked.

She shrugged. 'That's up to her, isn't it? I don't mind either way.'

He could tell that was a lie and plaited his fingers with hers, giving them a squeeze. This was not the time to debate the issue, but he sensed that he needed to let her know he'd be extremely pleased if Vigdis decided to marry one of Arnarson's men.

Anyone other than himself, in fact. He didn't care who she chose.

'Well, that was a stroke of good luck,' Hrafn commented on the way back to Stormavík. 'Arnarson had a lot of things to sell and I am confident I'll make a huge profit on all the goods on my way back.'

'I'm glad,' Geir said, but he sounded as though his thoughts weren't really on the subject of trade.

Maddie was watching him and followed his gaze along the ship to where Vigdis was chatting animatedly to a long-suffering Ivar. She'd been regaling him with stories of her triumph at Vik ever since they set off, even though Ivar had been present and seen it all for himself. The woman had seemed to really come alive in Arnarson's hall, animated and vivacious as she'd flirted with anything in trousers. She clearly thrived on male attention. Not that there was anything wrong with that per se . . .

'And that Aske, he was *most* insistent.' Vigdis's laugh rang out now. 'Wanted to marry me on the spot and told me exactly what his prospects were. Can you imagine? By Freya, I don't know when I was last courted this much. I must have received at least six proposals!'

As if she had ever been courted to this extent, Maddie thought sourly. Although perhaps she had – she was a pretty woman after all. Throughout her long recital of all the marriage offers she'd received this afternoon, though, Vigdis kept glancing at Geir under her lashes. Was she taunting him with how popular she was? Showing him that he should take advantage and grab her while he could?

The complete and utter cow.

The worst thing was, however, that Maddie sort of agreed with her. It was probably best for Geir if he did just that. What use was it having a wife who couldn't give him children? Sure, he still seemed keen to make love to her, but even that would fade, and she was sure the time would come when he'd simply go to sleep the moment his head hit the pillow.

Maddie swallowed down a huge lump in her throat. He was too honourable to divorce her for the sole reason that she was barren, but she couldn't in all honesty condemn him to a childless marriage. Nor herself to a life where she had to feel guilty about being infertile. It wasn't a crime, and back in her time there must be a man who'd want her, even knowing that about her. Now Geir had the opportunity right here to change his status, but since he was a stubborn man, it would be up to her to do something about it.

She just had to pluck up the courage.

If only they'd been in her time, and not his, it wouldn't have mattered. But this was the ninth century and it did, a fact she simply couldn't change.

In the end, Hrafn stayed for another week and Geir enjoyed having his brother there immensely. Never one to sit still and do nothing, Hrafn helped out with anything that needed doing, and the two of them worked in perfect harmony, whether they were ploughing together or heading out for some fishing. The only fly in the ointment was that he didn't manage to see much of Maddie during the day, though he tried to make up for it at night, when he made love to her as passionately as he could. He had the horrible feeling that she was slipping away from him, and he'd do anything to prevent that.

Hrafn was right – he was in love.

He didn't tell her, because he wasn't sure if she felt the same way any longer – if she ever truly had – but he tried to show her instead, taking his time to caress every inch of her, kiss her, and pleasure her to the point where he almost drove himself mad. He hoped she understood, and she melted into him the way she always did, but during the day it was as though she avoided him. Once Hrafn left, he was determined to talk to her properly. They needed to have a discussion and sort out whatever was bothering her so much. It had to be more than the fact that she hadn't conceived yet. Surely it couldn't be that important? It wasn't to him.

To his intense irritation, Vigdis was often around, sticking to him and Hrafn like tree sap to your fingers.

'She has no one else to talk to,' Hrafn said with a shrug when Geir complained. 'The other women don't seem to have taken to her. I suppose it was just as well you didn't want to marry her after all.'

'Yes. Perhaps she should make herself a bit more agreeable. She never actually says anything bad, but the way she looks at everything, as though a troll made it, that's not going to endear her to anyone.'

'I know. I'm sorry I didn't realise what she was like. She never showed this side back at Eskilsnes.' Hrafn made a face. 'Actually, Linnea did mention something, but I thought she was just feeling grumpy because of her condition, you know? Goes to show, I should always listen to my wife.'

Geir grinned at that. 'I'd say you listen to her quite enough.'

'*Hei*, are you calling me a henpecked husband?' Hrafn punched him lightly on the arm.

Geir held up his hands, laughing. 'I wouldn't dare.'

'Hmph.'

The following day he was in the byre, loading a cart with manure to spread on one of the fields, when suddenly a pair of arms snaked around his waist and a lush body pressed against his back. By now, he knew every curve of Maddie's body and realised at once that it wasn't her, so he jumped and swivelled round with a fierce scowl. 'Vigdis! Let go this instant!'

She didn't, though, her grip like the tentacles of an octopus. Instead she laughed up at him and batted her eyelashes, and he had a horrible flashback to the last time she'd done this. He hadn't welcomed her advances then and he didn't now. Why could she not understand this?

'Geir, Geir, always so grumpy these days. That's not what you used to be like when last we met,' she chided playfully.

He pulled her arms away forcibly and placed them at her sides. 'Then your memory is faulty,' he hissed. 'I resisted, remember?'

'Oh yes, you were pretending disinterest. Made it so much more enjoyable to chase you.' She sighed, as if happily reliving the memories. 'Looks to me as though you could do with a bit of entertainment now. That wife of yours is walking around with a face as long as a horse's. I don't know how you can stand it.'

'What? No, she isn't,' he protested, and took a step back. She was standing way too close for comfort, seemingly thrusting her large bosom in his direction. But she was right, damn her. Maddie did look constantly unhappy, or at least as though her mind was weighed down with worry.

'Oh, come now. I never took you for a liar, Geir. All is not right with your marriage, and you can do something about it, you know. When that sort of thing happens, there's only one thing for it – divorce.'

'I am *not* divorcing my wife,' Geir practically snarled.

'Well, perhaps you need a little more time to think about it.' Vigdis smiled at him and reached out a hand as if to pat him on the cheek like a little boy. 'Which is why I've decided to stay when Hrafn leaves. Just so that you will have options, *unnasti.*'

He gripped her hand to shove it away and was about to tell her in no uncertain terms that he was not her 'dear', but before he had time to do so, she rose on tiptoe, flung her arms around his neck and started kissing him. He froze with shock, then reacted violently and shoved her away so hard she fell backwards on to what was left of the winter hay. A small sound of distress made him look towards the door, and he caught sight of Maddie, her face devoid of all colour. One hand went to her mouth, as if to stifle further sounds, while her eyes grew enormous and filled with pain.

'Maddie, it's not . . .' he began, but she turned and fled without listening to him. He rounded on Vigdis, who was leaning on her elbows with a knowing smile. 'You're going to pay for this, by all the gods!' He'd never hurt a woman in his life, but right now he wanted to throttle her. 'I'll speak to you later.' He rushed out of the byre, followed by her tinkling laughter.

'Oh, I do hope so,' she called after him.

Geir caught up with Maddie in the sacred grove, where she was leaning against a tree feeling as if all the air had left her lungs. She didn't really want to talk to him, but knew she couldn't avoid it. Best to get it over with.

'Maddie! Please, listen to me. It wasn't what it seemed. I don't know how long you were standing there, but you must have seen that she just launched herself at me. I didn't touch her. I swear to all the gods!'

She turned slowly and nodded mutely. It was possible that it had happened that way. No, it was more than possible – it was probable, knowing Vigdis. But that didn't change the fact that perhaps he shouldn't have pushed her away. The tiny vixen would be a much better match for him, with her womanly curves and fertile womb. Maddie couldn't compete with that. Wasn't even sure she wanted to any longer.

'*Unnasta*,' he murmured, and gathered her into his embrace, leaning his cheek on top of her head. She flinched at that word, because she'd heard Vigdis use it about him not five minutes ago. As if he was her 'dear' from long before. As if she had the right to call him that because they had shared history. Geir didn't seem to notice her tiny movement. 'Maddie, sweeting, you're my wife and that is all I want. Vigdis is just stirring up trouble, but we mustn't let her. Please, don't let it disturb you. She's jealous, that is all. She wants what you have, but she'll soon see she can't. And I'll make sure she leaves with Hrafn after all.'

'After all?' The words came out sounding rather hoarse. Maddie hadn't known there was any doubt about this, but now she gathered that Vigdis planned to stay. Knowing the cunning woman and her wiles by now, she suspected she'd probably succeed in making this happen somehow. Perhaps she'd fake an illness, or find some other excuse why she couldn't leave right now. Maddie wouldn't put anything past her.

But it didn't matter. Nothing mattered any more.

'Yes, she was spouting some drivel about staying behind, but I won't allow it. Maddie? Do you believe me?' Geir lifted her face to his by cupping her jaw with both hands. His stormy blue-grey eyes were troubled but sincere, so she nodded. She did believe that he hadn't invited Vigdis's advances in this instance. But perhaps he soon would. And he could try to send her away, but the woman would find a way to circumvent his orders.

'Good. Because you know I'd never lie to you, I swear.' He bent to kiss her, and she allowed herself to melt into his arms, the way she always did. She wanted to remember how it felt, and stored up the memories in her mind – the feel of his mouth on hers, the taste of him, the outdoorsy smell that was so uniquely him. And the hard body that held hers so tenderly, restraining the latent strength so as not to hurt her.

She would never forget this – him – even if she lived to be a hundred.

'So will you make sure she goes with you? I really can't have her here creating discord, you must see that. She was enjoying stirring up trouble and the gods only know what she'll do next.' Geir had cornered his brother for a private chat, and pushed his fingers through his hair in an impatient gesture. He didn't add that the whole situation was of Hrafn's making – if he hadn't brought Vigdis in the first place, none of these problems would exist. Hrafn was nobody's fool, though, and caught on quickly.

'Of course I will. I know it's my fault, and I'll make it right. At least as much as I can – the rest is up to you.'

Like everyone else, he must have noticed the strained atmosphere that reigned between Geir and his wife. There couldn't be a single person in the whole of Stormavík who hadn't seen it. It was making Geir extremely tense. After that kiss in the sacred grove, Maddie had been largely silent and avoided his gaze. He had no idea what to do about it, but hopefully once Hrafn had left with Vigdis, her normal good spirits would return.

'Thank you, I would really appreciate it.' He changed the subject. 'Are you going straight home after you've sold the goods you bought from Arnarson, or doing some more trading along the way?'

Hrafn smiled. 'You know me – I can never resist a trading opportunity. And by the way, if you have anything more you'd like to sell, let me have it. Especially any spare *rosmshval* tusks.' He grew serious. 'We'd better set off tomorrow. I need to get back to Linnea or she'll fret. That's not good for her right now.' He clapped Geir on the shoulder. 'You'll see what it's like when it's your turn. Maddie will have you tied in knots.'

'I'm sure.' Geir didn't mention the fact that this might never happen. He hadn't given up hope yet and he'd been making sacrifices to the gods in the clearing. But there was no guarantee that would help, as the gods were capricious. 'We'd better tell the others that your time here is almost at an end. I'll give orders for a farewell feast.'

Everyone grumbled good-naturedly at the news, but Hrafn promised he'd return when he could. Geir looked at Maddie, expecting her to give his brother a message for Linnea, but she was staring into space as if she wasn't really listening. Perhaps she'd already charged Ivar with delivering it. He frowned and went to sit next to her, taking her hand. He caressed it with his thumb. 'Are you well, *ást mín*? You're not too sad to say goodbye to your brother? He'll come back.'

'Hmm? Oh, yes, probably.' She pulled her hand out of his. 'I'm fine. Just a bit tired.'

She didn't seem tired that night, however. In fact she took him by surprise and initiated their lovemaking, something she hadn't done for quite a while, now he thought about it. He smiled into the darkness and lay back, letting her do whatever she wanted. The pleasure was intense, and when she finally allowed him to enter her, he was ready to explode. They rode the waves together in perfect harmony, and he thought he would never tire of this. Ever.

She was his world and he loved her to the point of madness. He really should tell her that, and he vowed he would, as soon as everyone else had left.

But the next morning, both she and Ivar were gone.

Chapter Twenty-Six

When Maddie came to, she found herself lying in a field, surrounded by sheep. A couple of them stood nearby, peering at her curiously, and one snorted as if to show that he – or more likely she as, despite the horns, there were two lambs with her – wasn't impressed.

'Urgh! That was horrible,' she muttered, swallowing down the residue of the nausea she'd felt after she and Ivar cut their fingers with the folding knife. They'd decided to try and both use the same time-travel device, even though Ivar had one of his own.

'There's no guarantee we'd end up in the same time or place if we use different ones,' he'd argued, and she had to agree. The thought of arriving in modern-day Iceland alone was daunting, and they'd held hands as well just to make sure they weren't separated.

And here she was. Or so she hoped. She sat up and looked around, spotting Ivar getting to his knees next to her. 'Oh, you're here – thank goodness!'

'Mm, just give me a minute. I'll never get used to this. It's like the worst fairground ride ever, and I never liked those in the first place.'

'I know, but . . . did it work?'

'Only one way to find out.'

As soon as the world stopped spinning and their stomachs had settled, they headed inland and found a road. 'Look, asphalt! We did it!' Relief coursed through her. It was bad enough having to make the decision to leave, but if they'd ended up in some other time period, it would all have been for nothing.

'Yep. Let's just head south, and hopefully someone will come along and give us a lift.'

A couple of cars sped past, ignoring their outstretched thumbs, and Maddie couldn't blame them. She was dirty and unkempt, and they were both wearing Viking clothing, which probably looked extremely odd. Eventually, however, a kind old man stopped and picked them up. 'Did your car break down?' he asked, staring at them with unfeigned interest.

'Yes,' Ivar said. 'We left it back at the cottage we've rented. We've, um . . . been to a re-enactment party and I'm afraid we were burgled. The bastards took everything – our passports, wallets, credit cards – and then they punctured the wheels on the car. We need to get to Reykjavik to report it. Is that where you're heading?'

'What bad luck! Yes, I can drop you off at the police station, no problem. I'm sorry this has happened to you. We don't usually have much crime here.'

'Thank you, you're very kind.'

As Maddie sat in the back seat of the car, watching the scenery whizzing past, her thoughts whirled. On the one hand, the austere landscape was very familiar to her now, after a year on this island, but at the same time the modern houses, cars and tarmacked road were totally alien. Outside, the air had been more or less the same – cold and fresh – but inside the car she could smell plastic and a faint whiff of petrol fumes. It was nothing short of a shock to the system, and she wasn't sure how she felt about it. In fact it was all surreal and a bit hard to take in.

Less than an hour later, they were in the Icelandic capital, a fascinating mixture of modern architecture and old-fashioned clapboard houses in various colours. The nice man dropped them off outside a square building with '*Lögreglan* – Police' in big letters over the entrance. It seemed intimidatingly large to Maddie, after living in the turf hall for nearly a year, and almost too bright inside with a myriad of windows. The officers, when they told their story again – although changing it slightly and leaving out the bit about renting a cottage and a car, as they didn't want anyone to search for this fictitious place – were sympathetic. 'Mugged, you say? Lost everything?'

'Yes. Would it be possible for you to call our parents in Sweden, please? They can help organise emergency funds and plane tickets for us.'

'OK, let's try that. And you'll probably need temporary passports too.'

To Maddie's relief, no one questioned their story, and once her parents got involved, things happened quickly. She and Ivar were soon installed in a twin room at a hotel in the centre of Reykjavik. The bare wooden floor and minimalistic décor struck her as cold and unwelcoming after the clutter she was used to, but the springy beds with pristine sheets and comfortable pillows and duvets were extremely welcome. Compared to hard benches covered with straw and furs, it was like sinking into a cloud. The tea- and coffee-making facilities and the large flat screen TV were added luxuries as far as she was concerned, and she found the mini fridge stocked with soft drinks and snacks. Bliss.

They wolfed down a dinner of pizza, followed by the sweetest dessert on the menu, and took turns having long, hot showers before dressing in new clothes. Haakon and Mia had managed to transfer some cash so that they'd have enough for their immediate needs, and this enabled them to buy whatever they needed.

'This feels so weird,' Maddie murmured, zipping up her new hoodie. She didn't mention that she missed the sensation of skirts swirling round her legs. What was the use? She'd soon get used to wearing trousers all the time again.

Sooner than she'd thought possible, she was on a plane heading back to Stockholm, where her parents met her at the airport.

'Maddie! Oh Maddie, sweetheart. We can't tell you how relieved we are . . .'

She was enveloped in a group hug so fierce she nearly lost her breath, but they were all three crying with happiness and relief, so she barely noticed.

'Mum, Dad, it's so lovely to see you again.' And it was. She'd imagined this moment hundreds of times, especially at the beginning, when she'd first arrived in Iceland, and it was almost as sweet as she'd thought it would be. Almost, but not quite, because she hadn't planned on being alone.

As if they'd read her thoughts, her dad said, 'But where's Ivar?'

He wasn't the man on Maddie's mind, but she didn't want to mention that right now, and buried all thoughts of Geir for the moment.

'He went back to the past. He said to tell you he's sorry, but he had unfinished business and . . . well, you know where he is and he's fine.' He'd told her some of what had happened to him while he'd been in the Viking era, but she'd sensed that he was holding something back. She hadn't wanted to press him.

'Oh, right.' Her parents' disappointment only lasted a few seconds, as they were too busy hugging her and pelting her with questions as they drove home.

Ivar's decision not to come with her had taken her by surprise too, but she was so grateful for his help, she didn't question it. He'd always been a law unto himself, and he would come back to the future as and when he was ready. Or not, as the case may be. It wasn't for her to decide or try to influence him, just as he hadn't tried to persuade her to change her mind. Well, not much.

'Remember that Roxette song, "Listen to Your Heart"?' he'd said casually, then hummed a few bars. This was followed by a searching gaze and a quick 'Are you really sure about this? And don't try to tell me you're not head over heels in love with the guy.'

'Yes, I am sure. And it doesn't matter whether I'm in love or not.'

She'd tried to sound decisive, but recalling the words of that song definitely didn't help, because she *wasn't* sure. Nowhere near. The only thing she knew was that she and Geir couldn't go on as they had been. It would be like living with an axe hanging over her – sooner or later it would fall, when he realised that they'd never have children and he'd wasted years on her. She couldn't bear it. Surely it was better for everyone concerned if she ended it now? She clung to that thought even though the pain of what she'd done clawed at her insides.

They didn't want the police to know that Ivar wasn't going to Sweden with her, however, so he'd hung around the airport until it was time to go through security. By then, their escort had left, and he'd been able to sneak out the door without anyone being the wiser.

'Look after yourself, little sis,' he'd whispered before he left, giving her a huge bear hug.

'You too. Love you!'

'And you.'

And now she was home. She should have been happy, but instead tears were flowing down her cheeks as her parents continued to bombard her with questions.

'How could you do this to us? What is it with our children that they all have this need to time travel? Sheesh, isn't the twenty-first century good enough?' her dad joked.

'You just disappeared, Maddie!' Her mother's concerned gaze was more direct.

She was clearly expecting explanations, and Maddie tried to give them, but she was so tired. All she wanted was to go to bed, and not think. Eventually they let her.

As she sank under her duvet, she felt as though she was in heaven, but at the same time it was utter hell – because Geir wasn't sharing the bed with her. And no one else could ever take his place.

'What do you mean, we shouldn't look for her?' Steinthor stared at Geir as if he'd grown two heads and a tail. 'She must have been abducted again. We have to get her back, take revenge on the *niðingar* who took her, just like last time!'

'She hasn't been abducted. Her brother is with her. They must have left together.'

'But how? On foot? Because the ships are both here and so is the rowing boat.' The smith scowled at him. 'I can't believe you're just going to let your wife leave and not do anything about it. I thought . . . Well, never mind what I thought. I was clearly wrong.'

Geir reached out and grabbed Steinthor's arm as the man prepared to walk away. 'No, you weren't. It's just . . . it is very difficult to explain, and I fear you wouldn't believe me even if I tried.'

'You're not making any sense.' Steinthor's scowl wasn't letting up, but he crossed his arms over his chest and stood still, as if prepared to listen.

'Look, if I tell you a secret, do you swear an oath not to tell a soul? No one, not even your wife. Ever?'

'Yes, of course. I swear by all the gods. What is it? Tell me!'

Geir pushed his fingers through his hair, tugging at it in frustration, then tried to explain to Steinthor what he thought had happened. About time travel, and the gods choosing his wife for him. Although perhaps they had just been toying with him. That was what he'd thought in the beginning, and – Odin's ravens! – it would seem he'd been right. How could they be so cruel? Making him fall in love, marry and think he'd won Maddie at last, only to snatch her away again. It was unbearable.

And it hurt. *Skítr*, how it hurt. That Maddie would go back to her own time without saying anything, without at least talking it over with him. That she could just leave without any qualms. He'd known she wanted to see her parents and reassure them she was safe, and he'd been prepared for that, but this was something else. Deep down, he could sense that she wasn't coming back, and in a way, he could understand why she hadn't said goodbye. He wasn't convinced he would have been able to either. But still . . .

'To the future? You are certain?' Steinthor's eyes were wide now, blinking in disbelief.

Geir sighed. 'Yes, completely sure. I told you you wouldn't believe me.'

'It's not that. Of course I do, if you say so, although you must admit it does sound a bit fantastical, but then . . . you can't go after her. I mean—'

'I *know*.' He clenched his fists and bit down on the roar of frustration that wanted to escape. That must have been the whole idea – to leave and take the time-travel device with her. But there *was* a way he could follow. Hrafn – or his wife – had one too, and so did his other brother, Rurik. It would be possible to borrow one of them, but the question was, would Maddie want him to?

He just didn't know, and so he said nothing about this to Steinthor.

'I'm going to the hot spring. Please tell everyone not to disturb me, or they might regret it.'

'I will.' Steinthor gave him a bewildered look and patted him awkwardly on the shoulder. This wasn't something he could help with, and they both knew it.

Hrafn was the only one who disobeyed this order, but by that time Geir was sick of his own thoughts and welcomed the company. He didn't say a word until Hrafn had undressed and joined him in the pool.

'I take it I wasn't as good at being a husband as you or Rurik,' he muttered, sinking deeper into the warm water. 'Or the gods were having a joke at my expense.'

His brother sent him an exasperated glance. 'Don't be a *fifl*. There must be more to it than that. Did you have words? Was there something you disagreed about?'

'No. Nothing as far as I know. Well, you know Vigdis tried to come between us, but I thought we had sorted that out. And then there was the fact that she was becoming impatient because she hadn't conceived yet, but I told her it didn't always happen immediately. I've been pleading with the gods, but no luck so far. I don't know . . .'

'Hmm.'

'I need to speak to her.'

'Clearly.'

Geir swivelled round. 'You agree with me? But you know what that means.'

Hrafn gave him a small smile. 'Yes, I do understand what you're saying.'

'And you're willing to help me?' Without thinking, Geir grabbed his brother's arm and shook it, splashing them both with hot water.

A sad smile crossed Hrafn's features. 'How could you doubt it?

You're my brother. We leave tomorrow – I postponed our departure this morning because of what has happened – but I still need to do my trading along the way, so you'll have to be patient, even though that's probably the last thing you want at the moment.'

'Of course. Thank you.' What more could he say? Hrafn was on his side and he always would be. If anyone could help him find Maddie in the future, it was his big brother. Thank Odin for that.

'We can't find anything wrong with your reproductive system, Miss Berger. It all seems to be in working order.' The doctor smiled at her, but Maddie didn't smile back.

'Then why can't I get pregnant?'

'Oh, there could be a number of reasons – your husband's sperm count, incompatible blood groups . . . the list is long. The thing is, you're still very young, and until you've been trying for a few years, I really wouldn't worry about it. Not everyone conceives at the drop of a hat.'

She'd booked an appointment with a gynaecologist as soon as she'd emerged from the first few days of wallowing in misery. Her parents had wisely left her alone until she was ready to interact with them more, and now they were trying to be as supportive as possible. Her mum, Mia, was waiting for her when she came out of the hospital.

'Here, I bought you a hot chocolate. I thought you might need it.' She handed Maddie a polystyrene cup, which felt unfamiliar to the touch. Maddie missed the feel of the wooden beakers she was used to now. Missed everything about the past, which was insane really. And the hot chocolate, although nice, was almost too sweet. How was that even possible?

She sighed. Here she had access to a shower, lived in a warm, clean house, and didn't need to worry about whether there was enough food in the larder. The sheer variety of food, as well as all the things she'd missed – like pizza, burgers, ice cream, chocolate and cinnamon buns – was breathtaking. And yet she craved plain fare. Fish, smoked meat, stew, even gull's eggs and seaweed. The taste sensations back in her own time were overwhelming, a sugar and calorie overload.

But she didn't want to disappoint her mother. 'Thanks, Mum.'

'So how did it go? It's OK if you don't want to talk about it, but I'd like to know what they said. Come on, let's sit over here for a bit. There's a nice bench in the sunshine.'

Maddie shrugged, but sat down obediently. 'They said that they can't find anything wrong. That I should be able to conceive. I just have to be patient. But it could be years, and I don't know if . . .' She trailed off, not wanting to even say Geir's name out loud.

Her parents had been extremely surprised when she told them her time-travelling tale, but they agreed it had to have something to do with fate. And perhaps the Norse gods. Why else had all their children disappeared in this way? It couldn't be coincidence.

'Well . . . and I can't believe I'm saying this, but . . . maybe you need to go back and find out if the doctors are right. Give it a chance.' Mia shook her head and gave a tentative smile. 'I guess your dad and I will have to move to the ninth century too if we ever want to see any of our kids.'

That made Maddie smile back, at least a little. 'I'm sorry. We must be a sore trial to you both. And I can't believe Storm and Ivar both left, on purpose, when they didn't have to.'

Ivar had told her he'd travelled back in time because he wanted to meet one of his ancestors. His curiosity had been overwhelming, to the point where he'd felt he just had to go. Meeting up with Maddie was simply a fluke. However, she'd been dismayed to find that Storm had followed her to the past, to look for her because he felt guilty about her disappearance, according to the note he'd left behind.

She continued now, 'I mean, Linnea and I kind of just ended up there by mistake, but my brothers knew what they were doing.'

'Hmm, yes, but they're boys, or men, or whatever. They probably didn't want to miss out on the adventure.' Mia snorted. 'Typical!'

'Well, I guess in a way it's your own fault, Mum. Yours and Dad's. If you hadn't filled our heads with Viking tales and dragged us round to all those re-enactment events, maybe none of us would have been interested.'

'I suppose,' her mother conceded. 'Still . . . you didn't all have to go.'

Maddie finished her hot chocolate and leaned her head on her mother's shoulder. 'Well, I'm back now.'

Chapter Twenty-Seven

The day after Maddie's disappearance, Ivar came walking into the hall at supper time and threw himself down on a bench next to Hrafn, who almost spilled his ale and choked on the mouthful he'd just taken.

'Ivar! What in the name of all the gods? I thought you'd gone to—'

Geir shot out of his seat and surged towards the man, pulling him up by the front of his tunic. 'Where is she? What have you done with her? Tell me, or I swear I'll—'

'Whoa, calm down and I'll tell you whatever you wish to know.' Ivar carefully detached Geir's hands from his clothing and dusted himself off, ignoring the death glare he was receiving.

'Well? I'm waiting.'

'Should we do this outside?' Ivar enquired, sending Hrafn a look from under raised brows.

'Oh, yes, good idea. Come, little brother.' Hrafn got to his feet and gripped Geir's arm, towing him outside and down to the shore. It wasn't properly dark, and Ivar had no trouble following them.

Once there, Geir tore himself out of his brother's hold. 'Let go of me. I won't beat him to a pulp until he's told me what I want to know.'

'No need for that,' Ivar murmured. 'It's not me you should be angry with. Women, eh? We'll never understand them.'

'Get to the point!' Geir almost shouted, but he didn't want anyone else at the settlement to hear this discussion – his brother was right about that – and sound carried next to the water, so he restrained himself.

'Fine. Maddie has gone home. She should be with our parents by now. I saw her to the *plane* myself, and they were meeting her at the other end. She's safe.'

'*Plane?*' Bewildered, Geir stared from Ivar to Hrafn.

The latter shrugged. 'It's a vessel that flies people long distances through the air. I gather that from here it would only take a matter of hours, rather than weeks, to reach her destination.' He turned to Ivar. 'So she's back in Svíaríki?'

'Yes. And, er . . . she intends to stay there.' Ivar gave Geir a direct look. 'You are free to marry Vigdis.' He held up his hands in a peace gesture. 'Maddie's words. She asked me to give you that message.'

Geir swore most foully and kicked at a nearby stone. The resulting pain shooting through his foot did nothing to assuage his bad humour. 'The trolls take her! Why? For the love of Odin, tell me why. What did I do wrong?'

He didn't want to plead with the man, but Ivar was the only one who could provide him with an answer, and he would surely go mad if he didn't get one soon.

Ivar sighed and crossed his arms over his chest. 'Well, she made me promise not to tell you this, but in a gesture of solidarity between men, and because I think she was wrong not to discuss it with you, I'll reveal what I gathered. You two have been married for a while now. Since the beginning of the autumn, am I right?'

Geir nodded. 'Yes, and what of it? I can't believe she tired of me so quickly.'

Ivar's mouth hitched up a fraction and his eyes glimmered with amusement. 'Oh, I don't think she did. She didn't actually say it out loud, but she implied that you had been sleeping together rather frequently.'

'Yes, of course.' Clenching his fists at his sides, Geir raised his chin. 'I know she's your sister, but to me she is a very beautiful and desirable woman. Naturally I wanted her as often as possible. That's normal.'

'Er, quite.' Ivar cleared his throat and seemed to be stifling a smile.

'Are you saying I should have let her be occasionally? She could have just told me no. In fact, we discussed that very thing. I thought she understood.'

'That's not what I'm saying at all.' Ivar grew serious. 'The problem is that this did not result in her becoming with child. In short, she thinks she's barren, and because she knows that you will need heirs to take over here one day, she decided to be noble and leave the field open for Vigdis, who has already proved that she is, er . . . fertile.'

Geir stared at the man, his eyes widening. 'Noble! Of all the . . . *Fool of a woman!*' he roared.

'I take it this is not what you want,' Ivar commented drily. 'You don't care whether she's barren or not?'

'Of course not! And I wouldn't marry Vigdis if she was the last woman in Miðgarðr! She would drive me out of my wits within days. I love Maddie and I don't care if we never have a single child. It's not important. Hrafn here has plenty of them. I'm sure I could always give my domains to one of them in due course. Aargh!'

'I only have two and a half so far,' Hrafn murmured with a smile, but Geir ignored him.

'You really love her?' Ivar was looking serious now.

Hrafn burst out laughing. 'Can you doubt it? Look at him.'

'Very funny,' Geir muttered, shooting his brother a dark look. 'I distinctly remember the state you were in when you thought you'd lost Linnea.'

'Yes, well, that's how I know you are truly smitten.' Hrafn placed an arm around his brother's shoulders. 'Come, let us go and finish our meal. Tomorrow we sail for home, and then I'll take you to see Maddie. It will be up to you to persuade her you are serious.'

'He's coming with us?' Ivar fell into step beside them.

'Of course. We Eskilssons don't give up that easily, and we had already reached that conclusion before you returned.' Hrafn peered at him. 'Why did you come back, by the way? You could have gone with your sister on the *plane* and you would have been back in Svíaríki in no time. I thought it was your intention to go home after this journey.'

'It was, but I've had time to think and I need to go back to Hordaland first. There is something I have to do there. I was hoping you could drop me off? Besides, as I said, my feeling was that Maddie should have given Geir a chance to have a say, so I wanted to tell him her reason for leaving. A decision such as that cannot be made by one party.' Ivar sighed. 'You try persuading either of my sisters of anything, though.'

'Oh, trust me, I have a wealth of experience – and failure – of that.' Hrafn chuckled. 'Let's hope Geir is more successful.'

'You don't have to work quite so hard, sweetie. Those weeds aren't going anywhere.'

'Exactly, but they need to.' Maddie gave a grunt as she pulled out a particularly nasty nettle. She was spending time with her parents at their cottage on the shores of Lake Mälaren, west of

Stockholm. It was their refuge and summer paradise, a wonderful place for relaxing and recharging your batteries. But Maddie couldn't sit still. It was impossible.

'The beauty of this place is how wild it is,' her dad, Haakon, commented from the sunlounger, where he was soaking up some rays. His shock of white-blond hair was as thick as ever and provided a pleasing contrast to his golden tan. Maddie wished she had taken after him in looks instead of her mother, as the two of them always got burnt. Linnea was lucky to have inherited his genes.

She sighed. 'I'm sorry, but I'm not used to inactivity. At Stormavík we were working non-stop from dawn till dusk. It felt good to be active, doing something worthwhile . . .' She trailed off, not wanting to sound as depressed as she felt. Would she ever get back to normal? Or what passed for normal in the twenty-first century? She wasn't sure. A life of leisure definitely wasn't for her, though, and the only good thing about being back was that she'd been able to go to the dojo and do some training with her former teachers and friends.

'We get that, Maddie,' her mother put in, 'but you could perhaps try to take it just a little easier? Or why not go for a swim? The water is very refreshing.'

'Yes, OK, maybe I will. I'll just finish this patch.'

A while later, Maddie ran into the lake, drowning a shriek under the surface of the icy water. It was a far cry from the delightful hot spring she was used to bathing in, and that thought sent another dart of misery shooting through her.

'*Damn it!*' she shouted, still underwater, and opened her eyes to watch the bubbles from her mouth and nose escape towards the surface. Would she ever be able to put it behind her? Why did falling in love have to be so painful? And why had she gone and fallen for a Viking, of all people? The trolls take it, as he would say.

She should be blaming the gods, or fate, or whatever – and to a certain extent she did – but it was mostly her own fault.

'I should have stuck to my guns and not got involved with him,' she muttered under her breath, while swimming breaststroke as fast as she could in order to warm up. 'I *knew* it would lead to trouble. I just knew it.' But she'd been a fool, and now she was paying for it.

What was he doing now? He must have finished the ploughing and sowing, and there would be fresh fish drying in the breeze. Most probably he and the others would have started more building works. The hall needed an extension or two – that much had become obvious as they tripped over each other all winter, and they'd planned to remedy it. A separate house was going to be built for Steinthor and Lif, and if there was time, Ingimund and Fridgerd's new home would be established upriver.

But it would all be done without her help.

She ducked her head under the water again and held her breath, swimming below the surface. Why should it matter now? Those people had lived a thousand years ago. They were long dead and forgotten.

Except *she* didn't think she would ever be able to forget. She would always wonder.

A thought struck her. *Hrafn!* He'd be home soon, and hopefully Linnea would come to visit their parents during the summer months. Maddie could ask her for news of Geir and the others. She might not know much, but it would be something. Anything.

'Aargh!' In her frustration, she swallowed some lake water and had to stop and cough.

She was grasping at straws and she needed to put it all behind her. Stop mooning about. And she would, when they went back to town in the autumn, she promised herself. Until then, she was supposed to take time out to rest and recover. But was it possible to recover from a broken heart?

'You're coming with us? How wonderful! Does that mean you'll be returning to Svíaríki for good?'

Vigdis, not having been privy to any of the discussions of the night before, blinked in delighted surprise when she found Geir boarding the ship with her and the others the next morning.

'No, I'm hoping to come back here soon. There's just something I need to do first.' He turned away from her and stowed his travelling kist under one of the rowing benches, praying she would take the hint that he wasn't in the mood to talk to anyone, least of all her. Although Maddie had appeared convinced that he hadn't made any advances to Vigdis, he couldn't shake the thought that the woman probably still had much to do with his wife's decision to leave.

Vigdis was nothing if not tenacious, though, as he was all too aware, and put a hand on his arm and tugged on it. 'You're a free man now, or so I hear. I understand your wife has divorced you. Perhaps you'd like me to stay and wait for you here rather than travel all that way and back again.' She gestured to little Hilda, who was huddled miserably on the ship's planks. 'It's a long journey for a child, and she seems to like your settlement.'

Geir had heard Hilda screaming earlier that she didn't want to leave her new friends, but her mother hadn't paid her any heed at the time. Poor mite. It made the concern Vigdis was showing now all the more unbelievable.

Either way, the widow's words required an answer. He couldn't tell her the truth, but it was past time he made it clear to her where they stood. Fixing her with the fiercest gaze he could, he replied in a harsh but firm voice, 'No. My wife has *not* divorced me. And I do *not* want you to stay here and wait for me. I do not *ever* want to marry you. In fact, even if you were the last woman in the whole of Miðgarðr, I still wouldn't want you. Do I make myself clear?'

'But . . .' She stared at him, her mouth opening and closing.

'Do you understand me, Vigdis? I will never be your husband. Leave me *alone*! Find yourself another man. And while you're at it, treat your child with a bit more consideration. You should count yourself lucky you have her.'

'Well, really, there's no need for—'

'There's every need,' Geir interrupted. 'Since you appear to have skin thicker than a *rosmhval*.'

Her eyes narrowed and shot sparks of fury at him. 'I'll thank you not to insult me further,' she snarled, then turned on her heel and marched up to Hrafn. In an unnecessarily loud voice, she demanded that he drop her off at Arnarson's settlement. 'It seemed to me I was wanted there,' she added, 'and I'm not going on that long journey again unless I have to.'

'I'll be happy to let you off anywhere you wish,' Hrafn assured her.

Geir was fairly certain he wasn't the only person on board to heave a sigh of relief when they left the woman at Vik. He could only hope the poor men there knew what they were letting themselves in for, and that little Hilda soon found new friends to play with. He'd make sure to check on her on his way back. *If* he came back.

Four weeks later, the ship pulled up next to one of the jetties in Birka, the town closest to Eskilsnes. Geir left his brother and the other men to tie her up and made his way up the hill to his middle brother's house. He was hoping Rurik would be at home, which proved to be the case.

'Geir, by all the gods, it's good to see you!'

He found himself enveloped in a massive hug by his brother, and then released into the softer embrace of his sister-in-law, Sara. Hrafn had decided to stop at Birka rather than go straight home, because that was the best place to sell his trade goods. Not that he had much left, as they'd stopped at two other trading towns along the way, but he wanted rid of the lot. Rurik and his wife, who were both silversmiths, lived and worked in Birka, and they led the way into their home. It was situated on the edge of the town, overlooking the bay, where ships were coming and going, and a lot of trading took place on the large jetties.

'It's great to see you too,' Geir replied. And it was, but the circumstances could have been better.

'What brings you here? Tired of life in Ísland already? I assume you came back with Hrafn.' Rurik peered behind him, as if he expected someone else to be there. His next words confirmed this. 'Didn't you bring your wife back with you?'

'Wife?' Geir scowled. How did Rurik know about Maddie? But then it dawned on him what his brother was talking about. 'Oh, you mean Vigdis?' He snorted. 'She's not my wife and never will be, if I can help it.'

Rurik blinked at the vehemence in his voice. 'Oh, right, well . . . come in and tell us more.'

After reacquainting himself with their toddler son, Lars, and their huge dog, Beowulf, who both seemed pleased to see him, Geir sat down and gave them a brief outline of his woes. They didn't need to know every detail, although he was sure they'd have plenty of questions when he was done.

Sara's eyes grew round with amazement as he recounted his meeting with Maddie. 'I don't believe it! Why her? It seems like . . .'

'Fate?' Geir ground his teeth together. 'Yes, that's what I thought too. I immediately assumed the gods had had a hand in it – what else could I think? It appeared to be so obvious. But now . . . I'm not so sure. Or at least, they probably did plan it all, but they were toying with me. With us. Giving me what I thought was the perfect spouse, and then ruining it.' He sighed and bowed his head, feeling exhausted both physically and mentally. He'd had weeks to think it over, and with every day that passed, his doubts grew. Was he doing the right thing chasing after her like this? Or was he just making a fool of himself?

It had been a long journey, and having to wait around while Hrafn conducted his business had sorely tested his patience. While they'd been travelling, Maddie could have forgotten all about him. Resumed her old life. Met a new man . . . But he wouldn't allow his thoughts to dwell on that. Not until he'd seen her and knew for sure where they stood.

'So I take it you are going to the future?' Rurik's question broke into his ruminations.

'What? Oh, yes, of course. I mean, I must speak to her. There might be some way we can salvage our marriage. I will do my utmost to convince her of that. If not . . .' He shrugged.

Without Maddie, he didn't want to go back to Stormavík. There was no point. Although, come to think of it, he didn't want to stay here either.

Rurik and Sara seemed to understand that he didn't want to talk about it any more, and instead they began to regale him with tales of little Lars's misdeeds, which appeared to be many and varied. 'Honestly, you'd never think a two-year-old could get into so much trouble.' Sara shook her head. 'I have no idea how I'll cope when the next one arrives.' As soon as she'd said it, she turned pale. 'Oh, I didn't mean to—'

Geir held up a hand. 'It's fine. I'm not going to fall apart every time someone mentions children. Of course I would have liked some, but it's not as important to me as regaining my wife. Really,

I mean it. I'd rather have her than a dozen little ones.'

'Right. Well, good. I'll go and see about some food for us all. Come on, little scamp.' She took Lars by the hand and went off to confer with an older woman who was in a back room preparing a meal.

'Thank you for not snapping at her,' Rurik said quietly. 'I appreciate that this is difficult for you, and I will pray to the gods that you succeed.'

'Me too.'

Geir was saved from saying anything else, as Hrafn chose that moment to arrive, and it was his turn to tell his travel tales.

They spent the night with Rurik and Sara, catching up on all their news, and enjoying sleeping on a bench that didn't move, and set off again early the next morning. Geir sat in a daze, hardly taking in their surroundings, only rousing himself when the ship bumped against a jetty. He frowned as he looked up at a settlement that wasn't Eskilsnes.

'What's this? I thought we were going to your home.'

Hrafn shook his head. 'Wait for me on the jetty and I will explain.' He spoke to his men, then jumped up to stand next to Geir, and they watched as the ship set off again, leaving them behind.

'I don't understand. Isn't this your friend Haukr's domain?'

'Indeed, but we won't be visiting him today. Come, let's head into the forest before anyone spots us.' Hrafn led the way into the trees, ignoring the curious glances of one or two members of Haukr's household who had nevertheless caught sight of them. 'We should really have waited until after dark, but I know you're in a hurry, so we will take a chance that we end up somewhere without anyone about. Now, hold out your hand and on the count of three repeat the words *Með blóð skaltu ferðast*. Understand?'

'Yes, whatever you say.'

They knelt together on the ground and Hrafn counted them down. '*Ein, tveir, þrír* . . .' To Geir's surprise, his brother cut both their fingers with the sharp point of the massive brooch that normally held his cloak in place, and then they both recited the words.

He gasped as the world began to spin unbearably, and strange noises started up inside his head. Leaning forward, his hands encountered springy moss, but he hardly noticed. He was too busy trying not to be sick. 'What in the name of . . . ? Aargh! Hrafn?'

But his brother didn't reply, and in the next instant, everything went black.

Chapter Twenty-Eight

'Will you be OK if we pop over to the supermarket?'

Maddie opened her eyes and put up a hand to shield them against the sun. She squinted up at her dad. 'Of course I will. I'm not a baby. Stop fussing, please!'

'Sorry, it's just that . . . Sorry. We won't be long. Take care you don't get burnt.' He bent down to kiss her forehead, then set off towards the car. Soon after, she heard it take off down the dirt road and breathed a sigh of relief.

They were smothering her.

Naturally they meant well, and she knew they were concerned about her, but she didn't need to be mollycoddled. She'd survived a whole year in Viking-age Iceland, for crying out loud. And she was a woman grown, in every way. No, a bit of tough love might be better to jolt her out of feeling sorry for herself. Right now, her body was finally accepting that she needed a rest, and she'd slathered herself in coconut-scented sunscreen and was lying in the sun, soaking up the rays. It felt good. Peaceful. And she knew not to overdo it.

Half an hour later, she sat up and prepared to go for another swim. She was pleasantly warm – not baking, as the sun kept going behind the clouds – and needed some exercise. Enough with the resting. However, as she stood up, she caught movement out of the corner of her eye and swivelled towards the forest that abutted the garden on the right-hand side. She thought she was suffering from sunstroke as she watched two Vikings emerge from the trees and head towards her with purposeful steps. Then she blinked.

No, it couldn't be . . .

'Hrafn? And . . . Geir?' The towel she'd been holding dropped out of suddenly numb fingers, but she hardly noticed. Her gaze was fixed on the man who was now running towards her, while the other one turned and headed for the jetty. As he came to a halt in front of her, she stared at him, drinking in the sight of the man she loved more than anything. 'Wh-what are you doing here?'

He was looking her up and down, eyes wide, as if he wasn't sure what he was seeing, and she belatedly remembered she was wearing a bikini. A very tiny bikini that didn't cover much. Not that he hadn't seen every inch of her before, but it had been a while.

'Maddie?' His voice was a hoarse whisper. '*Unnasta*, why are you outside half naked?'

As if that was the most important thing here. She glared at him. 'None of your business. And I asked first. Why are you here? And how . . . Well, Hrafn helped you, I suppose.'

At least her brother-in-law had the decency to stay down by the lake, staring out across the water and giving them privacy for this confrontation.

'I came for you.' Geir was still staring at her and seemed to be having trouble speaking. 'You look . . . radiant.'

'Hot and red, you mean? Yes, that's what the sun does to me. I was just going for a cooling swim in the lake.'

'Right.'

She didn't know why she was being so waspish, because she

wanted to just throw herself into his arms and kiss him senseless. *He came!* He hadn't said why he was here, though, apart from . . .

'What do you mean, you came for me? You should be happy to be rid of me. Have you married Vigdis yet?'

It was his turn to glare. 'No, of course not. Why would I? I'm already married. To you.'

'Not if I'm here, in the future. You're free then. Or should I have sworn some sort of oath to that effect?' She looked down and scuffed at the grass with one bare toe. Her emotions were all over the place and she didn't trust herself to look at him without throwing herself at him.

'No, but what if I don't want to be free? Did you not think to ask me that?' His tone was accusing, but she thought she heard something else in it too. Desperation? Sadness? Anger? It stung, because he was right. She'd been a coward not to discuss it with him.

'I just . . . couldn't.' She took a deep breath, and her voice came out trembling and broken as she added, 'I didn't want to hear you say it. Couldn't bear it. I . . . Don't you understand? She can give you children and I can't. Well, probably not, and—'

He cut her off by grabbing her round the waist and hauling her up against his chest, looking down on her with the fiercest scowl she'd ever seen. 'Do you seriously think I care? After all we have shared, did you really believe I'd happily discard you just for the privilege of having children?'

'Well, I . . . Yes. It's important in your culture. I know it is.'

He pulled her even closer, to the point where she wasn't sure she'd be able to breathe.

'You are a fool, woman! But you're *mine*, and I'm not letting you go for such a stupid reason, do you hear me?' He was practically bellowing, seemingly at the end of his tether, and for some reason that made her want to smile.

'Um, I should think most of the neighbourhood can hear you. Good thing they don't speak your language.' She threw a glance towards the jetty and saw Hrafn turn away with a grin on his face. 'So that means you—'

'Love you, yes, to the point of madness! For the love of all the gods, have you not understood that yet? Have I not worshipped your body night after night, shown you exactly how I feel? If you can't reciprocate, then tell me that to my face, but don't ever – *ever* – just leave like that again!'

'*OK.*'

'*Oh kay?* Is that your answer?'

She put her arms round his neck and leaned her forehead against his broad and very warm chest. 'No, not all of it.' Looking up at him, she gave him a soft smile. 'I love you too, so, so much, and I promise never to leave you again without discussing it first.' She grew serious again. 'But are you absolutely sure? Because I don't want you to regret this in five or ten years' time. I was barely able to walk away now, after less than a year. Any longer and I'd be utterly crushed.'

'You have no idea, *ást mín* . . . I have been going frantic these last weeks, thinking you had come back here because you had simply tired of me. Of living at Stormavík in my time, and all the hard work it entails.' He seemed to take in his surroundings for the first time, frowning slightly. 'I thought perhaps you missed this too much and Ivar reminded you of that.'

She put a finger on his mouth and shook her head. 'I'll never tire of Stormavík. I loved it – all of it – and sharing it with you made it even more special.'

'So does that mean you'll come back with me? Hrafn tells me there are ways of getting there without spending weeks at sea. I brought all the silver I have to pay for passage.' He was regarding her intently, as if he wanted to see into her heart. And he was welcome to, because it belonged to him, and always would.

'Yes, I will. Of course, I will. But you don't have to pay. I—'

But he didn't give her a chance to say anything else, because his mouth came down on hers in a kiss so demanding and passionate, she felt it all the way down to her toes. He continued to kiss her until she wasn't sure her legs would hold her for much longer. When they came up for air, she was breathing heavily. 'Geir, I think we'd better go indoors.'

'Mm, good idea. I'll be tearing those scraps of material off you any moment now.' He sniffed her skin. 'You smell like a goddess. What *is* that? It's driving me insane with wanting.'

She giggled softly. 'It's *coconut*. I'll explain later. For now, come with me.'

As they turned towards the house, she sent Hrafn a little wave and received another huge grin in return. She hoped he'd have the sense to keep her parents talking if they came back any time soon. It might be better if they didn't catch her and Geir naked the first time they met their son-in-law . . .

'I'm pleased to meet you.'

Geir was dressed again and feeling calm and pleasantly languid, a wonderful contrast to the tension, anger and anxiety that had been running through him for the past few weeks. Being introduced to his parents-in-law was a bit daunting, but Maddie had assured him they couldn't force her to stay in their time and had no jurisdiction over her. Not that he would have let that stand in his way, but still, it was good to know.

'And you.' Maddie's father, Haakon, appeared to be scrutinising him. 'But you have come to take our daughter away.' It wasn't an accusation, just a statement accompanied by a sigh. Geir cast a glance at Maddie, silently appealing for help.

She smiled and went to hug her father. 'I had to leave home at some point, you know. And at least now you know I am happy and well.'

'As long as you're sure . . . ?'

'I am.'

They were all speaking Old Norse, out of politeness to him and Hrafn, Geir guessed. Haakon and Mia's speech was a bit halting, but they could make themselves understood and had clearly been practising. It showed that they were willing to adapt for the sake of their children. It couldn't be easy to have them all disappear a thousand years back in time.

When they'd come downstairs, they had found Hrafn sharing a meal with them at the back of the dwelling in a curious room that appeared to be wholly made out of glass. It was beautiful, and he was hoping to explore his surroundings a bit more before going home. It was all so very different to what he was used to, and he was intensely curious about everything here.

Maddie's sleeping chamber had been small, but contained the softest bed he'd ever lain on, with a mattress that moved. That was a bit disconcerting, but he'd become used to it after a while. Her sleeping quarters were up a narrow staircase, and there appeared to be two more chambers up there – one where his parents-in-law slept, and one for bathing.

'I need to clean off the *coconut*,' Maddie had told him, then added with a glint in her eyes, 'and you can come and help me.' She'd made him stand in a strange white bathtub with a curtain in front of it while she poured water over them both from a handle attached to the end of a metallic snake. 'A *shower*,' she explained. It was intriguing, but just then he'd been more interested in applying sweet-smelling soap to her sun-bronzed skin. He'd find out more about that snake later, he vowed.

Downstairs in Haakon and Mia's dwelling, there were three chambers. One that appeared to be for cooking in, one filled with odd-looking chairs and benches made out of huge pillows, and then this glass construction at the back overlooking the lake. It was interesting, and he was keen to study the workmanship of the carpentry surrounding the pieces of glass, but it could wait. For now, he needed to get to know his parents-in-law better, and he was grateful to his brother for having kept them occupied while he and Maddie made up their quarrel – if that was what you could call it – in spectacular fashion. He was sure he wouldn't forget the smell of *coconut* for as long as he lived.

'We'll have to go to Iceland as often as we can,' Mia said, taking her husband's hand and giving it a squeeze. It warmed Geir to see that they were still so obviously in love, even though they must have been married at least twenty years.

'Yes, as long as one of our children is kind enough to lend us a time-travelling object,' Haakon muttered.

Mia gave her husband a tiny shove. 'Maybe we can find one of our own. You have access to thousands of artefacts at the *museum*. There might be another one there. Or in someone else's collection.'

'I suppose. No harm in looking.'

Hrafn got to his feet. 'I had better go back now. Linnea will be waiting and I'm anxious to see how she fares.'

'Yes, of course. Do send her our love, and we hope all goes well with the birth. You will let us know, won't you?' Mia's gaze became troubled, and Geir could understand her concern. Childbirth was a dangerous business.

'I will. Thank you for your hospitality.' Hrafn bowed to them and gestured for Geir to follow him outside. 'A word before I go, brother.'

They walked together down to the jetty, which was becoming shrouded in darkness as night fell. 'Is all well?' Hrafn peered at him through the gloom.

'Yes. She's coming back with me, but I have agreed to stay here for a short while so that she can show me her world. It's only fair, and to tell the truth, I'm curious to see it.'

'Who wouldn't be? You'll enjoy it, but there is much to take in.' Hrafn gripped one of Geir's hands with both of his. 'Will we see you before you leave?'

'No, we are going straight back to Stormavík. There is so much to do, and Steinthor and the others will need our help.'

'Of course. We'll try to come for a visit next summer.' Hrafn turned to go, then stopped. 'Oh, there is something I've completely forgotten to tell you – Aunt Estrid died.'

'She did? When?'

Estrid had been more like a mother to Geir than an aunt, because his mother had died giving birth to him and his aunt had stepped into the breach. He couldn't believe she was gone. The last time he'd seen her, she had given him her whole-hearted approval of his schemes, which meant a lot. She'd been one of the few people who hadn't doubted him.

'A couple of months back. The thing is . . . you know she and her husband inherited a large farm not long after they were married?' Hrafn chuckled. 'Just as well, since she was never going to agree to live in her new brother-in-law's house where she had no authority.'

'Yes, what of it? I suppose her husband will take a new wife now.' Geir didn't really care one way or another.

'No, he died too, before her. That left her free to give her possessions to anyone she wanted, as neither of them had any children, and she designated you as her heir. The farm is yours now.'

'What?' Geir goggled at his brother, shock reverberating through him. 'But I live in Ísland . . .'

'Yes, I know. Although she admired your intrepidness and spirit of adventure, I think she was hoping you'd come back. She always believed family should be close to one another, able to help if necessary. At least she wanted to give you that choice.'

Taking a deep breath, he dry-washed his face. This was a lot to take in. 'A farm of my own, here? Not far from Eskilsnes?'

'No more than an afternoon of rowing.' Hrafn clapped him on the shoulder. 'Think about it, eh? I am overseeing the running of it for now, as her closest kinsman, and I'll keep it safe for one of my children if you don't want it. But any time you wish to come back, it will be waiting for you.'

'Thank you. I don't know what to say. It's . . . so unexpected.' He didn't add that it was a shame their aunt hadn't died a year ago, before he set off on his adventures, because he'd liked her too much to wish anything of the sort. It was simply bad timing. And he couldn't regret his new settlement either. It had been a great experience and he'd enjoyed it. Well, most of it . . . 'I'll see you next year. Take care of yourself and your family. And thank you for helping me with this too.' He gestured back at the strange dwelling, where the love of his life waited for him in her glass chamber.

'Any time, you know that. Good luck, and enjoy yourself in this strange era!'

He didn't stay to watch Hrafn disappear. It was weird enough experiencing it for yourself, and he knew his brother would be fine.

Chapter Twenty-Nine

'Does it hurt?'

'Huh? Oh, no, I was just admiring the patterns. That man was very skilled at drawing. It's exquisite.'

Geir was lying in bed with Maddie, holding his wrist up to the morning light to admire his newly etched tattoo. It was the same sort of pattern as she had on her arm, done by the same person, and gave him a more or less identical black cuff of swirling snakes, dragons and mythical creatures. It was glorious and he was very pleased with it. The pain had been negligible.

'It does look nice.' She grinned and held up her own next to his. 'Almost a perfect pair, as though binding us together.'

He turned and swooped on her, giving her a deep kiss. 'We *are* bound together. For life. And I don't need any visual reminders of that. However . . .' Pushing himself over to the edge of the bed, he rooted around inside the pouch he'd left on top of his clothing.

'However what?' Maddie was leaning up on one elbow, regarding him with a quizzical look.

He smiled and returned to her side, holding out his hand palm up. 'I was advised by my sister-in-law, Sara, that you might want a token of sorts as proof of my love. She and Rurik made this, and I hope you like it.' A ring of pure gold glinted in the light from the window, and a row of small green gemstones twinkled around its top edge as he proffered it to her.

'Geir! It's beautiful. Thank you so much! I . . . You didn't have to.'

Her eyes appeared to have misted over, and a tear trembled at one corner. He reached out to wipe it off while she slid the ring into place on the third finger of her left hand. 'I hope that's a happy tear, *ást mín*?'

She threw her arms around him and gave him a bear hug. 'Of course it is! I'm so happy I could burst. It's perfect, I love it!' Her gaze grew dewy again. 'I love *you*! So much.'

'I'm glad you like it. It's a bit daintier than the silver ring I gave you when we were wed.'

Maddie cupped his face with both hands and gazed into his eyes. 'I like that too, but you know I don't need any tokens really, don't you? I just need you. But it was a lovely gesture and I shall treasure it always.' She gave him a tender kiss, making him forget everything else for the moment.

He felt sure it would always be thus between them.

They spent two weeks in the twenty-first century, and Maddie tried to show Geir as much as she could of her world. Not because she missed it or wanted to make him jealous or anything, but just so that he would understand her better and know what she was talking about if she tried to explain something to him. He took it all in his stride, marvelled at most things, asked endless questions, and delighted in every type of food she introduced him to.

'It's a good thing you keep taking me to the training place with you,' he commented, 'or I'd be practically rolling back to Stormavík.'

Her friends at the dojo had accepted him as her Icelandic boyfriend and they'd all had fun sparring and hanging out together after the training sessions. No one seemed surprised when she informed them she was moving to Iceland with him.

'Just make sure you visit from time to time.'

Her parents said the same thing, of course. 'Although your father is going through the museum collection with a fine-tooth comb at the moment, trying to find another time-travel device,' her mother told her. With a rueful smile, she added, 'I wonder how many parents have to travel a thousand years back in time to see their kids?'

Maddie gave her a hug. 'It's a lot to get your head round, isn't it. Thank you for being so understanding and not making a huge fuss. I know this must be hard for you.'

Mia hugged her back. 'Yes, well, it could be worse. Not everyone's children are as radiantly happy as mine. I'm very grateful for that.'

And Maddie knew she was extremely lucky to have such wonderful parents.

When they arrived at Keflavik airport, just outside Reykjavik, Geir was still a bit wide-eyed from the plane ride. He'd been staring through the window at the strange landscape of mountains and volcanic rock on the Reykjanes peninsula below them. To her surprise, he'd relished every moment of the journey and hadn't shown any fear whatsoever. 'What is there to be scared of?' he'd asked, when she questioned him about it. 'You told me it was perfectly safe.'

'Well, yes, but . . .' How could she explain that she was in awe of his fearlessness? The way he went through life never worrying about what might be. He just accepted whatever happened as fate and got on with what he had to do. From now on, she was determined to do the same.

In truth, she'd been terrified herself the whole journey – not of the flying part, but because they'd had to borrow Ivar's passport and pretend that Geir was her brother. It hadn't occurred to any of them until Maddie went to book the plane tickets, but then Haakon had suddenly exclaimed, 'Oh my God, Geir doesn't have any legal documentation! And we can't obtain any either, since technically he hasn't been alive for over a thousand years.'

It seemed like an insurmountable obstacle at first, and they'd discussed the possibility of hiring a boat to sail to Iceland, but in the end they'd agreed to try something illegal first. Haakon and Mia had a key to Ivar's apartment, and a quick search there had unearthed his old passport. Ivar himself had kept the temporary one he'd been issued with in Iceland.

'If you grow a beard, you might be able to pass for him,' Mia said doubtfully. 'You're both tall, with blond hair. If anyone asks, just say you grew yours out since this photo was taken.'

Maddie was sure it wouldn't work and they'd be busted, but somehow it had. The passport officials had barely glanced at him, just frowned at the long hair and beard and waved them through.

'The gods helped us,' Geir told her, and she truly believed that, because surely it couldn't be as easy as all that otherwise? 'Which reminds me,' he added, as they made their way out of the modern airport, 'there is something I need to discuss with you.'

'Oh? Sounds serious.'

'It is, but not in the way you think. Hrafn told me I've inherited a property half a day's boat ride from Eskilsnes from our aunt, Estrid, who passed away. He's looking after it for me, but I think he was hoping we would go and live there.'

'In Svíaríki? But what about Stormavík?'

Sure, the idea of moving back to Sweden and living closer to all her relatives was tempting, but they had worked so hard to establish the settlement here and they weren't finished, not by a long shot.

'I know. I'm not ready to move back yet, but it's good to have the option, don't you think? And if it's what you would prefer, I'll do it.'

'No, I feel the same as you.'

'How about we stay here for a couple more years and then make a decision? It may be that we've had enough of this island, and we can always sell Stormavík to someone else. Or gift it to Steinthor and the others to share. If we have a property in Svíaríki, we don't need to be paid for this.'

'That sounds like a great plan.'

At the moment, living in Iceland felt like a huge adventure and she wasn't tired of it, but she could imagine the time would come when she would want to be near Linnea and Sara, and within easier reach of her parents. For now, however, she was content to remain here.

She and Geir were welcomed back to Stormavík with shouts of joy, and to Maddie's huge relief, no one asked why she'd left in the first place. Perhaps they merely accepted that arguments happened in marriages, and none of them – apart from Steinthor – knew where she'd really gone. The most enthusiastic greeting came from Blár, who'd been left behind when Geir travelled to Sweden. He nearly knocked them over as he came hurtling towards them, and his joyous barking was deafening.

'Yes, yes, we're very happy to see you too. Down, boy, down!' Geir and Maddie both laughed and fussed over the ecstatic dog.

'How did you get here?' Ingimund was smiling, clearly relieved to see them. They must have been short of manpower for the last month, and Maddie felt a twinge of guilt.

'We walked. I found Maddie, er . . . further down the coast, and no one could be spared to take us back.' Geir shrugged as if it was nothing. 'We managed.'

In truth, they'd taken a taxi from Reykjavik and the driver had let them off not far from where Maddie reckoned Stormavík was. No one here would understand about that, though, so there was no point trying to explain. It had felt strange being back in the starkly beautiful landscape of Iceland, with its wide-open spaces, long empty roads and distant mountains. Especially now she was used to being surrounded by either the massive Swedish forests or the myriad of houses in Stockholm, teeming with people. But as soon as they'd walked out of the airport doors, she'd had a strong sensation of coming home, as if she belonged here, at least for the moment. Sweden was a possibility for the future, but right now, this was where they were meant to be.

'Are you ready to do some hard work?' Steinthor challenged them now. 'There is plenty to be done, I can assure you.'

Geir and Maddie smiled. 'Lead the way. We can't wait to get started.'

Chapter Thirty

Nine months later

'I don't believe it – two of them! Are you sure? I mean, I can see that there are two, but are they really both ours?'

The normally unflappable Geir was floundering, and Maddie laughed, despite the bone-deep tiredness. Childbirth was no walk in the park, and she had no idea why she'd been so eager to undergo this torture, but it was definitely worth it to see the utter joy on her husband's face.

'Yes, a boy and a girl. They're a bit small, but Lif thinks they'll be fine. If I run out of milk, one of the others will help.'

There were two other babies at Stormavík at present, a few months older than her twins, and their mothers had plenty of milk.

'I am lost for words. You are amazing, *ást mín*. Have I told you how much I love you?' Geir was holding her hand as if it was made of glass.

Maddie grabbed his shirt front and pulled him down for a kiss. 'Yes, you have, but I'll never tire of hearing it, so please say it as often as you like. Now, would you like to be introduced to your son and daughter?'

'Yes, most definitely.' He beamed at her, and after one more kiss, he moved aside so that she could shuffle over to the side of the bench and reach into the cradle he'd made. 'I suppose I'll have to make another one now. They won't be able to sleep head to toe in that for long.'

'True.' Maddie lifted the first baby and placed it in the crook of his right arm, then put the other one in his left. 'Make sure their heads are supported at all times. Their necks aren't strong enough yet.' She smiled at the sight of this huge man holding two such tiny human beings. Tears of joy ran down her cheeks as her heart melted. She was the luckiest woman alive.

'We'll have to visit your parents more often if this is what happens,' he quipped, but he was gazing with reverence at the two small faces, so peacefully asleep at the moment. They had joked that her parents' summer cottage must be magical, as that was where she had conceived at last.

'Hmm, not for a while, please. I feel like I've just been through a *hólmganga*.'

'Sorry, *unnasta*. Are you crying?' He peered at her with concern. 'Am I doing this wrong?'

'No, not at all.' She sniffled. 'These are happy tears. I'm just overwhelmed. Lif says I will be doing this a lot, so please don't mind me. It's normal.'

'Oh, if you say so.' He kissed each tiny head in turn. 'So what will we call them?'

'Isn't that meant to be your choice? According to your traditions, aren't I supposed to give them their first feed with everyone looking on? Not something I'm very happy about, I can tell you.' How embarrassing to have to attempt breastfeeding for the first time with a bunch of people staring at her. But it was the custom and a sort of formal initiation of the babies into their community. 'Then you're to take them and give them a name.

That's what Steinthor and the others did.' Apparently that was the way the men here acknowledged paternity, and the fact that they were responsible for the child henceforth.

'That is so.' Geir grinned at her. 'But I know my wife, and I have a feeling you have strong preferences. Perhaps if you were to give me a few choices, I can select two and we will both be satisfied.'

She reached out and caressed his cheek, rasping her nails through the golden stubble. 'You really are the best of husbands.'

'So tell me then. I'm listening.'

A short while later, the entire population of Stormavík assembled to watch Maddie feed her babies for the first time. Lif had given her whispered instructions, and sat nearby ready to help if needed. She handed her her son first, and after a couple of near misses, the little boy latched on and seemed to know exactly what to do. Maddie was so entranced by the way his tiny mouth worked that she forgot to be embarrassed, and when the baby had had enough, she held him out to Geir.

He accepted the child and cradled him, careful to support the head as he'd been instructed earlier. With a huge grin, he swept the assembled company with his gaze. 'I present to you mine and Maddie's son – Gisli Berger Geirsson.'

A huge cheer went up, startling the infant, and Geir soothed him by bouncing him gently up and down. Maddie beamed at him, pleased that he had agreed with her first choice of name, but then she'd known he would, because he was like that: kind and thoughtful, and always mindful of her wishes. It was probably more than she deserved.

The ritual was repeated with the second baby, and Geir again made his announcement. 'I present to you mine and Maddie's daughter – Gytha Berger Geirsdottír.'

Another cheer, slightly quieter this time, and then a clamour of voices, all wishing the new parents and babies the best.

Tears ran down Maddie's cheeks again, but she was smiling so much her face hurt. This was what pure happiness felt like, and to share it with the man she loved was just marvellous.

He came and sat next to her, holding Gytha while she attempted to burp Gisli. 'You're going to be kept busy with these two, aren't you, my love.' He leaned over to give her a gentle kiss. 'I hope you'll still have a little bit of time for me occasionally.'

'Always. There are plenty of people here to help with the twins, and I'll hopefully be back to normal in a few weeks, then we can make our escape. We have our own bedchamber now, and these two must surely want to sleep sometimes!'

Geir laughed. 'Let's hope they sleep a lot. But if not, I look forward to our stolen moments.'

'Me too.'

And she was looking forward to sharing the rest of her life with this gorgeous man. She'd be eternally grateful to the gods, because they had given her the best gift ever. There was no longer any doubt in her mind that she and Geir had been destined to be together – he'd been right about that. And no matter what fate threw at them, they would overcome it, because they had each other and a love that would last for all eternity.

Life couldn't be more perfect.

Acknowledgements

This book was written during the Covid pandemic when travel was more or less impossible, and setting a book in Iceland – a country I had never visited – proved quite a challenge! Thankfully, there are some incredibly nice people in the world, and I want to start by saying a huge thank you to Birna María Ásgeirsdóttir, Project Manager at the Settlement Exhibition in Reykjavik, who came to my rescue. Following my plea for help, she very kindly sent me the books I needed from the museum shop and went above and beyond the call of duty – I am so grateful to her!

Other friends who had been to Iceland told me of their experiences – many thanks to Catherine Close, Dagny Hlín Ólafsdóttir and Gill Stewart for taking the time to do this.

Fortunately, when restrictions eased up, I was finally able to visit Iceland myself and it's an amazing country! I'd like to thank all the lovely people we met who were unfailingly kind and helpful, especially the lady who showed us around Eiriksstaðir (the reconstructed turf longhouse on the site where Eirik the Red lived in the tenth century). She spent ages patiently answering all my questions and was a fount of knowledge. A huge thank you also to the young man at the Settlement Centre in Borgarnes who opened up the museum just for us, and then let us have a taste of whey – incredibly useful for research purposes! And many thanks to the restaurant at Hotel Viking in Hafnarfjörður where they served me fermented shark and dried stockfish – Viking delicacies – even though it wasn't on the menu.

I couldn't have made it through the lockdown without the help of my amazing friends who kept me sane by weekly WhatsApp chats – Sue Moorcroft and Myra Kersner; emails – Gill Stewart, Henriette Gyland, Tina Brown, Carol Dahlén Fräjdin, Nicola Cornick and all the Word Wenches; and text messages – Chicki Jonsson and Gunbritt Lager. A massive thank you to all of them for always being there when I need them!

As always, thank you to Dr Joanne Shortt-Butler for all her help with Old Norse words, phrases and pronunciation – I learn something new every time and I'm loving it!

A huge thank you to my wonderful editor Kate Byrne and her team at Headline, as well as Lina Langlee, my lovely agent, and her colleague Julie Fergusson – it's a huge pleasure working with you all!

To Richard and my two daughters Josceline and Jessamy – love you and I'm so glad we got through this pandemic! Also other family members, especially my mother, my niece Lea and nephew Anthony, who kept everyone safe in Sweden so I didn't have to worry – thank you!

Finally, I really want to thank all the readers, reviewers and book bloggers who have been so supportive of me and my books – I appreciate your reviews very much and interacting with you on social media is always a pleasure – THANK YOU!

Tempted *by the* Runes

Bonus Material

Read on for an exclusive short story featuring Geir and Maddie's daughter, Gytha!

Birka, Svíaríki, AD *896 – nineteen years later*

'Why on earth did you let her come along? It might be dangerous!'

The words were hissed in an undertone, but Gytha Berger Geirsdottír heard them clearly, and resented them no end. The speaker, her brother Gisli's best friend Bryn Hauksson, had always hated her tagging along whenever they went anywhere, and didn't understand the special twin bond that existed between the siblings. He didn't know that Gytha had been raised by a mother who came from the future, and who believed that girls were just as capable as boys of doing whatever they wished. Including going on dangerous journeys.

'She can take care of herself, you know that,' came Gisli's laid-back response, and Gytha could have hugged him. He always had her back, but he trusted her to know what she was doing. The pair of them had been trained in combat almost from birth, with no distinction made between them because of her being female. And although he was bigger and stronger, she knew perfectly well how to defend herself.

'Is there something amiss?' She walked over to them where they stood on a jetty next to her uncle Hrafn's ship, which was laden with trade goods – furs, iron ore, amber and much more. She sent Bryn a narrow-eyed glance and tried to ignore the jolt that always ran through her at the sight of him.

Handsome as sin, he was a younger son of Haukr Erlendersson, Hrafn's best friend and one of their neighbours. Ever since her family had moved from Ísland to live on her father's property in

Svíaríki ten years ago, Gytha had known Bryn because their families met up often. And right from the first, he had seemed to resent her being included in whatever game he and Gisli were playing. Because she was a girl, he didn't want her hanging around, but that had only made her insist more strongly. Call her contrary, but no one told her what to do.

Bryn had his father's height and build, but his Celtic mother's chestnut hair and green eyes. They surveyed her now and something shimmered in their depths. Anger? Awareness? Disdain? Gytha wasn't sure, but it made her shiver. She hated that he always had an effect on her – one look and she was all aflutter, like some silly adolescent, but she hid it well. No one must ever know that she was attracted to him, least of all Bryn himself. He'd probably laugh himself silly since he'd never liked her. She stood her ground now and waited for his reply.

'Nothing, apart from the fact that you should not be coming along on this expedition,' he bit out.

'Oh, I suppose you think I ought to be at home having your babies?' she snarked.

'You wish,' he muttered, those emerald eyes shooting sparks at her, although a slight tinge of pink crept up his cheeks, as if he knew he shouldn't have said that.

Gytha saw red and lunged to push him off the jetty, but Gisli caught her arm and stepped in between them, shaking his head. 'For the love of Odin, enough!' He sighed, then turned to Bryn. 'You should be used to it by now. She'll be fine.'

'I don't understand why your father allows it. She's well past marriageable age. Shouldn't she be at home practising housewifely skills?' Bryn grumbled.

Gisli just smiled. 'Let it go.'

After a brief staring contest, the two combatants turned away from each other. Gytha climbed down and took her seat on one of the rowing benches of her uncle's ship, as far from Bryn as possible. She was more shaken by the encounter than she cared to admit, and what he'd said was true. Having seen nineteen winters – one less than him – she should have been married long ago. She couldn't hold out for much longer. But yet again her mother's influence had spared her – Maddie didn't believe in marrying too young or in arranged matches.

'I want you to find love, sweetheart,' she'd told her daughter. 'Without that, a marriage is meaningless.'

And judging by the way her parents acted towards each other, fathoms-deep in love after so many years together, Gytha didn't want to settle for less either. But what if the object of your affections never felt the same way? Should she accept second best or simply not marry at all? She had no idea.

The first part of the journey went smoothly. Hrafn was heading to a city in Garðaríki called Aldeigjuborg, where he often went to trade. He had friends and connections there and usually made a small fortune each time he went. Gytha knew that Bryn had gone with him before, as he wanted to be a merchant as well. As a younger son, there wouldn't be much for him to inherit from his father – his older brother Cadoc would get most of it – and he had to make his own way in the world. Gisli was his and Gytha's father's heir, and she had a large dowry, so neither of them needed to make a profit, but they'd wanted an adventure and Hrafn had agreed to let them come along.

They made landfall on an island off the coast of Svíaríki the first night, pulling the ship high up on a long, sandy beach. Gytha helped with building fires and cooking the evening meal, but she noted that Gisli and Bryn did their fair share of the work as well. Seeing her glancing at them, her uncle smiled and whispered, 'I don't allow anyone to come on these voyages with me unless they're prepared to help out. We don't normally bring women, except for your aunt Linnea, so my crew members need to be able to cook for themselves.'

He winked at her and she laughed. Hrafn was married to a woman from the future as well, and his daughter Estrid was as independent as Gytha, although she was now happily married. Headstrong women didn't faze him at all.

To her surprise, after the meal, Bryn sank down on to the sand next to her and placed a board game in between them. 'Fancy a bout of *hnefatafl*?' he asked.

She raised her eyebrows at him. Was this a peace offering? But he didn't apologise for his earlier comments so she couldn't be sure. She shrugged, trying her best to appear unaffected by his nearness. 'Why not?'

She noticed that Gisli threw them a quick glance, but when he saw that they weren't currently fighting, he went back to talking to the man beside him. It was nice that he cared, but as he'd said, she could look after herself.

They played in silence, slightly strained at first, but becoming easier as they settled into the game. Having won one round each, Bryn challenged her to a final, deciding one.

'Very well, but if I beat you, you have to promise not to say another word during this whole journey about how I should have stayed at home.'

'Gytha, I—'

She interrupted him, not wanting to hear his arguments. They were growing old. 'Do you agree?'

'Very well, you have my oath. But what if I win?' He gave her a considering look.

'I'll promise not to come on Hrafn's next trading venture.' She hadn't planned to anyway, so that wouldn't be a hardship.

'Fair enough.'

She won the game and Bryn held up his hands. 'My lips are

sealed. Good night, Gytha.'

As she bedded down for the night in the tent she shared with Gisli, she couldn't help but feel that Bryn had cheated in her favour. She'd won too easily. But why? Perhaps she'd been right, and it was his way of apologising. She would rather he'd just have said it outright.

The following morning, they were up before dawn and set out across the Baltic Sea. The crossing was fairly rough, but Gytha managed to hang on to her morning meal somehow. She breathed a sigh of relief when they reached the coast on the other side and made camp on yet another beach, but the peace was short-lived. Not long after they'd eaten, shadowy figures appeared from behind the sand dunes and Hrafn shouted out a warning. 'An ambush! Arm yourselves!'

Gytha had her sword strapped to a baldric wrapped crosswise over her torso, and she reached for it immediately, jumping to her feet. There was no time to run to the ship to retrieve her shield, but she had learned to fight both with and without it, and wasn't unduly concerned. A group of men were upon them in an instant, and she began to defend herself instinctively. One or two of the attackers halted for a moment at the sight of her long, curly blond hair, loosely tied behind her. That gave her the advantage and she didn't hesitate to wound them, although she drew the line at killing unless she had to.

'Get behind us!' Bryn came hurtling over to shield her, with Gisli close on his heels.

'Don't be a *fifl*,' she shot back, lining up next to him to spar with another foreigner. 'There are too many of them – you need my help.'

She thought she heard Bryn swear, but ignored him. He ought to know by now that she could fight just as well as Gisli, even though she lacked some of his brawn. Whenever she managed to disarm an opponent, however, she used her mother's fighting techniques and instead of wielding the sword, she executed high kicks and what Maddie called 'karate' to incapacitate them. Thankfully she was wearing men's clothing, something else she knew Bryn strongly opposed. Well, he should be glad of it now.

When the fight was over and everyone accounted for – only one man badly wounded, while their opponents were all either dead or had run away – Bryn turned to her, his gaze furious. 'You should have stayed back, like I told you. You could have been killed!'

She merely regarded him coolly. 'So could you.'

'Yes, but—'

'Leave me alone, Bryn. I am not your concern,' she snarled and stalked off, tired of his carping. If this was how he kept his promises, she didn't think much of them.

Gisli found her sitting on the ship's planks, leaning her head against the gunwale. 'Are you hurt?' he asked, sinking down beside her.

'No, I'm fine. You?'

'A few scratches, that's all.' He was silent for a moment. 'He meant well, you know. It was concern for you that prompted his outburst.'

She knew he was talking about Bryn. 'Yes, well, he can keep his concern to himself. I know he doesn't want me here, but it's not his decision to make so he'll just have to put up with it.'

Gisli opened his mouth as if to say something else, then shut it. 'Go and get some rest,' he told her after a while. 'I'm taking first guard duty.'

For the rest of the journey, she didn't exchange a single word with Bryn, but she felt his brooding gaze on her several times. She ignored it, and whenever he looked to be heading in her direction, she moved away. If she couldn't get over this stupid infatuation with him, she'd simply have to avoid him. Surely, it must pass one day?

In Aldegjuborg, when they reached it safely, they stayed with a merchant friend of Hrafn's who welcomed them into his hall. He and his wife evinced no surprise that he'd brought a niece dressed like a man, and Gytha was grateful for that. She felt exhausted, mentally and physically, and appreciated their quiet acceptance and warm welcome.

On the second evening, she'd had enough of resting and insisted on taking her turn at guarding Hrafn's ship. He always posted two men at a time, taking no chances with his cargo. Gisli went with her, and they sat in companionable silence until dusk fell. Since it was summer, it didn't become properly dark, which was good as it meant they could see anyone coming near the ship.

After a while, footsteps could be heard on the jetty and when she looked up, Gytha saw Bryn approaching.

'Gisli? A word, please,' he called out.

Gytha turned to look out over the meandering River Volkhov, next to which the town was built. It was beautiful in the half-light, with reeds along the banks, billowing in the slight breeze, and the occasional fish flipping its tail fin near the surface of the water. She heard the murmur of the men's voices but not their words. Soon after, footsteps headed off along the jetty and the ship moved slightly as Gisli jumped on board to join her again. Only, when she turned towards him, it wasn't her brother, but Bryn who sank down next to her.

'Good evening,' he murmured.

'Bryn! W-what are you doing here? Did uncle send for Gisli?' Her stomach was suddenly alive with butterflies. He was too close, too overwhelming, too . . . everything. She didn't want him so near. It was sheer torture and she clenched her fists in her lap.

He regarded her solemnly. 'No, I came to talk to you.'

She frowned. 'Why? You don't even like me.'

'Don't I?' Amusement glinted in the green depths of his eyes, confusing her.

'Well, no. Ever since we first arrived from Ísland, you've been trying to get rid of me. You didn't want a girl tagging along, you made that abundantly clear. Still don't – I heard you in Birka before we left, loud and clear.' And it had hurt, but she didn't add that.

He shook his head. 'At first, maybe it was like that,' he admitted. 'When we were children. But as soon as we began to grow up a little, I had another reason.'

'I know. You think it's unseemly and I should be a wife and mother, not a warrior.' She heard the bitterness in her tone and turned away, not able to bear seeing these sentiments reflected in his expression.

'That's not it at all, Gytha.' He sighed. 'I just want you to be safe. I was utterly terrified during that fight the other night in case I'd lose you.'

'What?' She swivelled back towards him. 'Lose me?'

'I . . . I care about you.' Closing his eyes he grimaced. 'I know you don't feel that way about me, but I like you. Too much perhaps. And I want you. Badly. Have wanted you since you first started to grow curves. You have no idea . . . But even though I can't have you, the thought of you being hurt, it just kills me! I can't bear it. Do you understand? I'm not trying to be mean, which is what Gisli said you believe.'

Gytha blinked. 'You want me?' she repeated, dumbfounded.

'Yes, no need to rub it in.' His mouth tightened. 'I just wanted to explain so that you'd understand my reasons for acting a bit high-handed. I'll go and fetch Gisli.'

He made as if to stand up, but she grabbed his arm and pulled him back down. 'You fool!' she exclaimed. 'I want you too! Have done for years. Why do you think I haven't married anyone yet? I was hoping one day you'd finally notice me.'

Bryn had gone completely still and was staring at her in wonder. 'You do?' He brought one hand up to caress her cheek. 'You don't hate me?'

A laugh bubbled out of her. 'No, very far from it. Oh, Bryn . . .'

She didn't have time to say anything else, because his mouth came down on hers in a fierce kiss and his strong arms encircled her waist, pulling her close to his hard, muscular chest. Her heart was beating madly but she could feel his doing the same, as if they were trying to reach each other. His lips were warm and firm, and he tasted of mead – sweet and delicious. She kissed him back with all the pent-up passion she'd been storing up for years. No one had ever kissed her before, but somehow she knew just what to do and she welcomed his tongue as he delved deep, stroking hers in a sensuous rhythm. And she didn't protest when his hands began to roam across her back, along her waist, and down to cup her behind. Instead, she crawled onto his lap to encourage him further.

Breathing heavily, he pulled away after a while and held her to him. 'Gytha *mín*, wait, we can't . . . but, Odin's ravens, I want you so much!'

They were both shaking and she didn't want to stop, but reality intruded. 'Oh, we're supposed to be on guard, aren't we. *Skítr!* Uncle Hrafn will kill us if we don't pay attention.' But she couldn't make herself let him go, and her mouth gravitated towards his like a lodestone to the north.

He kissed her back, but murmured in between playful nibbles, 'No, not that. Gisli is keeping guard at the end of the jetty, but . . . I'm a younger son. I have nothing much to offer you yet, maybe not for a few years. Your father will skin me alive if I . . . if we go any further.'

Gytha stopped kissing him long enough to look into his eyes. She smiled. 'A very good reason for not stopping. If we've already anticipated our wedding oaths, he can't refuse. Besides, he's told me I'm allowed to make my own choice. Now I have. I want you.'

A slow smile spread across his features and he leaned his forehead against hers. 'Are you absolutely sure, *ást mín*? Because once I have you inside a tent, I'm not letting you go. Ever.'

'That's what I was hoping for.' She matched his grin. 'Come.' She took his hand and pulled him up and over to a tent that had been raised at one end of the ship as shelter for the guards, if necessary. Before crawling inside, she stopped and looked up at him. 'You haven't asked me yet, you know.'

'What? Oh. Gytha, will you make me the happiest man alive and be my wife? I love you more than I can ever say.' His arms tightened around her and the look he gave her was so intense it almost melted her insides.

'Yes,' she whispered, 'gladly. I love you too, so much, Bryn.'

'Then you're right, we're not waiting another instant. We've wasted too much time already.'

As he pulled her into the tent and closed the flap behind them, she sank down onto the soft furs that covered the ship's planks and chuckled. 'Did you just admit that I was right about something? That's a good start.'

'Oh, you . . .' He lay down on top of her, fitting his body to hers without crushing her. 'Actually, I'll let you be right about anything, as long as you keep wanting me.'

'I think I can safely promise that. And will you let me come on trading journeys with you or is marrying me your way of keeping me safe at home, the perfect wife?'

He kissed his way along her eyelids, cheeks, neck and shoulder, while he replied. 'No, I want you with me always. And you *are* perfect – for me.'

Gytha sighed happily and reached down to unbuckle his belt. 'Thank you. Then you're definitely the perfect husband for me.'

'Believe me, I'll prove that to you in a moment. Now let's get you out of these men's garments.' He tugged her tunic over her head. 'They've been driving me wild because I could glimpse every luscious curve of your body and my imagination filled in the rest. Now I want to see them for real.'

'As long as I can see you too. I want us to be equals.'

'Always, my love, always.'

When they emerged from the tent some time towards midnight, Gisli was sitting cross-legged on the jetty, and he gave them a huge grin. 'At last! Now can we have some peace or are you going to be unbearable as man and wife as well?'

Gytha and Bryn looked at each other and laughed.

'Unbearable,' they replied, as one.

'You really don't mind?' Bryn added, searching his friend's gaze.

Gisli shook his head. 'No, I think you're well matched and everyone will be relieved you've finally realised it yourselves. And I might take my revenge – I have my eye on one of your sisters.'

'What? Which one?'

Gytha swatted Bryn on the arm, then stood on tiptoe to give him a kiss. 'Stop looking like a bear protecting his cubs. You owe him.'

'She's right, and it's none of your business. You'll find out soon enough.' Gisli's smile was smug.

'Oh, very well. As long as you make her happy, that's all I ask. As happy as I feel right now.' Bryn kissed Gytha back, lingering for emphasis.

Gisli sighed. 'Honestly, you two! You are definitely going to be insufferable.' But it was clear that he was pleased for them, and with twin intuition Gytha knew he approved of her choice of husband as she would approve of his intended, whoever she was.

She leaned into her betrothed. All was right with the world – at last.